INDIGO RAIN

Elise Noble

Published by Undercover Publishing Limited

Copyright © 2019 Elise Noble

v5

ISBN: 978-1-912888-01-6

Edited by Nikki Mentges, NAM Editorial

Cover design by Abigail Sins

www.undercover-publishing.com

www.elise-noble.com

If you act like a rock star, you will be treated like one.
- *Marilyn Manson*

CHAPTER 1 - ALANA

"AIEEEEE!" TESSA SHRIEKED.

Huh? My neck creaked as I turned my head to the side. I'd fallen asleep—or rather, passed out—on the sofa, and between there and the kitchen, the apartment I shared with my brother looked as though the love child of a hurricane and a tornado had rampaged through it.

Tessa poked her head around the kitchen door. Once, she'd been my best friend, but not anymore seeing as last night's get-together had been her idea.

"You're either gonna love me or you're gonna hate me."

Judging by the apologetic grimace on her face, it would be the latter.

"What have you done?" I croaked.

"Tell you what, why don't you get up and have a cup of coffee first? Or some more wine? There's half a bottle of..." She ducked back into the kitchen. "Euuuch! That is *not* wine."

How about I go and puke in the bathroom instead?

"I can't believe you talked me into having a party."

"Oh, come on, Alana. You haven't lived until you've had to grovel to the police at three o'clock in the morning."

Yes, that had really happened. Which meant my

brother was sure to find out what I'd done when he got back from his honeymoon, and he'd probably lecture me for twenty-four hours straight. The police had actually been quite understanding. Possibly because I'd unplugged the stereo straight away, or maybe because Tessa had cried—crying on cue was her party trick, quite literally—but when everybody scuttled away, we'd been left with the mess to clean up.

"Please just make the coffee."

"When does your brother get back?"

"Tomorrow morning."

Which meant we only had one day to make the apartment look perfect again.

Perhaps you're thinking it was a strange arrangement, me living with my half-brother and his new wife, and I guess you're kind of right. But Zander had raised me from the age of fourteen, so to me, sharing a home with him was normal—first a crappy bedsit in Sydenham, and now our riverside apartment in Chelsea. Plus I adored Dove. They'd only been together for a few months, but they were perfect for each other, and I couldn't have been happier for them when they'd decided on the spur of the moment to tie the knot in Las Vegas. I'd even played bridesmaid. But then they'd decided to travel around South America for a month, and since I'd just started my summer break from university, I'd been left home alone. Then *this* had happened.

Carnage.

I rolled off the sofa, tripped over a cushion, then paused to pick up a lamp on my quest to find caffeine. Was that a red wine stain on the carpet? Or worse, blood? With Tessa and a blow-up doll as my witnesses,

I was never holding a party again. Or even attending one. What were the symptoms of an aneurysm? Something in my head felt as though it was about to burst.

Tessa slid a mug of coffee across the kitchen island in my direction, and I propped myself up on a stool. Someone had drawn a smiley face on the clock above the sink. Dammit.

"So, tell me why I'm gonna hate you more than I already do right now."

"Well, you might not hate me."

"Why? What did you do?"

"It's actually really good news if you decide not to be boring for the rest of your life."

"I already tried that last night, and look how it turned out. The whole apartment stinks of vomit. What did you do, Tessa?" I asked for the third time.

"Remember how last night, someone put on an Indigo Rain song and we started perving over pictures of Rush Moder on Instagram?"

No, *we* didn't. Tessa had been perving over Rush Moder, something she'd started doing almost three years ago when Indigo Rain had their first UK number one. I could understand why—dark hair, designer stubble, a strong jaw, piercing blue eyes... He was incendiary. She even had a shirtless photo of him set as the screen saver on her phone. And last night, it hadn't only been pictures of Rush Moder we were looking at, but his words too. He'd posted a snap of himself holding his middle finger up to the camera then gone on a rant at the paparazzi, accusing them of printing lie after lie about the band to sell their "shitty, hate-filled gossip rags." A proper meltdown.

"Rush is the lead guitarist, right?"

"Right." She paused to take a sip of her coffee. "Uh, I might have messaged him."

That's what she was panicking about?

"I wouldn't worry. He's a rock star—I'm sure he gets loads of messages from tipsy girls."

"You don't understand. He freaking replied!"

"It probably wasn't him. I bet the band's PR person confiscated his phone right after he unleashed that tirade on the press."

Tessa shook her head. "No, it *was* him. I didn't believe it at first either, but he even sent a photo."

"Why? Why would he do that?"

"It was a trade. I had to send one first."

"Let me get this straight... You were flirting with Rush Moder last night, and now you don't know what to say to him?"

"Not exactly." Tessa shifted so the granite expanse of the kitchen island was between us. With hindsight, I should have realised something really, really bad was coming, but my alcohol-addled brain was still functioning at half capacity. "I borrowed your phone, so technically, *you* were flirting with Rush Moder."

"You *what*?" I picked up my coffee, contemplated throwing it, then realised I needed the caffeine too much. "My phone was locked."

"And your PIN number's one-two-three-four. I've watched you type it in a thousand times. But before you go crazy, I was doing you a favour, okay? You know how you need to get a job?"

A job? How did we go from drunken sexting with one quarter of the world-famous bad boys of rock to my employment status?

Although, yes, I did need a job.

Tessa and I had met at school soon after I moved to London, and now, seven years later, we were both studying for journalism degrees and about to start work for our placement year. Or at least, Tessa was. She'd already landed her dream internship with *NewsFlash* magazine, the perfect career move for a girl who wanted to become an investigative journalist. Me? I hadn't had so much as an interview, probably because I hadn't applied for any jobs, and I wasn't even sure I liked journalism anymore. It had all seemed so glamorous when I signed up—flying around the world to report on breaking news and interview the rich and famous—but when I'd temped at a newspaper last summer, I'd spent my time fetching countless cups of tea for a boss who thought patting me on the arse was an acceptable form of greeting. And most evenings, I'd still been sitting at my desk at ten o'clock, correcting typos.

Honestly, working in a fast-food restaurant would've been more fun, because at least they offered free fries, but when I broached the subject of dropping out with Zander, he'd looked so disappointed that I'd rapidly backpedalled. He did pay my tuition fees, after all.

So, until now, I'd been burying my head in the sand. My ex-boss said I was welcome back anytime, probably because my replacement was male and built like a wrestler, but I guess I figured if I ignored the work situation, it would go away. So why had Tessa brought it up now?

"Yes, I know I should look for a job. What's that got to do with anything?"

"Because I might have found you one. Well, sort of."

"Can we back up a bit here?"

My brain was struggling to process all the information. I'd missed something.

"Okay, okay." She talked slowly, as if I were a small child. Better. "Rush Moder is sick of the media printing rubbish about him and the band, so I came up with a total brainwave."

"Did this brainwave happen before or after you almost set fire to the curtains with flaming sambuca?"

"After, but that doesn't mean I'm not a genius."

A groan escaped my lips. Even before the sambuca, Tessa had been a little worse for wear, and although I loved her dearly, genius was stretching things a smidgen.

"Just tell me what you did, will you? Get it over with."

"I sent Rush Moder a pitch on your behalf. What better way for them to set the record straight than to write their own story? A biography! That way, they can tell the world the truth."

"And?"

"Well, you're the perfect person to write it. Duh."

"Tessa, I don't know the first thing about penning a biography."

"Don't be so negative. Didn't you win a creative writing contest once?"

"I was thirteen years old!"

That was back in the days when I used to translate my pain into words. I'd submitted one of my efforts to the short-story section of a local arts festival, and I could still see the judging notes in my mind now.

This heart-wrenching tale of the abuse suffered by

a young girl at the hands of her stepfather moved us all to tears. A gritty and well-written piece of fiction.

Too bad it wasn't fiction.

No, it was a cry for help, I saw that now. A cry for help that my mother either hadn't heard or had chosen to ignore until Zander rescued me a year later. Thanks to the therapist my brother had worked his ass off to pay for, I could talk about my past more easily now, but it still hurt.

And Tessa wasn't done. "We write stuff at uni, and you always get better marks than me."

"There's a world of difference between essays and articles and a whole damn book." But then curiosity got the better of me. "Are you serious? He actually replied?"

"Yup. And he thought it was a brilliant idea. You start next week."

"Wait, wait, wait. What?"

"Your new job. Indigo Rain arrives for their UK tour a week from tomorrow, and you need to join them next Monday. You know, to see what goes on and do interviews and stuff."

"Show me these messages. Someone must've been pulling your leg. Like an intern having a joke or something."

Silently, she slid my phone over, and the cheeky mare even had the balls to unlock it first. My hands sweated as I loaded up Instagram. What the hell had Tessa done?

It all started out quite innocently.

Raven: Rush, I just wanted to say I totally agree with your post. Publishing those pictures of your girlfriend naked was a horrible thing for that magazine to do.

Then things quickly degenerated.

RushModer: That really you in the bikini, babe?

Uh, didn't Rush Moder have a girlfriend?

And as for the bikini, I was on the beach, okay? I'd pulled a wide-brimmed hat low over my eyes so nobody could identify me.

Because this was the Instagram account Zander didn't know about. He could get a teeny bit overprotective, and if he saw a picture of me in swimwear on the internet, he'd get one of his hacker friends to remove it before I had time to change my password. Think I'm exaggerating? Well, when Tessa and I holidayed in the Algarve last summer, one of Zander's colleagues from the Lisbon office of Blackwood Security had just happened to be staying in the villa next to ours. A total coincidence, according to my brother. And I only found out when I overheard the guy on the phone. Yes, I know I shouldn't have been eavesdropping, but he was hot, and Tessa had encouraged me.

So secret me had started using Instagram to share my photography hobby with my friends, but as my portfolio grew, so did my number of followers. I didn't stick to a particular theme. Rather, I photographed whatever called to me that day, anything from London's hidden history to nature's beauty to arty self-portraits, some of which may have been a little risqué. But I never revealed my face.

Raven: Yes, it's really me. I went to Portugal last summer.

RushModer: Prove it. Blow me a kiss.

Any normal girl would have backed off at that point, wouldn't they? But not Tessa. Now I thought about it, I vaguely recalled her lining me up for a selfie last night and encouraging me to make a duck face at the camera.

Raven: Here you go. But it's only fair that you recite
    Recipe
    Recuse
    Damn autocorrect!
    Send me a picture back...

RushModer: Lol.

Rush Moder actually did send a photo, one of him puckering up while holding a bottle of Jack Daniels in his other hand. Guess we knew what was fuelling this little conversation, didn't we? Alcohol. 80 proof.

Raven: Aww, partying alone?

RushModer: Why? Wanna join me?

Raven: Maybe. I have a proposal for you.

RushModer: Already had four of those this week, babe. One girl even gave me a ring.

Raven: Not that kind of proposal. This is totally a

business one.

RushModer: Don't be boring, bikini girl.

Raven: Give me two minutes of your time, and then I'll send you another bikini pic.

She didn't. Tell me she didn't…

RushModer: Deal.

Raven: Here's my proposal. I'm a journalism student, and I want to write a behind-the-scenes piece on the music industry as part of my degree. If you give me access, I can totally tell your story. The real story of Indigo Rain, not trash about you and your friends. I don't need to sell papers, so I've got no incendiary to make stuff up.
    *incentive

RushModer: You got big coconuts, bikini girl.
    *colonials
    Duck.
    Fuck.
    Cojones. Balls. Big balls.

Raven: No, that's totally you.

Did I mention that the drunker Tessa got, the more she used the word "totally"? Oh, and she tended to lose her flipping mind.

RushModer: I like you, bikini girl. Gonna send

me that pic?

She did. She freaking did. Tessa sent a photo of me stretched out on a sun lounger in the same bikini I wore in my profile picture, drinking a cocktail *sans* hat. The only saving grace was that it had been taken before I fell asleep and got sunburned.

"I really hate you right now."

She pointed at a bakery bag on the counter. "I went out to the patisserie and got fresh pain au chocolat for breakfast."

Pain au chocolat? I almost smiled, but I stopped myself just in time. "I still don't like you very much."

"Have you read to the end?"

"Not yet. Just to the part where you decided to send a half-naked picture of me to a complete stranger."

"Rush Moder's a rock god."

"I don't freaking care, Tessa! I've never met him, therefore he's a stranger. I barely even listen to Indigo Rain's music."

"Keep reading, okay?"

Why? Was I going to get to the end and find it was all just a terrible joke?

No.

No, I wasn't.

RushModer: Are you single, bikini girl?

Raven: Totally single.

I. Was. Going. To. Kill. Her.

Raven: What do you think of my idea?

RushModer: What idea?

Raven: Writing your biography? Interviews and stuff?

I imagined the idiot pausing to take a slug of his whisky before he replied.

RushModer: Right. A biology. Where do you live?

Raven: London.

RushModer: We'll be in London soon. Come and meet me, bikini girl.

Raven: For an interview?

RushModer: Sure. But Dex will want to check out anything you write. He's a control feet.
    *freak.

"Who's Dex?" I asked Tessa.

"Indigo Rain's bass guitarist. He's kind of serious compared to the other guys. Hardly ever smiles. So, you're gonna meet Rush? I mean, this is a dream. I'd totally go myself if I wasn't pretending to be you."

Totally. There was that word again. "Tessa, are you still drunk?"

"Maybe just a little tipsy. Well?"

"No! Of course I'm not going. He was probably as drunk as you when he wrote this garbage."

"Who cares? He said yes, and this is the chance of a lifetime."

"He'll come to his senses."

"Have you read the last part?"

No, and I wasn't sure I wanted to. I also made the mistake of taking a mouthful of coffee before I lowered my gaze to the screen again.

Raven: Where should I come?

RushModer: On my dick. Or on my fingers. Or in my mouth. All three? Your choice.

I spat the coffee across the table.

"I see you've got to the good bit," Tessa said. "He just sent that, like, two minutes ago."

"What about his girlfriend?"

"She dumped him after the whole naked-pictures thing."

"Rush Moder's a pig. You asked a reasonable question, and he twisted it into...into *this*." I stabbed at the screen and hurt my finger. "Ow."

"At least you admit my suggestion was reasonable."

"No! No, now *you're* twisting things too. On the scale of one to utter depravity, your idea was merely stupid."

"Well, Rush liked it."

My phone pinged again.

RushModer: We're staying at the Hamilton House Hotel. Meet me there at eleven a.m. a week from Monday.

Moder was the cockiest asshole I'd ever met. Well, not met, exactly, but you know what I mean.

"There's only one thing for it."

Tessa grinned. "You'll meet him a week from Monday?"

"No, I'll have to block him on Instagram, and we're never mentioning this again."

And I also needed to change my PIN number to something trickier. Four-three-two-one, perhaps.

"But—"

"Zip it. Unless you want me to put one of *your* bikini pics up on Plenty of Fish with a note that says you like threesomes."

"I've never tried one, but it could be fun."

Good grief.

"I mean it. We're never discussing this again, and while I think about it, you're banned from wine too."

"Where's your sense of adventure?"

Somewhere in Surrey, in a mock-Tudor mansion inhabited by my ex-stepfather. Mother divorced him three years ago, but for the whole of their marriage, she'd brushed his abuse under the carpet in return for a platinum credit card and vacations in San Tropez. I still refused to speak to her unless it was absolutely necessary. Tessa knew about my past, but I didn't want to bring it up now and send her on a guilt trip. Not when I tried so hard to act normal.

"I'm not going to the Hamilton House Hotel to catch an STD next Monday morning, Tessa. I'll start applying for proper jobs instead."

I'd been putting it off for far too long. My tone said I was serious, and her sheepish look said she'd finally got the message.

"Sorry. I was only trying to help."

"I know. And I appreciate it, really I do. But I'm not into rock stars, and they're not getting into me."

Absolutely no way. I may have shared almost everything with Tessa, but the one thing I liked to gloss over was my complete lack of experience with men who weren't paedophiles. I dated occasionally, drooled over sexy men on the internet, and read every issue of *Cosmopolitan*, but the one time I'd ended up naked in bed with a man as an adult, I'd flipped out, made an excuse, and left. Then, when Tessa questioned me the next day, I panicked and told her it was amazing.

And I'd felt guilty about my lie ever since.

"No Rush Moder? You're seriously turning him down?"

"No Rush Moder." I forced a smile. "I'll write some application letters after we've got the apartment straightened out. Will you help?"

"With both things? Sure." She looked around and grimaced. "Did you see someone broke a leg off the coffee table? We'll have to go furniture shopping."

This promised to be a really long day.

CHAPTER 2 - ALANA

"NEW COFFEE TABLE?" Zander asked the moment he walked through the door.

Damn my brother for being so observant. Although I suppose that trait did help him in his day job as a private investigator.

"Uh, yes. I thought we could do with a change."

Dove sniffed the air. "Did you get an air freshener too?"

"I burned dinner last night. It smelled really bad." I managed a smile, although that took quite an effort since I'd spent twenty-two of the last twenty-three hours cleaning. "But I made lunch—quiche and salad." Okay, the deli down the road had made it, but I picked it up and that was practically the same thing. "Welcome home!"

Dove abandoned her two suitcases and flopped onto the sofa. "Boy, am I glad to be back. Who knew travelling could be quite so exhausting?"

"But you had a good time, right?"

I'd seen the pictures on Facebook, and I hated to say I was jealous, but... I was insanely jealous. First, they'd rented a convertible to drive parts of the old Route 66, and after they reached California, they'd flown to Mexico and spent a week on the beach. Then they travelled to Peru and walked the Inca Trail to

Machu Picchu. The trip of a lifetime.

Apart from my four-day jaunt to Las Vegas to be their bridesmaid, I hadn't made it out of Europe since I was a baby, despite the fact that I had dual English and American nationality. Mother was from Colorado, and I'd been born there by virtue of being a month premature, but I'd spent my whole life living in England and France. When Mother went on holiday with her various husbands, she'd always left me at home with the nanny so I didn't get in the way.

"An amazing time. I'll show you the pictures of the cloud forest later." Dove pinched herself. "I still can't believe all the places we went."

I giggled. "And I still can't believe Zander got married."

A year ago, if I'd had to nominate one person who'd stay a bachelor for the rest of his life, it would've been my brother. But now he'd fallen head over heels in love, and my new candidate was Rush Moder. Surely no woman would ever put up with him? Even thinking of the late-night conversation he'd had with Tessa made me want to vomit.

"Are you okay?" Dove asked. "You look like you've swallowed a wasp."

"I'm—" A knock at the door saved my life. "Totally fine."

Gah! Now *I'd* started with the "totallys." Tessa was a bad, bad influence.

I practically ran to the door and yanked it open.

"Hi."

Mrs. Galbreski from next door looked up at me. And I mean looked up. At five feet nothing, she stood seven inches shorter than me.

"Hello, dear." She held out a foil-covered plate. "I thought you might be hungry after all the cleaning yesterday, so I made you a cake. I saw you out scrubbing the balcony during the ten o'clock news."

Oh, bless her.

"Why were you scrubbing the balcony?" Zander asked from behind me.

Dammit. Because someone had spilled a bottle of beer over the wood and it stank, but I couldn't tell my brother that.

I conjured up a smile. "I just wanted everything spick and span for when you and Dove came home."

Mrs. Galbreski patted Zander on the arm. "Don't worry, dear. Everyone likes a good party. Well, almost everyone. There's always one stick-in-the-mud who calls the police. I bet it was that young couple who moved in downstairs last month. They wrote me a nasty note complaining about my Zumba dancing the other day."

Zander raised an eyebrow, and I sagged back against the doorjamb.

"Lanie?"

"It was only a few friends."

"Back in my day, we'd have been fishing people out of the river," Mrs. Galbreski told him. "Enjoy the cake."

Busted. I closed the door and turned to face my brother. "Honestly, it wasn't that bad."

Zander sucked in a breath, pinched the bridge of his nose, and let the breath out again in a long exhale.

"I just worry about you, that's all. If I'd known, I could have arranged for someone to keep an eye on things."

Exactly, and what kind of fun would that have

been?

"Honestly, it wasn't a big deal."

Behind him, Dove shifted on the sofa, then her brow furrowed as she fished a pair of knickers out from behind the cushions.

"Are these yours?"

No way. And I had no clue who they belonged to. I couldn't even blame one of Zander's pre-Dove girlfriends because he'd never brought them back to the apartment.

"Uh, possibly some people might have been messing around?"

"Lanie, next time you want a party, just let me know, okay?" Zander said. "I'll get a couple of the guys from work to stand at the door and make sure nobody does anything stupid."

My brother wasn't completely unreasonable, far from it. No, he just worried too much. Nobody at a Zander-monitored party would dare to let their hair down, and he'd probably insist on background-checking everyone first. Not even kidding. He'd already informed me that Greg from my journalism course had gotten arrested last year for being drunk and disorderly, so guess who would have been banned from the party if Zander was involved?

As it was, I'd invited Greg, and he'd brought a whole shopping trolley full of beer then had us in stitches with his dad-dancing. Tessa had wheeled the sodding trolley back to Sainsbury's yesterday evening.

"Okay, I'll tell you next time."

Zander had saved me from my previous life, so I could hardly act ungrateful. But sometimes, just sometimes, I wanted a little bit of freedom.

He wrapped an arm around my shoulders. "Did you say you'd got lunch?"

I swallowed down my sigh. "Give me ten minutes to heat up the quiche."

With Zander and Dove both back at work on Monday morning, I started my job-hunting in earnest. If nothing else, Tessa's stupid stunt on Friday night had spurred me into action.

The lady in the university careers office tutted and gave me a lecture on leaving things till the last minute. Apparently, all the good placements had already gone, but she did grudgingly send me a list of possibilities. Did I want to do social media, copywriting, editorial work, or digital marketing? None of the positions paid more than minimum wage, and some didn't pay anything at all. Luckily, I didn't need the money—Zander had inherited our father's fortune, which covered our living expenses—but I didn't want to be taken advantage of either. Call it a point of principle. One of the job descriptions was basically for a PA by another title, and the PAs where Zander worked sure as hell earned a lot more money than these cowboys were offering.

Still, I did my research, filled in application forms, and sent off emails to anywhere that looked reasonable. And by reasonable, I mean I skipped the place where the boss got Twitter-shamed for timing his employees' bathroom breaks.

By Thursday, I'd scored one interview and a whole bunch of rejection letters. Overqualified, underqualified, sorry, we've already hired somebody else. To make matters worse, Tessa had been messaging me all week, raving about how much she was enjoying her internship. And I was thrilled for her, really I was, but every time my phone buzzed, my heart sank a little lower.

"How's the job-hunting going?" she asked when we met up for dinner on Thursday evening. She'd picked the restaurant, a hip new place where none of the food came on plates.

"I have an interview tomorrow."

"Ooh, where?"

"Fly Boy Media."

She crinkled her little ski-jump nose. "I've never heard of it."

Neither had I until I sent in my CV. "They provide news and content aimed at the under-thirties."

The company had been around for over twenty years, according to their website, so they had to be doing something right. It was run by a father-and-son team, and they offered the opportunity to gain a rounded experience by working in all departments.

"Sounds good. At *NewsFlash*, we still have a few dinosaurs who insist on using shorthand. Where are they based?"

"Shoreditch."

"It's nice around there now." She held up her glass of wine. "Here's to your new job."

"I haven't landed it yet."

"But you will. They'll love you. Although I won't lie —I'm super disappointed you turned down Rush Moder. You could have introduced us."

"I'm pretty sure Rush Moder's offer had nothing to

do with my professional capabilities."

He'd kept calling me "bikini girl," for crying out loud.

"Who cares? Most girls would crawl to that hotel on their hands and knees just to lick his feet."

Eeeeuw. "Good thing I'm not most girls. And I've never understood the whole foot-fetish thing."

"Me neither. I tried sucking a guy's toes once, but he'd been wearing trainers the whole day and it was gross."

"Yuck. Were you sober?"

"Of course not. And speaking of not being sober..." She waved at the nearest waiter, all cute and smiley, and he came over right away. "Can we get two more glasses of white, please?"

"Chardonnay or Sauvignon blanc?"

"Hmm, I can't decide. Just bring two of each."

Thanks, Tessa. Her insistence that we drink everything on the menu meant I didn't check my phone until we got home, which meant I missed seeing the message from Roy Flynt, my potential new boss at Fly Boy Media, until almost midnight.

Alana, forgot to mention it earlier, but could you write a brief article on a hot topic among twenty-somethings and bring it with you to the interview? See you at two!

Oh, shit.

At that point, I could barely even focus, let alone start researching an article. I racked my brains for anything I'd written recently that I might be able to repurpose, but there was nothing. Was this a test? A challenge to see how I coped with impossible deadlines? I groaned out loud, but with no other opportunities on the horizon, I couldn't afford to screw up this interview. Finding a placement was even harder than I thought, and I'd gone from being picky at the start of the week to being desperate by Friday as the harsh realities of the London jobs market revealed themselves.

I had to nail this.

The alarm rang at six, and I rolled out of bed to make coffee. Zander sauntered past on his way to the gym.

"You're up early," he said.

"I have to prepare for my interview."

"I won't bother wishing you luck. They'd be crazy not to hire you."

I appreciated his confidence, but it would be misplaced if I couldn't get a bloody article written in time. And what should I write it on? At that time of day, tired and a bit hungover, my mind was blank.

Panicking slightly, I thumbed through my phone for inspiration. What topics mattered to people my age? Unfortunately, I made the mistake of clicking on Instagram, and Rush Moder's grinning face made me groan. His drunken rant had got hundreds of thousands of likes and comments in the past week. Why was he so popular? What made girls go crazy over the assholes in Indigo Rain when they acted like idiots all the time? Hmm... *That* could actually make an interesting article.

I turned to my old friend Google. None of the four band members were men you'd want to take home to meet your mother. Especially *my* mother—she'd probably end up dating one of them since they appeared to have more money than sense.

If I had to rank them from bad to, well, less bad, the tattooed lead singer and occasional guitarist, Travis Thorne, would take the top spot. My heart might have skipped a beat when I saw his picture because there was no denying he was as handsome as sin, but no amount of messy brown hair or scruffy beard or dimples or hooded hazel eyes could make up for his character flaws.

Following a late-night party, he'd gained his first DUI conviction six weeks ago and been banned from driving for half a year. Since he most likely had a chauffeur, I imagined that wasn't as much of a hardship as the course at DUI school, the counselling sessions, and the thousand-dollar fine he'd also been landed with. Despite breaking his arm in the incident at the beginning of May, he'd allegedly managed to push his girlfriend down two weeks later—she had a black eye to prove it—although he wasn't charged by the police over that. Unsurprisingly, she'd dumped him, and since then, he'd been pictured falling drunk out of a club with a different bimbo every night. How he ever managed to do any actual singing was beyond me.

Rush Moder took the number two spot, and from the amount he seemed to drink, I concluded he'd have been better off at Alcoholics Anonymous sessions than meet 'n' greets with his fans. No wonder he'd made so many typos in his messages to Tessa. But he didn't seem short of female company either, even if he struggled to keep his temper in check on social media.

Jethro David Altierre—more commonly referred to

as JD—played the drums for Indigo Rain when he wasn't too busy doing drugs. He'd been arrested for possession last year and let off on a technicality, but a grainy picture that appeared on a gossip website six months later of a blond guy snorting white powder suggested he hadn't changed much.

Finally, there was Dexter Reeves, the bassist. He never smiled, rarely spoke, and had—miracle of miracles—avoided significant scandal since he started with the band. A true enigma.

In all my research, the words most commonly used to describe the members of Indigo Rain were "talented but troubled," and that about summed it up. I played some of their songs as I worked, and although I'd always been more of a pop fan than a rock chick, I could hear why they were so popular.

In fact, I got lost in the music for almost half an hour, then gave myself a mental slap when I realised how little time I had left to write the damned article. A title. I needed a title.

Five reasons why girls go for bad boys... And six reasons why they shouldn't.

I picked up my favourite pen and began to write.

Since Tessa liked to visit Old Spitalfields Market in Shoreditch, and she also liked to drag me along with her, I had a reasonable idea of where I was going. Or at least, I thought I did. When I traipsed along a side road near Shoreditch High Street, I found a dusty storefront with a sign for Brightwell's Books where Fly Boy Media should have been. I checked the email again. Number forty-four—I definitely had the right place.

I pushed the door open and hesitated on the threshold. "Hello?"

A plump man with a comb-over popped out from behind a musty stack of paperbacks.

"Can I help?"

"I'm looking for Fly Boy Media, but I'm not sure I'm in the right place."

"Alana?"

Oh, shit. I *was* in the right place.

"Yes, that's me."

He stuck out one pudgy hand. "Roy Flynt. Why don't you come through to the office? My boy will be back any moment. He's been looking forward to meeting you."

"Really?"

"Oh yes, he's been looking at your Twittergram."

I didn't know what was worse—a so-called media company boss who didn't know the difference between Twitter and Instagram or the fact that his son had been stalking me through them. At least they could only have found my regular pages, not bikini girl. Bikini girl masqueraded as Raven du Walt. Raven was my middle name, and I'd borrowed the du Walt from my maternal grandma. She died when I was five, but until then, she'd spent more time caring for me than my so-called mother had.

"Coffee?" Roy asked as he showed me into a grubby room full of mismatched desks and chairs.

"Yes, please."

"The kettle's over in that corner. Milk and two sugars for me, love."

Did he just...? Oh my goodness. Welcome to the

dark ages. I should have walked out right then, but two qualities my mother had instilled in me were tolerance and politeness, no matter how misplaced they might be. Plus I couldn't afford to have any rudeness reported back to the careers advisor at uni. At that moment, I envied Rush Moder for his ability to let rip with whatever was on his mind.

"Sure, no problem. Milk and two sugars."

The kettle boiled—slowly—and even though I took my time, Flynt junior still hadn't arrived by the time I set a mug of coffee on the desk in front of Roy. The old man seemed to have forgotten what I was there for, and he'd started work on some invoices.

"It was two o'clock, wasn't it?" I asked. "The interview?"

"That's right. Terry's never been so good at timekeeping, but I'm sure he'll be along soon."

"Perhaps you could call him? Or text him?"

"Eh, I'm not so good with all that modern technology."

I gingerly slid my article towards him. "I printed this out. Perhaps you'd like to read it while we're waiting?"

Because at least then I wouldn't need to attempt conversation.

In the early hours, I'd come to the conclusion that dating a bad boy really wasn't a smart idea. Sure, they were sexy, tough, and exciting, but if you wanted a project, building flat-pack furniture was a better bet. At least it wouldn't break your heart when it got bored. Bad boys were bad news.

Roy fished around in his drawer and came up with a pair of reading glasses, and I breathed a sigh of relief.

As soon as Terry arrived, I'd ask a few basic questions, then make an excuse and leave.

Ten interminably long minutes passed before a guy younger than me slunk through the door. From his clothing, he aspired to be in Indigo Rain, although he sadly lacked the looks and presumably the talent since he was working in a place like this. He fiddled with his lip ring as he slumped into a chair opposite me.

"You're the new girl, yeah?"

"I'm here for an interview."

He looked me up and down, pausing on my chest. "You're hired."

"Hold on a second—I don't even know what the job entails. The description was kind of vague."

"Oh." He glanced at his father, then shrugged. "We've got this website, like the Huffington Post but for our generation, and you'd be writing the articles for that."

"All of them?"

"Pretty much, yeah. Unless you can get other people to help you out."

"And what do *you* do here?"

"Load the stuff onto the website."

So he basically hit copy and paste.

"What about affiliate income? SEO? Traffic generation? Ads?"

"Huh?"

"How do you make money?"

"We just need to get everything up and running before we worry about that."

In other words, they had no plan, no work ethic, and no idea how the internet functioned.

"Your website says the company's been going for

twenty years?"

"Indeed it has," Roy said. "Up until now, we distributed religious pamphlets, but everything's going online now. Times are a-changing, and so are we."

Great. I'd wasted an entire day.

"Thanks for your time, but I don't think we'd be a good fit."

I strode towards the door, and Terry came to life, shifting into a new gear as he chased me to the door.

"Wait! How about we throw in some stock options?"

No. Just no.

CHAPTER 3 - ALANA

AS IF TO rub salt into the wound, my phone vibrated as I hurried along Shoreditch High Street towards the Tube station. My university supervisor just wanted to remind me how important it was to secure a suitable work placement so my final degree classification didn't suffer. She'd helpfully attached a project brief to the email—in order to get the course credits I needed, I had to write up what I'd learned during my spell in the real world and show how it tied into my studies.

Hurrah.

Dove was already home when I got back, and so was Bear, the dog she'd rescued with Zander. He was a bouncy ginger thing—Bear, not Zander—who drooled a lot and had a habit of eating Zander's boots at every opportunity. During the week, Dove and Bear lived in a cottage at the fancy estate where she worked, outside of London in Northbury village. Zander usually stayed with her for two or three nights a week, which gave me breathing space, but they'd both be around for the weekend and the last thing I wanted to do was rehash my disaster of an interview.

"How did it go?" she asked.

"It wasn't quite what I was looking for."

"Aw, I'm so sorry. Do you have anything else lined up?"

Nope. "One or two possibilities."

I didn't want dinner to turn into a pity party.

"That's great! You can tell us all about them over dinner. Maybe we can help you to prepare for your next interview? Not that I've had loads of practice, but I know Zander interviews staff for Blackwood."

On second thoughts...

"I promised Tessa I'd watch a movie with her tonight."

"Anything good?"

"Something about dragons and, uh, space. And it's got hot guys in it."

"Any idea what time you'll be back? Not that it matters, it's just, you know..."

She blushed because I *did* know. Dove wanted to do dirty things with my brother, things that I didn't even want to think about, let alone hear.

"I'll just stay the night."

"You don't have to..."

"It's no problem, honestly."

Except it was. Because Tessa had gone out on a date, which most likely meant she'd be doing naughty things of her own later. Instead of ruining everyone's evening, I threw a change of clothes and some toiletries into a bag and slunk off to a cheapish hotel around the corner.

"Single room again, Miss Alana?" the receptionist asked.

No, that wasn't the first time I'd stayed there, and it wouldn't be the last.

"Yes, that tiny one on the third floor's fine."

He beamed at me. "I give you discount."

"Thanks, Marek."

Alone in bed, I turned on the crappy TV and tried to concentrate on a detective show, but I'd missed the beginning, so nothing made sense. Much like my life, really. That hadn't truly begun until I moved in with Zander. And now relationships confused me, and I didn't understand boys.

Especially Rush Moder. Out of morbid curiosity, I opened Instagram and checked out his profile. The rant had disappeared, replaced by a picture of him playing the guitar on stage, complete with thousands of comments pledging to have his babies. Ugh.

Had a responsible adult finally reined him in? How did it work? I'd always figured that with their millions of dollars, rock stars would have assistants running their social media accounts for them. That was partly why I'd been so incredulous when Moder replied to Tessa in the first place.

I checked my inbox, and yes, the whole thread was still there. It hadn't been a figment of my imagination. And possibly I *had* been a little harsh on Tessa over her idea, because after my visit to Fly Boy Media, spending a year writing about four spoiled man-children looked like an attractive option. At least I'd be able to pick my own hours. And it'd be easy enough to fulfil my supervisor's brief and tie the whole project back to my studies. There was the writing I had to practise for the journalism skills module; the ethical dilemmas that had to be weighed up when considering privacy, objectivity, and public interest; the need to expand my research capabilities; and the constraints of media law.

What if I could wangle my way close enough to Rush Moder to write an article about the band? It wouldn't need to be anything epic, just enough to satisfy my supervisor, and Moder *had* been open to the idea because he'd mentioned Dex wanting to sign off on anything I came up with. And the meeting time he'd suggested—eleven o'clock in the morning—hardly said one-night stand, did it?

Should I consider it? There'd be no naughtiness, and I definitely wouldn't wear a bikini, but I'd be willing to put on tight jeans and make-up in the name of a story.

To message or not to message... I drummed my fingernails on the cheap veneer of the bedside table as I considered my options, which were depressingly few.

Oh, screw it.

Raven: Still on for Monday?

Nothing. The screen stayed stubbornly blank. Either someone had confiscated Rush's phone completely, or he hadn't noticed my message. Or possibly he'd come to his senses. Realistically, that last option was the most likely. Dammit. I'd have to start hunting for a proper job again next week.

I'd all but lost hope when a notification popped up on my phone in the middle of my Sunday-evening Netflix binge. My fingers trembled as I read the whole message.

RushModer: Yeah, babe. I'll leave your name at the desk.

Holy shit. I had a...a what? Not a date, but a meeting with Rush Moder. A *business* meeting. A very businessy business meeting. And thank goodness Zander would

be at work tomorrow because I absolutely couldn't tell
him about this. He'd flip out.

He'd *totally* flip out.

"Hi." I smiled at the receptionist at the Hamilton
House Hotel even though the butterflies in my tummy
threatened to force their way up my throat. "I'm here to
see Rush Moder."

Her polite expression faded to mild distaste. "Your
name, please?"

"Raven du Walt."

It felt strange calling myself that, but Rush only
knew me by my Instagram handle. My left foot began
tapping all of its own accord as I waited, and my
fingernails were about to drum out a staccato on the
wooden counter if she didn't hurry up.

Finally, she shook her head.

"Sorry, you're not on the list. I'll have to ask you to
go outside. Indigo Rain's management has set up a
waiting area for fans, and some of the band members
may come down later to sign autographs."

"Could you check again? I only spoke to him
yesterday, and he promised to leave my details with
you."

"You *spoke* to Rush Moder?"

"Well, I messaged with him."

"I'm sorry, Miss du Walt, but he definitely hasn't
given us your name, and we're under strict instructions
not to let anybody else up. Perhaps you could message
him again and clear up the confusion?"

Her voice stayed sweet, too sweet, while her tone

said she absolutely didn't believe me. As for Rush, I hadn't even met him yet, and I already wanted to shake the guy. Was it so difficult to remember one simple task? I took a step back and pulled out my phone, ready to berate him for wasting my time, when I had a horrible thought. Rush had never called me Raven. He'd only ever called me "babe" or...

"Uh, could you try looking under 'bikini girl'?"

"I'm sorry?"

"My name. Try 'bikini girl' rather than Raven."

"*You're* the bikini girl? We were wondering who that was supposed to be."

"Yes, that's me. It's a nickname."

"Where's your bikini?"

I was in a five-star freaking hotel, lady. "I only wear it on special occasions."

And meeting the dick that was Rush Moder didn't count.

"I suppose that makes sense. Okay, take the express elevator up to the top floor. The band has all four penthouse suites."

The security guard stationed in front of the lift stepped to one side as I approached.

"Top floor?"

I nodded. Obviously, he'd seen the receptionist pointing me in that direction, and he swiped a card that allowed me to select the uppermost level. As I sped skywards, the butterflies took a leaf out of JD Altierre's book and got high. They were having a rave in my freaking stomach. I checked my reflection in the mirrored wall, relieved to find I was still presentable after my dash from the Tube station. I wore my make-up like a shield, and I was just touching up my scarlet lipstick when the doors dinged open on the penthouse floor.

The band has all four suites.

I paused in the hallway as the elevator whooshed back down to the ground floor. Suites A and B were to the left, C and D to the right. What was I supposed to do? Knock on each door until I found Rush Moder? Everything about today's escapade screamed "bad idea."

Voices came from the left, and I headed in that direction. Maybe I could ask whoever was there for help?

The door of Suite B was closed, but A's was wide open. I knocked anyway, but when nobody answered, I ventured inside. Further... Further...

"Oh my..."

A naked blonde lay handcuffed to the king-size bed, long hair flowing over the pillow. Three men crouched next to her, whispering amongst themselves while she slept on, oblivious.

One guy turned at my muttered interruption, his eyebrow raised. "Yes?"

JD Altierre. I recognised him from the pictures I'd been studying all weekend.

"Hi, I'm... I'm..." Speechless.

Fortunately, Rush Moder picked that moment to look up. "Bikini girl?"

"You really have to stop calling me that."

After all, I'd worn jeans today, tucked into sensible mid-heel boots, plus a top that covered everything.

"You know her?" JD asked.

"Sort of. She wears less clothes on the internet."

Great. Now he'd made me sound like a porn star.

"On *Instagram*. Rush was looking at my holiday photos. Apart from that, I remain clothed at all times."

"Well, that's disappointing."

JD turned his attention back to the blonde as Dexter Reeves straightened.

"Clothes or no clothes, you need to leave."

"But I was invited."

"Yeah, I get that. But we're dealing with a situation here, so unless you know how to undo a pair of handcuffs without the key, you'll have to fuck around with Rush later instead."

What a pig! And worse, I couldn't even correct him on his mistaken assumption because Rush did indeed think that I was there to fuck around with him. All I could do was stop myself from getting thrown out before I convinced the band that I had a higher purpose.

"As it happens..." I slid a bobby pin out of my hair. "I may be able to help you."

Handcuff locks weren't complicated. I'd found that out one morning three or four years ago after I received a desperate call from Zander. Please could I come and rescue him? His friends thought it would be funny to handcuff him to the balcony in some girl's flat, and he was terrified she'd wake up at any moment. I'd had to climb a freaking tree to get to him, and did I mention he was wearing boxer shorts and nothing else? Remind me again, who in our household was supposed to be the responsible adult?

"Are you for real?" JD asked. "You can undo the handcuffs?"

"Yes, but how did you lose the key?"

"We didn't lose the key. Travis cuffed her to the

bed, and we lost Travis."

What the hell had I walked into?

I bent a ninety-degree kink near the end of the bobby pin and got to work. Following my first ever attempt, which had taken me a good ten minutes, I'd practised on the spare pair of cuffs Zander kept at home until I could get them open in seconds. Then I'd started practising with a bunch of other locks while I watched TV in the evenings. Call it a strange little hobby. A moment later, the cuff around the girl's wrist popped open, and I quickly removed the other end from the bedpost too.

Rush held up his hand for a high five. "That's my bikini girl."

I ignored the hand. "You and me, we need to talk."

JD snorted a laugh. "Sounds bad, buddy."

"And someone needs to find her clothes." I looked around the room, and something red and slinky sticking out from under a chair caught my eye. A dress, I presumed, although I had underwear that gave me more coverage. I stooped to pick it up. "Here. Put this on her."

Rush took the garment and held it up by one strap. "How does this work?"

Oh, for goodness' sake.

When I left home this morning, this was the last thing I thought I'd be doing. Fending off Rush Moder and his wandering hands, yes, but not stuffing a voluptuous blonde back into an overly complicated outfit. Finally, I got her decent, and she still hadn't woken up. What had she taken? I'd checked her pulse just in case, and she wasn't dead.

"Now what?" I asked. "Do we just leave her here?"

"Where's Gary?" Dex asked.

JD shrugged. "Still getting his beauty sleep, probably."

"Who's Gary?" I whispered to Rush.

"The world's biggest asshole."

Really? I'd have said he had some stiff competition from the members of Indigo Rain.

"You'll have to elaborate."

"The minder sent by our record label. Apparently, we bring the company into disrepute."

I looked pointedly at the sleeping girl.

"Babe, we're Indigo Rain. What are we supposed to do? Sit around drinking cocoa and playing shuffleboard?"

"I don't even know what shuffleboard is."

"Me neither." He took my hand and tugged me towards the door. "So let's do something else instead."

Before I got a chance to protest, we were in another bedroom with the door closed. Rush backed me up against it and moved in, pressing his body against mine. Wasn't this every girl's dream? Being kissed by Rush Moder?

Not mine. My mouth went dry as I lowered a mental portcullis on my girly bits.

"Hey, wait. Stop!"

He paused, his lips an inch from mine.

"What's wrong?"

"This isn't why I came here." He tried to kiss me again, but I turned my head away. "I mean it. I came to write a story, remember? We messaged about it."

"You weren't serious about that, were you?"

"Yes!"

"It wasn't just an excuse? Believe me, I've heard

them all. Girls pretending to be singers and models and reporters and masseuses. Pointless. If a chick's hot, I'm not gonna say no." He leaned in, now just millimetres away, and I could practically taste the whisky he'd drunk for breakfast. "And you're hot, bikini girl, even if you're dressed like a nun today."

"Can't you listen to what I have to say for five minutes instead of acting like a sex-starved gorilla?"

He huffed but shifted back six inches. "You slay me, bikini girl."

"My name's Alana, not bikini girl."

"I thought your name was Raven?"

Ah, so he *had* read my profile properly. "Raven's my middle name. And I really am a journalism student." I took a deep breath. "A journalism student who's hit a tiny snag with her coursework."

"What kind of a snag?"

I gave him a brief précis of the past week, and when I got to the part about making Roy coffee, Rush leaned his forehead against mine and began chuckling.

"He really said that?"

"He really did. And I still can't believe I obeyed."

"Fuck, babe, I'm an asshole and even I'd have made you coffee."

Well, at least Rush admitted to his character flaws. "So, how about it? You let me do a few interviews at a time to suit you, and I'll write a story from your point of view. You or Dex can approve everything before it's printed."

"And where would it be printed?"

"I don't know exactly, not yet." I tried for a smile, even as my last hope began to slip away. "But I have three hundred thousand Instagram followers. Some of them might like to read about you."

"Do you take the pictures you post yourself?"

"All but one. A friend took that damn bikini photo."

Rush tucked a lock of hair behind my ear, and I'll admit, his proximity was making me slightly hot and bothered. Maybe, just maybe, I was beginning to understand why Tessa never shut up about him.

"I'll cut you a deal, Raven du Walt. Access to our On the Run tour and an interview with me in return for you taking photos for my social media profiles. I'm always too drunk to hold the fuckin' camera. You can write your article, and if the others approve it, you can publish it."

"I always figured you'd have a proper assistant to handle your social media."

"We've tried that, but they all quit because of Travis."

"Why? What did he do?"

Did he yell at them? Throw things? Make unreasonable demands? I needed to know what I'd be letting myself in for.

"Charmed their panties off, then kept forgetting their names. Or sometimes he called them the wrong names, and they didn't like that either."

Okay, perhaps that wasn't so bad. "That's not a problem, because I won't be sleeping with Travis."

Rush grinned.

"Or you. This is strictly business."

"You're killing me, bikini girl."

"I'll bring my camera to the funeral."

"Babe, you're gonna drive the rest of the guys crazy."

"Is that a yes, then? I can work with you?"

"You'll have to pay your own way. The bean counters at the record label are tighter than a mosquito's ass."

What a lovely visual. "I can do that."

Finally, he pushed away from me, and I didn't know whether to sigh or collapse in relief. My knees had turned to liquid, and until now, Rush had been holding me up.

"Give me half an hour," he said. "I'll have to sell this to the others. In case you haven't noticed, Dex is a grumpy fucker." He took a step back. "Do me a favour and get me a coffee while you wait."

Hold on. Was he...?

"Kidding." He threw his hands up. "Don't give me that look, bikini girl. I like my junk where it is."

Rush opened the bedroom door and motioned for me to walk out, so I took that to mean my presence wasn't wanted. Before I knew it, I was in the hallway again. Now what? I could hardly hover around like a groupie while Rush explained to his colleagues that he wanted to hire an amateur biographer purely because she looked good in swimwear.

A green sign ahead pointed towards the stairwell. Perhaps I could hide out in there while Rush worked his magic? Yes, that was a good plan.

At least, I thought so until I walked through the door and pitched headfirst onto the floor.

CHAPTER 4 - ALANA

"HEY, ARE YOU okay?" a man asked. Deep voice, American accent, a hint of concern.

I rolled over and blinked a few times, trying to clear the fuzz. Where was I? The stairwell. Right. Except instead of finding a quiet corner for a moment of reflection, I'd tripped over somebody's legs and fallen flat on my face. Who the hell sat in the way like that?

His face came into focus, brown hair flopped forward and tickled my chin, and I got my answer. Travis Thorne, complete with a cast on his left arm.

"Oh, crap."

"Are you okay? Did you hit your head?"

I tested each limb in turn. My knees would be bruised tomorrow, and my wrists hurt where I'd used my hands to break my fall, but my head was fine. The biggest dent was to my pride.

"I'm fine, just mortally embarrassed."

"Don't be. I've fallen on my ass a hundred times."

But never when he was sober, I bet.

"Why were you sitting on the floor?"

"There wasn't a chair."

A little clarity returned. "You handcuffed a girl to your bed and left her there!"

"The blonde? She handcuffed herself to my bed. I don't even know where she came from." Travis helped me into a sitting position and propped me against the wall. "Who are you? And how do you know about her?"

"I came to see Rush."

"Aah."

"Not in that way. You've got such a dirty mind."

"And I promise you I've got the sweet tongue to go with it."

Travis's flirting seemed forced, a habit rather than a heartfelt attempt, and when I met his gaze, a certain sadness lurked behind his soft hazel eyes. Eyes that locked on mine with an intensity that left me squirming.

"Are *you* okay?" I asked.

The shutters slammed down. "Why wouldn't I be?"

"Because you're hiding away in here."

"I needed a few minutes on my own."

"Why?"

"What is this? Twenty fucking questions?"

Well done, Alana. Alienate your potential sort-of-employer before you've even landed the internship.

"I didn't mean to upset you."

Travis's shoulders sagged as if a boulder was pressing down on him. "Sorry, I shouldn't have snapped. I just got some bad news, that's all."

"Do you want to talk about it?" Dammit, now I sounded like my therapist.

"No."

"Should I let the others know to stop looking for you?"

He shook his head, and that was it. Since I couldn't get through the door without him moving, I stayed put, trying not to fidget as the silence turned from oppressive to merely awkward to contemplative. Travis was a thinker. Absent-mindedly, it seemed, he lifted one of my hands from my knees and stretched out each digit in turn, lining his own hand up against it from palm to fingertip.

"A friend died last night." He spoke softly, staring straight ahead. "An overdose. I partied with her three days ago, and I warned her to go easy on the drugs, but she couldn't quit."

"I'm so sorry. Had you known her for a long time?"

"Since we were kids. We weren't from the same neighbourhood—she had money, and we didn't—but we hung out in the same places. Back when JD got hypothermia sleeping in his car, she snuck him in through her window every night until her momma caught him in her bedroom and kicked his ass. She left home soon after that. A free spirit, JD always said, but she wasn't, not until now. Heroin had her trapped."

"Does JD know?"

Travis shook his head. "I'm supposed to tell him. Because I'm the strong one, right? Sure as hell doesn't feel that way."

Words seemed inadequate, so I squeezed his hand. If he wanted to talk, I'd listen.

"You know the worst part? This'll be all over the gossip sites later, and no one'll care that Marli had a beautiful smile and loved her friends and volunteered at the animal shelter on her good days. They'll only care that she was a junkie and she knew me and JD." Travis screwed his eyes shut. "Fuck. Listen to me, unloading like an asshole. I don't even know you."

"It's okay. I'm prone to oversharing myself."

A bad habit I'd picked up from therapy. I'd spent years bottling everything up, and now my mouth ran away from me on occasion.

"So tell me something about you, stranger. Like your name."

"I'm—"

The door crashed into Travis, and a brown-haired man squeezed through the gap. His face matched my lipstick, and when Travis groaned, I got the impression it wasn't just because of his bruised leg.

"What the hell are you doing in here? I've told you a hundred times not to bring groupies upstairs." He jerked a thumb towards the door. "Off you go, sweetheart."

Travis's arm snaked around my waist. "She's not a groupie; she's a friend of Rush's, and we were trying to have a private conversation."

"You don't have time for that. We need to go over today's schedule."

"Ten minutes."

"Now."

The man sounded like a petulant child.

"Five minutes."

"Two minutes. Everybody's waiting."

The prick backed out of the doorway, and Travis slumped against the wall. "Behold, the glamorous life of a rock star."

"Who was that guy?"

"Gary, our babysitter from the record label. He's supposed to stop us from getting into trouble."

"Does it work?"

"Nope. But he annoys the shit out of us while he tries." Travis got to his feet and held out a hand. "C'mon, blue-eyes. You were on your way out?"

"Not exactly," I said as my hand found its way into

his. "It's kind of a long story, but I'm waiting for Rush to message me back."

"About what?"

"A job."

"What job? I didn't know we were hiring anyone."

"You weren't. We had this drunken conversation on Instagram, or at least he thinks we did, but it wasn't me, it was my friend Tessa, and I was wearing a bikini, and..." I covered my face with my free hand. "This sounds so much worse than it is. Anyhow, I'm a journalism student, and he offered me a sort of internship taking photos and writing an article on the band if the other guys agreed, and I guess that's you. I think I'll stop talking now."

"You gonna write the truth?"

"I plan to, and you get to approve any copy."

He used up a full minute and a half of his two minutes contemplating my words. What was going on in that head of his? I wanted to know, but at the same time, I didn't.

"You'd better get your camera ready, blue-eyes."

"You're agreeing?"

"None of us can take pictures for shit." He steered me back towards Suite A. "Just show some compassion, okay? I've gotta break the news about Marli to JD."

"Absolutely. Yes, I will, I promise."

Rush, JD, and Dex were all lounging on the sofas in the living area when we walked in. The blonde was nowhere to be seen, no doubt doing the walk of shame towards a Tube station somewhere.

"Hey, you found bikini girl."

Travis raised an eyebrow, and the barbell stuck through the end of it glinted in the light from the chandelier.

"Bikini girl?"

"Forget I said that. She's not wearing a bikini anywhere near you."

"Or you. She's working for us now?"

Rush glanced at JD and Dex, and Dex glowered at me but didn't speak.

"Yeah. Raven's our Instababe. Make sure you keep your hands off this time."

"Raven?"

"That's her rocker name."

A rocker name that had never suited me, not one little bit. That was why it made the perfect online disguise. Raven was cool and sexy with a dark edge, while Alana was a sheltered blend of emotional confusion and gawkiness. But since I'd somehow blagged myself into the ultimate internship, I had to at least pretend.

"She doesn't look like a Raven," Dex said. "More of a sparrow. What's her real name?"

Gee, thanks. "My name's Alana."

"Where's Gary?" Travis asked. "I thought he wanted to talk to us."

Dex's mask of contempt cracked long enough for him to answer. "He got a phone call."

"Well, Alana, I need to talk to JD." Travis jerked his head towards the door, and JD ambled in that direction. "See you later."

Travis's smile didn't reach his eyes, and I knew why. Like so many other people, I'd assumed that stars like him led a charmed life, but an hour into my assignment, I'd already realised appearances could be deceptive. Until now, my goal had been to get enough fluff to write a bullshit article that would satisfy my uni supervisor, but as I watched Travis trailing JD out of the room with his head down, for the first time, I wanted to actually tell their story. The men behind the music. The truth behind the glitz.

Although if I'd known at that moment how twisted the tale would become, I'd have run straight back into the express elevator, sprinted out of the Hamilton House Hotel, crawled back to Fly Boy Media, and made Roy all the coffee he could drink.

To tell Zander or not to tell Zander?

On the plus side, his inevitable background check wouldn't turn up many skeletons lurking in the boys' closets because they were already widely available to anyone with Twitter. On the minus side, my brother would most probably lock me up in my bedroom until Indigo Rain's UK tour was well and truly finished.

The first concert was tomorrow, in Sheffield, and I was supposed to be at their hotel by eight so I could travel on the tour bus rather than having to catch the train. *The tour bus.* It still felt surreal. Although I was under no illusion as to why I'd got this job, if you could call it that, and the reason had nothing to do with my abilities as either a journalist or a photographer and everything to do with me panic-buying a gold bikini two sizes too small from the sale rack because it was end-of-season and all the high-street shops were getting ready for winter.

But did I care? No.

Resisting Rush's limited charms would be easy, and

I giggled as I fired off an email to my uni supervisor informing him I'd found something to do for the next year. Not that I intended to work for the whole twelve months, obviously. A month putting up with Rush Moder—six weeks tops—and then I could take my time writing everything up. Job title? *Instababe*. Hmm, maybe not. *Digital media assistant*—that sounded better.

For Zander, I decided to go with a variation on the truth as we sat down for dinner. Well, I waited until we'd almost finished eating so I could make a quick getaway.

"I got a part-time job. You know, for my placement."

Zander's head snapped up. "What kind of job? I thought the guy last week was a prick?"

"This is a different job. I had an interview this morning, a last-minute thing."

"Doing what?"

"Uh, it's freelance work photographing venues and writing copy for an events company." That wasn't entirely untrue. I just neglected to mention the part about the venues having rock stars in them. "I'll have to travel to take the pictures, but I can do the rest from home."

"Writing adverts? Are you sure you'll be happy doing that? Two years ago, you wanted to win a Pulitzer."

The chances of me winning a Pulitzer were negligible, while long hours and eye strain were a certainty. Once, I'd aspired to become a famous journalist covering Washington, DC, but now every time I got near a politician, I wanted to punch them in the mouth. So much of journalism focused on politics, and if I had to listen to those idiots spouting their lies every day for the rest of my life, I'd have a permanent headache.

"Things change."

And investigative journalism could be dangerous. Nobody liked reporters or anybody else poking their noses into places where they weren't wanted. Dove had nearly died when she got tangled up with a criminal a few months ago, and I didn't want to admit how much that had scared me.

Taking photos and writing Instagram posts was much more compatible with my current goal. I didn't want to be a hard-hitting reporter anymore; I just wanted to be happy.

Maybe I could start a travel blog when I finished uni? Or do something that used my photographic skills? Fashion shoots, perhaps? Grandma had always told me the world was my oyster, even if I didn't like shellfish.

"As long as you're happy with that," Zander said.

"I am." Sort of.

"What venues do you need to photograph?" Dove asked.

"Uh..."

Zander's phone buzzed, and I muttered a silent thanks to the heavens.

"Shit. There's a problem at the office." He pushed his plate away and leaned over to kiss Dove. "I might be a while."

"Shall I keep your dinner warm?" she asked.

"No, I'll get something at work if I'm hungry." He hunted for his jacket, already distracted. "Good luck tomorrow, Lanie. Call me if you need anything."

"Thanks."

He vanished out the door, and I quickly changed the subject to plants. Dove could talk for hours about greenery, and if she was explaining why bananas were technically classed as herbs and not trees, she wasn't asking questions about Indigo Rain. Phew.

CHAPTER 5 - ALANA

AS I STEPPED onto the tour bus in the morning, a green-haired guy three inches shorter than me thrust a spiral-bound book into my hands.

"Tour rules. Read them, remember them, obey them."

"That's Ian, our tour manager," Rush told me. "He spoils our fun."

I thumbed through a couple of pages, and the first thing written, in big, shouty letters, was *DO NOT SHIT ON THE BUS*. Well, that sounded quite sensible to me, along with *do not vomit on the bus*, *no sex on the bus*, and *no drugs allowed*.

JD grabbed the book and tossed it out the door. "Don't worry about that. Those guidelines apply more to the supporting acts and the crew bus."

"Then maybe I should ride on the crew bus."

Rush took my hand and tugged me forward. "No, babe. You need to take pictures of us, remember? Let me show you around."

There was a lounge at the front with a tiny galley on one side, complete with a kettle, a microwave, and a huge flat-screen TV. Gary had set his laptop up on the dining table, and when he saw me, he beckoned me closer.

"Just so you understand, I agreed to your presence

here under duress. If I hear you've broken a single one of Ian's rules, you'll be off this bus before you can pull your panties up."

Wow. Wasn't he just delightful?

"I'm here to do a job. Nothing more."

"Yes, your photos. I've made my feelings on that quite clear to Rush. If you post anything unflattering, our lawyer is on standby to sue you for every cent you've got."

Was he trying to scare me off? Because his rudeness only made me more determined to stay. I curled my toes into the soles of my shoes and smiled sweetly.

"I won't—"

"Ignore him," Rush said, pushing me farther into the bus. "He likes to throw his weight around."

"Ian's such a hypocrite," JD added, wrinkling his nose. "He's already broken the 'no shitting on the bus' rule. And I like you, bikini girl."

The tiny toilet had a neon sign stuck to the outside. *NO SHITTING.* Beyond that, eight bunks took up the middle of the bus, four on each side—two by two—with curtains for privacy. Belongings lay scattered on the mattresses—phones, laptops, a wallet. A few clothes. Condoms. A plastic baggie full of suspicious-looking pills. Uh-oh.

"Is that your camera?" Rush asked, tapping my bag.

"Yes. And my laptop and a ring light for close-ups."

"Put it on my bed so nobody trips over it." He patted one of the top bunks. "Put yourself on there too if you want."

I dumped my bag, then folded my arms.

"You'll change your mind, bikini girl."

"No, I won't."

In another lounge at the back, Dex had stretched out on a leather couch with a computer-game controller in his hand. Icy air blasted from an air conditioner in the ceiling.

"This is the band's private area," Rush told me. "Ian's banned from here."

"Private means *private*," Dex said.

"Chill, man, she needs to take pictures."

"Not of me, she doesn't."

"Dex hasn't taken his meds this morning."

"Fuck you."

I backed away. "Don't worry, I'm leaving."

In the narrow aisle outside, I had to squeeze past JD to get back to the communal area. The On the Run tour was scheduled to go on for three months, but my sanity didn't have that much stamina. How long could I last packed into a bus with two people who hated my guts and another who wanted to take advantage of me? A week? Two weeks? *Just block out the horror, Alana.* I didn't need to stay for the whole tour, just long enough to do my research. I could do this. After all, I'd spent fourteen years living with my mother.

"Where the hell is Travis?" Ian asked.

Two girls had appeared in the lounge, a blonde and a brunette. The blonde spoke.

"Still in his hotel room, but he said he was just coming."

"Coming. That's about right," Rush muttered. "Alana, meet Reagan..." He gestured towards the blonde. "And Courtney. Our assistants. Girls, this is Alana. She's helping with our social media."

"Good luck with that," Reagan said. "They've been through six social media girls so far this year."

"Call Travis again," Ian demanded. "We should've left five minutes ago."

But she didn't have to. Travis swanned out of the hotel with a rucksack over one shoulder and a redhead on each arm. Tall, thin, and beautiful, so similar they could almost have been twins. He kissed each of them on the cheek, and they were still giggling when he climbed onto the bus.

"You're late!" Ian squawked.

"Yeah, well, I can't shower properly with my arm in a cast. I need help."

"Next time, I'll throw a bucket of cold water over you. Get in your damn seat."

"Is it always like this?" I asked Rush.

"Nah, usually Travis is at least fifteen minutes late." Rush rummaged in the refrigerator, which as far as I could see, only contained beer, white wine, and a packet of cheese. "Drink?"

"No, thanks."

"C'mon." Rush herded me back to the rear lounge. "We need to talk strategy."

Since Dex had bagged one couch and JD decided to spread out on the floor with his headphones on, I found myself squashed onto the other couch between Rush and Travis and someone's guitar. Great.

Thousands of girls would kill to be here, Alana.

"So what now? We just sit here for five hours?"

Rush gave me a one-shouldered shrug. "Maybe six or seven if we get stuck in traffic. Sometimes they let us out for rest stops if we get lucky."

"Really?"

"Yup. Welcome to our world. And people wonder why we like to let our hair down in the evenings."

Dex had his own copy of the tour book, well-thumbed and dog-eared around the edges, and he turned to the itinerary at the back.

"Today, we have interviews, interviews, interviews as soon as we get to Sheffield, so you'd better lay off the beer, bro."

"You should drink more of it. Might loosen you up."

"Guys," Travis interrupted. "Why do we have to start every trip with an argument? Dex, pass me a pill, would ya? My arm hurts like fuck."

"Why? Did it get twisted by one of your bitches?"

"Nah, she slammed it against the headboard."

Dex tossed Travis one of the packets I'd seen earlier, a plastic baggie filled with white pills.

"Knock yourself out." Then to me, "Don't get excited, little girl. These are prescription."

Yeah, but whose prescription? And why was Dex so nasty? I could understand him being upset with me, the interloper, but he didn't seem to like Travis or Rush either.

Rush just ignored him, and that suggested the animosity was a regular occurrence.

"Gimme your phone, Instababe. I need to add my account so you can write nice things about me." He flipped his hair and mock-pouted. "Make sure you get my good side."

"Which one is that? I thought you were all bad?"

He grabbed a bottle of beer and hammered the cap off on the edge of the window frame. The scarred plastic suggested he'd pulled that move before.

"Yeah." He paused, thoughtful. "You might be right about that."

Like every journey, the trip north went faster if a person fell asleep, and I wondered if the boys partied as a strategy—you know, exhausted themselves by having fun all night so they slept like the dead during the day.

I wouldn't have minded, but Rush keeled over sideways and pinned me into my seat, and he smelled worse than a day-old corpse. Since he was actually easier to deal with while he was unconscious, I left him like that the whole way to Sheffield.

Opposite, Dex creaked into life when we neared the venue, and I watched him from under my eyelashes. He stretched back, sniffed his armpits, and grimaced before pushing himself to his feet. Then he staggered forward, even though the bus drove smoothly, and his jaw clenched. Those first few steps... That wasn't normal. And his face scrunched up in pure pain.

Dex had a problem? My hasty research hadn't mentioned any injuries, but I hadn't imagined that expression. What was going on?

Beside me, Rush stirred awake and wiped drool off his shirt.

"You'd better not post that picture, Instababe."

"I won't. But get your hand off my thigh, rock god."

"Yes, Mom."

Rush stopped to use the bathroom before we disembarked, meaning everyone else had gone on ahead when we emerged blinking into the sunshine.

"Which way?" he asked.

"How the hell should I know?"

"Reagan usually tells me where to go."

"I can't say I blame her for that."

"I meant she gives me directions." Rush put one hand on my back and steered me towards a door. "Let's try in here. If I'm wrong, we can just make out instead."

"Don't you ever stop?"

"No, but most women say that's one of my better qualities."

We ended up in a corridor, and I was trying to think up a witty comeback when two men walked towards us and my worst nightmare came true. *Shit, shit, shit.* I recognised both of them because they worked with Zander. Why were Max and Bryson here? Tell me Blackwood wasn't involved in security for the tour... Zander hadn't mentioned that, but why would he? As far as he knew, I was photographing a conference centre today.

Oh, crap. If I didn't do something fast, they were gonna see me, and my internship would be over before it even started.

"Rush?"

"Yeah?"

"I changed my mind."

"Huh?"

I dragged him in front of me and stood on tiptoes to kiss him. Thankfully, he got the message and kissed me back—with tongues, the asshole.

Max cleared his throat as they approached, and Bryson muttered something along the lines of, "Shoulda been a rock star." Then the outside door slammed, and I sagged in Rush's arms, willing my lungs to take in air. Air that felt like a wave of fire rolling off Rush's body.

"What was all that about?" he asked.

"I'm sorry."

"So am I, because I don't think you really want me to fuck you against the wall in this hallway."

"I know those men."

Rush's eyes widened. "Like, know them, know them?"

"No, not that way! They work with my brother, and he doesn't know I'm here. He can get a teeny bit overprotective."

"And you think he might not like you hanging out with us?"

"Exactly. I mean, you're nicer than I thought you'd be, but Zander doesn't understand that, and he'll just go by your reputations, and... I'm sorry. Word vomit."

Rush just stared at me.

"Do you want me to leave?" I asked.

"Nah, babe. You act all cool, but inside, you're just as screwed up as the rest of us, aren't you?"

"Uh, yes?"

What else could I say to that? He was absolutely right.

"Look, I've seen those guys before. We've got a regular security team, but last year, some crazy woman got into my dressing room and attacked me with a knife." Rush lifted the edge of his shirt and showed me a thin scar on his stomach. "Now the label likes to hire in outside help to assess the safety of each venue."

"She stabbed you?"

"Yeah. She'd been writing crazy letters for ages, and the label assumed she was just a kook."

"I didn't hear anything about that."

"They buried it. The venue screwed up, the label screwed up, the crew screwed up, and I got taken down by a girl. Nobody wanted it splashed across the news."

"I'm sorry that happened to you."

"I grew up in the south side of Chicago, babe. Getting stabbed was practically a rite of passage." Brave words, but his weary voice told a different story. "But if you ever see a girl go into my dressing room alone, do me a favour and call security, okay? Because they're all banned."

CHAPTER 6 - ALANA

OH MY...

NO, I had no words.

I stood at the side of the stage, clutching my camera and waving my pass every time someone gave me a suspicious glance. The concert was almost over, and in the two hours the boys had been playing, they'd blown my mind.

I'd been to concerts before, everything from corporate hospitality at the Royal Albert Hall with my mother and the pervert to a muddy Glastonbury trip with Tessa, but nothing—*nothing*—had come close to watching Indigo Rain at Sheffield Arena. In terms of music, energy, and sheer volume, they were in a class of their own. Apart from the people in the accessible viewing area at the front, the whole audience had been on their feet, and even the guys and gals in wheelchairs had waved their arms in the air.

Everyone was still screaming when the band finished their encore and ran off stage, and I scrambled to get my camera ready.

Travis with sweat pouring down his face.

Snap.

Rush waving his guitar.

Snap.

JD pausing to throw his drumsticks into the crowd

below.

Snap.

Dex forgetting he hated me for a second and sticking his tongue out as he made devil horns with one hand.

Snap.

Holy hell.

Now I knew why people did it. Why boys started drumming on plastic buckets and playing cheap guitars in their garages at home, and why women threw themselves at the men those boys became. The four idiots who'd made me want to tear my hair out for the last two days had transformed into divine beings before my very eyes. And ears.

Luckily, only an hour later, they shattered that illusion.

I'd managed to get the last room available in the hotel the band was staying in, a tiny single tucked away by the fire exit on the ground floor. The boys, of course, had suites again, up on the top floor. Apparently, they were having a post-concert get-together, but I had to finish editing photos before I could consider having fun. I had the perfect shot for Rush's Instagram feed, him lifting his guitar strap over his head after he came off stage with his shirt riding up high enough to show a hint of his six-pack while he did so. I just needed to play around in Lightroom to enhance the contrast and bring out the blue in his eyes.

When I'd asked if he wanted to check out the photos, he'd told me to go ahead and post whichever one I liked best. It felt kind of strange that he trusted me like that, but I guess he was used to delegating.

I loaded up the photo and added a caption—

Thanks, Sheffield!—and a bunch of hashtags.

"Well, here goes."

Posted.

That wasn't so difficult, and best of all, uni counted it as work. My supervisor had emailed back this morning, surprised but pleased that he wouldn't have to spend his precious time dealing with my inability to find a temporary job.

Hmm... Was anyone still around upstairs? I kinda wanted to sleep, but Rush had invited me to join the band for a drink, and I figured I should probably make the effort if they hadn't gone out to a club or something. I touched up my lipstick, checked my hair, and hopped into the elevator, only to get stopped by security at the door of Rush's suite. Not Blackwood, thankfully. I'd seen this guy getting off the crew bus earlier.

"I'm with the band."

"If I had a dollar for every time I heard that..."

"No, I really am. I'm Rush's—" Dammit, I nearly said "Instababe." "I'm his social media coordinator. He invited me. I even have..." No, I didn't. "I've left my backstage pass in my room."

"Sorry. If I let in everyone who told that story, nobody would be able to move from all the women."

I was about to give up and slink back to my room when JD pushed past me from behind.

"Hey, bikini girl! Rush showed me the picture. Whatcha drinking?"

Thanks, Rush. I did a mental eye-roll, then flashed a *Ha!* smile at the guard as JD dragged me farther into the room, then wished with all my heart that I'd stayed in bed because—*freaking hell*—Travis was lying on the sofa right in front of me with a girl's head in his lap, and I didn't know where to look. Heat flashed through me from my cheeks, through my thumping heart, and straight between my legs. Fuck. Thank goodness he had his eyes closed or I'd have died on the spot.

"Are you looking for Rush?" JD asked, acting as if watching his mate get a blowjob was perfectly normal. Probably in his world, it was.

"Uh, yeah. I guess."

JD led me into a bedroom, then stopped dead so I bumped into the back of him. "Looks like he's busy right now."

I stood on tiptoes to look over JD's shoulder and got an eyeful of Rush's naked ass, complete with a pair of shiny purple stilettos digging into it. The heels were shaped like daggers. That had to hurt, but Rush didn't seem to notice. I could barely see the girl, just a glimpse of long black hair as Rush sucked her tonsils out.

"That's fine. Perhaps I'll just have one drink and leave."

"Drinks I can do. What do you want? We've got... Yeah, we've got everything."

Including, it seemed, illegal substances. Inside, I was horrified, but I fought to maintain a neutral expression because this was what I'd come to see, wasn't it? Their world.

"Hey, JD! Did you get the stuff?"

JD threw a package in the man's direction, and I noticed a residue of white powder on the massive dining table.

"Save some for me."

Shit. Zander would have a fit if he found out I was here. What if the police came? I'd never knowingly been to a party where drugs were being taken before, although I guess I shouldn't have been surprised at their presence since this was Indigo flipping Rain. Perhaps because Rush and Travis had been nice until now—not the lunatics the newspapers made them out to be—I'd let my guard down.

Seeing the chaos there in the hotel suite, the casual way people snorted cocaine and screwed around, brought home what a sheltered life I'd led. During my time with Mother, I'd attended an all-girls prep school and spent my weekends watching movies and hanging out at the tennis club. When we lived in France, I'd even been junior regional champion, mainly because every time I hit the ball, I pretended it was stepfather number two's head.

"Jack and Coke?" JD asked. "Vodka? Beer? Hang on, we're in England. Gin and tonic?"

"Anything. I don't care."

"Hey, someone get Instababe a drink!"

A tumbler full of clear liquid was thrust into my hand. If any day called for alcohol, it was this one.

"Thanks. Do you know everyone here?"

"I hardly know anyone."

Even so, JD seemed determined to play the congenial host, and I would have been grateful if he hadn't stopped to snort a line of coke in the middle of it. He wiped the traces away from his nose and carried on as if nothing had happened.

"This is Zephyr from Vendetta, one of our openers. That guy on the floor over there is Pete, our merchandise guy. And there's Verity from Styx and Stones, our main support act. Hey, Verity! Where's Meredith?"

Verity looked up at me, three inches shorter despite chunky platform boots. Her platinum-blonde hair was tinted blue at the ends, a vivid blue that matched her eyes and the sapphire stud in her nose.

Now she giggled. "Meredith's with Rush."

So Miss Spiky-Shoes had a name. And now the girl who'd been with Travis walked in too. I recognised her fancy hair clip—a skull set with jewels. From the front, I saw she wasn't English but Asian. Asian, slim, elegant, and beautiful.

"Who's that?" I asked JD.

"Jae-Lin. She used to have a thing with Travis."

Used to? Still did, surely? I was way out of my depth here. No, not just out of my depth. I was freaking drowning.

A crash from the dining area made everyone spin around. The guy next to JD spun too fast and fell over completely. On the other side of the room, an expensive-looking wooden chair lay splintered on the floor, but nobody nearby seemed to care or even acknowledge that fact. No, two of the guys simply heaved a girl in a skimpy dress off the floor and lifted her onto the table so she could carry on dancing.

Just another day in the life of everyone's favourite rock band.

Apart from Dex. I couldn't see Dex anywhere. I tried a sip of my drink as I looked around and almost choked. Holy shit. This was basically neat gin. JD had lost interest in me, thankfully, so I sidled in the direction of the door, hunting for somewhere to abandon my glass, but every surface was littered with empty beer bottles and glasses and random pieces of clothing.

"Leaving so soon?" the door guy asked.

"Past my bedtime."

"Aye, if you keep hanging around this lot, your body clock'll adjust soon enough."

Or not.

Once again, I ran for the stairs, and once again, I went flying over a pair of denim-clad legs the instant I got through the door. By some miracle, I kept hold of the glass, but I fell on my knees and twenty quid's worth of Bombay Sapphire flew over the far wall.

"Shit!"

"We've got to stop meeting like this, blue-eyes."

"Why the hell do you keep sitting in stairwells? It's dangerous."

I took a deep breath as I willed myself to stop shaking. At least Travis had his trousers done up now. That was something.

"Because everyone else takes the elevator and it's the only place I can get any space."

"What about going to bed?"

"Rush was fucking Meredith next to my bed. I tried lying on the sofa, but I couldn't get any peace there either."

"Yes, I noticed."

He raised his barbelled eyebrow at my tone. "I didn't ask Jae-Lin to do that. She offered."

"But you didn't stop her."

"No, I didn't. You seem shocked."

I thought about it. "I guess I am."

Silence wrapped around us like steam. Hot, heavy, but oddly comfortable.

"Why do you all act that way? I'm not judging. Just curious."

"Why?" Now it was his turn to think. "Because we can. That's not really an answer, is it?"

"No."

"How much do you know about the band? You're not like the other girls who hang around us."

"The honest answer? I read your Wikipedia page."

He barked out a laugh. "Honesty's refreshing. Everyone lies in this business. Our manager lied when he told us we got a great record deal. Women lie when they say they like us as people and not as a conquest to brag about to their friends. The crew lie when they say playing the next venue will be easier. The staff at the record label lie when they tell us they care. *Nobody* cares. You know the only people who didn't lie?"

"Who?"

"The lawyers."

"The lawyers?"

"Yeah, the lawyers, when they told us we're stuck on this fucking treadmill for two more years if we want to get paid."

"But I thought..." What was he talking about? "The press said you got a huge record deal. Twenty-five million dollars."

"You don't understand how the industry works, blue-eyes. We don't actually get twenty-five million dollars up front. We get small milestone payments as long as we keep doing what makes the label happy— performing on stage, releasing albums, doing endless interviews—and at the end of the five-year contract, if I haven't thrown myself off a building in the meantime, I'll get one quarter of twenty-five million dollars. Right now, I'd earn more serving up fries."

"You're kidding."

His face stayed stony.

"You're not kidding?"

"They own us."

"Then what do you live on?"

"Per diems. Two hundred dollars a day to cover food and expenses, and half of that goes on an apartment I never sleep in and a car I can't even drive. The label pays for our hotel rooms, which is why we smash them up when Gary's not around. Because we fucking hate them." He flashed a grin, but once again, it didn't reach his eyes. "That and, hey, we're rock stars."

Wow. "I had no idea."

I'd always thought of myself as trapped, but now I saw I had more freedom than I'd realised. And more money. Zander never complained if I went shopping, I lived rent-free in a nice apartment, and I owned my car free and clear.

"Livin' the dream, blue-eyes."

"How did you end up in this situation? With the contract, I mean?"

"Because we came from nothing, and when you've got nothing and someone waves a few thousand dollars in your face, it seems like all the money in the world. When we started off playing the underground club circuit in LA, we had fans, but no cash to live on. The four of us shared this shitty two-bedroom house with no heating and no hot water. Ever lined up at a soup kitchen to eat?"

"No."

"Back in those days, we dreamed of getting signed, and then we ended up in this nightmare. I can't even walk down the street without getting pulled around by fans or hassled by the paparazzi. If I stop to sign autographs, I'll never get away. When I tell them to fuck off, that makes the papers." Travis did that thing with his hand again, lining our fingers up so our palms pressed together. "And that, blue-eyes, is why I sit in stairwells."

I believed him. A piece of paper fluttered to the floor, and I picked it up.

"You're writing song lyrics?"

"Yeah. Work never stops. Entertain or die. That's gonna be the name of our next album if the fuckers at the label don't make us change it."

"Can I see?"

He shrugged, and I took that to mean yes. Travis's writing was neater than I thought it would be, tidy lines of printing in blue ink.

A smile, a kiss, a backward glance,
But now she's fallen still.
In my head I hear her laughter,
In life I never will.
Those that spark,
They go too young.
Stolen by the devil,
Now I'm under his gun.

"Is this about your friend? The girl who died?"

He nodded. "It's all I can do. They won't even let me go to her funeral."

"That's crazy! Why not? Does it clash with a concert?"

"No, it clashes with an interview. The other guys said they'd handle it, but Gary spouted his usual bullshit about us being a team."

"A team he's clearly not a part of. Hasn't he heard of the carrot-and-stick approach?"

"First he beats us with the stick, and if that doesn't work, he fucks us with the carrot."

"What a douche canoe."

Travis laughed again. "A douche canoe? You're so fuckin' polite."

"Compared to you, maybe."

This time when Travis smiled, it was genuine, and my heart did a funny little skip that was obviously a delayed reaction to having fallen over him once again. Outside, he was all attitude and leather and confidence and filth, but in the insulated bubble of the stairwell, he turned into the boy-next-door with a little more facial hair.

But alas, that wasn't to last, and he got to his feet.

"Bet I'm boring the shit out of you. I should go throw a TV through a window or something."

I took his proffered hand, but as he pulled me up, a scream ripped through the air. A girl's scream that made every hair on my body stand on end.

"What was that?" I asked, a tremble in my voice.

Should we investigate? Or run for our lives down the stairs? Travis's eyes had gone as wide as mine as he stared towards the door.

"I don't know, but we'd better find out."

CHAPTER 7 - ALANA

TRAVIS RAN INTO the corridor, and I followed even though my feet wanted to go in the opposite direction.

"What's going on?" he shouted.

When nobody answered, he carried on into the suite where Jae-Lin lay on the living room floor, clutching her stomach as she tried to suck in air. Her chest heaved as she gasped, and she'd turned deathly white.

Rush knelt at her side, trying to pull her hands away.

"I dunno, man. We found her in the bathroom like this."

There had to be fifty people in that suite, but every single one of them just stood there, staring.

"What did she take?" I asked.

Because she had to have taken something, surely? There were drugs lying on the freaking table, for goodness' sake! But nobody answered.

"Rush? What did she take? Anyone? Has someone called an ambulance?"

I dropped to my knees and checked her pulse, finding it weak and fluttery. Was she overdosing? What did an overdose even look like? In my posh, sheltered little life, the only things I'd ever been in danger of overdosing on were Godiva chocolates and Zac Efron movies.

"Jae-Lin? Stay with us, okay? We'll get help." I locked my gaze onto Rush's. "Call a damn ambulance!"

The poor girl jackknifed up, hands clawing at her throat, coughing and wheezing. What was happening?

"What are the symptoms of an overdose? Anybody?"

With the number of junkies in that bloody room, somebody had to know.

"We've only got coke and speed, and that's not either of them," JD said, his voice soft. Scared.

"She didn't take anything," a girl said. "She was just drinking rum and cola."

Then what was wrong with her? She couldn't speak, but then I noticed her lips were beginning to swell, and that triggered a memory. Every Blackwood employee had to go on a first aid course, and last year when someone called in sick, Zander had arranged for me to take his space so it didn't get wasted. Something about last-minute cancellations being non-refundable. And one of the things the instructor talked about was anaphylaxis, how it made your airway swell up so you couldn't breathe.

"Is she allergic to anything? Nuts? Bee stings?"

After what seemed like forever, Travis spoke. "Shellfish. She can't eat shellfish."

"Does she carry an EpiPen? Where's her handbag? Her purse? And has somebody called an ambulance?"

"I'm calling," Rush said, phone pressed to his ear.

JD came to life. "We need to get rid of this shit before the cops get here."

Oh, now people started moving. Avoiding being caught with drugs was more important than saving a girl's life, was it? Until then, I'd been shaking with worry, but as the activity grew frantic, the heat of anger pulsed through my veins.

"Will somebody find her fucking bag?" I screamed.

Travis thought I was polite? I begged to differ.

People murmured to each other. What did the bag look like? Where had she left it? Had she even brought a bag? The crowd began searching, tossing the contents of any unattended handbag on the floor in the hopes it might yield something useful. The toilet flushed in the background.

"Hey! I think I see a purse under the bed. We need to lift it."

Muffled *thud*s came from the bedroom, and a minute later, someone shoved a tube into my hand. An EpiPen. My fingers trembled as I tried to get the stupid thing out of its protective outer case. How did it work? Thankfully it came with pictures on the side, which was about as much as my brain could handle at that moment. Remove the blue cap. Stab the orange end into her thigh. Hold it in place for three seconds.

Thirty seconds passed. A minute, but Jae-Lin stopped gasping and started breathing again. Then her tears came, a flood of them, and I wrapped my arms around her, holding her in a seated position until a paramedic finally arrived.

"What's wrong with this young lady?" he asked, and now I started crying too, with relief because someone who knew what he was doing was there to take over.

"I-I-I think s-s-she's gone into anaphylactic shock."

"You used an EpiPen?"

"Y-y-yes."

"Then you did good. We can take it from here. Have

you got the EpiPen you used?"

Somebody handed it over, and I squashed myself into a little ball on the sofa as the ambulance crew loaded Jae-Lin onto a stretcher and took her away. The police arrived and started questioning everyone, and I'd never been more grateful for my safe, boring life with Zander than at that moment. Would he find out about this? I'd take his anger, but I hated the thought of losing his trust. I wasn't cut out for this. When my mother turned twenty-one, she'd already moved from America to Italy and married her first husband. Me? I still hid behind photos that didn't include my face and ordered most of my food through an app so I didn't have to talk to people.

A cop sat next to me, notepad in hand.

"Can you talk me through what happened here? I understand you were the person who administered the adrenaline?"

"I learned about it on a first aid course."

"Any idea what set off the allergic reaction?"

"Sorry. I wasn't in here when it started."

"Oh? Where were you?"

"In the corridor outside."

"Doing what?"

"Talking."

"To who?"

"Travis."

"Travis Thorne?"

"That's right."

"Talking, you say?"

"Yes, talking. That was all. We were discussing song lyrics, and then someone screamed."

"We heard reports that there may have been drug

use involved. Did you see anything?"

Oh, shit. I'd go straight to hell for this, but although taking drugs was wrong, I couldn't risk ruining people's careers and livelihoods over a moment of stupidity. Not when everyone who'd got high tonight had done so voluntarily.

I shook my head. "All I saw was alcohol. Will Jae-Lin be okay?"

"It looks that way. They'll keep her in overnight in case there's a secondary reaction."

He closed his notepad, and the band around my chest loosened a smidgen.

"Are you done with the questions? Can I go now?"

"I'll need to take your details first."

"Sure."

I gave my name and address, seething. Tessa had always said there was a bad girl inside me waiting to escape, but I wasn't sure lying to the police was quite what she had in mind. I didn't know who I was crosser with—Indigo Rain and their buddies for putting me in that position, or me for allowing them to.

And that anger bubbled over into words once the emergency services had left and Rush tried to give me a hug.

"Nice going, Instababe."

I shoved him halfway across the room.

"Don't you dare 'Instababe' me. My name is Alana. Not that it matters to you anymore, because I quit." I stared daggers at everyone left in the room, with a particular focus on Rush, Travis, and JD. "The three of you need to re-evaluate your fucking priorities."

I stomped out of the room and slammed the door behind me. Who cared if it fell off its hinges? With all the other damage in the suite, nobody would even notice.

Downstairs, I threw myself onto my bed. Well, that was my illustrious showbiz career finished. Just for good measure, I uninstalled Instagram and turned my phone off. I'd find another job. One that didn't involve illegal activities. Writing stories about a bunch of crusty old politicians had never looked so appealing.

The knocking at my door was soft at first, so soft I thought I'd imagined it. But it kept going, insistent, and I stumbled across the room in a baggy T-shirt and yoga pants to inform whoever had woken me up at three o'clock in the morning of the error of their ways.

"What are you doing here?" I asked JD.

"Can I come in?"

"Why?"

"I need to talk to you."

"Then you can say whatever you need to say here."

JD didn't look like a rock star anymore. Floppy blond hair fell over his face, and his eyes were puffy. Bloodshot. He'd gone fuzzy, as if someone had tried to erase his lifeblood.

"Okay." He grasped the doorjamb for support. "I need to apologise for what happened earlier. We all behaved like assholes, but I was the worst. I've never seen anyone sick like that before. I was scared, and I panicked, and I know that's no excuse but I guess self-preservation kicked in or something."

Tempting though it was to shut the door in his face and go back to bed, I appreciated that it had taken a lot for him to come down to my room. Had he ever had to apologise for anything else in his life?

"You'd better come in. We can't talk about this out here."

Secretly, I was curious about JD. Call it my inner journalist. What made him tick? How had he gone from sleeping in his car, as Travis had mentioned, to trashing hotel rooms?

I sat on the edge of the bed, and JD turned the desk chair around to face me. When he sat, he leaned forward, elbows on his knees so we were less than a metre apart.

"Jae-Lin could have died tonight, JD."

"I know. If Zeph hadn't broken the bathroom door down, and if you hadn't come..."

"He broke the door down?"

"Verity was mad because she needed to take a piss."

"And that necessitated destroying the door?"

"She heard someone moaning and thought they'd gone in there to f—"

"Okay, okay, I get it."

"It's rude when there's only one bathroom."

It was also rude out in public, but I sort of understood his point.

"So they broke in and found her?"

"Yeah."

"It's dangerous when people with serious allergies get so drunk they don't know what they're eating. She obviously realised there was a problem if she carried an EpiPen."

"There wasn't any shellfish. Hell, the only food we had was pizza. The cops said it must've been cross-contamination from the kitchen. It was an accident. A stupid accident, and then we made it even worse."

"Yes, you did. I can deal with most things, but not the drugs. What if I'd been arrested?"

"Getting arrested isn't that bad."

Don't kill the rock star, Alana.

"Forgive me if I don't want to try it," I said, with as much piss and vinegar in my voice as I could muster.

"Sorry."

Dammit, he looked so contrite that now I was the one who felt bad. "Fine, apology accepted. Can I get some sleep now?"

"Are you really gonna quit?"

"I'll get the train back to London."

"Rush doesn't want you to quit. Neither does Travis."

"Well, they should have thought about that earlier. Actions have consequences, JD."

Shit, now I sounded like someone's mother. Not mine, obviously, because she'd delegated my upbringing to a series of nannies and the occasional au pair.

"What if we cut down on the parties?"

"I don't care about the parties, just the illegal substances. Can you cut down on those?"

JD sat back and sighed. "That's mostly me, and I've tried. Gary and Ian started fining us five hundred bucks every time one of us got drunk or high."

"And?"

"I couldn't afford to pay my rent, and my landlord took back my apartment. Rush had to sell his car."

Freaking hell. "What about rehab? Have you tried rehab?"

"I don't have time for rehab right now. I think Gary

and Frank are gonna send me after the tour ends. If it ever does. They keep adding more dates."

"Who's Frank?"

"Our manager."

"I thought that was Ian?"

"No, he's the tour manager. Frank's the band manager."

The band manager who put profits above JD's health. Travis was right—nobody cared. Was there any hope for them? The three amigos made Dex look almost normal. And speaking of my favourite grumpy bassist...

"Where was Dex tonight?"

"Who knows? He doesn't party much."

Sometimes, I had to concede Dex had the right idea.

What should I do? Despite their many shortcomings, Rush, Travis, and JD were oddly likeable, and I'd had a great time at the concert. Now that my adrenaline had seeped away, I understood I'd lashed out earlier in shock and fear, and perhaps I'd been too hasty. This wasn't my dream job, but it was a chance to sneak a glimpse into a world normally closed off to girls like me.

"I'll stay, but I'm not going to any more of your parties if you have drugs there. Or if people are having sex in front of me because I really don't need to see that. And I'm not travelling on the tour bus if you've got illegal substances on board."

"We don't have coke on the bus. Our dealer delivers."

I held up a hand. "Stop! I don't want to know any of this."

"Sorry."

"Just let me get some rest. We're in Liverpool tomorrow?"

"Leaving at nine."

I closed the door behind JD, then leaned on it and closed my eyes. *Dammit, Alana.* How badly would I regret this in the morning?

CHAPTER 8 - ALANA

IT WAS A subdued rock band that climbed onto the tour bus on Wednesday morning. Either that or they were still asleep, which was entirely possible. I felt like a zombie myself.

According to Google, the journey to Liverpool would take two and a half hours, and I'd hoped to spend most of that snoozing. But Ian had other plans.

"What the hell did you think you were doing last night?" he yelled at everyone. "You promised you'd go straight to bed, then you destroyed an entire hotel suite. Again."

Rush shrugged, unapologetic. "A few people came over."

"It's splashed across the internet. The police were called, and everyone's saying a girl overdosed."

"She didn't overdose. She had an allergic reaction."

"You really think people will believe that?"

"Who cares?"

"Frank's flown in to sort out the mess, and I'll warn you—Gary's not happy."

"What's fuckin' new?"

"I'll tell you what's new—from now on, we're implementing an extra tour rule. Anyone caught with more than two visitors in one hotel room gets a thousand-dollar fine."

"That's you fucked, buddy," JD said to Travis. "You'll have to cancel the triplets tonight."

Rush snorted. "That's him not fucked, you mean."

"You can't keep sabotaging your careers like this," Ian said. "Thousands of people have booked to see you on this tour, and your fans don't want to witness you acting like hooligans."

"Bullshit. That's exactly what they want. You think they'd pay to see choirboys?"

"Everybody's patience is wearing thin. Anyone would think you wanted this tour to end."

"We do."

Ian ignored that comment and pointed to the back of the bus. "Get some sleep."

I tried to follow, but Ian put out an arm to stop me. "Not you."

"Why? I need sleep too."

"The boys have had quite enough distractions for one day. If you want to sleep, you can do that on the seat here."

What an asshole. Four spare bunks and an empty lounge, and I had to squash onto a bench beside Reagan and Courtney.

"Do you think it's true?" Courtney whispered.

"Think what's true?"

"That the girl last night had an allergic reaction?"

"She did. I was there."

Reagan's eyes narrowed. "You were there?"

"Not for very long. I was on my way to my room when Jae-Lin got sick, but somebody screamed, and I ran back."

I carefully left out any mention of my little chat with Travis. Everyone here seemed to have a different agenda, and I hadn't yet worked out whose side the two girls were on. Wow. This tour was actually more political than Parliament.

"And?"

"And she'd gone into anaphylactic shock, so I used her EpiPen."

"*You* did?"

"Yes."

Why did they look so surprised? I may not have understood how the world worked yet, but I wasn't entirely stupid.

"But I thought you were just here to do Instagram?"

"Right. Next time there's a girl dying at my feet, I'll just post pictures instead."

"There's no need to get snippy."

Reagan turned away from me in a huff, and I mentally filed her in the "too stupid to live, too mean to die" category.

Courtney gave me a helpless "she's always like this" smile. I rolled my eyes back, and she giggled. Yes, Courtney was okay, but I'd have to watch my back when it came to Reagan.

The band killed it on stage again while I slumped against a stack of equipment boxes in the wings and tried desperately not to fall asleep. Even with earplugs in, the noise was deafening, and the bass vibrated through my core with every chord Dex played.

Gary had been incandescent with rage when we arrived in Liverpool, shouting red-faced about professional behaviour and potential cancellation costs and legal fees. Dex had walked off first, and Gary had only yelled louder as the others followed.

I'd started making notes for my article in the afternoon, but as the saying went, truth was stranger than fiction. Who would believe all the crazy stuff I'd seen so far? A rock group at the pinnacle of their career who hated their jobs, the secret personalities of four so-called bad boys, and a record-label exec who popped antacids like candy.

Especially as I told a different story with my photos. Yes, I'd reinstalled Instagram, and the boys put on a show for the camera, leaping around the stage as they played their hearts out.

Perhaps I should suggest a few more candid shots to Rush? Rehearsal pictures, snaps from the tour bus, that sort of thing. Real life without the sparkle.

Rush grabbed me and spun me around as they came off stage. Great. Now I was sweaty as well as tired.

"Did you get good pictures, Insta—"

I glared at him.

"Instalana?"

Better. At least he was trying. *Very* trying.

"I got some good shots, but I'll need to edit them when we get back to the hotel. No party tonight, right?"

"No party."

And no more hotel suites either. From now on, Gary insisted the boys got basic rooms only, and worse, they had to share. JD grumbled about Dex's snoring, and Travis complained about Rush's untidiness, but Gary refused to budge. Four guys, two rooms, no minibars, and he'd even cleared the alcohol out of the fridge on the bus and replaced it with juice and mineral water. Wasn't this the funnest tour ever?

At the hotel, Rush clutched the bottles of whisky and vodka he'd managed to score at the venue while Travis carried their bags. Teamwork, rock star-style. I half expected Travis to have at least two out of the three aforementioned triplets in tow, but tonight, he'd returned alone.

He didn't break all of his habits, though. When I went out in search of ice just after midnight, he was back in his favourite spot. The good news was that I didn't trip over him this time. The bad news? Dex was with him.

"I'm just looking for ice," I said, holding out my glass to prove I wasn't lying.

"One floor down," Dex told me.

I tried to squeeze past, but Travis reached up and grabbed my hand.

"Hey, wait."

"What?"

"I never thanked you. For last night, I mean. I know JD spoke to you, but me and Rush owe you an apology too. We'd have been in so much shit if you hadn't done what you did."

"Do you mean the part where I saved Jae-Lin's life or the part where I lied to the police about your drugs afterwards?"

"Fuck." Travis dropped his head back against the wall with a quiet *thunk*. "All of it."

"I don't like clearing up your mess."

"Cut him some slack," Dex said.

"Oh, you mean like you do with me? You've been nothing but hostile since I arrived."

"She's right, buddy."

"Shit." Dex slithered down the wall, wincing as he landed. "I figured you were the same as all the others."

"What others?"

"The brainless bimbos that buzz around Rush and Travis, sticking phone numbers in their pockets and poking holes in condoms."

"Seriously? They do that?"

Travis nodded. "Rule number one of being a rock star, blue-eyes. Always bring your own protection."

"Wow." I shook my head to clear the image of an evil bitch with a pincushion. "For your information, my only goal in this whole debacle is to write an essay that convinces my university supervisor I can take all the waffle I've learned in my journalism studies course and apply it to the real world. I don't want a notch on my bedpost or a nasty surprise in nine months' time. Nor do I want to get arrested or appear in the press myself. Got it?"

Dex chuckled. He actually chuckled. "Rush was right. You're a ball-buster."

That was what he thought? No, I wasn't tough. I'd just gone into this game with a kill-or-be-killed mentality, and my emotions were all over the place. Three days with Indigo Rain felt like a year.

"I am *not* a ball-buster."

"Sweetheart, that's a compliment."

"I'm not your sweetheart either. And if you'll excuse me, I was on my way to get ice."

This time, it was Dex's turn to grab my arm.

"Trav, get her some ice, would you?"

Oh, no, no, no. Because that would leave me alone with Dex.

"I can get it myself."

But Travis was already on his feet, holding out his good hand for my glass. "Sure."

His footsteps receded down the tiled stairs while I stood opposite Dex and his attitude with only a chasm of awkwardness separating us.

He spoke first. "My problems can't go in your article."

"I won't publish anything you haven't approved. I've already said that."

"Yeah, well, journalists lie."

"I'm a journalism student, and a lot's changed since I started my course. I don't even want to be a journalist anymore. But I need to finish my degree and get that piece of paper because otherwise, I've wasted two years of my life."

So many employers wanted you to have a degree. Without one, it was difficult to get interviews. Unless you wanted to be a doctor or a lawyer, it often didn't matter what you'd studied as long as you had letters after your name. They just wanted to know that you could apply yourself and learn.

Dex stayed silent, so I carried on. "It's obvious there's something wrong. I don't need to be a journalist or a genius to see the pain in your eyes."

Which he closed, blocking me out. Where was Travis with the damn ice?

"Arthritis," Dex finally said. "I have osteoarthritis in my knees. Some days I can hardly walk."

"Arthritis? But you're so young."

"Nobody told my bones that."

"But why is it such a big secret?"

"Rock stars drink. They do drugs. They screw girls, and they smash up hotel rooms. They don't walk around like old men at the age of twenty-five. And Gary thinks the cost of our tour insurance would go up if the news got out."

"Then Gary's an even bigger asshole than I first thought."

Dex opened his eyes again and smiled, just for a second. "Gary's got an ego the size of the Coliseum and a dick the size of a peanut."

"Is there any treatment for your knees?"

"I need osteotomies in both legs, but that'll take me out for at least six weeks, so it has to wait until the end of the tour. If that ever fucking comes."

"That's crazy."

"The devil's got us by the balls. We sold our souls to a corporation, and it's not letting us go. Which is why you need to go easy on Travis. He lost one friend this week, yesterday he almost lost another, and he's more shaken than he'll admit."

"Marli was friends with JD too, wasn't she?"

"Yeah, but not in the same way as Travis."

"They dated?"

"For a while. We've all got our problems, Alana, and for Travis, that's women. He falls for them too easily, and he ends up getting hurt."

"But he has a different girl every night."

"A coping strategy. He never used to be that way. Just like Rush didn't used to drink whisky for breakfast and JD didn't have his dealer on speed dial. This world's changed us all. The only good part is the music."

Heavy boots on the stairs signalled Travis's return. He hadn't changed out of his stage gear yet, although he'd left his leather jacket somewhere.

"Ice, milady. The machine on the next floor's broken, so I had to go ask at reception, which meant signing twenty autographs and posing for selfies." He held up a plastic bag. "Got some for you too, buddy. Figured you'd need it. Did you tell her?"

"Yeah."

"So now you know why he's such a miserable fucker." Travis gave me my ice, then reached out a hand and hauled a creaking Dex to his feet. "Just don't make any jokes about walking canes. He hates that."

"No canes. Got it."

Another piece of the jigsaw puzzle that was Indigo Rain slotted into place. Dex was in constant pain, and he used his attitude as a defence mechanism. I wouldn't just need to cut Travis some slack, I'd need to cut Dex some too.

CHAPTER 9 - ALANA

"SHE'S DEAD, DEXTER. She won't know whether Travis is at her funeral or not."

"But—"

Gary held up a hand, his voice irritatingly calm. "Travis is not, I repeat *not*, going to that girl's funeral. You've all got interviews tomorrow afternoon, and you're headlining at Glastonbury on Saturday. No way."

"If he flew tonight, he'd be back by midday on Saturday, and our set isn't until nine thirty."

"No. That's my final word on the subject. Just make sure you're on the bus by nine o'clock sharp tomorrow morning."

What an asshole.

Back at the hotel with the after-show interviews done, Dex, JD, and Rush had made one final plea on Travis's behalf. Travis had sunk into a depression during the day and spent the whole bus trip to Manchester writing song lyrics, which would have been good if they weren't borne out of such pain. At Manchester Arena, he'd spent half an hour on the phone to Jae-Lin, who'd thankfully been let out of the hospital, and then he'd picked up his scruffy notepad and pen again.

I'd snuck a look at some of the words.

I wanted to be there, but I left you to die,
The music machine shut me out.
Now I can't even say a proper goodbye,
Grinding gears silence my shout.

"This isn't good," Rush said. "Travis has these black moods, and they can last for weeks. Everything suffers —our music, our performance, our fans. But mostly Travis."

Frank had pleaded Travis's case too, but his reasoning fell on deaf ears. Gary was simply the most pig-headed man I'd ever had the misfortune to meet.

"Does he know I'm supposed to be a journalist?" I asked Rush as Gary headed for the elevator. "Isn't he worried about what I might write?"

"I might have left that part out. I just said you were our new social media girl."

"That's good, I guess."

"And I may have implied we're fucking because then he'll think you're too stupid to string a sentence together."

Deep breaths, Alana. "Gee, thanks."

"Hey, don't knock it until you've tried it."

"We've already had this conversation. I'm not trying anything with you. As Gary would say, that's my final word on the subject." I mimicked his annoying voice. Gary was that kid at school who ran whining to the teacher whenever he didn't get his own way. "But the bigger issue is Travis. What can we do to help him?"

Maybe I *had* lost a few brain cells, because I kind of liked him. Liked him in the same way I might like a skinny puppy kicked one too many times by its master.

"What *can* we do?"

"Couldn't he fly to LA anyway?"

Dex shook his head. "Gary would lose his mind. You've seen the way he is. He'd think up some vindictive punishment and make our lives hell for the next six months."

"He'd lose his mind if he found out."

"What do you mean, if he found out?"

"What if you said Travis was sick? That he needed to stay in his hotel room to recover?" My brain began working overtime. "Gary doesn't ride on the bus with you guys, right?"

"No," Rush said. "He's rented a big-ass Mercedes, and our music's paying for that too."

"So we'll just say Travis got on the bus first and went to sleep in his bunk. By the time anyone notices he's not there, he'll be in LA."

Now Dex got all negative. "Wouldn't work."

"Why not?"

"Because the moment he set foot in Manchester Airport, the internet would go crazy. Gary has people who track that shit. He'd haul Travis back here before the plane took off. And Trav would get mobbed in LA too. Can you imagine him waiting in line for a cab? There'd be a riot."

"He could rent a car."

"He doesn't have a licence, babe. He got banned, remember?" Rush said. "Plus he's wearing a cast."

"Fine. I'll go with him and rent a car. And I have an idea for the flight."

It was Tessa who'd taught me about the joys of empty-leg seats. We'd flown to Spain and back by private jet last year, and it had barely cost more than a regular ticket. Basically, whenever some rich person hired a plane to fly them somewhere, it would have to fly back, and when it flew back, those seats always used to be empty. Now it was possible to book them at bargain-basement prices via various apps, as long as you could fly at short notice. And short notice was precisely what we needed. So, what were the chances...?

Got one! A small jet leaving Manchester at six a.m. on Friday morning, seven seats free. We could be in LA by six p.m. UK time, ten a.m. PST, which would give Travis time to get to Marli's funeral at one o'clock. I explained all that to the others.

"What about coming back?" Dex asked.

"We could try for another empty-leg, but we might have to fly commercial."

"Which would mean sanctions from Gary."

"But at least Travis would be able to say goodbye to his friend."

What would it be? Would his three bandmates risk Gary's wrath? By my estimation, we probably had a fifty percent chance of getting in and out of LA without being spotted, and worse odds of his absence going unnoticed in the UK. But Gary was an utter prick for vetoing the trip in the first place. If he'd helped, Travis could have gone to the airport right after tonight's concert and been on a plane by now.

"I say do it," Rush said.

JD nodded his agreement. "Me too. Dex?"

After an unbearably long wait, Dex finally shrugged. "It's not as if this tour can get much worse. Just make sure he's back in time for our festival set, or we're all dead."

There was something strangely illicit about sneaking out of a hotel in the dark. Perhaps it was because Gary was still asleep—in his suite, no less—or perhaps it was because I had the world's hottest rock singer in tow. Yeah, okay, I admitted it. Travis was hot. But hot in a don't-get-too-close-or-you'll-burn-up sort of way, not a fling-your-knickers sort of way.

"This is crazy," he whispered as we headed towards the cab I'd booked.

"That's a bit rich coming from the man who took a blow-up doll as his date to an awards show last year."

"Hey, I liked her. The perfect woman. She didn't keep talking, her bits were in the right places, and she didn't get hysterical or wake me up at five a.m. the next morning begging for—"

"Okay, okay, I get the picture."

Travis opened the car door for me, and I slid into the back seat. We were travelling light—just one small bag each with a change of clothes and other essentials. Half an hour later, we boarded an eight-seater jet, and as our pilot taxied down the runway at a quarter past six in the morning, I sent a silent thank-you to Tessa and her goal to live a champagne lifestyle on a Prosecco budget. So far, so good. We'd be flying into LAX, and I'd booked a rental car at the other end. *Remember to drive on the right, Alana.*

"Are you okay?" I asked Travis.

He'd barely spoken since we left the hotel. I'd snuck glances at him on the drive, but he'd spent the whole time staring out the window.

"No, but I'm better than I was yesterday." He reached across from his plush leather seat to squeeze my hand. It was just the two of us at the back of the cabin—no flight attendant, and the only other passenger was a grey-haired businessman engrossed in his laptop at the front. The old guy nodded in time to music on his headphones. "And I need to say thank you. I can't remember the last time someone dropped everything to help me like that. Maybe it seems dumb that I want to go so much..."

"It's not dumb. You want closure."

"Yeah." He gave a heavy sigh. "I really liked Marli, you know? Once, I even thought we might have a future together, but then she started on the heavy stuff... Injecting... Shit, I should have tried harder."

"It seems to me that a person has to want to give up before they can quit."

"If I'd been there..."

"You didn't force her to take the drugs, Travis. Did she have other people around her?"

"Always. Everybody loved Marli."

"You can't blame yourself for what happened. She wasn't alone."

"I know, but... I guess I thought she'd be around forever, and now she's not."

"How long were you with her? Together, I mean."

"Six months? Seven? Something like that, at the beginning when the band was taking off. Marli was a rebel. We never saw each other every day or anything, but for me, there wasn't anyone else in that time. Her parents were loaded, wanted her to be a lawyer like her daddy, but she only cared about having fun. I had no money, but she didn't give a shit." He smiled for a brief moment, but it faded just as quickly. "She bought me my first guitar."

"You play rhythm guitar, right?" I'd been doing my research.

"Yeah, sometimes. And I also play the keyboard, but not live."

"You're full of surprises."

"Marli used to say that too. *You're full of surprises, Trav, some bad, some good.* I missed her when we left LA. I still miss her. I'll always miss her."

"First love?"

Another flicker of a smile. "Second. Caitlin came first. My girlfriend in high school. Well, sort of. I didn't spend much time actually in the school building."

"Did she?"

"Catie was a good girl. Too good for me. She's a nurse now."

A good girl. Those words made me shudder, but I fought to maintain my cool. "You're still in touch?"

"We call each other every few weeks. I know you think I'm an asshole with women, but I do care."

"No, I can see that you care." Why else would we be flying five and a half thousand miles to Los Angeles? On the outside, Travis was bad from the roots of his messy brown hair to the toes of his scuffed leather boots, but inside, he had a heart. I saw that now. "What about your parents? Are you close to them?"

"My biological parents? No. I don't even know what they look like. But I probably get on better with my last set of foster parents now than I did when I lived with them. They took so much shit from me, and all they ever gave me back was love. If I'd grown up with them my whole life, I probably wouldn't be the dick I am today. They're the closest thing to family I have."

"You grew up in foster care?"

"Partly. I spent six years in a children's home. They just sent me wherever there was space."

No wonder Travis found relationships difficult, if he'd been shipped from pillar to post that way. How was it possible to form bonds if you never knew where you'd be the next month?

"Do your foster parents live in LA too?"

"Not too far from the funeral home. If I had another hour today, I'd visit."

"When did you last see them?"

"At Christmas." He sighed. "Too long ago. We only got one day off, and I'd barely finished dinner before it was time to leave. How about your family? I've only heard you mention your brother."

"Zander's the only family I care about. My mother's a professional divorcee, and my father's dead."

"I'm sorry."

"Don't be. I'm not. He spent his whole life ruthlessly squeezing every last drop of money out of his investments, cheating on his many wives, and pretending I never existed. He hardly ever talked to my brother—half-brother—either, but Zander got bonus points for having a penis. I think maybe Father hoped he'd take over his business someday, but when I was seventeen and Zander was twenty-three, Father died of cancer. Of his oesophagus. For ages, he thought it was acid reflux, so he ignored it, although it really shouldn't have been a surprise because he smoked and drank and ate all the wrong things and... I talk too much."

Travis squeezed my hand. "If talking helps, then talk."

"I won't burden you. I have a therapist for that."

"Gary tried sending me to a therapist once. For my 'womanising.'"

It didn't seem to have helped Travis much, did it?

"What happened?"

"She was thirty years old, blonde, and her husband didn't pay enough attention to her."

"You didn't...?"

"Like I said, I'm an asshole." He waggled his eyebrows. "But she gave me a good report."

"I bet she did. Wow. My therapist is a middle-aged lady who speaks in questions and always wears pearls."

"You still see her?"

I nodded. "I had to cancel this week's appointment, so you get to put up with me instead."

Travis reached across and reclined my seat, couch-style, then leaned over, elbows propped on the arm.

"If you want to talk, I'll listen."

"I was kidding."

"I wasn't."

The air thickened and turned cloying. One of my hands went to my throat and pulled my sweater away, but that didn't help, not one bit. Why did it always hurt when people were nice to me? Those kind words needled at my heart and left it raw.

Travis leaned closer and wiped my cheeks with his sleeve. "Hey, don't cry. You don't have to say a word if you don't want to."

"No, I..." How did I explain that my emotions were a big tangled ball of string, and whenever I tugged at the end, I never knew whether the whole lot would come loose or get knotted tighter? "I'm so screwed up inside."

"Welcome to the club, Alana Graves."

I screwed my eyes tightly shut. "I lost my virginity when I was thirteen years old." The words just fell out of my mouth. "To the man who became stepfather number three."

"Fuck."

"Do I win?"

"You got me beat, blue-eyes. I was seventeen."

"Really?"

"Late starter, but I've made up for it since."

"I can't believe we're even having this conversation."

Travis fell silent for a long moment, and when he spoke again, his voice was almost a whisper.

"Alana, I'm sorry if I've made you uncomfortable when I've touched you. If any of us have made you feel uncomfortable. I didn't realise at first how...how fragile you are."

"You haven't made me feel uncomfortable. You all flirt, and that's okay. I guess in a weird way it makes me feel normal. Because you're not going to do anything more, are you? I do my job, and you do yours, and I don't have to worry about waking up in the middle of the night to find you slipping into my bed or jacking off next to me or wrapping my hands around—" I choked out a sob. "I'm sorry."

"You've nothing to be sorry for, blue-eyes. What happened to your stepfather? Did he get convicted?"

"I was fourteen when Zander found out what was happening and got me out of there. Fourteen, and it took me three years of therapy to be able to talk about it. I didn't want to go to court, not if I had to face him again."

"You're braver than I've ever been. I promise you none of us will ever hurt you, but if I ever get the chance, I'll smash my guitar in your stepfather's face."

"That's the rock-and-roll thing to do, right?"

"Right." Travis stroked his thumb over my knuckles. "What about boys? Did you ever...?"

I shuddered automatically. "Nuh-uh. I'm only interested in window shopping. I have friends who are guys, but most of them are gay, and none of them know about my past. Not many people do—my brother, his wife, my best friend, my therapist, and now you. That's it. I don't even know why I told you. Sometimes, my mouth just runs away from me. But my therapist said I'd find it easier to talk about as time goes on, so I guess all those thousands my brother's spent on her fees have been worth it."

And it *was* easier. Those first months, I'd barely spoken a dozen words in each session. Now I could vocalise how angry I was with the man whose job it had been to take care of me. Just thinking of him gave me the shivers. And my mother, who'd stood by and let it happen.

Travis took off his jacket and tucked it around me. It was the one he wore most, and it smelled of leather and man with just a hint of cologne. Yes, Travis was a womaniser, but only when the women in question were willing. Around me, he behaved himself, and for that I was grateful.

My mouth opened in a yawn as a lack of sleep caught up with me, and I covered it up with my hand.

"Sorry."

"Get some rest, blue-eyes. You've earned it."

I managed a smile. "Wake me when we get to LA."

CHAPTER **10** - ALANA

"ALANA? WE'VE LANDED."

"In LA?"

"I sure hope so. You slept through the refuelling in New York."

I willed my gummy eyelids open and groaned when I caught sight of Travis. Mornings weren't my friend, and while I felt as if I'd been dragged through a rubbish dump backwards and probably looked worse, Travis had changed into a suit. I hadn't even realised he owned a suit. Black, single-breasted, with a thin tie and tailored trousers. He'd combed his hair and tied it back and also trimmed his beard.

"What's up?" he asked.

"I've flown out of Manchester and into a fairy tale. *Beauty and the Beast*. Guess which one I am?"

"Can I plead the fifth?"

"My mouth tastes like a compost heap."

"Here." He held out a packet of gum and a bottle of water. "I came prepared." A wink. "I've had practice at this."

Memories slowly surfaced, snippets of conversation and confessions and tears. Shit.

"Uh, what I said earlier... Can you just forget all that?"

"No, blue-eyes, I can't." Now I got solemn Travis.

"But I wish I could help *you* to forget."

"I'll be fine." I went for perky. "Let's go find this rental car."

"At least one of us still has a licence."

"DUI, huh?"

"Yeah, and it was bullshit. They caught me the morning after, and I only got into my car so I could move it off the drive to let someone else out. Technically I shouldn't have done it, but I was on the road for, like, five seconds, and I wasn't even going anywhere."

"But you broke your arm?"

"I told the cops to take a hike, and my arm got fractured when they slammed me on the kerb."

"But...but that's illegal, surely?"

"They said I resisted arrest. And then the judge said he wanted to make an example of me."

"Not a fan?"

"Guess not. I probably screwed his wife or something."

"Why do you do it? All the women, I mean."

I struggled to reconcile the Travis I'd talked to last night, the one who mourned over Marli and spoke so fondly of Caitlin, with the man-slut I'd been hanging out with for the past week. Why the difference?

"Why?" He chewed his lip as he stuffed his jacket into his duffel bag. "Because at the moment, it's my only option. I like women's company, I won't lie about that, but my lifestyle isn't compatible with a stable relationship. What girl wants to live on a tour bus? Wants to see groupies throwing themselves at her man every night? There has to be trust, and trust isn't easy to come by in this business."

"I suppose I can understand that."

He held out his hand, the one with the cast this time, and I took it without thinking as he picked up both of our bags. Then I realised I shouldn't be getting so familiar with Travis Thorne, but I didn't want to offend him by snatching my hand away. That and it didn't feel as scary as I thought it might.

"What will you do in two years, when your contract's up?"

"In two years, I'll be free. I'm gonna buy a shack on a beach somewhere and spend my days messing around with my guitar and eating pineapple."

"Pineapple?"

"What's wrong with pineapple? It's my favourite food."

"Nothing's wrong with it. It's just not very rock-star."

"We don't always bite the heads off small mammals, you know. Only on stage." Travis waved to our pilot. "Thanks, buddy."

I giggled as we hurried down the steps and into a car waiting to take us to the terminal. "What about the others? Indigo Rain will split?"

"For a few months at least. We all need a break. After that? Who knows? We've gone full circle now—when we first got signed, we were best buds, last year we hated each other, but when Dex punched Rush out the day before Thanksgiving, we realised we'd been taking our frustrations out on each other and agreed things had to change."

"And now you're okay again?"

"We got into this shit together, and we'll get out of it together."

The private terminal at LAX was nicer than any other airport I'd ever been to, quiet too, and small enough that getting to the exit didn't burn more calories than a gym session. We were almost there. So near. I could practically taste the LA smog when it happened. When what happened, you ask? The worst thing imaginable.

Somebody recognised me. Not Travis. *Me*.

"Alana?"

I'd been so busy checking my phone for the rental car details that I hadn't noticed the blonde woman approaching, and now I found myself three feet away from Zander's boss. Not his London boss, but the owner of the whole freaking company. Emmy Black. I'd met her once or twice when I'd gone to Blackwood social events as Zander's plus-one, and quite frankly, she'd scared me.

And now she scared me even more because I was in a city I wasn't meant to be in with a man I wasn't meant to be with, and if Zander found out, he'd go mental.

"Uh, yes?"

Now her gaze homed in on Travis. "Travis Thorne? Aren't you supposed to be playing Glastonbury tomorrow?"

"I'll be there."

"Cutting it a bit fine, aren't you?"

"We've just flown in for a funeral," I told her. "We'll be leaving again in a couple of hours."

She looked down at our joined hands. "Should I be offering my congratulations?"

"No!" I hastily stuffed the offending hand into my pocket. "I mean, I'm just here to help out with organising stuff."

"Like a job?"

"Yes. A job. Exactly like a job."

"Does Zander know about this job?"

"I may have glossed over some of the details."

"Fuck me. Your brother isn't gonna be happy."

"It's fine, honestly. I'm just going to drive Travis to the service, I'll book us a flight home while he's inside, and we'll be back in the UK before anyone's even noticed we're missing."

"You plan to go commercial?"

"Unless we can get another empty-leg."

"Honey, he'll get eaten alive in the airport." She ticked off on her fingers. "Today, you've got Scott and Connor Lowes flying in. Armand Taylor's arriving, President Harrison's just left, and the entire cast of some reality show is causing chaos in Terminal Four. There's paparazzi everywhere."

"Oh." Dammit.

Travis stepped forward. "Look, lady, I don't know who you are, but this is none of your business."

"Since my company's tasked with assessing security for your tour and ensuring the safety of your band, this literally *is* my business." She checked her watch. Tapped long purple fingernails on her phone screen. "Follow me." Then, under her breath, "What the hell did I do to deserve this?"

Travis looked as though he wanted to argue, but if I'd learned one thing from Zander and the work-related tales he told me over dinner, it was that you didn't mess with Emmy Black.

"We need to do as she says."

Whatever that might be.

She strode ahead, muttering instructions into her

phone. I hurried to keep up because even in stilettos, she glided like a freaking combat-ready swan. As we emerged into the sunshine, a black SUV skidded to a halt in front of us, and a man leaped out of the driver's seat.

Emmy gave him a tight smile. "Thanks, Kelvin. I'll be back in a couple of hours. Just have a coffee or something." She turned to Travis and me. "Get in. What time is the funeral?"

"One o'clock."

"And the address?"

"Uh, I booked a rental car."

"Cancel it. I'm driving."

"Is she sane?" Travis whispered.

"I don't think so. But do you want to argue with her?"

He sucked in a breath. "Not really."

I slid into the back seat, all the way over to the far side, and Travis climbed in next to me. Emmy peeled out of the parking area, speaking hands-free into the phone as she drove.

"Brett? I need you to change the flight plan. We'll be taking off at four now, and we need to make a pit stop as near to Glastonbury as possible to drop a couple of people off before we carry on into London."

"Glastonbury?"

"Somerset. West of England."

"Got it."

"You're flying us back?" I asked.

"Your brother would kill me if I left you to fend for yourselves. Besides, I'm going in that direction anyway."

"Thank you."

"Thanks," Travis added.

"Thank me after Cinderella here gets back to play his set."

Talk about awkward. Travis went to the funeral alone, creeping in last so he could stand at the back of the chapel, and that left me in the car with Emmy.

"Skittle?" she asked, holding out a packet.

"No, thanks."

The butterflies in my stomach wouldn't have appreciated that.

"So, Travis Thorne, eh? I'd never have seen that one coming."

"It's not what you think. I'm actually working for Rush Moder, doing his social media stuff for my uni work placement."

"And yet you're here with Travis."

"Only to act as chauffeur, although you seem to have taken that over."

"He could've booked a cab."

"It's not a good time for him at the moment. His friend just died, and his boss from the record label is a grade A cockwomble."

"Gary Dorfman?"

"You've met him?"

"No, but my husband has. Although he described him as a skid mark on the ass of humanity rather than a cockwomble."

A giggle escaped. "He's horrible. We only snuck here because he said Travis couldn't come. What kind of man stops someone from going to a funeral?"

"You already answered that question."

"I know you probably think I'm mad for helping him, but he's been so depressed for the last few days, and he needs to say goodbye to her."

"They were close?"

"They used to date." The knot in my stomach grew bigger. "Are you gonna tell Zander?"

"No, but I think you should."

"How? He'll forbid me from going near the whole band."

"You honestly think he won't find out anyway? Bryson and Max go to half of Indigo Rain's concerts, and they're both good friends with your brother."

"They almost saw me the other day."

"Well, there you go. It'd be better coming from you. How long is this work placement supposed to last?"

"It's kind of ongoing. Originally, I thought a few weeks, long enough for me to convince the university I did something worthwhile, but it's fun."

"And you like Travis?"

"No! I mean, yes, but not in that way. We're just friends." Having rock-star friends felt surreal, but that was what they were, weren't they? "All the guys are nice."

"I'm not sure Travis has bought into the 'just friends' part."

"Sorry, but you're wrong there. I've... I've had some problems in my past, and he knows about them, which means he looks out for me."

Emmy rolled her eyes. "O-kaaay."

"Really!"

"Sure."

Thankfully, my phone rang and saved me from an

argument I couldn't win. Not against Emmy. But what did Rush want?

"Babe, we've got a problem."

Out of the frying pan and into the pits of hell...

"What problem?"

"So the first issue was when we told Gary that Travis was sick and couldn't do the interview. He insisted on calling a doctor. Frank found this old dude —"

"Frank knows now?"

"We had to tell him. Anyhow, he found this old dude who's never heard of Indigo Rain, so we pretended Dex was Travis and put a hot towel on his head so it felt like he was burning up."

"And...?"

"We thought Gary cancelled the interview, but it turned out he only rescheduled it. Now it's in an hour."

"At Glastonbury? But it's almost nine in the evening."

"It's with some female blogger. He drove her down here, and he'll invite her to his hotel afterwards as well. Five bucks says he's using our interview to try and buy himself party favours."

"Uh, yuck." Even if we left that very second on Emmy's jet, we couldn't get back in time. "Dammit. Why does everything always have to go wrong?"

"What's gone wrong?" Emmy asked.

I muffled the microphone against my chest. "Travis's presence is required at an interview in an hour."

Fascinating. I could almost see the cogs turning in Emmy's head. Zander always said she was scarily devious, and right now, I crossed everything in the hope that she'd come up with a miracle.

"How well does the interviewer know Travis?"

"I don't know."

"Put us on speaker."

I did so, and she repeated the question.

"Who are you?" Rush asked.

"Trust me; you don't want to know."

"My brother's boss," I told him. "We ran into each other at the airport, and she's helping us out here. Please, just answer the question."

"We've never met the woman before."

"Good," Emmy said. "How do you feel about the Ghost?"

"As in the music producer?"

"The one and only."

Everyone had heard of the Ghost, also known as Ethan White. Not only did each track he collaborated on shoot straight to the top of the charts, but he'd also been front and centre of every news bulletin in the last few months after he got accused of murder. Until then, nobody knew what he looked like because he always performed in a mask. He'd been cleared now, and he was rumoured to be planning a collaboration with Red Bennett, a former boyband star who'd recently reappeared on the scene.

"He's a legend, man," Rush said. "If the label let us have any say in it, he'd be top of our list of people to work with."

"So what about doing your interview in Ghost masks to show solidarity with one of your fellow artists? I know it's not your normal style, but then we could get a stand-in for Travis."

"I'd do it." Murmurs of agreement came from Dex

and JD in the background. "But where the hell do we get a stand-in with zero notice?"

"I have someone in mind. Just leave it with me, and when he arrives, sit him at the back and don't let him speak much because his voice is smoother than Thorne's. Got it?"

"Uh, yeah. Alana?"

"Yes?"

"Is she for real?"

"Just roll with it, okay?"

I hung up and leaned through the gap in the seats. "Do you *really* have someone in mind?"

"Of course."

"Who?"

"Red Bennett. He's at Glastonbury with Ethan, he's the same height and build as Travis, and they've got similar hair. Red'll just have to wear a scarf or something to hide his lack of a beard. Put a cast on his arm, and we'll be golden."

"You know Red Bennett?"

"Honey, I know everyone."

Last to arrive, first out. Travis hurried to the car the moment the service ended, head down. Quiet.

"Are you okay?"

He nodded, but he wasn't okay. I reached over and took his hand, ignoring Emmy's raised eyebrow in the rear-view mirror. Let her judge. She didn't walk in my shoes.

Should I tell Travis about the problems in England? Ultimately, I decided against it because what good would it achieve? Whatever happened with the interview was out of our hands, and he didn't need the extra stress.

Emmy drove like a Formula One driver on amphetamines, but by some miracle, we made it back to LAX without crashing. When we stopped, she picked up our bags from the boot and ushered us on board a bigger jet than the one we'd flown out on.

"This should get us back to England at around one p.m. My assistant's arranged for a car to meet you at the airport, and it's another hour to Glastonbury."

"Thank you for doing all this. I don't know how I can repay you, but if there's ever anything…"

"I'll come up with a way, don't worry. In the meantime, think about telling Zander what's going on, yeah? The longer you leave it, the more hurt he'll feel."

I did think about it. I thought about it while Emmy took her place beside the pilot in the cockpit and when I stowed our luggage next to the seats in the spacious cabin. I thought about it while I sat cross-legged beside Travis on the bed in the tiny bedroom to the rear. I thought about it as I wiped a tear from his cheek. I didn't think about it when I slithered down the headboard and fell asleep next to him, but I sure as hell thought about it when I woke up in his arms four hours later.

Fuck.

By rights, I should have freaked out, but this was Travis. He wouldn't hurt me. And I should have moved, moved all the way back to my seat in the main cabin, but something deep inside me overruled my brain, and I snuggled closer against his chest.

It was official. I'd lost my freaking mind.

Bad boys were bad news, remember?

Chapter 11 - Alana

"WHAT DO YOU mean, it went 'mostly okay'?" I asked Rush.

Emmy's driver had dropped us off at the performer's entrance, and Rush came out to meet us with the passes we needed to get inside. He'd sent me that cryptic message after we landed, and although I'd replied asking what the freaking heck "mostly" meant, he'd been annoyingly silent on the issue. Now we were in the lounge on the tour bus, and I needed answers.

"Whoever that woman on the phone was, she's a genius. Red Bennett turned up with four Ghost masks and a fake cast, we sat him behind Dex, Twitter's gone crazy, and even Gary's happy because we've scored some publicity that didn't involve us breaking shit."

"Nobody noticed Red wasn't Travis?"

"Nah, the woman couldn't take her eyes off JD, and Gary couldn't take his eyes off her legs."

"So what's with the 'mostly'?"

"Reagan walked in just as Red was taking off his mask."

Travis groaned. "Will she keep her mouth shut?"

"Not sure. We had to tell her where you'd gone, and she got real funny after she realised Alana went with you."

"Fuck."

"Why would that matter?" I asked. "It was just work."

Well, apart from the falling-asleep-in-Travis's-arms part on the way back, but I didn't even want to think about that because it confused the hell out of me. Thankfully, I'd come to my senses and crept back to the main cabin before he woke up.

Rush and Travis looked at each other.

"Do you want to tell her or should I?" Rush asked.

"I've been trying to erase it from my mind."

"Me then. A month ago, Travis accidentally slept with Reagan, and since then, she's been pushing for a repeat."

My stomach dropped faster than a runaway freight elevator. "He *what*? How do you accidentally sleep with someone?"

Travis pinched the bridge of his nose. "Jack Daniels. Haven't touched alcohol since. I don't remember a thing about it except waking up with her on top of me, and my... Well, one part of me was still functioning properly."

"And you didn't encourage her?"

"Might be hard to believe, but I have to like a girl to fuck around with them, even if I've been drinking. And I've never liked Reagan. Gary hired her, for one thing."

"But... But... If you didn't participate, or consent, then surely that's assault?"

Rape, even. And if he'd forgotten everything, maybe it'd been more than just alcohol. What if she'd slipped a roofie into his drink or something? I wouldn't have put it past her. I'd poured out my secrets to Travis, and he'd been bottling this up inside.

"And who would believe me if I told them?" he

asked.

"You should…"

I trailed off because Travis was right. Who *would* believe him? He'd spent years cultivating his reputation as a womanising party animal, and unless you knew the real him, which I liked to hope I was starting to, you'd assume he'd stick his dick into anything with breasts.

"Exactly," he said, following my thoughts. "And can I be a hundred percent sure I didn't encourage her? No, because I don't remember. But I'm ninety-nine percent certain about what she did."

And now he had to see her every day. Work with her every day.

"I don't know what to say."

He gave me a sad smile. "Nothing you *can* say. This is my mess."

"And now it's even messier," Rush said.

"I'll rip her bloody nails off," I muttered.

Travis paused to flick a pesky bug off my shoulder. "No, you won't, blue-eyes. I'll fix it. Placate her somehow. Better to do that than to have Reagan take her jealousy out on you."

"You shouldn't have to make a single concession to that bitch."

"For the next two years, my life doesn't belong to me. I'll do whatever it takes to get through it. I'm a survivor, Alana. We all are, and we always have been, even if JD does his best to self-destruct on a nightly basis. In a few weeks, you'll leave, and I don't want you to go back home tainted by the stench of Indigo Rain."

"He's right, babe," Rush said. "This is our world, and we're used to it. Let Travis do his thing."

"If I argue, will it make any difference?"

Travis shook his head.

"For the record, I hate this."

"So do we all, blue-eyes. So do we all."

"You'll need to help Courtney on Monday," Reagan told me as we waited for the boys to finish their soundcheck at Glastonbury.

"Why?"

Helping Courtney wasn't in my job description. Not that I actually had a job description, but Rush hadn't mentioned anything about doing PA work when he sort-of-hired me.

"Because on Monday, I need to buy a dress in Paris, and Courtney can't do everything by herself."

That I could believe. Courtney seemed to spend most of her time staring vacantly into space, just as she was doing right now. But why did Reagan need to go shopping?

"What's the dress for?"

She puffed out her chest and gave me a smug smile. "Because Travis has invited me to go to the Euro Rock Music Awards with him, and I don't have anything suitable to wear."

This? *This* was how he placated the little witch? By asking her on a date? Boy, sometimes Travis could be a real idiot. Surely leading her on like that would only make the situation worse?

The ERMAs were being handed out in Paris next Tuesday. The band was due to travel there on Sunday, record a segment for a TV show on Monday morning, play a private party for some obscenely rich socialite in the evening, sit through interview after interview for the whole day on Tuesday, then walk the red carpet and smile for the cameras. Hopefully, they'd win Best Rock Band too. I'd already made my travel arrangements, but now I wasn't sure I wanted to go at all.

But I knew damn well Reagan would prioritise her outfit over everything else, which meant the band would suffer because of Courtney's shortcomings. Dammit. Adulting sucked.

"We'll see," I said through gritted teeth. "Part of my family lives in Paris, so I need to fit in a visit while I'm there."

In reality, I'd rather have drowned myself in the Seine than spoken to my mother and my new stepfather, the French *salaud* she'd gotten hitched to after she divorced the pervert. But Reagan didn't need to know that. And speaking of family, I had to call Zander. Emmy was right—I couldn't keep skating around the truth with him, because he'd find out eventually.

Might as well do that now. It was less painful than talking to Reagan, anyway. So far, I'd been keeping both him and Tessa at bay with texts, but that wouldn't work forever. If he decided to pop into the office and track my phone...

Okay, Alana, get it over with.

The tour bus was empty, and I set my camera on the table and dialled, hoping I'd go through voicemail so I could delay the inevitable by another day. But no such luck.

"Lanie? You've stood us up for dinner again. Dove made spaghetti bolognese."

"Sorry."

"Are you at Tessa's?"

"Uh, not exactly. I sort of got a job."

"You already told us that."

"I may have skimped on the job description, but I'm having a good time."

"I'd congratulate you, but your tone says I'm not gonna like it. Is this why you've been avoiding me all week?"

"I haven't been..." I totally had. "Sorry."

"Go on, spit it out. How bad is it?"

"I'm working as a social media coordinator for Indigo Rain."

The silence was broken only by Zander sucking in a breath.

"They're a rock band, and they're on a UK tour at the moment."

"I know who they are. I also know they're bad news. Blackwood does some work for them, and I've heard the stories. They take drugs, Lanie."

"Only JD does that."

"Fucking hell, that doesn't make it okay."

"Please don't be mad. I tried applying to other places, and I only got that one offer where they wanted me to run the entire company and make the coffee too. This is much easier, and it's fun."

"Fun until you get slung in jail for possession."

"I'm not touching any drugs, I promise. I've literally had one drink since I started, and most of that got spilled when I tripped over somebody's feet."

"And where are you now?"

"Glastonbury. Please don't make me come home."

"You're an adult, Lanie. I can't make you do anything."

"You know what I mean."

"Yes, you're asking for my blessing to carry on hanging around four men who dabble in every illegal substance known to man, ruin women on a nightly basis, and think they're above answering to anyone."

"That's not true."

"Oh, and you know that for certain, do you?"

"Most of it's an act for the public. It helps them to sell more records."

"But some of it isn't an act?"

"Don't twist everything I say, Zander. Like you said, I'm an adult. Let me form my own opinions."

"Fine. But I want you to call me every day to let me know you're okay." Zander sighed. "I'm only pissed because I care."

"I know. And I appreciate that you care."

"Max and Bry are around at most of the gigs too. If you see or hear anything that worries you, tell one of us immediately."

"I will. I'll do all of that. And Zander?"

"Yes?"

"Thanks. Not just for this, but for everything you've done."

"You're my sister, Lanie. I love you, and I'll always take care of you. Sometimes, you just make that difficult."

"I won't do anything stupid, I swear. I'm just taking photos and writing social media posts and one news article."

"And enjoying yourself, but not too much."

"I love you too, Zander."

"Go listen to some music."

I didn't realise how fast my heart had been beating

until I hung up the phone. I'd done it. I'd told Zander what I was doing, and he hadn't been as upset as I thought. Once again, Emmy had been right. Next time I saw her—if there was a next time—I'd have to thank her, although words were inadequate for everything she'd done. She hadn't even let me pay a penny towards the flight back from LA, just told me to donate a few quid to the local dog shelter instead. Wow.

The call to Tessa should have been easier, except it turned into more of an interrogation. A cross-examination that would have made any trial lawyer proud, asked with the urgency of a rapid-fire quiz show host.

"Is Rush Moder as hot in person as he is in pictures?"

"He's nice. A bit flirty."

"OMG, he flirts with you?"

"He flirts with everyone."

"Fanning myself here. What about the others? Do they talk to you much?"

"Travis and JD do. Dex is quieter."

"I heard a rumour he's dating that red-headed model. You know, the one who wore the strawberry cheesecake dress on the catwalk for Ishmael last year. Is it true?"

Ah, the strawberry cheesecake dress. The fashion designer had made headlines last year when six male models licked the dress off at the end of the show. Hashtag censored.

"I haven't seen her around."

"Is Travis still sick? I heard he cancelled an interview, and he was real quiet yesterday. They dressed in Ghost masks. Did you see those?"

"Uh, yes."

Just not on their faces.

"Are you staying to see the last day of the festival tomorrow?"

"We're all going to Paris in the afternoon."

"Can't. Breathe." Yes, she could. In fact, she was hyperventilating. "Paris? That's so freaking romantic."

"It's work, Tessa. Trust me, there's nothing romantic about it in the slightest."

"Do they walk around shirtless on the tour bus?"

"Wait. How did we get from Paris to shirtless?"

"I have a list. I'm working my way through it."

Good grief. "Uh..."

"How about naked?"

"Tessa! No, they don't."

"Shame. The Red Hot Chili Peppers performed on stage with only socks on their—"

"Enough!"

The opening wail of Rush's guitar saved me from further questions.

"Gotta go. They're just starting their set, and I have to take pictures."

"Don't hang up, don't hang up. Let me listen. Pleeeeeease."

"Sure, I'll let you listen, at least until the battery runs out."

"Love ya, Lanie."

"Love you too, Tessie."

CHAPTER 12 - ALANA

IT TURNED OUT that when you were literally the only person in the whole crew who spoke fluent French, and the band's self-proclaimed number one assistant swanned off on a shopping trip for almost the entire day—allegedly with Gary's blessing—you ended up really, really busy.

I spent hours scheduling transport, arranging for laundry to be done, explaining where instruments needed to go, sorting out meals—including Courtney's vegetarian option, which the hotel chef just laughed at —and doing my very best not to shout at Gary or Frank or Ian. I even went to the hospital with Travis and waited while he got his cast removed. The joy on his face at being able to scratch his arm after eight weeks in plaster was something to behold.

Finally, seven p.m. came around, and I collapsed onto a chair in the lobby while we waited for the cabs to take us to the party the band was playing. Tonight, their show would be different, a stripped-down version with a few acoustic numbers because most of the equipment was already en route to Leeds for Thursday's show. It was the only way they could play the Paris party, and Gary was determined to squeeze every last drop of blood from the band. How much was the label making compared with what they paid out? It had to be a fortune. What did it cost to put on a show? To hire a venue? To pay the support staff? Tickets started at fifty pounds for the cheapest seats, so someone was clearly raking it in. I made a note to do a little research on that. It might make an interesting addition to my article if I ever managed to get it written in between hauling racks of stage clothes.

"You're coming with us, right?" Rush asked.

"I just want to go to bed."

"Sleep's for pussies."

"Meow."

"Want me to carry you?"

No, because I'd probably end up slung over his shoulder, caveman-style. "I can walk."

"That's my girl."

"Not your girl, Rush. Not anybody's girl."

"Not even Trav's?"

Rush looked sideways at his friend, which was just as well because my cheeks heated.

"No, not even Travis's. If I have to come tonight, I'm leaving straight after you've played the last song. You may be able to keep going twenty-four-seven, but I need a rest."

"You can come back with Dex. He never stays out late either."

At least I knew why now. The longer Dex spent on his feet, the more his knees hurt. At Glastonbury, he'd headed straight back to the tour bus after Indigo Rain's set, pausing only to pose for a handful of grumpy-faced selfies before he staggered up the steps. Then he spent the rest of the evening lying in his bunk with bags of ice packed around his legs.

Gary? He seemed oblivious to the pain he caused

the boys, both physically and mentally, although tonight, he appeared to be distracted by a blonde wearing a belt for a skirt. I overheard one of the crew say he'd invited the blogger back to his hotel after the interview at Glastonbury, so Rush had been absolutely right about Gary's motives, except the woman had declined then slapped him when he got pushy. Gary should have gotten together with Reagan. They'd have suited each other perfectly.

"Okay, I'll come back with Dex."

I was glad I went to the show, even if I couldn't stop yawning. I got to hear a different sound from Indigo Rain, rawer, more intense. That was the way I imagined them playing when they first met all those years ago in LA, back when they played for love rather than money.

The women—and it *was* mostly women—at the party seemed to like it too. Travis had barely started his second song when they started throwing underwear at him. Lacy thongs and frilly satin—at one point, he had to pause to pluck a bra off the neck of his guitar. Yes, he was playing tonight too, the first time he'd been able to since he broke his arm. And he was every bit as good as I knew he would be.

And when the guys put their instruments down? Think wasps on jam, complete with sticky little fingers that pawed and clawed. Being honest, Tessa would probably have joined them, but I took the opportunity to slip away unnoticed. I didn't need to watch Travis getting sucked off again. Once was quite enough. No, my job was to get Dex back to the hotel while the crew packed up the gear, and the cab I'd booked was already waiting downstairs.

"*Vous quittez la fête de bonne heure?*" the driver

asked.

Was I leaving the party early? He sounded surprised.

"*Oui, je suis un lève-tôt.*" Yes, I'm an early riser.

Dex appeared, covered in lipstick with his shirt ripped open. Wow. Women could be really demented. He sank into the back seat with a groan, and I was about to tell the driver to get going when my door was wrenched open.

"Move over a bit?"

"Travis? What are you doing here?"

"Escaping." Well, almost. A girl shouted his name, a pretty blonde, and he groaned. "Don't go anywhere." His stage smile came back, the fake one. "Peyton? Why are you in Paris?"

My inner nosiness got the better of me, and I leaned sideways to listen.

"Mom had a business meeting in the third arrondissement, so I tagged along." She giggled. "Isn't this a crazy coincidence?"

"Crazy's right," Dex whispered.

"Who is she?"

"Travis's stalker. They met six weeks ago when he started his DUI offender program, and it was obsession at first sight."

"Isn't following him to Paris slightly drastic?"

Dex rolled his eyes. "Love knows no bounds. She turned up in Chicago and Düsseldorf too."

Outside, Peyton was still babbling on about music, the Louvre, and Paris being the most romantic city on earth as Travis edged closer to the car. Poor guy.

"Uh, I have to go now."

"Back to your hotel?"

"It's been a long day."

"Aw, never mind. I'll see you next week, right?"

"Yeah, that's my final session."

"You're so *lucky*. I still have ten months left."

"Luck's got nothing to do with it," Dex muttered. "Travis was barely over the limit. Peyton drank so much she passed out behind the wheel and crashed into a parked car, and it was the second time she'd done that."

Wow.

Travis slid in beside me and slammed the door harder than was necessary.

"Let's go."

"Are you sure you want to come back with us?" I asked. "You're missing the party."

"Yes, I'm sure."

"But I thought..." Free, easy, posh women. Surely that was any rock star's wet dream? "Are you feeling ill?"

"Maybe I'm just getting old."

"What about Rush and JD? Are they coming?"

"No, they're having fun. Some scary bitch just ripped JD's pants off. Those women are like Stepford wives gone rogue."

I was kind of squashed in the middle, but I didn't mind. Not when Travis had blown off fifty horny women to come back to the hotel with us. That gave me hope. No, not *that* kind of hope. Hope that he wouldn't die of exhaustion before he hit thirty. What did you think I meant?

Inside the hotel, Dex leaned on Travis as they walked along the hallway, while I went to fetch ice. I'd scouted out the machine earlier, and it was close by.

Teamwork. I was starting to feel as if I was a part of something, and I liked it a little more than I should. Because as Travis had reminded me at Glastonbury, I'd be leaving in a few weeks.

With Dex as comfortable as he could get, which was to say, tanked up on painkillers with his knees frozen solid, Travis and I exited into the hallway.

"Look on the bright side," I said. "At least you can get some sleep without Rush snoring."

I'd never heard him snore on the bus, but Travis swore he did.

"I'm still buzzed. Reckon I'll be awake for hours."

"Why don't you watch a movie or something?"

"Maybe. I spend half my life watching TV on the bus."

"You could order some food?"

"I thought I might go out for a walk instead. See if there's a café open. I hardly ever get the chance to do that."

"Do you know where you're going?"

"No, but I'll figure it out. Wanna come?"

Did I? I'd felt knackered earlier, but fresh energy buzzed through my veins at the thought of exploring. I'd been to Paris on many occasions as a child, but not so much in recent years. Last time I came, it was to rescue Zander after one of his drunken escapades left him stranded. Perhaps his own experiences were why he'd been so lenient with me on the phone on Saturday.

"Just let me grab a jacket."

Travis pulled a knit cap low over his eyes, and we started off on the banks of the Seine, ambling along side-by-side as the lights of the city twinkled around us. In a few hours, he'd be back in the chaos of the music industry, but right now when I snuck glances across at him, he was relaxed, a secret smile playing at the corners of his lips.

"What are you thinking?" I asked.

"That this is how prisoners feel when they're released from jail." He sucked in a lungful of air. "Freedom. I smell freedom."

All I smelled was rather pungent cheese from a nearby café, but Travis's version sounded more romantic. No, *not* romantic. More, uh, expressive. There was a reason he wrote the band's songs while I could barely string together the sentences for an article I didn't want to write. When Tessa first came up with the idea, I thought it might be fun to be a showbiz journalist, an intrepid reporter who ferreted out the secrets of the rich and famous and splashed them around for the world to see. But now I understood that those secrets were theirs to tell and nobody else's. How would I like it if somebody followed us on this quiet walk, taking pictures and yelling questions? I wouldn't. I'd hate it.

"What are *you* thinking?" Travis asked.

"That it's nice to get some peace and quiet. That Paris is pretty at night. That I want to quit my degree course because I'm a different person now than when I started it and wasting two years is better than wasting three. If you could turn back the clock, would you still be a musician?"

"I'll always be a musician. It's in my blood. Would I go in pursuit of money and fame? Never. I'd get a day job to earn cash, then sing in my spare time."

"What would you do instead?"

"Before the band took off, I was an artist. Tattoos,

mainly. I should have carried on with that."

I'd seen pictures of his tattoos. At the moment, he had a sleeve on his right arm plus the four horsemen of the apocalypse cantering across his back. Beautiful in a macabre sort of way. Follow him through the years, and you'd see the designs evolving as he did, from the music notes he'd started off with on his left biceps to the darker themes he rocked today.

"Did you design all of yours?"

"Yeah. And most of the other guys'. Art and music were the only lessons I went to in high school. And English, but that was because the teacher was hot. Miss Kirby. Thirty-five years old with tits the size of watermelons." He smiled to himself and shook his head. "She should've been called Mrs. Robinson."

No way. "Tell me you didn't..."

"When I was seventeen."

When he was seventeen...

"You lost your virginity to your *teacher*?" I squeaked.

"She taught me a lot. Nothing about verbs and metaphors and all that shit, but plenty about what women like in bed." Travis chuckled. "We almost got caught by the principal once. I was under her desk and —"

"Stop! I don't want to know. Your teacher? Wow. The most rebellious I got in school was hacking the smartboard."

"What did you put on there?"

My cheeks heated. "A dick pic. Not a real one—I drew it on a dare."

A dare from Tessa. Who else? I'd scrawled it out, short and hairy just like my stepfather, and I'd been so angry at the memory, I broke the pen. Call it my own kind of therapy.

"An artist and a rebel. I like it. So, what will you do if you're not gonna be a journalist?"

"Truthfully? I have no idea." I groaned out loud when I realised I'd just shot myself in the foot. With a cannon. "Ah, shit."

"What?"

"If I quit my degree, I don't need to be here with you anymore. With the band, I mean."

"Are you sure you want to quit? That's kind of a hasty decision. Maybe you should think about it for a few weeks?"

"Maybe I should."

The outcome would still be the same, but I'd have fun in the meantime. Yes, there were ugly parts to this job, but I'd grown to like being around Rush and JD and Dex and Travis. Okay, mostly around Travis. That little revelation hit me like an arrow, an arrow that pierced my brain, obliterated my common sense, carried on through my heart, and came to rest in a pool of fire between my legs.

Oh, freaking hell.

If there was a list of men in this world who were completely and utterly unsuitable for me, Travis Thorne would be right at the top. Like he said, his job was totally incompatible with a relationship. He had a wealth of experience with the opposite sex, whereas mine consisted of being abused by my stepfather and running out on my one and only ex-boyfriend when he went for third base. Literally running out. I hadn't even stopped to do up my shoes. Then there was the small matter of Travis being a superstar with women throwing themselves at his feet, plus the fact that my brother would kill him if he touched me or even looked at me funny.

As if perfectly in tune with my feelings, the universe voiced its agreement and rain began to fall. The occasional fat drop quickly became a deluge, and guess who hadn't worn a waterproof jacket?

Travis grabbed my hand and we started to run, but instead of heading for the hotel, he tugged me sideways into a dimly lit little café, empty save for an old man staring out the window as he sipped a cup of coffee.

I slammed into Travis's chest, and my breath caught as he tilted my chin up so our eyes met. Was he...? Was he...?

"Hungry, blue-eyes?"

No, he wasn't. With all the supercharged hormones rushing around my body, I'd thought that maybe he'd been about to kiss me, but it was just my stupid imagination running wild. Wild like the herd of mustangs stampeding through my chest.

"I guess I'm a little peckish."

Rain splashed on the pavement outside as Travis led me to a corner table by the window. People scurried past, sheltering under umbrellas as the storm unleashed her sudden fury. Mental note: next time, check the weather forecast. If there *was* a next time. For Travis, freedom was a hard-won prize.

"*Que voulez-vous?*" an older man wearing an apron and a scowl asked.

"*Un plateau de charcuterie pour deux, s'il vous plaît. Et une bouteille de vin rouge. Tout ce qui est bon.*"

"What did you order?" Travis asked when the old

guy had stomped off.

"A charcuterie platter to share. Bread, cheese, and meat. And red wine. Unless… Are you still avoiding alcohol? After the Reagan thing, I mean."

"I'll drink wine with you, blue. You're not gonna molest me." He lowered his head and muttered something.

"I didn't catch that?"

He flashed me a shy smile, and my stomach did a backflip.

"I said I wouldn't mind if you did."

Oh. Oh! Wait. Was he serious, or was he joking? He had to be joking, right? I laughed to show I realised that.

"You've been spending too much time with Rush. He's a bad influence."

The waiter dumped a bottle down between us. "*Vin rouge.*"

"Friendly guy," Travis said.

"He probably has a whole cabinet filled with his employee-of-the-month awards."

"I bring you to all the best places." Travis poured a slug of wine into his glass, swirled it, tasted it, then filled both of our glasses halfway. "Cheers."

I clinked my glass against his. "What are we drinking to?"

"To moments of light in dark days."

"But it's after midnight," I joked.

"Maybe I do know what a metaphor is after all."

So did I. When I wasn't busy projecting hastily scrawled dicks onto the classroom wall, I'd actually listened in school. And now my belly turned into a turbulent sea.

"Cheers. To moments of light in dark days." I spotted the waiter approaching again, and the waves turned into an embarrassing gurgle. That's what happened when a girl skipped lunch and dinner. "And cheese. Cheese is good too."

This was a moment I'd no doubt look back on and tell my grandchildren about. Well, not *my* grandchildren, but probably Zander's grandchildren. Or my roomie in the old-folks home. The night I nibbled on bread and cheese with a world-famous rock star while our knees bumped together under the table. The night he wrapped his arm around my waist and tucked me close against his side on the walk back to the hotel. The night he pressed his lips against my forehead outside my hotel room.

The night I dreamed filthy, dirty, bad things about Travis Thorne.

Okay, perhaps I wouldn't mention that last part.

CHAPTER 13 - ALANA

"VERITY'S DONE *WHAT*?" Gary snapped.

Meredith shrugged. I'd met her properly now, and she came straight out of the rock-chick mould. Jet-black hair with purple streaks, more earrings than I could count, and everything she wore was ripped in some way. But she seemed friendly, which was a relief.

"She got arrested. Shit happens. It was all a misunderstanding."

Yes, trying to buy dope from an undercover French police officer was totally a misunderstanding. According to Meredith, Verity's lawyer was busy sorting out the problem, and Gary probably wouldn't have minded so much if the incident hadn't happened right before the Euro Rock Music Awards. Verity was supposed to be Dex's date, you see, and Gary didn't want an empty seat at the table because "it doesn't make great TV."

And now he turned to me. "You'll do. Find a dress. You've got an hour and a half."

"I'm sorry?"

"And wear more make-up. Nobody in rock goes for that innocent look." He rolled his eyes. "Do I have to spell it out? You're going to the ERMAs with Dexter."

"Do I get a say in this?"

"Look, blondie, I've made concessions by even

allowing you on this tour. Nobody gets a free ride. Just find a fucking dress, and don't be late."

Gary disappeared in a cloud of overly pungent aftershave, and Dex shrugged.

"Sorry."

It wasn't that I minded going with Dex. Since he thawed out towards me, we'd gotten on quite well. But I hated giving in to Gary's demands, and where the hell was I supposed to find a dress? All the good boutiques were closing right about now. Then there was the fact that I'd have to watch Reagan pawing Travis for the entire evening, and if I let my guard down for just one second, I'd break her bloody fingers.

"It's okay," I said weakly. "I've never been to an awards show before. It'll be an experience."

"I'll buy you a dress."

What, with his crappy per diem? I couldn't take that, not when he got paid so little and most of his money went on medical bills. Nor did I want to rub it in by pointing out that I had more money than he did.

"Don't worry; I'll find something to wear."

Reagan had been listening to the conversation from the sidelines, and now she stepped forward with an oh-so-fake smile.

"Such a shame you didn't know you were going earlier, or you could have gotten an appropriate outfit. Still, I suppose you could dress up a pair of slacks or something."

Grrr.

"What about borrowing Verity's dress?" Meredith asked, sizing me up. "Actually, I don't think it'd fit."

No, it definitely wouldn't fit. In bare feet, Verity was six inches shorter than me, and she had proper curves while I relied on chicken fillets in my bra and careful use of stripes. Meredith was thinner than me, so I couldn't even beg an outfit from her. Rush had managed to bag himself a date with a French supermodel.

Dammit. An hour and a half, and I hadn't even brought anything sparkly with me.

"At least it'll be dark," Reagan said. "I don't suppose anyone'll even notice you."

Oh, that bitch. I'd already seen her dress because she'd shown it to absolutely everyone. A bright red number slashed to the thigh that showcased her cellulite perfectly. And what did I have? Five different pairs of jeans, three of which were being laundered.

"Do we need to go out somewhere?" Dex asked. "I can find a cab."

"Yes, we do." My stomach sank to my feet as I realised there was only one viable option. Only one place in Paris where I could get a gown at short notice that would be glamorous enough to wipe the arrogant smirk off Reagan's face.

I'd have to call Marianna Odette de Montfort, formerly known as Marianna Graves. Also known as my mother.

She lived a five-minute drive away, and we were the same size. Occasionally, she sent me her cast-offs for Christmas. While I kept trim by going to the gym three times a week when I was home, Mother simply forked out thousands to have bits sucked out or filled in as necessary. And she always had kick-ass clothes because she liked to dress twenty years younger than she actually was. In fact, she told everyone she was thirty-four when she was really forty-seven.

I stepped out of the room and dialled the number I'd been hoping to avoid.

"*Oui*?"

"Mama, it's Alana." I always used my name just in case she'd forgotten it. "I'm in Paris this evening, and I —"

"*Desolé*, Francois and I have tickets for the opera tonight. But if you need somewhere to stay, Gaspard can open up a room for you."

Ah yes, Gaspard—her poor, long-suffering butler.

"Actually, I was hoping to borrow a dress. I need to go out to a fancy dinner tonight—short notice—and I didn't bring anything with me."

"A dress? Of course you can borrow a dress."

At this point, I should probably mention that the only mother-daughter bonding activity we'd shared when I was a child was traipsing around an endless parade of beauty pageants. Marianna loved to dress me up like a little doll and watch me sing and dance and turn cartwheels. As a three-year-old, my cheeks had ached from being forced to smile for hours on end, and I was the only toddler at my kindergarten with a vocal coach. Once the pervert started his sick games, I'd refused to participate anymore because I hated the way he watched me and the other kids on stage, and Mother had mostly ignored me after that.

I hated her.

But tonight, I could use her to take Reagan down a peg or two. Mother's Paris apartment might be the same elaborate clusterfuck of extravagance that every other one of her homes had been, as ostentatious as it was tasteless, but she had a closet full of designer clothes plus the shoes and handbags to match.

"Can I come over right now?"

"*Oui*. The stylist was just about to leave, but I'll make him stay. What kind of dress do you want? I'll pick out a selection."

"Something edgy. Black. I'm going to the Euro Rock Music Awards."

"Rock music? There's money in rock music. Some of those bands earn millions." Little did she know. "Just remember; only smile at the rich ones."

Wear a nice dress and smile at rich men. That, ladies and gentlemen, was my mother in a nutshell.

"Holy fuck." Dex gave a low whistle. "Who are you and what did you do with Alana?"

"Very funny. I *can* wear something other than jeans, you know."

"Travis is gonna bust a nut."

"I doubt that. It's just a dress."

A tightly fitted, dangerously low-cut dress with a funky skirt made of black mesh and slinky silver fabric. Goodness only knows why Mother had bought it, but it was perfect for the ERMAs. Her stylist had straightened my hair into a sleek blonde curtain before taping my boobs in and giving me smoky, dramatic eyes. Oh, and then there were the five-inch spiked heels.

"Dress and shoes," Dex said. "How can you walk in those?"

"Ask me later. I'm not sure which of us'll be holding the other up by the end of the evening."

"At least I don't have to run around a stage all

night. We're only performing one song." Dex touched the tip of his index finger to the choker around my neck. "Diamonds?"

"Created white sapphires."

Mother had bought them for a costume party, apparently. She'd happily give me a dress, shoes, and make-up, but she drew the line at expensive jewellery. The cheap option would have to do.

"I feel like I should bow at your fuckin' feet."

"How about you just hold me back if I get tempted to stab Reagan with one of my stilettos?"

"You'll have to wait in line for that."

I wasn't sure what was sweeter when I climbed out of the cab and into the rented limousine outside the band's hotel—Travis's jaw dropping or Reagan's. I smiled sweetly at her.

"Turns out I managed to find a dress after all."

"What... How..."

"It's by Ishmael?" Rush's supermodel asked.

"Yes. One of a kind." Victory was so, so sweet. "But your dress is nice too, Reagan, for something off the peg."

Meredith bit her lip beside JD, obviously trying not to laugh. She'd gone with a classic little black dress, or so I thought until she turned away. The back was made from ripped purple mesh and showed off her tattoos nicely. I couldn't help wondering whether Travis had designed them, and a hot little ball of jealousy rolled around in my stomach.

Stupid, Alana.

Not only had she gotten her ink before I even met Travis, but Meredith was also far better suited to him than I was. Another singer, used to life on the road. I forced myself to focus on Dex. He was my date for tonight, and he'd been nothing but kind to me today.

And I was super grateful for his help on the red carpet. Whenever anyone asked who I was, he simply said "a friend" and hurried us through the gauntlet of photographers and autograph hunters and screaming fans like the seasoned pro he was.

Once inside, it only took ten seconds for my phone to buzz.

Zander: What the hell, Lanie?

I looked around, noticing the stern-faced security guards for the first time, each with Blackwood's shield logo on the badge around their neck. Oops. Not only did I have the eyes of the press on me, but fifty of Zander's colleagues were watching my every move too.

Me: Dex's date dropped out at the last minute, and I'm standing in. THAT'S ALL!

Zander: Dexter Reeves had better keep his hands above your waist.

Shit. I leaned in close enough to whisper.

"Dex, someone told my brother I'm here. He's not very happy."

"Because you're with me?"

"Because I'm not sitting in a convent, clutching rosary beads. Uh, if you could just not touch my ass, I'd be really grateful."

"It's Travis he should be worried about, not me."

"No, Travis always behaves like a gentleman."

"Travis is walking on a tightrope of propriety, and sooner or later, he's gonna fall off."

Before I could question Dex further on what he meant, a lady with a clipboard waved us towards the auditorium. Time for the fun and games to begin.

CHAPTER 14 - ALANA

"AND THE BEST rock group of the year is..."

Oh, get on with it. On stage, a reality TV starlet made a drama out of opening the envelope, drawing the process out for as long as possible to make the most of her precious seconds in the spotlight.

"Indigo Rain!"

Thank goodness. The tension I'd been carrying all night escaped in one long exhalation as Rush squashed the breath out of me. His date would probably have snapped in half if he'd tried the same trick with her. The poor girl looked so thin and brittle, and she'd only drunk sparkling water for the entire evening. Dex hugged me too, but Travis didn't, because Travis was sitting opposite me between Reagan and Meredith. Every so often, he moved his chair another half inch in Meredith's direction, but as soon as the winner was announced, Reagan flung her arms around him, squealed, and made a show out of kissing him on the cheek. Meredith rolled her eyes, and I giggled while at the same time plotting Reagan's murder.

"Put the fork down," Dex whispered as he stood up.

"Huh?"

I looked at my hand. Hmm... Yes, I suppose I was holding it rather tightly. I forced my grip to relax, then applauded as the boys got up and walked to the stage.

Even Dex had a spring in his step tonight.

This was the last award, and once the boys had made a speech thanking their crew, the Jack Daniels distillery, Fender, their support acts, their fans, the women of Pornhub, the manager of the club in LA where they'd played their first gig, Frank, JD's former pet rat, hotel housekeeping—in fact, everyone but Gary and their record label—the whole show began to wind down as people headed off to various after-parties.

"What do you want to do?" I asked Dex. "Carry on or go back to the hotel?"

"I've saved up today's quota of painkillers for this evening."

"I'm not sure you're supposed to take them all in one go."

"Done it before, and I'm not dead yet."

"Try leaning on me instead."

"Are you okay walking in those shoes?"

No, I needed the bloody painkillers myself. "Absolutely fine."

"In that case, thanks."

Someone's record label—not Indigo Rain's because the execs were too cheap—had set up shop in a local hotel, and the alcohol was already flowing by the time we arrived. Dex slung an arm over my shoulders, and I clung onto his waist as we made a circuit of the top-floor bar, Dex talking to reporters and women and fellow musicians and women and talk-show hosts and yet more women. Fortunately, none of the conversations lasted long.

"The trick is..." Dex told me as he washed a painkiller down with neat whisky. "The trick is to insult everyone in the first sentence, and then they move on to their next victim." He nodded in Travis's direction. "Or take Reagan with you. That works too."

Poor Travis. He'd definitely drawn the short straw tonight. Reagan made catty remarks to everybody, and I suspected the glass in Travis's hand contained orange juice and nothing more. Rush's supermodel had already gone home, but he looked quite in his element surrounded by girls, and JD and Meredith were talking to a bunch of industry suits.

"This is the ultimate in people-watching, don't you think?"

"The first time or two, it was okay, but now it's just a chore. At least JD has Meredith to help him tonight. Last time, he got mauled by a drunk Z-lister."

"Ouch."

"Yeah. Meredith was supposed to go with Travis until the Reagan thing happened." He cut his eyes left to a singer I recognised backing away from the bitch in question. "Poor guy. Now do you see why he took a blow-up doll last time Gary insisted we all needed dates?"

"Should we try to do something?"

"Reckon that would only make the situation worse."

Unfortunately, Dex was right.

"Did you go out much before your knees got bad? You seem different from the others. Much more..." I couldn't think of a way to put it without sounding insulting.

"Dull? Boring? Conservative?"

"Sensible?"

"Not sure sensible's much better."

"How did you end up playing with the band, anyway? I mean, I know from Wikipedia that you answered an advert on the internet, but you're each so different."

"Back then, the music was all that mattered. Yeah, we did our own shit in our spare time, but when we jammed together, everything fit."

"Opposites attract?"

"More times than you'd think."

A guitarist from another band came over to talk to Dex, and when Dex didn't immediately go out of his way to be rude, I figured they must be friends.

"I need to visit the little girls' room."

"You know where it is?"

"On the floor below." I'd heard one of the waiters mention it earlier.

Whew, the relief as I peeled down my control underwear was indescribable. Lucky I didn't need to dress up like that every night. How did my mother do it? To Marianna de Montfort, appearances were everything, but I preferred jeans or sportswear. Or even pyjamas.

Tempting though it was to camp out in a toilet cubicle for the rest of the evening, I sucked in my stomach and tugged everything back into place, then touched up my lipstick. At least the tape was still secure. What the hell had Mother's stylist used? It would probably take a layer of skin with it when I peeled it off.

I was still puzzling over the conundrum when I walked out of the bathroom. Straight into Travis.

"Oops. Sorry."

He smiled, the first time I'd seen him look happy since the awards were handed out.

"Hey."

"Hey."

"Shit, blue-eyes, you're killing me tonight."

"I'm killing myself. If the government ever needs to convince terrorists to talk, they should just put them in these shoes and this dress, and they'll spill everything."

"Sore feet?"

"Walking across a red-hot barbecue grill would be less painful."

Travis caught me by surprise when he scooped me up into his arms, bridal-style, and strode off along the hallway. My squeal sounded like a passable impression of Reagan.

"What the hell are you doing?"

He shoved open the door to the stairwell, then settled me onto my feet inside. Actually, I preferred being carried.

"I'm taking a moment to tell you that you look pretty."

"Oh."

"Oh?"

What the freaking heck was I supposed to say to that? Logic flew out the window, and I started babbling instead.

"Well, that's actually a good thing, because I think I might be stuck in this dress forever. The stylist used tape, and even if I get that unstuck, I can't reach the zipper, or I might break an ankle on the way back to my hotel room and having to go to the hospital in this outfit would be mortifyingly emb—"

Travis pressed a finger against my lips. "Blue, stop talking."

His kiss caught me by surprise, the softest brush of his lips against mine, but he might as well have struck a match against my skin because fire burned all the way through me.

"Travis?"

He rested his forehead against mine. "I want you, but I don't want to hurt you."

Travis Thorne wanted me? *Me*? A ditz from London who didn't know the difference between a melody and a harmony? A girl who'd shoehorned herself into a world where she didn't really fit? Except I fitted quite nicely into his arms, right there in the empty stairwell. Zander better not have set up any spy cameras.

"You won't hurt me."

"Not deliberately. But in the end, I won't be able to help it."

I knew what he was saying. That there was no hope for us. He'd be living on a tour bus for the next two years with women throwing their undergarments and themselves at him every time it stopped, and I'd be back in Chelsea.

But dammit, I really, really liked him. For the first time in my life, I felt both safe and ridiculously turned on around a man, and my girly bits were just one big bowl of hormone soup.

"You're worried about the future?"

He nodded.

"I'm more worried about the here and now. I've... I've never done more than kiss a man before." I buried my face in the crook of his neck and mumbled into his shirt. "If I ever got out of this stupid dress, I'd probably die of embarrassment or fear."

There it was—my soul laid bare. I'd exposed myself to a man I'd met little more than a week ago, but one I felt I'd known for much longer.

"Fuck, I—"

A door opening on the floor above us interrupted our awkward discussion, and I groaned out loud. Why hide my feelings anymore?

Travis didn't miss a beat, just tugged me out of the stairwell and along the hallway until we found a dimly lit alcove complete with two leather armchairs and a table full of car magazines. Was this the place men went when they needed to escape from their wives?

Backed into a corner with Travis a millimetre from me, I didn't feel threatened the way I'd thought I might. No, I felt safe. Protected. The man did crazy things to my insides. Think fireworks going off in the middle of a spin cycle.

Fireworks that fast became damp squibs.

Things started off hopeful. Travis ran his thumb over my bottom lip, and my mouth dropped open as a low moan escaped. Then he shook his head.

"I can't do it, blue. I can't do this to you."

"What? Why?"

"You'd be so easy to fall in love with, but you deserve better."

"But I want you," I whispered.

"I'm not a good guy, Alana. You've seen how I behave."

"I also understand why you do it."

"The press would rake over your life. Every damn detail. Gary and Reagan would give you hell. And even if your brother didn't kill me right away, what have I got to offer? Nothing. Nothing but a bunk on a fucking tour bus and a whole world of trouble."

"I don't care."

"But *I* care. It might not matter today or tomorrow,

but a month down the line, a year if we're lucky... You'd be cursing the day you ever met me."

I rested my hands on his arms, conflicted over whether I wanted to hold him at bay because everything he said made perfect sense or pull him closer because I desperately wanted those lips on mine.

"I'm right, blue. You know I'm right." He kissed me on the forehead, already backing away. "I need to go."

My knees turned to jelly, and I sank into one of the ugly chairs, shaking, as he disappeared along the hallway. Why did it feel like I'd been dumped from a relationship that had never even existed? If this was how love felt, then perhaps Travis *was* right. We were better off apart.

Breathe, Alana.

My eyes prickled, but I couldn't wipe them because I'd end up looking like a heroin-addicted panda. A minute passed, two, five, but the dampness didn't subside. Maybe I could just dab at the corners if I had a tissue or—

For the second time in as many weeks, a scream tore through the air, high-pitched and terrified. My spine went rigid, and I scrambled to my feet, trying to decide between fight or flight. Okay, in these shoes, running wasn't an option, but I heard rapid footsteps approaching.

"Thank fuck." Travis skidded to a halt in front of me. "I was scared that was you."

"I'm fine. Where did it come from?"

"Somewhere close. Keep behind me, okay? We'll go and find out what the hell's happening."

CHAPTER 15 - ALANA

A SMALL CROWD had gathered near the stairwell, and as we approached, a girl staggered her way towards us and puked.

"What's going on?" Travis asked nobody in particular.

"There's a dead girl at the bottom of the stairs," a British guy said.

"Who?"

"Dunno. Some blonde."

"How do you know she's dead?"

"It's obvious, innit?"

"Stay there," Travis told me, then pushed through the wall of bodies. I heard his curse even over everybody talking.

"Fuck."

Who was it? Did I want to see? Not really, but nosiness won out. A bead of sweat rolled down my back as I slipped between two men wearing leather trousers, mentally steeling myself for a gruesome scene.

"Holy shit."

Reagan lay crumpled in a heap on the floor, her neck twisted at an unnatural angle. Blood trickled from the corner of her mouth as she stared at the wall, unseeing.

"I thought I said to stay back," Travis said.

"I'm not very good at doing what I'm told, okay?" Wow, that was creepy. Reagan looked like a broken doll, not a human being who ten minutes ago had been alive and well and irritating everyone who crossed her path. "Has somebody called the police?"

Some shakes of the head, some shrugging, and one more person threw up. Great. I pulled out my phone and did the necessary, and exactly ten seconds after I hung up, Zander called.

Just when I thought this evening couldn't get any better.

"Hello?"

"Why did you just dial the emergency services?"

"Are you monitoring my freaking phone?"

A beat of silence. "Certain numbers may be flagged."

"Do you know how to spell 'invasion of privacy'?"

"Just answer the question, Lanie."

"Someone fell down the stairs. The band's PA."

"Which band? Indigo Rain?"

"Yes."

"Badly hurt?"

"I think so. She looks dead."

"Fuck. Where are you?"

"About three metres from the body."

"I meant where are you in Paris?"

"Uh, the Hotel Nova. On the ninth floor."

"I'm sending someone to help. Don't speak to anybody until they get there. Got it?"

"Yes. I'm so, so sorry."

"Just try not to get involved."

Try not to get involved? Yeah, right. Someone I knew had just died. True, I didn't like her, but she was only a year or two older than me and until that moment, I hadn't really considered my own mortality. I shuddered involuntarily, and Travis squeezed my hand.

"Want to go and sit down, blue?"

"Will you come with me?"

He scrubbed a hand through his hair. "I don't know. I mean, I knew her. I was supposed to be with her tonight. What if they think I...?"

"Think you what?"

Then I realised. Until that moment, it hadn't occurred to me that this was anything but a terrible accident, but what if Reagan had been pushed?

Travis wouldn't have done that, though, would he?

No, of course not. Not Travis.

Although he did have a motive. First, Reagan had screwed him while he was unconscious, and then she'd practically blackmailed him into bringing her tonight. He'd had to be nice to her all evening, even as she bitched about everything to everyone. Hell, I'd been dreaming up ways to kill her myself earlier, although my plans had been more creative. Strapping her to the back of the tour bus then reversing into a wall. Strangling her with one of her definitely-not-designer necklaces. Lacing her coffee with rat poison. At no point had I envisioned something so simple as a swift shove down the stairs.

But I wouldn't have actually done it, not a chance, and I couldn't imagine Travis resorting to vigilante justice. Emmy Black? Yes, in a heartbeat, but not Travis. In the two weeks I'd known him, he'd been an arsehole at times, but a kind arsehole.

Dammit. Two weeks. I'd only known him for two weeks. Was that long enough to judge a person's character?

And he'd had the opportunity to push her, because he'd walked away from me several minutes before the body was found. Mind you, somebody could say the same about yours truly—I'd been alone, and I'd certainly been gunning for Reagan too.

What a shambles.

The crowd parted momentarily, and I caught a glimpse of Reagan's silver stilettos. They weren't quite as high as mine, but she hadn't looked too stable in them earlier, plus she'd been drinking. Me? My feet might have hurt, but I'd been wearing heels since I was three years old, and I'd never fall, no matter how much I might joke about it.

"Where did you go after...you know?" I whispered to Travis.

He tugged me away from the crowd. "You can't think...?"

"No, of course not." Maybe. "But did you see anything? Anybody?"

"I wasn't anywhere near the stairwell." He jerked his head in the other direction along the hallway. "I was down there, looking out the window."

Where had he appeared from when he came back for me? I tried to recall, but my eyes had been too blurry to see straight. And Travis had a penchant for stairwells, I already knew that.

What if he *had* pushed Reagan? Could I blame him? Reagan's demise was karma at work, surely? Did the truth matter?

Not to the media, it didn't. The rats who chased Indigo Rain day and night would never let facts get in the way of a good story, and if they could make a quick buck by dragging Travis or any of the other celebs present through the mud, they'd do it for sure.

"Did anybody see you?" I asked.

Travis shook his head. "I don't think so. It was quiet; that's why I stopped there."

A simple solution would be for us to say we were with each other, but then people would ask why. Fibbing to the cops about drugs at a party was something I didn't feel too guilty for, but giving someone an alibi for murder? That was a dangerous game, and one I didn't want to play.

"We need to stay apart."

"Why?" Travis asked.

"Who did you tell about what Reagan did to you?"

"Just Rush, Dex, and JD. And you."

"Frank? Gary?"

"No."

"Then you haven't got a motive for wanting to hurt Reagan. Hell, you brought her as your date tonight. But if people see you close to me, they might start to ask questions. Like you said, nothing's gonna happen anyway, so you need to keep your distance."

"I fucking hate this."

"Me too." Another awful thought struck me. "Oh, hell."

"What?"

"I remember reading a story a while back. A story that you pushed your ex-girlfriend."

"Ah, fuck." Travis tore a hand through his hair again, and it went from artfully dishevelled to messy.

"It was a lie, right?"

"Two lies. Firstly, she tripped over a coffee table, and secondly, she wasn't even my girlfriend. Just a hook-up in search of column inches."

And she'd sure gotten those, hadn't she? This was a mess. A big, huge, giant mess.

"I'm so sorry."

"Nothing for you to be sorry about, blue. This is *my* life. My problem. And it's going to stay that way."

He stepped to the side, putting more space between us. Zander would look after me—of that I was sure—but would Gary go to bat for Travis? Hopefully, if it meant the record label's investment in the band was threatened.

"Just say as little as possible," I whispered.

Authoritative voices signalled the police's arrival, and a gendarme moved the small crowd back. A man in a long-sleeved black shirt and grey slacks appeared, thirty or so years old, and I didn't even have to ask to know he worked for Blackwood. All the Blackwood men radiated the same quiet confidence as Zander, and this guy was no different.

He scanned the scene, then made a beeline straight for me.

"Alana Graves?"

"Yes."

"Mathis Guerin. I'm here to assist."

"Assist with what?" Travis asked, sizing Mathis up.

"Anything Mademoiselle Graves requires."

"Travis, it's okay. My brother knows them. They work for the same company."

Now Gary appeared, carrying the band's award. The prick had claimed it as his own the moment the boys got back to the table.

"What's going on?"

"Reagan fell down the stairs," I told him.

"I'm not surprised with those dumb shoes she insisted on wearing. Can you believe she tried to claim them on her expense account? What'd she do? Break an ankle?"

"No, her neck."

"Well, shit. Who's gonna pick up my dry cleaning?"

I searched for some indication Gary was joking, that this was his misplaced attempt at gallows humour. But I got nothing. The asshole was actually serious.

"Perhaps you could pick it up yourself?"

"She had the tickets."

Wow. Even Mathis rolled his eyes as if to say, *Who is this dick?*

"Gary, Reagan just *died*."

"Yes, Alana, I know that. But we have to look at the bigger picture. There's no room for sentimentality in this business."

"Then maybe there should be. Music's created with passion, not spreadsheets."

"And you're the expert now, are you?"

Mathis stepped away and began murmuring into his phone as I resisted the urge to increase tonight's body count. Part of me wanted to quit and tell Gary to take a long walk off a short plank, but I couldn't because that would mean leaving Travis too. And even after what he'd said to me tonight in the alcove, I couldn't walk away completely. Call me a glutton for punishment.

"I just think you could show a bit more sympathy, that's all. What will the public think?"

"Hmm, good point. I should call our PR director."

He turned on his heel and strode off, and I sagged back against the wall as I watched him disappear down the hallway.

"Don't worry," Mathis said. "He'll still get questioned."

"On what grounds? Being an asshole?"

"*Oui.*" He held up his phone. "I have a friend. He will arrange, how do you say...a cavity search?"

Yes, I knew it was a dire situation, but I still choked back a laugh. "Are you serious?"

"Very much."

Thanks, Blackwood. "Do you think the police will question me too?"

"I'll ensure they keep it brief."

The highs of the award ceremony faded into nervousness and exhaustion while I waited for permission to leave. Due to the sheer number of people hanging around, the cops herded us upstairs to the bar, but I steered clear of the complimentary drinks and dragged an extra chair over to the corner table where the boys were sitting. Mathis hovered in the background, glaring at anyone who tried to approach while Travis stared into a glass of water.

"Reagan's really dead?" Rush asked.

I nodded. "Yup."

"I guess I should be upset, but I'm struggling."

"Let's look at the positives," Dex said. "She's still creating drama. Her legacy lives on."

I'd had enough drama over the last fortnight to last a lifetime. Why couldn't Reagan have faded quietly into the night instead?

Finally, a detective took me to one side.

"Can you describe your movements prior to the discovery of Mademoiselle Eckert's body?"

"I went downstairs to use the bathroom."

"You were in the bar prior to that?"

"Yes."

"Did you use the stairs or the elevator?"

"The stairs."

The detective glanced at my shoes.

"It was only one floor, and the elevator was taking ages to arrive."

"Okay. And did you see Miss Eckert at any point?"

"No."

"And how long elapsed between you using the stairs and the discovery of the body?"

"Maybe twenty minutes."

He raised an eyebrow. "You spent twenty minutes in the bathroom?"

"Ten minutes. Have you ever tried wearing control underwear?"

Mathis, standing at my elbow, snorted and turned it into a cough.

"And the other ten minutes?"

Deep breaths. This was the part I didn't want to talk about.

"I was on my way back upstairs when I bumped into Travis Thorne. We started talking, and I sat down for a few moments because my feet hurt."

"Travis Thorne?"

"Yes. I work for one of his bandmates."

"I see. And where did you meet him?"

"Outside the ladies' loo, but we walked back down the corridor until I found a seat around the corner."

"Did you go past the stairwell?"

"Uh, we went into the stairwell for a second." The cop sucked in a breath, and I almost wished I hadn't told him. "We were gonna go upstairs, but then we changed our minds."

"Why?"

"Like I said, I wanted to sit down because my feet hurt."

That sounded better than admitting we'd run from a stranger.

"And at that point, Mademoiselle Eckert was not in the stairwell?"

"No."

"For how long did you speak to Monsieur Thorne?"

"About five minutes."

"And then he left?"

I nodded. "But I stayed where I was until I heard someone scream."

"Why?"

I just pointed at my shoes.

"*Oui*, I understand. And that's when the body was found?"

"I believe so."

"Do you know where Monsieur Thorne went in that time?"

"No."

I didn't want to admit to having spoken with Travis afterwards in case the police thought we were colluding. As Mathis instructed, I kept my answers to the bare minimum.

"And did anybody walk past you?"

"Not that I noticed."

"I'll need your contact details, Mademoiselle Graves."

"Is that it?"

"*Oui*. For now."

Thank goodness. Mathis trailed me back to the

table, and I slid into the empty seat beside Dex.

"Did it go okay?" Travis asked.

"I said we talked and neither of us saw Reagan, but that was it. They didn't ask me what we talked about." I tried to keep my voice steady, but it trembled along with my hands. "I think I'll have a glass of wine now."

Or perhaps a bottle.

Chapter 16 - Alana

"WHO ARE THEY?" I whispered to Travis as we climbed onto the tour bus.

We'd travelled back to London on the Eurostar first thing in the morning, and now the bus would deliver us to Leeds in time for the evening's concert, the first of three that week. We also had Newcastle on Friday and Glasgow on Saturday, and on Sunday, Travis would fly back to Los Angeles for two days to fulfil his obligations under the DUI program. Right now, I had four hours to catch up on sleep, and I needed every second.

But first, I was curious about the two new faces in the front lounge. On the left, a pretty black girl who smiled, and beside her, a timid blonde who looked as though she should still be in school.

"The girl on the left is Vina. She won a reality TV show Gary made us go on as guest judges, and she sang on one of our tracks last year."

At least Vina looked happy to see me. "And the other?"

"No idea."

Gary appeared at that moment, fresh from first class. He'd made the rest of us travel in economy, where the boys had spent most of the trip speaking to fans until Dex got sick of being pestered and threw half a sandwich at one girl who refused to stop filming us.

"Guys, meet your new PA, Jeanne. She'll be helping Courtney to do whatever Reagan did. And you know Vina. Her record label thought it would be great if she joined you on stage for your remaining UK tour dates so you can sing 'Burn' together."

Oh, they did, did they? And what was in it for Gary? I'd quickly learned that he never did anything unless it benefited him personally, so he was probably getting a kickback.

"'Burn' isn't even on the set list," Travis said. "It doesn't fit in with the show."

"It was a number one in eight countries."

Dex backed Travis. "It was some bullshit song we had to sing for a TV farce. This is Indigo Rain's tour, not a showcase for washed-up reality stars." He turned to Vina. "No offence, sweetheart."

Her face crumpled, and I wanted to give her a hug. Dex may have mellowed towards me, but he could still go full-asshole whenever the mood took him.

Gary's mouth set in a thin line. "The deal's already been agreed to. You'll have to swap out one of the other tracks."

"We haven't rehearsed," Rush pointed out. "We haven't even seen Vina for months."

"You'll have an hour this afternoon. You're all professionals, people. If you can't handle a simple song change, you shouldn't be touring."

Gary backed off the bus, and the drink JD threw at him splattered against the closing door and dripped down the glass.

JD wasn't minded to be polite either. "Hey, Jeanne. Clean that up, would ya?"

"What with?"

"Do I look like a fuckin' housekeeper? Find a cloth. Or tissues. Or lick the damn stuff up for all I care."

I laid a hand on his arm. "It's not her fault."

"Yeah? She works for Gary."

A tear rolled down Vina's cheek. "I'm so sorry about this. My management told me you guys loved the idea, or I wouldn't have come." A sniffle. "I was supposed to be going on holiday to Portugal this week."

Travis tugged at his hair. I'd noticed he did that when he got stressed. "Ah, fuck."

I squashed onto the seat next to her and gave her shoulders a squeeze. "Gary Dorfman lies to everybody about everything. There's no reason he'd be any different with you."

"How about if I just leave?" she asked. "I signed something, but maybe my manager could undo it?"

Travis cursed again, but more softly this time. "If Gary made you sign something, it'll be watertight. Look, we'll work with this somehow."

"If I'd known..."

"It's okay, we get it. Gary's a dick."

Courtney got up to help Jeanne, and I glanced around at the people gathered in the lounge. Without exception, everyone looked unhappy. Nervous, pissed off, or downright miserable.

"Guys, we can't let Gary do this."

"Do what?" Travis asked. "Induct Vina into hell? Because he already did that."

"No, turn us all against each other. I know I shouldn't speak ill of the dead, but Reagan wasn't the easiest person to get along with, and she only divided us further." Courtney didn't seem as bad. Just way, way out of her depth. "So it's us against them. Well, us against Gary mainly, although I don't trust Ian, and hand-on-heart, I don't understand why you keep Frank as your manager."

Travis leaned in close so the other girls couldn't hear. "Because Frank gets a percentage of our royalties forever. Yeah, we didn't know any better when we signed that contract either. Back then, we were just happy to have someone—anyone—to represent us, and we weren't making shit. Now, if we get a new manager, we'll have to pay him as well as Frank, and at this stage, none of us are sure what benefits that would bring."

"Oh. Shit."

"Exactly."

"But my point still stands. We should be working together, not against each other."

JD got up silently and rummaged through a locker until he found a cloth.

"Sorry," he said to Jeanne.

That was better.

"We need to get some sleep because the police kept us up for most of the night. Courtney, can you wake us if anything important happens?"

"Yup. Uh, I'm not really sure what else I'm supposed to do. Reagan mostly made me fetch coffee."

Figured. Reagan had always struck me as a control freak who liked having an assistant because it made her feel important.

"We'll figure it out, okay? Can you try to get the boys' stage clothes ready? Do you know what they wear?"

"I think so."

"And then ask Ian if he can put together a list of tasks for you and Jeanne. The man created an

instruction manual for the bus, for crying out loud—
he's probably already got one."

"Okay."

"And if—when—Gary acts like a prick, don't take it
personally." Rush yawned, and that set me off. "I'm
going to bed."

At least, that was the plan. Travis pulled me into the
rear lounge and closed the door before I made it to my
bunk.

"Travis, I'm too tired for this."

"I... I... Fuck, I don't know what to say. Sorry and
thank you. Sorry for everything that happened last
night. For what I said, because I know it hurt you, and
for putting you in a position where you got questioned
by the police."

We'd only got the briefest of chances to speak last
night because the others had been around. Travis had
told the cops the same story as me, except in a stunning
case of double standards, they'd interrogated him for
twice as long, and then taken his fingerprints "for
elimination purposes."

"I understand why you said it. I just wish it didn't
have to be this way."

"If I was still playing dive bars and living on ramen,
I'd be crawling after you on my hands and fucking
knees, begging for a date. You walked into my life like
this...this ethereal being and ruined me for all other
women from the moment I laid eyes on you."

"I hate to mention this, but what about Jae-Lin?"

"I had my eyes shut, and I was thinking of you the
whole time."

"And the two redheads?"

"They did each other while I watched."

"Are you joking?"

"No."

And he really wasn't.

Freaking heck. I almost choked. Should I be flattered or upset by that little revelation? Travis's bluntness shocked me, but considering how accustomed I'd become to men lying throughout my childhood, his honesty was refreshing.

"I'm not sure what to say."

"You don't have to say anything, blue." His smile was tinged with sadness. "But thank you for being here. Right now, you're the glue that's holding us together. We were on the verge of walking away from the whole fucking industry before you turned up."

I wished I could offer more encouragement, but two years was a long time to go when you were stuck in a role you hated. When I was living with my mother, every night had seemed like an eternity.

"You guys took a chance on me, and I'll do everything I can to make this easier for all of us."

Travis gripped my hands, and my traitorous heart stuttered. Why couldn't it stay strong?

"I'd hate to lose you as a friend, blue-eyes."

"You won't."

And I knew at that moment I'd wait those two years. If Travis still wanted me at the end of it, I'd be there, standing in the wings.

CHAPTER 17 - ALANA

TRAVIS WAS ABSOLUTELY right about Vina. Yes, she could sing, but the song didn't fit. They'd performed it in Leeds last night, and although the audience didn't boo or jeer, they hadn't joined in either, and I spotted an awful lot of people nipping out for a bathroom break.

"Who wrote 'Burn'?" I asked Rush.

"Travis."

"Really? It doesn't sound like his style."

"Travis writes everything from love songs to metal. He's just not allowed to sell any of it to other artists."

"The contract?"

"Yeah. Vina was an exception because we were working together."

Vina was sweet though, not at all egotistic and also happy to help out with the endless list of chores Courtney and Jeanne had to do. Much as I hated to admit it, Reagan hadn't been a bad PA. A horrible human being, yes, but she'd been good at her job.

We were sleeping on the bus this week—the band, me, Vina, and Ian. Gary said it was for convenience, but the truth was, he was just being a cheapskate again. He still took Courtney and Jeanne to his hotel at night so they could cater to his ridiculous demands, which included finding a mattress topper at a quarter to midnight and ensuring his decaffeinated cappuccino was waiting for him at breakfast, together with a copy of *The Times* and a bullet-pointed summary of his overnight emails.

Secretly, I much preferred being on the bus, even while Ian constantly reminded everyone of the no-shitting rule, Rush fought with the Nespresso machine, and JD wandered around in his boxer shorts, although I did have to nag him several times to stop scratching his balls. This was the human side of the band. I started taking more photos, and Instagram went mad for my video of a shirtless Rush strumming his guitar in the rear lounge.

Our time in Leeds was good, and when we travelled on to Newcastle, I cautiously hoped that the second half of Indigo Rain's UK tour might go a little more smoothly than the first. Well, that was the kiss of death, wasn't it?

I'd just got back to the bus on Friday, having raided the catering table for lunch, when Courtney let out a shocked gasp.

"Ohmigosh!"

"What?"

"Have you seen this?"

"Seen what?"

"Some girl's done a kiss-and-tell on Travis."

My heart lurched into my throat. "She's what?"

"You know, a kiss-and-tell. Where she describes their night together and everything he—"

"Yes, I know what a kiss-and-tell is, thank you." I screwed my eyes shut, as if that made any difference. "Sorry, I shouldn't have snapped. Where is it?"

Courtney passed her iPad over, and sure enough,

there it was. *Confessions of a Rock Chick: My Night with the Bad Boy*, a feature piece on a gossip website famed for pushing the boundaries of taste, complete with pictures. Yes, the pornographic parts had been covered with black rectangles, but the pair were clearly fucking. The girl was riding him like a prize freaking stallion. And although their heads had been cropped out, there was no mistaking Travis's tattoos.

"She doesn't give her name, but man, there're a lot of details," Courtney said. "Do you think it's true? Or were the pictures Photoshopped?"

Oh, how I wished it was fake, but it could just as easily be real. Travis wasn't exactly famous for his discretion. I devoured the article, juicy titbits about what Travis had done with his tongue, his staying power, and how he'd nailed the aforementioned rock chick against the wall, and my knickers were decidedly damp when I finished. Wow.

And then the man himself walked in.

"What's up?"

"Nothing!" Courtney and I said in unison.

He raised an eyebrow, and we must have looked guilty as hell.

"Everything," I said, passing the iPad across.

Rush looked over Travis's shoulder. "Bad lighting, buddy."

"I didn't fuckin' pose for this."

Travis chewed on his bottom lip as he read, and by the time he got to the end of the article, a spot of blood had appeared.

"Fuck."

Yes, that was the whole problem. "It certainly appears you did that."

"Think positive," Rush said. "She gave you a glowing report."

"There shouldn't be any kind of report. I've never let chicks take pictures in the bedroom because I knew this was exactly where they'd end up. She did this without me knowing."

"Any idea who?"

He glanced sideways at me, and his shoulders slumped. "It could have been any one of thirty women. Forty."

Forty? And that was just the blondes. The girl had been careful, but in one shot, a cascade of golden hair tumbled down her back. Multiply Travis's admission by the brunettes and the redheads, and we were talking over a hundred women that he'd slept with. Maybe it was good he'd backed away on Tuesday night. That I hadn't battled my fears only to become another notch on his bedpost. Although what a notch it would have been if just a fraction of that article was accurate.

"What can we do?" I asked nobody in particular.

Travis sighed. "Nothing. This shit's out there now. Yeah, I could sue for breach of privacy, but it'd cost me more money than I have in legal fees, there's no guarantee I'd win, and even if I did, it wouldn't undo the damage."

Like Rush said, we had to think positive. "There's not actually that much damage. I mean, it paints you in quite a good light."

Travis brushed a lock of hair away from my face. "I meant the damage in your head, blue. I don't give a shit what anyone else thinks."

Whoa. That was the first time he'd hinted at his feelings in front of other people, but luckily, it went right over Courtney's head.

"We should tell Gary," she said. "He hates it when he's the last to know stuff."

"Who gets that job?" I asked.

"Uh, perhaps we could send him an email?"

Rush barked out a laugh. "He'll probably read the article for tips, although nothing's gonna compensate for his two-inch dick."

"Two inches? Dex said something about a peanut, but I thought he was joking."

"He wasn't." Which explained a lot. "Seen it in the bathroom."

"I'll tell him," Travis said. "He hates me already, so this won't make much difference."

"No, let me do it. You've got a concert to get ready for, and Gary's got no hold over me." Plus, now I knew what he was compensating for, I found him a whole lot less intimidating. "I'll go with Courtney."

"Blue, don't do—"

I didn't hear the rest, because I was already out the door.

"What do you mean, you already know?"

Gary peered at me from behind his laptop in the temporary office he'd set up inside Newcastle Arena. Courtney hovered in the doorway, no doubt looking for an escape route.

"Google Alerts, Alana. Don't worry, it's all in hand."

"You're getting it taken down?"

He let out a high-pitched cackle. "Why would I do that? This thing's gone viral." Viral like herpes. "No, I contacted the website and got them to include a purchase link for Indigo Rain's latest album at the bottom. Downloads are up already."

"Hold on. You think this is a *good* thing?"

"No publicity is bad publicity."

"Then why did you get so cross when the band smashed up their hotel room?"

"Because the column inches they gained didn't justify the expense. But this... This didn't cost us a cent."

"What about Travis's feelings?"

"It's business, Alana." He flicked his wrist at me. "Off you go, back to the playpen."

That... That...

That was the moment I vowed to take Gary Dorfman down. I had no clue how, but I'd bloody well find a way.

Outside Gary's office, I leaned against the wall, fists clenched, determined to calm down before I accidentally yelled at somebody. Gary obviously didn't share that sentiment, because he started shouting into the phone the moment the door closed.

Did I listen? Of course I listened.

"Verity thinks someone spied on her in the shower? How is that my problem?"

A pause.

"Dex's guitar tech? Does she have proof?"

The answer was obviously no.

"Then tell her to get over herself and remind her to close the bathroom door properly next time."

Slam.

Gary really was a misogynistic prick, wasn't he?

Oh no, not again.

Another day, another city—Glasgow this time—and Courtney's gasp alerted me to a new problem.

"What is it this time?"

"You know those pictures of Travis from yesterday?"

"Yes?"

"Well, somebody's gotten hold of the uncensored versions."

Holy shit.

"Where? Let me see."

Well, it was safe to say Travis had nothing to be embarrassed about in the shower. One photo showed him full-frontal, and my gosh, I winced just looking at it.

"Courtney, shut your mouth."

It had dropped open, more in shock than desire it seemed since she screwed her eyes shut and pressed the heels of her hands against them for a moment.

"Sorry." She opened her eyes again. "It's just... I really didn't want to see that."

Eight X-rated vignettes of Travis's most private moments, laid bare for all to see. The girl didn't feature as heavily, but when we got to the bottom of the page, Courtney spat her drink across the table.

"What?" I looked again. The blonde bitch was draped over Travis, but it wasn't as brazen as some of the other snaps. "This one isn't that bad."

Courtney had a coughing fit, and I thumped her on the back until she started breathing normally again.

While I waited, I snuck another look at the picture above. Wow. Travis packed some serious heat.

"I..." More coughing. "I think I know who it is."

Ohmigosh. "Who?"

"Reagan. I recognise her watch."

So did I now that I looked closer, an ugly thing covered in fake diamonds that she'd worn every day. It had still been gracing her wrist when she took a nosedive down the stairs.

Bloody hell.

I scrolled through the pictures again, more slowly this time. Travis lying there naked. The girl riding him, holding his hands on her hips. The pair side by side on the bed. Travis gripping his cock with her hand over the top. At no point was he actively participating in any of those scenes. This wasn't a groupie's tale of a night of passion, this was the delusions of a sick mind and evidence of assault.

Now Travis would have a permanent reminder of what she'd done, and—a chill ran through me as I realised the broader implications—this tell-all gave him a motive for Reagan's murder. What if the police connected the two and thought Travis killed her in an attempt to stop the article from being published?

He couldn't have, could he?

No, the shock on his face yesterday when he first saw the pictures had been genuine, of that I was certain. But the police didn't know that. This nightmare had just taken on a whole new dimension.

"Why? Why would she do that?"

"I had no idea she went with Travis," Courtney said. But neither did he at first. "She never mentioned anything."

"Well, the pictures suggest otherwise."

Courtney seemed as stunned as I'd been when I first found out about Reagan and Travis, even though she didn't know the full, horrific story. And I wasn't about to tell her. That was Travis's decision, not mine.

"I think she'd been having money problems. With her rent and her credit card. I overheard her on the phone a couple of times, asking for extensions to payment terms."

"So she sold the pictures to pay her credit card bill?" I suggested.

"Maybe."

Ouch. That was cold. Did she plan it all along? Set Travis up with the intention of making a quick buck? Or did she merely take advantage of a convenient opportunity afterwards?

Either way, I had to tell him, and that promised to be more awkward than talking to Gary.

CHAPTER 18 - ALANA

SUNDAY MORNING, AND Travis was still as shaken as he'd been when I showed him the uncensored pictures yesterday. Wouldn't you be if pictures of you being abused had been made public and you couldn't explain the truth?

He'd started drinking on stage last night. *On stage.* The audience loved it, but by one a.m., he'd passed out on the tour bus and Rush and JD had to drag him into bed, a feat easier said than done since Rush was also drunk and JD was high.

And now Travis was preparing to fly to LA, and I was terrified he'd do something stupid. The rest of the band was going too, for two rare days of R and R, as were Meredith and Verity. And when I say R and R, I mean Gary had only pulled one more dickish move and scheduled a TV interview for Monday afternoon right after Travis's counselling session ended.

"Will he be okay?" I asked Dex.

"We'll make sure someone stays with him at all times."

"Do you really think he'd try anything?"

A shrug. Boy, that was comforting.

"Hey, Travis?" Meredith didn't know all the facts, but she tried to help. "Wanna get together on Monday night after your interview and write some songs?"

He shook his head. "Gonna stay with my folks."

"I could come over?"

"Rather be on my own." Travis looked around, still under the influence. "Where's my guitar?"

"In the lounge. I'll go get it for you, okay?"

"He writes songs with Meredith?" I asked Dex.

"Yeah, for Styx and Stones."

"I thought he wasn't allowed?"

"He's not allowed to *sell* songs or lend his name. But he wrote most of their hits and just didn't take any credit for them."

"That sucks."

"Yeah, it does. But we've known Meredith for years, so he doesn't mind. She bought us our first decent amps when we began to take off. You wouldn't think she's a trust-fund baby from looking at her, would ya?"

"No, but so am I, pretty much."

"You're different though. More...refined."

Dex didn't mean to be unkind, but his words were just one more reminder that my face didn't quite fit around there. Nobody had invited me to go to the US, which was understandable since I was basically crew. But with some of the things Travis had said to me... Why did men have to be so freaking complicated?

The next leg of the tour would be in London, starting on Thursday at the O2, which meant I could stay at home for a week instead of camping out on buses and in hotels. Having some space would be good, right? Some time away from this circus to make sense of everything that had happened over the last three weeks? Time to catch up with Zander and Dove and Tessa. I needed that.

"Want to share a cab to the airport?" Vina asked.

She was flying back to London too.

"Why not?"

"Aaaaaaaah!" Tessa squealed, flinging her arms around me. "I've missed you so much!"

"I've only been away for three weeks."

"Which is *forever*."

"And I've been sending you photos."

"Totally not the same. But speaking of photos, did you see Travis Thorne's dick pics?"

"I saw them."

"They had to have been Photoshopped, right? I mean, people could trip over that thing."

"I don't think they were."

"Seriously? Holy cannoli. Does he know who the girl was?"

"He's not talking about it."

"I guess I can understand that. Say, what do you think the chances are of any Rush Moder nudie pics coming out?"

"Not good. And I hope they don't. So many people treat those guys as pieces of meat, as meal tickets, as a way to get free publicity, but they're living, breathing people with feelings."

Tessa's smile dropped, and her bottom lip quivered. "Sorry. I just didn't think."

Dammit, stress had turned me into a bitch. "And I'm sorry for snapping. Being on the tour's like getting stuck in a pressure cooker."

And I'd only endured it for three weeks. For the boys, that crushing burden was multiplied a hundredfold.

"Then tonight we should relax. Want to go out? Stay in?"

"Can we stay in? I've been living on cold buffets and restaurant food for too long."

Eating out used to be a treat, something to look forward to, but do it too often and it became a chore. I'd never been the world's best cook, but tonight I craved a simple meal like a salad or beans on toast on a proper plate with a glass made of actual glass instead of plastic. And I wanted to do my own laundry and use my own shower with its rainfall head and side jets. And did I mention the space? The apartment I shared with my brother wasn't huge, just two bedrooms, a combined lounge/diner, two bathrooms, and a kitchen, but the sheer joy of being able to stand in the middle of a room with my arms out and not hit a wall was something I'd never appreciated until now.

"Sure. Want me to make dinner?"

"I'd *love* you to make dinner." Tessa was much better at cooking than me. "But something simple."

"Pasta?"

"Pasta's good."

"Are Zander and Dove coming home tonight? Should I make extra?"

"I'm not sure; I just got in myself."

Zander's office was in King's Cross while Dove worked as a gardener an hour north of London. But her boss, Marlene, a nutty lady in her seventies who drank like a fish and surrounded herself with sparkly trinkets and tanned hunks a third of her age, was an absolute legend, and she never minded if Zander stayed over too. Which meant that during the week, I didn't have to sleep with earplugs in every flipping night.

With no sign of them and no note on the hall table, I fired off a text to Zander.

Me: Are you coming home tonight? Do you want dinner?

A moment later, he replied.

Zander: Picked up a case in Hemel Hempstead, so staying in Northbury with Dove all week.

Me: Say hi to Marlene for me.

"It's just us," I called out to Tessa, who'd already started rummaging through the fridge. "Zander and Dove are away all week, and no, we're not having another party. I'm partied out."

"I bet. Is that girl who almost died okay now?"

"Apparently so."

Travis had kept me updated on Jae-Lin, and she'd flown home to LA as soon as the doctors gave her the all-clear. She wanted to spend some time with her family following the reminder of her own transience.

"And that girl in Paris—do they know whether she fell or got pushed yet?"

"I haven't heard anything."

Zander had promised Blackwood in France would keep an eye on developments, but so far, the police were holding their cards close to their chests. According to Mathis, there were no cameras in the stairwell or the hallways nearby, so the investigators would be reliant on footage from inside the bar, witnesses—most of whom were drunk—and forensic evidence. And, of course, the search for a motive should foul play be suspected.

"But there's plenty of drama for your article on the band, yes? Will they let you include that stuff?"

"Honestly? I haven't even thought about the article. I'm not even sure if I want to write it."

Tessa whipped her head around. "*What*?"

"I'm thinking of dropping out."

"Wait, wait, wait." She grabbed a bottle of white from the fridge and rummaged in the drawer next to the hob for a corkscrew. "Why? You've done more than half the course."

"My heart's not in it anymore. I've got no desire to report on politics or hang out in a war zone or analyse economics. And now I've got to know the band, I don't want to write anything bad about them, and I'd probably feel that way about most celebs." I managed a weak smile. "We can't all be hard-hitting investigative journalists like you. How's your placement going?"

"Don't you dare try to change the subject. We're discussing your crisis of confidence right now."

"It's not a crisis of confidence. More a change of direction."

"Ah. And which direction are you going in now?"

"I'm not exactly sure."

Tessa got the bottle open and poured me a generous glassful. Whenever possible, I'd been trying not to drink on tour, but since I was at home tonight and I didn't have to go anywhere, I took a long swallow. And another. And another. Yes, this was much better.

By the time Tessa finished making her favourite tomato sauce with olives and artichokes and slid a plate of pasta in my direction, the room had gone a bit spinny and the alcohol had loosened my tongue.

"Gary's a dick, did I tell you that?"

"Gary?"

"The guy from the record label. In fact, everyone at

the record label's an asshole. They take all the band's money and make the boys work every freaking day, and Gary drinks decaf and complains about everything and drives a big-ass car to go with his tiny penis."

"You've seen his penis?"

"No! Rush told me. I say all this other stuff, and that's the thing you focus on? Have we got any more wine?"

"No more wine, sweetie. How about I get you a nice glass of water?"

"Can it be tonic water with gin in it?"

"Nope. I'll be generous and add ice and lemon." Thirty seconds later, she shoved a full pint glass to my side of the table. "Drink this. Now, what was all that other stuff you said?"

"I don't know. Did I say stuff?"

"Let's talk in the morning, eh? I'll stay here with you."

"Sure, stay. Okay."

CHAPTER 19 - ALANA

"WAKEY, WAKEY. RISE and shine."

Tessa yanked open the curtains in my bedroom, and I blinked in the glare from the sun.

"What? No, close them. Please, make it go away."

"I have to get ready for work."

"What time is it?"

"Six thirty."

Freaking hell. Touring with Indigo Rain had knocked my body clock off-kilter by a few hours, and now it felt as if someone was beating on my skull with Thor's hammer. Minus Chris Hemsworth, of course, because there was literally nothing good about this morning.

"You're inhumane."

"And you're hungover. I've put paracetamol on your nightstand. Are you planning to get out of bed today?"

"I'm not sure. Maybe."

"Well, while you think about it, I'm gonna take a shower then go research the correlation between fizzy drinks and exam results in primary school children."

"That's what they're making you do?"

"Everyone's got to start somewhere, right?"

By the time Tessa put a steaming mug of coffee on my bedside table and leaned over to give me a hug, I still hadn't moved. Perhaps I'd just stay in bed all day. I liked my bed. A comfortable memory-foam mattress, enough room to stretch my arms out, and if I wanted to, I could sit up without bashing my head on the bunk above.

Where was Travis right now? He'd planned to stay with his foster parents rather than at his apartment, so at least he had people around to keep an eye on him. I knew from my own experiences how hard it could be to live with abuse, how easy it was to blame yourself and constantly ask *what if?* What if you'd done something differently?

Would he tell his foster parents? Would he let them help him?

Tessa bustled around in the living room, and I wished I had her energy. Today, I felt like a chewed-up piece of string.

"Your phone's ringing," she called.

"Can you bring it?"

"Don't know where it is, and I'm late."

"Okay, don't worry."

"I'll be back for dinner."

The door slammed, and the ringing stopped. Gah. What if it was Zander? His boss, Nye, lived on the top floor here—well, sometimes, because he and his wife also had a country home in Northbury village—and if I didn't call back, he or someone else from Blackwood would turn up to make sure I hadn't died in my sleep.

My vision twinkled as I got up too quickly, and I steadied myself with a hand on the wall. Now, where the hell was my phone? It took ten minutes of searching before I remembered I could use the house phone to call myself, and another thirty seconds to find my mobile stuffed behind a cushion. Another ten seconds to realise it wasn't Zander who'd phoned me but Travis, and my heart did a crazy little dance which ended with it tripping over its own ventricles.

What did he want? Was everything okay?

My fingers shook so much I accidentally dialled my mother first, and I swore under my breath as I hung up. She wouldn't call back. She never did. Second time lucky...

"Hello? Travis?"

"Sorry, he's asleep. Can I take a message?"

My spine stiffened as though someone had hammered a metal stake straight through the middle of it. Who was she? Who was this girl with Travis's phone? She sure didn't sound old enough to be his foster mom. No, she sounded my age, peppy, a California surfer chick or a cheerleader, perhaps.

And she was with Travis while I wasn't.

"Uh, no, no message."

I hung up and stared at the screen, only now thinking of all the questions I should have asked. Starting with, *Who are you and why are you answering Travis's phone?*

What time was it over there? Eleven o'clock in the evening, and he'd fallen asleep with her close by. I realised he wasn't a saint, and of course I couldn't expect him to stay celibate for the rest of his life, but it still hurt that he'd run away from me and gone straight to another woman.

Oh, dammit all to hell. Travis Thorne had promised me nothing, and here I was, getting upset about what never was and never would be. He was just a stupid, hopeless crush, and I was just a stupid, hopeless girl for feeling the way I did.

"What the hell happened in here?" Tessa asked.

I turned around with a can of spray polish in my hand.

"Uh, I was feeling depressed, so I thought I'd do some spring cleaning."

"Next time, can you come and feel depressed at my place?" She ran a finger along the top of the kitchen door, and it came back clean. "Wow. You dusted *everything*."

Dusted, vacuumed, wiped, scrubbed, polished, washed, and swept. I'd even picked up the stray leaves Dove's plants had shed on the balcony in a desperate attempt to take my mind off a certain singer who'd left me feeling empty inside.

"And dinner's almost ready."

"Tell me you didn't cook from scratch."

Of course not. I didn't want to kill us both. "No, I ordered Chinese, but I need to reheat it."

"Sorry, I thought I'd be back earlier, but the Tube randomly stopped in a tunnel for twenty minutes, and then the escalator was broken."

"So a totally normal day in London, then."

"Mostly, except I got talking to this cute guy who runs a marketing company in Camden, and he's taking me out for drinks tomorrow."

"Nice move. How was work?"

"Fizzy drinks are evil incarnate. Refined sugar's bad for you, but artificial sweeteners are worse. I'm only drinking water and fruit juice from now on. And wine, obviously, because that's just fruit juice with added benefits."

"I'll go grab a bottle."

"And one glass. You're not drinking wine, not after last night."

"But—"

"And once you've brought the drinks, you can tell me what's eating at you."

"Travis had a girl with him last night," I blurted.

"Travis Thorne?"

"How many other Travises do I know?"

"But why does... Oh. You like him? You *really* like him?"

I nodded miserably.

"Okay, two glasses. But if you look as if you're about to fall off the stool again, I'm pouring the rest of the wine down the sink."

Tessa didn't wait for me to fetch the wine—she poured it herself instead. Now I understood how Rush felt. Alcohol numbed the pain.

"Tell me what happened," Tessa said. "Then I can work out whether I need to buy cream cakes or a voodoo Travis doll. Did he lead you on?"

"No, the opposite." The whole story came out—minus the sexual assault part—along with a million tears and, embarrassingly, some snot. Boy did I lead a glamorous life. Sometimes, I wished I could be more like my mother—focused on money and appearances rather than affairs of the heart. "You have to promise not to breathe a word of this to anyone."

"Pinky swear."

She held out her finger the same way she'd done when we were fourteen, a teenage pact not to tell anyone that we'd been the ones who sprinkled hot sauce in the geography teacher's coffee. Mr. Punter. He'd been a sadistic old coot, a relic left over from the days of corporal punishment. Every time he got annoyed, he'd thwack a wooden ruler against his hand, angry both at us and at the pesky rules that prevented him from tanning our insolent backsides.

Tessa was the first friend I'd made when I came to London. I'd been the new girl, and she'd been the chubby outcast sitting on her own in maths class. Our bond had been forged over a shared hatred of quadratic equations and a desire not to eat lunch alone, and it had only grown stronger since. When she hit fifteen, Tessa's braces had been removed and she'd gone on a diet, and she'd turned from an ugly duckling into a swan. A slightly annoying swan who borrowed my Instagram account to send messages to rock stars, but I loved her anyway.

And now I wrapped my finger around hers.

"You see why I'm feeling a little unsettled?"

"Yeah, I mean, whoa. Travis Thorne really said he liked you?"

"He really did. And the night before that in Paris, when we walked around the streets together... I'd begun to think it might actually mean something. And then another girl answered his phone."

"It could be perfectly innocent. What if she was just a friend? Or a foster sister?"

"I guess. I don't know."

"And he *did* try to call you. Did you ever stop to think you might be blowing this out of all proportion?"

See what I meant when I said Tessa was slightly annoying? Why did she always have to be right?

"Maybe."

"Just call him, okay? You should stay friends. Every girl needs a really hot guy friend. Bonus points if he's gay."

I choked out a laugh. "Travis Thorne is definitely not gay."

"I totally get that. Anyhow, I'm more interested in the whole contract thing. They honestly got shafted by their record label?"

Classic Tessa. She'd been the editor of the student newspaper at school, and although she liked to gossip, she loved a juicy story more. If I was honest, it was Tessa's enthusiasm rather than mine that had led me to study journalism at uni, that and a complete lack of direction when it came to my future career choice. Sticking with Tessa had seemed like an excellent way to delay the decision-making progress.

"It seems so. I haven't actually seen the contract, but—"

"Can you get a copy?"

"Tess, this isn't a story you can print. They told me the details in confidence."

"I know that—pinky swear, remember—but I'm super curious now. I always thought that record label was kind of odd."

"Odd in what way?"

"In that they don't have many acts, but the ones they do have are super successful until they leave, and then nobody ever hears from them again."

"That kind of fits with what Travis told me. Bands get so tired and disillusioned that they quit the industry completely."

"Why don't they just take a break, then find a new label?"

"Who knows? Maybe because they've lost momentum?"

"Look at other big artists who take time off. Their fans are ravenous for new stuff."

"If they've made their millions, perhaps they just want to lie back and relax on a beach somewhere? How do you know all this stuff, anyway?"

Tessa turned bright pink. "Uh..."

"You were stalking Rush Moder, weren't you?"

"Possibly. I like doing research, okay? It's good practice for my future career. And you have to admit, the label *is* weird."

"I'm just annoyed that Gary lives better than the boys and yet they do all the hard work."

"I'll do some digging."

For a moment, I considered trying to talk her out of it, but then I remembered that this was Tessa we were talking about. I'd have a better chance of trying to convince a toddler that vegetables really were tasty. And yes, I was a tiny bit curious myself.

"Just be careful, okay?"

"Can you get a copy of the contract?"

"Tessa!"

"Hey, it's always worth asking. Pass the prawn crackers?"

I pushed the plate towards her, together with a bowl of chilli dipping sauce.

"Aren't you eating?" she asked.

"I'm not all that hungry."

The events of the last week had made me lose my appetite.

Chapter 20 - Alana

"HEY," TRAVIS SAID.

"Hey."

Wow, this wasn't awkward at all. Wednesday evening, and the band had arrived back at their hotel in London, having travelled halfway around the world to spend just one day with their nearest and dearest. And now they needed to go act perky in a studio while a radio host grilled them about subjects they'd rather avoid. Rush had messaged me yesterday, begging me to bring coffee and take pictures.

And there I was, in the hotel lobby, complete with a tray from Starbucks. A sucker for punishment.

"Didn't you get much sleep?" I asked.

Travis scraped his hair back. "Is that a British way of telling me I look like shit?"

"Not shit, exactly. A little rough around the edges?"

"At least you're honest."

Rush squeezed the breath out of me from behind, lifting me clear off the floor.

"Instababe!"

I gave up. I didn't really mind him calling me that anymore, and when I smelled the whisky on his breath, I knew any protest would fall on deaf ears anyway.

"Are you drunk?"

"Best way to fly, baby. JD has this deal with the

check-in girl. He gives her orgasms, and she gives us upgrades."

"Let me explain the concept of 'too much information,'" I said as Dex walked past us towards the reception desk, stony-faced. "Is he okay?"

"We had to walk about fifty miles at the airport."

"Where's JD?"

"Getting supplies. He'll be here in two minutes."

Shit. It didn't take a genius to translate. JD was getting drugs. He'd been slightly better over the past week, but now it seemed he was on a backwards slide.

"You didn't try to stop him?"

"Hard to reason with an addict," Travis said softly. "He goes off the rails every time he has to come back after a trip home."

"Like going back to school to face the bullies on Monday morning?"

"Were you bullied?"

"Not me. My friend Tessa."

"Some little punks tried picking on JD once for the way he dressed. He smashed the mouthiest asshole over the head with Rush's guitar." Travis shook his head at the memory. "Rush went fuckin' purple. We had a gig that night, and he had to steal a new guitar so we could play."

"I'm not sure I want to know."

Rush leaned on my shoulder. "We went to this music store with an empty guitar case, and Travis and JD distracted the girl behind the counter while I picked out a sweet, sweet Gibson and put it in the case."

"Like I said..."

"Don't worry; the girl did well out of the deal."

Travis didn't look happy. "Shut up, buddy."

Was this what life would be like if I stuck around? Having to listen to tales of Travis's past conquests while praying nobody got arrested?

Courtney appeared, clipboard in hand. "Uh, guys? We need to go. The cars are outside."

What followed was vintage Indigo Rain. JD was quite clearly high, and Rush slurred every other word. Dex barely spoke. The show host made a comment about Vina that was borderline racist, and Travis threatened to smash his fucking face in. The girl working the bleep machine certainly earned her money.

"Well, that was an interesting experience," I said as we rode back to the hotel. It was nearly midnight, but that hadn't stopped fifty fans from waiting outside the radio station, clamouring for pictures.

Travis shrugged. "The guy was an asshole."

I'd never advocate violence, but I was oddly proud of him for sticking up for Vina. "Yes, he was."

In truth, the host was known for it, and I was surprised the band had agreed to appear on the show, but that was Gary for you. His willingness to eschew morals in return for publicity knew no bounds.

"What did social media think?" Rush asked.

"Your fans are arranging to boycott the station."

"Shame. Anyone want to go out and celebrate?"

Dex and Travis groaned. JD didn't, but only because he'd passed out.

"Instababe?"

"I have to go home."

"You're not staying at the hotel?"

"Not when I have to pay for my own room and I live a twenty-minute cab ride away."

Rush dropped his head back and closed his eyes.

"Guess I'll just stay in and watch porn instead."

Oh, what a lovely image.

The car pulled up outside the hotel, but because it was a limo arranged by the label, I couldn't simply pay the driver to carry on to my place. Thank goodness for Uber. I trailed the guys into reception to wait.

"Want me to stay with you until your car comes?" Travis asked.

Yes. "No, it's fine. You'll get mobbed by selfie-hunters."

"Text me when you get home. I want to know you're safe."

Sometimes, he reminded me of Zander except with longer hair and a beard.

"I will; I promise."

"Night, blue."

I got a hug from Rush, nothing from JD because he'd zoned out, a grimace from Dex, and an awkward little wave from Travis. Hashtag friend-zoned.

My Uber turned up, a ubiquitous Toyota Prius with disco lights on the dash, and I was about to climb in when I heard running footsteps behind me. Shit! I fumbled in my handbag for the illegal pepper spray Zander insisted I carry, but before I could get it out, Travis pulled the car door open and half lifted me inside. He followed, no doubt trying to stay out of sight of prying eyes.

"What the hell are you doing?"

"I need to talk to you."

"What about?"

Travis eyed up the driver, who seemed a little too interested in our conversation.

"Can we go somewhere more private?"

"Uh, okay. Where? A café? Back into the hotel?" I hesitated a second. "My place?"

"Will your brother give me grief for coming home with you?"

"He's not there tonight." Which meant he'd never know.

"Then we'll go to your place."

Why did I feel as if I were inviting a fox into the henhouse?

"We can leave now?" the driver asked.

"Yes, please."

In Chelsea, Travis stared up at my apartment building. Admittedly, it did look beautiful at night, the steel and glass lit by strategically placed spotlights. We lived on the sixth floor, which gave us a balcony and a nice view across the River Thames.

"Your apartment's much nicer than mine," Travis said.

"Really?"

"I just rented somewhere cheap to leave my stuff. I haven't even unpacked most of it."

"You didn't go there this week?"

"No, I went to my folks like I said."

"Oh."

"What's 'oh'?"

"It doesn't matter."

"Yeah, it does, because now you won't look at me."

I used my fob to let us through the outer door, then led Travis over to the lift. I might as well be honest with him. Yes, I knew he messed around with women all the time, but I really didn't want to know about it.

"You had a girl over, that was all. I just figured you'd go to your place rather than your parents' for that."

"How do you know?"

At least he didn't try to deny it. "You called me, remember? On, well, I guess it would've been Sunday night for you."

"You didn't pick up."

"No, but I tried to call you back, and *she* answered and said you were asleep."

"*She* was Caitlin. She came over for dinner with me and my parents. And on Monday and Tuesday, she drove me to my DUI sessions because my parents were working."

"Then you didn't..."

"No, blue. Anything between us was over years ago, but we're still friends, and we still talk. Hell, she's got a boyfriend. A doctor at the hospital where she works, except they're keeping it quiet because his divorce isn't finalised yet. They bought a fuckin' puppy together last week. She brought it over, and it shit in the lounge. I spent Sunday evening disinfecting the damn carpet."

"I'm sorry. I just assumed..."

Travis crowded me as I unlocked the door, and sweat beaded on the back of my neck. The man made me lose my mind when he got this close.

"We talked about you too."

"What? Why?"

"Catie helps me to get my head straight. She was the one person who told me not to sign that fuckin' record deal, you know. Back then, I accused her of being selfish, of wanting to stifle my career. Took us six months to speak again after that, and I'm lucky she spoke to me at all. She was right, and I was a fool."

"At least you can admit it now."

"Yeah. I've changed, and so has she."

"Why did you talk about me?"

"I wanted advice. Told her I'd met the right girl at the wrong time."

My heart began thumping against my ribcage, an insistent beat that drowned out rational thought.

"And what did she say?"

"That I was an idiot for walking away. That if you were the right girl, we'd find a way to make things work, like her and her damn doctor."

"So what are you saying?"

He gave me a lopsided smile, and my heart lurched out of my body and splatted on the living room floor.

"I'm saying that I like you, blue. I really fuckin' like you. I don't know what the future holds, but I can't just walk away."

I didn't know what to say, and I also thought I might cry, so I stood on tiptoes and kissed him before I could tell myself it was a bad idea. And he kissed me back. Softly at first, with his hands fisted in my hair, then he licked along the seam of my lips and they parted automatically. My experience with men may have been limited, but the way he tangled his tongue with mine felt pretty damn good, judging by the zaps of heat that ran through me from my scalp all the way to my toes. Travis's beard scratched against my chin, a sharp contrast with his lips, and his hands went everywhere—on my back, around my waist, squeezing my ass. The faint taste of coffee still lingered on his breath, but who needed caffeine? I'd never felt so awake—so alive—in my life.

But the longer we kissed, the faster the pool of heat in my belly began to boil, until eventually it fizzed into full-on panic. I was getting off with *Travis Thorne*. His list of conquests was into triple figures, and he'd quite literally been schooled in the art of sex by a teacher. I had no freaking clue what I was doing.

I tore my lips away, panting. "Stop. Please."

He did, instantly, and I missed his arms when they dropped away.

"Blue?"

"I... I..."

He took a step back, face ashen, but I grabbed his hands and pulled him towards me again.

"I'm scared. I've never... Not since..."

"I thought I'd hurt you. I never want to hurt you."

"No, no, you didn't. It's just that I don't know what to do next, and you obviously do, and I'm worried I'll end up acting like an idiot, well, more of an idiot because quite clearly I'm acting like an idiot right now, and—"

"Shh." Travis put a finger to my lips. "That innocence is part of what makes you special. I'll teach you. We can do things as fast or as slow as you want."

"I need an A to Z manual."

Now I got a new kind of smile, a filthy grin that turned my insides to jelly.

"I can help with that. Let's start with A."

"Please don't say anal." I clapped a hand over my mouth. "And please forget I said that."

Travis smoothed my hair and gently cradled my face.

"A is for arousal." He traced one finger across my cheek. "Your skin flushes. Your pupils dilate. Your lips get fuller." The finger continued downwards, across my collarbone, farther. "Your nipples harden." He laid a hand on my chest. "Your heart speeds up. Your breath quickens." A soft kiss. "You're getting wetter."

And my knees were about to give way. I gripped Travis's arms to stop myself from tumbling to the floor.

"Am I right?" he whispered.

All I could do was nod.

"B is for breasts. Men are fascinated by what we don't have, which means we like to play with these." He cupped my boobs in his hands. "Yours are perfect. As is your oh-so-English bottom." His hands moved downwards and lifted, tipping me towards him. "Better."

"At this rate, I'm not gonna last past E. Uh, what *is* E?"

"Patience, baby-blue. We're on C. C is for clitoris." His fingers brushed over my mound, the merest touch, and then they were gone. "But that's for later. C is also for confidence. I hate that somebody stole that from you, and I want to give it back."

C was also for crying. A tear rolled down my cheek, and Travis licked it away with the tip of his tongue.

"D is for..." Tell me he wasn't gonna say "dick." He'd been so freaking amazing until now. "Dreams. You've been in mine since the day I met you, but I won't tell you what we've been doing." That filthy smile came back. "Don't want to scare you off."

"I know what E is for now. Emotion." A sniffle escaped. "I never thought it would be like this."

Travis trailed kisses along my jaw. "I knew it would when I met the right person."

"What's F?"

Fucking? Because the way he was making me feel, I was about ready for that. Terrified but ready.

"Foreplay. Gonna take my time with you, baby-blue. But first I'll skip ahead to T. Talking. If anything makes you feel uncomfortable, or if we're moving too fast, you need to tell me, okay?"

"I thought T was for tearing each other's clothes off."

Travis chuckled and lifted his arms up. "Tear away."

I pulled off his shirt and got my first close-up look at those tattoos. A microphone on his right shoulder with a snake slithering around it. Music notes on a stave below it, then a guitar with its neck tied in a knot. I traced the outline with a fingertip.

"Why did you get this one? The guitar?"

"Stifled creativity."

I turned him around so I could look at the masterpiece on his back, the four horsemen of the apocalypse.

"This is a metaphor for the band?"

"It is. Indigo Rain, bringers of chaos and doom, but nobody truly knows us."

"Which one are you?"

"The dark horse, baby."

Travis didn't have a gym body, no big muscles, but he kept fit from running around on stage every night, and it showed. As did the growing bulge in his jeans. Bloody hell. I wasn't sure what to do next, which part to touch, so I kissed him again. I understood the kissing part. And this time when Travis lifted me, I wrapped my legs around his waist and clung to him like a monkey.

"We can't stand in the living room all night," he said. "Well, we could, but it wouldn't be very comfortable."

"How long are you staying?"

"Until you kick me out."

"That's not gonna happen. Shall we move this to the sofa? Or...or the bedroom?"

"Are you ready for the bedroom?"

With anyone else, the answer would have been no, but what Travis had said earlier resonated. When I met the right person, everything fell into place.

"Yes."

"Then tell me where to go."

I jerked my head to the right. "Down that hallway. First door on the left."

I'd always liked my bedroom with its dark pink curtains and cream bed linen, but now with Travis present, it suddenly seemed childish.

"It's a bit girly," I said, apologetic.

"I'd be more worried if it was a bit manly."

He carried me over to the windows, floor-to-ceiling glass that took up an entire wall. Zander had the same view in the master next door, and since the balcony rail was also made of glass, I could lie in bed and watch the boats on the river.

"Can people see in?" Travis asked.

"It's one-way glass."

"Good. I don't want more fuckin' pictures on the internet."

His hard cock nestled between my legs as he sat on the edge of the bed, and I wasn't just wet, I was soaking. I glanced down, and sure enough, there was a dark spot spreading on my jeans. Travis's gaze followed mine.

"Fuck. That's the hottest thing I've ever seen."

"Just get me out of these clothes, would you?"

I raised my arms, imitating his pose from earlier, and he peeled off my shirt and tossed it away. I expected my bra to follow, but he pulled the cups down instead, leaving my nipples pointing to attention over the top.

"You're perfect, blue."

I looked down at myself, but I didn't see what he saw. Instead, I tried to suck in the roll of stomach pressing over my waistband as he kissed and licked and sucked his way across my chest. *Come on, come on, come on.* Things were getting mighty uncomfortable.

"You okay?"

"I'm still wearing too many clothes. We're both wearing too many clothes."

"P is for patience."

"Don't give me that bullshit. You missed out 'cock' and 'dick,' so P is for penis." I gasped. "I can't believe I just said that."

Travis burst out laughing. "Hot and bothered, blue? I like your dirty mouth."

"I like your mouth too. Especially when you kiss me with it."

Infuriatingly, he only offered the faintest brush of his lips. "Since you seem determined to skip ahead in the alphabet, how about we try the letter O?"

"O?"

"Oral."

I glanced at his crotch, and visions of the first party came back to me. Of Jae-Lin going down on him with practised efficiency.

"You mean I..."

"No, me. I want to taste you."

Of all the things my stepfather had done, that

wasn't one of them. He hadn't stolen that pleasure from me, which only made me more eager to try it.

"Okay."

If Travis Thorne ever quit singing, he could still make millions with his mouth. His tongue in particular. Perhaps I should have been jealous of the hundred other women he'd been with, but at that moment, I didn't care because all the practice and all the experience gave me *this*. I arched off the bed as he pressed my thighs apart and went to town on me, bringing me to the brink time after time but pulling me back each time I got too close to the edge.

"Dammit, will you let me come?"

His response?

He pushed one slim finger inside me and pressed, and I nearly hit the ceiling. The asshole looked up, pleased with himself.

"G is for G spot."

"H is for hurry up."

Finally, he let me go, sucking with just the right amount of pressure as I shattered, the scratch of his beard on my skin countering the sweet touch of his lips. And when I broke, he gathered me up in his arms and hugged me back together again.

I rewarded him with a stream of gibberish. "Wow. I can't even... I've never... Words are gone."

He kissed my forehead. "We don't always need words. Time for you to get some sleep."

"Huh? Wait. What about you?"

I'd have been freaking blind if I'd missed the effect of our games on Travis, but just to be sure, I went in for a feel. Denim over rock-hard cock. Holy hell.

"Too much, too soon, blue. I'll go take care of

myself in a minute."

I should have been appreciative of his consideration. Told him how sweet he was, or perhaps kissed him to show my thanks. But since he'd turned my brain to mush, what actually came out was, "Can I watch?"

"Fuck me. You really are filthier than you look, aren't you? An angel with the mind of a sewer rat."

"Is that a problem?"

"Hell, no." He gave me a quick kiss on the lips, his beard still damp with my juices. "Yeah, you can watch. Join in if you want."

I sucked in a breath as I got my first glimpse of naked Travis and nearly swallowed my own tongue. If there were an awards show for dicks, he'd win every prize.

"Are you talking about acting like a dick or physical dicks?"

"Did I just say that out loud?"

"Yeah, babe."

"Three weeks ago, I would have gone with the first option, but now I've changed my mind."

"Do I need to make an acceptance speech? You know, first, I'd like to thank genetics, and also Trojan for keeping everything in good working order, but mostly Alana Graves for creating this replica of the Washington Monument we see here today."

"Shut up and show me what to do."

Travis spat on his hand then wrapped it around his cock, his fist moving slowly to start with. His earlier efforts had left me drained, but watching him now, my energy levels replenished with every stroke.

"Can I try? H is for hands."

He didn't speak, just wrapped my hand around the shaft under his. My fingers didn't even meet, which was a daunting prospect for later on. Because there was no question I'd go all the way with Travis. The man had me in every way possible.

"Shit, blue, I'm not gonna last long."

"Will you..." I screwed my eyes shut. "Will you come on me?"

Quick as a flash, he changed positions, straddling me as he pumped his cock. Cum squirted across my breasts, and I stared at it, scarcely able to believe that in twenty-four hours, I'd gone from hopelessly miserable to borderline depraved. And Travis Thorne watched me, a smile tugging at the corner of his lips.

"H is also for happy ending."

"And hot as hell."

"I'm burnin' up, blue." He reached forward to grab a handful of tissues from the box on my bedside table and wiped away the mess. "I'd like to roast all night, but we need to get some sleep."

"What time do you need to start work?"

Travis sighed, his earlier good humour gone. "I should get back to the hotel early. Alana, we need to keep this quiet for a while. What's happening between us. Not because I'm not proud as hell to have you as my girl, but because I don't want you gettin' scared off."

"It's okay; I understand."

I didn't like it, but I understood. And yes, I was nervous as hell about whatever would come next.

"I just want to be absolutely solid before we go public. I know my reputation, but this isn't some game for me."

"Me neither. I'll have to break the news to my

brother as well."

"Will I need to duck?"

"Possibly. Like I said, he can be a bit overprotective."

"Then we're on the same page. I'd do anything to keep you safe, blue."

"Just don't break my heart."

He placed a hand on my chest, and I pressed my own over the top.

"Our hearts are bound together now, so I'd be breaking my own as well."

CHAPTER 21 - ALANA

SIX THIRTY, AND Travis hopped around my room as he pulled his jeans on, swearing under his breath. Three hours of sleep hadn't left either of us particularly coordinated.

"Are you sure you don't want coffee before you leave?"

"Stay in bed, blue. I'll get it back at the hotel."

"What if someone sees you sneak in? The press?"

"They won't. I never get up this early, so they don't arrive till noon."

It was true; the band really didn't do mornings. A year or so ago, Gary had tried to make them do a run of eight a.m. public appearances, so they'd lain on stage at the beginning of a show and taken a nap in protest. One of the few times they'd stood up to the record label.

"I'll get there by ten. Save me a seat at breakfast?"

Travis leaned down to kiss me, a chaste peck on the lips that turned into something entirely more heated.

"You can't sit next to me, or I'll be hard all day. I'll save you a seat next to Dex or JD."

"Why not Rush?"

"Because Rush likes to hug you, and I don't want to have to kill him." Another kiss. "Bye, blue-eyes."

"I miss you already."

He messaged me the moment the door closed.

Travis: Miss you too xx

The texting theme continued when I got to the hotel. Squashed onto a bench seat beside Dex, I fished my phone out of my pocket when it vibrated.

Travis: I is for innocence or indecent behaviour. Which do you prefer?

Oh, hell. I glanced across at the man himself, but he was eating muesli with Vina, Meredith, and Verity, not a care in the world. Meredith gave me a wave when she caught me looking, and I forced a smile back. Gah! Travis Thorne was the most amazing, frustrating, sweet, sexy, filthy asshole I'd ever met. The sensible part of me said to pick innocence, a low-risk strategy, but the girl who'd lain there last night while a man came all over her was kind of tempted by option two.

"What did that toast ever do to you?" Dex asked.

"Huh?" I looked down and realised I'd destroyed a slice of wholemeal, and now I was spreading Nutella on the plate. "Oops. I'm a little tired."

"Didn't sleep well?"

I'd slept better than any other night in my life, just not for long enough. "Do you ever feel really restless?"

"Nah, my pain pills knock me out every time."

I got a new piece of toast and focused on spreading the Nutella properly. I figured I'd earned the right to a decent breakfast after all the calories I'd burned last night. Innocent or indecent. Innocent or indecent... In the end, I decided to live dangerously.

Me: Indecent behaviour. And J is for jam. I'm gonna lick it off you later.

Travis looked across just as I dropped a miniature jar of strawberry jelly into my handbag, and I saw him suck in a breath. Good.

Tonight's show was at the O2, and we headed there after breakfast. I'd been to plenty of events in that arena, but I'd never seen it empty like that. I stood centre stage and took a picture for my own Instagram. Looking out at the cavernous space gave me a strange feeling of vertigo, a fear that everyone was watching even though there was nobody there.

"Impressive, huh?" Travis said, walking up behind me.

"Scary. What's it like, being up here with thousands of people screaming at you?"

"The biggest rush you can imagine. That's why we're still in the business. Otherwise, we'd have said fuck it and walked, then waited for the label to sue our bankrupt asses."

"Do you ever worry about falling?"

"Nah, I jump instead. The fans always catch me."

"You're crazy."

"Crazy about you, blue."

"And cheesy. Did I mention cheesy?"

"Perhaps in a few years, I can make a living singing Barry Manilow covers."

I was about to suggest adding Cliff Richard to his repertoire when one of the crew called him over. But as he walked away, my phone buzzed.

Was that Travis?

It sure was. A black-and-white photo, taken of him naked in bed with his hand over his cock. Flipping heck. It had begun. He'd cropped out any identifying marks, obviously mindful of the Reagan incident, but I knew it was him. And if he'd taken it earlier, he must have known which option I'd pick. Was I really that predictable?

And how was I supposed to follow up? Did he expect me to send a picture too? Maybe, but he'd also never push me to do anything I wasn't comfortable with. After a moment's hesitation, I nipped into the ladies' loo and took a picture of my mouth, just my mouth, with the tip of my tongue licking my lips. A little artistic editing and a pretty filter later, I sent it over. Take that, Thorne.

He got his own back an hour later as I walked down a corridor in search of coffee. I didn't have the best sense of direction, and it was all too easy to get lost, but I didn't care when I saw Travis approaching. He glanced over my shoulder, shoved me into an alcove, and snogged me senseless.

"K is for kissing."

Five seconds later, he'd gone, and I'd almost come.

Things only degenerated as the afternoon wore on. First, Travis sent me the ultimate dick pic, which I unfortunately opened right after I'd taken a mouthful of coffee.

Vina hastily passed me a handful of tissues to blot the mess off my keyboard. "Are you okay?"

"Uh, fine. It just went down the wrong way."

Oh, dear goodness. He'd lined glacé cherries up along his length and decorated it with whipped cream. How in the hell was I supposed to compete with that? The best I could manage was a heart drawn in jam, the pointy part tucked into my cleavage.

Me: L is for laughter.

And possibly love too, because with every passing

moment, my feelings for Travis grew stronger. Love was a strange creature. My mother had tied the knot five times without experiencing it once, Tessa swore she fell in love every other week, and my brother had been the king of one-night stands until he met Dove. I guess it was different for everyone.

The show kicked off at seven with Vendetta, then Styx and Stones, and finally Indigo Rain. I'd started taking pictures of everyone now, and people just looked at them on my screen and picked out the ones they wanted me to send to them. Yes, it was kind of slave labour since I wasn't getting paid, but apart from dealing with Herr Führer Gary, I enjoyed being there. I suppose that even though my father hadn't been much of a dad, I had to thank him for giving me the financial means to be able to do this.

Because there was nothing on earth that compared to watching an Indigo Rain set from the edge of the stage, seeing Travis Thorne turn to wink at you, then clutching your chest in panic as he swan-dived into the crowd below. Like he said, they caught him, and he carried on singing as he crowd-surfed on his back around the arena, eventually returning to the stage minus his shirt.

Freaking heck. I was *dating* that guy.

And tonight, he'd be in my bed again. At the hotel, he headed upstairs with the others while I lingered in the lobby, but I knew he'd be back. Five minutes passed. Ten. It didn't matter because the black cab waiting at the kerb had its meter running. The driver would wait as long as I wanted. Finally, Travis jogged down the stairs with a messenger bag over his shoulder and a cap pulled low over his eyes.

And ran right into Vina as she came out of a different door.

Shit.

"You're going out?" she asked, then turned and saw me. It took her five seconds to put the puzzle pieces together, and her eyebrows flew into her hairline as realisation dawned. "You're going out together?"

I gripped her hand. "Please, please don't tell anyone. We're trying to keep it quiet."

"I won't." She mimed zipping up her lips and throwing away the key. "I won't say a word."

"Thank you."

"I don't suppose you've seen my room card? I can't find it anywhere."

"Sorry. But the desk'll just code you a new one if you ask."

"That's what I figured." She smiled. "Have a good time."

The cab driver grudgingly put away his packet of crisps when we climbed in, and I snuggled against Travis as we once more headed for Chelsea. What a difference twenty-four hours made. Last night, I'd been freaking out about Caitlin answering Travis's phone, whereas tonight, I was panicking in case jam leaked all over my handbag.

And now Travis dumped his bag on my lap.

"Hey, what are you—" His hand slid underneath. "Ahh."

"I've been waiting all day to get my hands on you. Put me out of my misery, blue."

"So M is for misery?"

"No, M is for masturbation. I had to jack off in the bathroom after lunch."

Travis! I smacked my palm against my forehead. "I'm not sure I needed to know that."

"Take it as a compliment. Besides, it's fun. You should try it sometime. I could help you."

He ran a finger over the seam of my jeans, and I bit my bottom lip to keep from whimpering. Twenty-four hours, and I'd turned into a puddle of lust. I thought Travis might go for my zipper, but he didn't, just kept his touch infuriatingly light as he made me squirm in my seat.

If my legs hadn't been so wobbly, I would've run into my apartment building, but as it was, I had to settle for a fast stagger with Travis holding me up. Believe it or not, I hadn't even been drinking. The elevator took forever, and he pushed me against the wall and kissed me breathless on the journey to the sixth floor.

"You seem like you're in a hurry, baby?" he said as I cursed my key and the lock, neither of which wanted to talk to the other.

"F is for foreplay, that's what you said. And we've basically been doing that for the entire day, so excuse me if I'm a tiny bit flustered. F is also for faster, and that's how you need to move."

This time when we got inside, he really did tear off my clothes. Buttons went flying, and I accidentally ripped his T-shirt when his arm got stuck. Oops. But I had him right where I wanted him, naked and ready on my bed.

"Blue, wait. Shh, slow down. This isn't a race. We've got all night, and we're not rushing. I know what happened in the past, but I'm treating this like it's your first time, and I don't want to hurt you."

Hormones sizzled in my veins, and my libido wanted to straddle him like a desperate cowgirl, but logically, I knew he was right. It was gonna be uncomfortable. It always had been. With all the other stuff we'd been doing, I'd managed to shove the bad memories to the back of my mind, but now they returned with a vengeance.

"Okay," I whispered, the heat in my veins simmering down. "Tell me what to do."

"M is also for missionary, and that's how we're gonna do this. Lie on your back and raise your knees."

Yes, it stung as Travis stretched me, but he made up for it with his sweetness. Kisses, caresses, and a slow rhythm that let me savour the connection between us. My stepfather had always told me I was a good girl, and even today, those words made me feel sick to my stomach. But Travis did the opposite, whispering filth and smut and telling me how bad I was as he erased the worst parts of my childhood.

"N is for nails, blue. Rake them down my back. I'll pay for as many manicures as you want."

"You like that?"

"Yeah, I fuckin' do." His head dropped forward as I clawed at him, and he let out a low groan. "Gonna come. Can't hold out much longer."

"Do it."

Travis stiffened against me, peppering my cheeks with soft kisses as he grunted his release, and I knew at that moment the love thing was going to cause me a big problem. Travis Thorne had entwined his soul with mine, and untangling them would be impossible.

"You okay, Alana?"

"I think so."

"Sore?"

"A little."

"Do you want to sleep now? Or play with your jam?"

Travis couldn't keep a straight face as he asked, and I giggled with him.

"I'm still hungry."

"Give me a minute to get rid of this condom, and then you can do whatever you want to me." He pulled out, then rummaged in his bag before he went to the bathroom. "You can try this too."

He tossed me a can.

"Whipped cream?"

"Whipped queam. We did O and P yesterday, and I was struggling for Q."

The giggles turned into full-blown laughter. "You're such an idiot."

"Yeah, I know. But now I'm your idiot."

CHAPTER 22 - ALANA

ON FRIDAY MORNING, the dream turned into a nightmare when I heard the front door slam.

My first, sleep-deprived thought was that Travis had run out on me. My second, when I realised Travis was still asleep with his arm around my waist, was *oh fuck*.

"Travis, wake up! I think my brother just came home."

"Huh?"

Sleepy Travis was normally cute, but not today.

"My brother's outside."

"Aw, fuck. Are you sure?"

"Well, it's either him or a burglar." At that moment, a burglar actually seemed preferable. I had my phone, and my pepper spray, and, uh, half a can of squirty cream. "Wait here. I'll check."

"Alana, if you think it's a burglar, you're not going out there alone."

"I'm almost ninety-five percent sure it isn't."

"What about—"

"Lanie?" Zander called. "Are you okay?"

Dammit.

"Sure, why wouldn't I be?"

"Just wondering why there's a pair of size-ten men's boots in the hallway?"

Of course there was, and Zander took a size eleven.

Travis had turned out to be surprisingly well house-trained, but now I cursed his foster parents for instilling that sense of tidiness in him. If he'd just thrown the damn boots down the side of my bed, I could have hidden him on the balcony or something.

"Boots. Yes. Give me two minutes, and I'll come and explain."

Clothes. I needed clothes. An invisibility cloak would have been ideal, but I had to make do with pyjamas. Travis pulled on his jeans sans underwear, but when I handed him his T-shirt, one arm was hanging off, the stitching torn at the shoulder.

"It's okay, I brought a spare."

So he did, but it had a foot-wide parental advisory label on it, complete with a warning for explicit content.

"Could you turn it inside out?"

He glanced down at his chest. "Shit."

"Lanie?" Zander called.

"I'm coming, okay?" I turned to whisper to Travis. "Stay here, and I'll talk to him."

"No way. This is *our* problem, not yours."

Deep breaths. Okay, forget about the T-shirt. Travis was a rock star. It was almost appropriate.

Zander was leaning against the wall opposite my bedroom door when I opened it, his arms folded. He looked Travis up and down, assessing, then recognition dawned and his eyes widened in surprise.

"How long has this been going on?"

I said, "Two days," at the same time as Travis said, "Three weeks."

"Well, which is it?"

"I met Travis three weeks ago. He's been staying here for two nights."

"No offence, mate, but I've heard how fast you go through women." Zander's words were mostly civil, but there was no mistaking the hostility in his tone. "Alana isn't one of your groupies."

"I know that."

"I won't stand by and let you use her. Lanie, are you okay?"

"Zander, I'm fine." I put my hands on my hips. "Better than fine. Travis isn't using me."

"He has a different girl every night. I've heard the stories from the guys at the office."

"*Had* a different girl every night. Exactly like you did before you met Dove."

"That's different."

"How? How is it different?"

"I don't tour the world with women throwing themselves at me, for one thing."

"No, just London and Northbury. Shall I recap?" I ticked off the girls on my fingers. "There was Kelsy, who got hold of our home phone number and called fifty times a day for weeks, and you kept making me answer. Nye's weird second cousin Phoebe, who sent us an actual freaking pheasant she'd shot. That red-haired girl who used to sit outside on the steps for hours, and Sammi, who claimed you were the father of her baby."

"I wasn't."

"Yes, I know that. I'm just making the point that you screwed a lot of girls and most of them were lunatics. Oh, and Laura. Who can forget Laura? I got into a fight with Laura after she kneed Zander in the balls," I explained for Travis's benefit.

"Did you win?" he asked.

"Of course I did."

Zander's frown didn't ease, but he did at least unfold his arms.

"I don't want Alana getting hurt."

"Neither do I. She's worth a thousand of any other girl. A million."

"And what happens when your UK tour ends? You're only here for another week."

Travis and I looked at each other. That was the elephant in the room.

"I'm not sure," Travis admitted. "There are some difficulties, but we'll get through them somehow."

He reached out to squeeze my hand, and I clung to him. I couldn't lose him, not now. I *couldn't.*

"Please don't be mad, Zander. He makes me happy."

"Ah, fuck."

"And please don't tell anyone. We're trying to keep this quiet for now."

Zander fixed his gaze on Travis, hard, unyielding. "If you do anything to hurt my sister, I'll make your life hell. Do you understand?"

"Yes."

"And if you cheat on her, I'll remove body parts."

"I won't."

"Bry and Max need to know."

I nodded. "Okay."

Finally, Zander pushed away from the wall. "Who wants coffee?"

The tension seeped out of me. We were okay. Zander wasn't exactly overjoyed, but we'd got a grudging acceptance from him, which was as much as I could hope for at the moment.

Travis relaxed a little too. "Thanks, but I need to get back to the hotel before the others wake up."

"I'll drive you," Zander said.

"I can take a cab."

"No, you don't get it. My priority is my sister's happiness, which unfortunately seems to hinge on you right now. And since I don't want people asking questions about your movements any more than you do, that means I'm driving you back to your hotel so you stay out of sight. Understood?"

"Understood."

"We leave in ten minutes. Put some socks on. Lanie, I'm going straight to the office for a meeting afterwards."

"Are you staying here tonight?"

"Yeah, so try and keep the noise down, would you? I don't want to hear what you're doing in your room with Ozzy Osbourne's love child."

"You don't mind Travis coming back with me?"

"Better that you're both here than camping out in some hotel. Just don't eat all my bacon."

"I'll buy you as much bacon as you want."

Zander tapped his watch, trying not to smile. "Ten minutes."

I walked into the hotel at half past nine, slightly sheepish after this morning's drama. Travis had texted to say Zander hadn't tried to throw him over a bridge on their journey, so that was something at least.

Travis was sitting with the rest of the band this

morning, but there was an empty seat next to Vina, so I grabbed a bowl of fruit and headed in her direction. Hotel breakfasts were ridiculously overpriced, but today, I'd get my money's worth from the buffet because I needed to replenish my energy after last night. Travis was exhausting.

"Hey," Vina said. "You didn't get much sleep?"

"Is it that obvious?"

"Your eyes are a bit puffy."

"Shit."

"Was it...?" She cut her eyes in Travis's direction.

"That and my brother came home early this morning and woke me up."

"Have you got much to do this afternoon?"

"Just a session of photo editing, but I thought it'd look weird if I turned up late. I got some nice shots of you yesterday, but I want to make the colours pop more before I hand them over."

"I've got a desk and a spare bed in my room you're welcome to use."

"Are you sure?"

"As long as you don't mind me doing a Facebook live chat with my fans later on, but that should only take about half an hour."

"I don't mind at all. Is it me, or is it quiet in here this morning?"

"Vendetta and Styx and Stones are both off making public appearances, and the crew's gone to set up at Wembley."

"Gary?"

"Shopping. He took Courtney and Jeanne to carry his stuff. I honestly don't know how they put up with him."

"Me neither. I'd have snapped by now."

As soon as I'd shovelled down the fruit plus a fry-up —which I felt was totally deserved—I sleepwalked to Vina's room, set my alarm for two hours' time, and curled up on the bed. This thing with Travis was amazing, but we'd need to find some way of fitting in sleep along with everything else or we'd both die of exhaustion.

At eleven in the morning, as I drifted off, an overly horny boyfriend seemed like my biggest problem.

How little did I know.

A scream ripped through my world for the third time in as many weeks, and I bolted upright as Vina ran out of the bathroom. At first, I didn't connect the two events, assuming she'd heard the cry too and come to help.

Then I realised the awful noise was coming from her mouth as she clawed at her face.

"What's wrong? Vina, what happened?"

Her eyes were closed as she stumbled around the room like a zombie on speed. I leapt towards her, my heart thrashing at my ribcage, and up close, I saw her skin had turned red and begun to blister. A burn? What from? The hospitality tray sat untouched on the desk, the kettle unplugged.

Stop overanalysing, Alana. A burn needed cold water, and it needed it now. I turned her back in the direction of the bathroom, propelling her forward, and now her hands were red and angry too. Whatever had caused this, it was on her face.

Which meant I had to avoid touching her skin. I

grabbed a handful of her bathrobe and half lifted her into the bath, then slammed on the shower and turned the temperature as low as it would go.

"Vina, stay under the water, okay. Keep your hands away from your face."

She didn't answer, just wailed, an inhuman sound that made every hair on my body stand on end. I pulled the showerhead out of its holder and aimed it at her face. She hadn't opened her eyes, not once. Were they damaged? Or had she screwed them shut in a desperate attempt at self-preservation?

"It's okay, sweetie. We'll sort this out."

What had caused the problem? And could it hurt me too? I looked around the room, and my gaze alighted on a glass jar of white gloop on the countertop, its lid lying on the floor by the toilet. Had Vina been using it? Was that moisturiser?

Whatever, I didn't have time to think too much about it at that moment. We needed help.

"Can you hold this?" I tried to put the shower attachment into her hands, but she screamed when it touched her skin. I had no choice but to clip it back into place above her while I grabbed my phone.

A call to the emergency services came first, and once the ambulance was on its way, I dialled Travis with trembling fingers.

"Vina's hurt. Room three-twelve."

"Hurt how?"

"Burned, I think. Can you come?"

"Leave the door open."

Back in the bathroom, Vina hadn't moved from under the water, but the blisters were still spreading. I gently grasped her wrists to make sure the stream covered her hands as well.

"Help's coming. Just don't move, okay?"

"It hurts so bad," she gasped.

"Was it the cream you put on your face?"

She nodded, then began to sob.

I heard running footsteps outside and quickly tugged Vina's gaping bathrobe closed. Two seconds later, Travis burst in with Rush behind him.

"What happened?"

"She got burned by her moisturiser."

"What, this stuff?"

Travis moved to pick the pot up, the idiot.

"Don't touch it!"

He peered closer instead. "It looks like she hardly used any."

"However much she used, it was too much." Was this some crazy allergic reaction? I shuddered as I remembered what happened to Jae-Lin, although her anaphylaxis had been a known issue. "Can one of you go downstairs and show the ambulance crew where to go?"

"I will," Rush said.

"What should I do?" Travis asked. "Hey, your phone's ringing."

"Who is it?"

"Your brother."

"Can you tell him what's happening? He monitors my phone, and if nobody answers, he'll drop everything and come racing over."

"He monitors your phone?"

"Just answer it!"

Of course, telling the story made little difference with Zander. Once he found out what was going on, he raced over anyway. He turned up just as the ambulance crew was strapping Vina onto a stretcher, her face twisted in agony even after painkillers. The paramedics said I'd done the right thing by getting her into the shower straight away, but she still looked like Deadpool on his day off.

"Lanie, what the hell happened this time?" Zander sat on the bed where until forty minutes ago, I'd been sleeping peacefully. "The control room's started a pool on how many more times you're gonna dial 999 this month."

"I was asleep when she screamed, and when I got up, her freaking face was dissolving. I thought she'd burned herself at first because she'd gone all red, but it was her moisturiser."

"A chemical burn?"

"I guess."

"Where's this moisturiser?"

"In the bathroom. None of us touched it."

"Why didn't this happen the last time she used the stuff?"

When someone's skin's melting off in front of you, you tend not to think about those little things.

"I don't know."

Zander got up. "Where is it? This white stuff by the sink?"

"Yes."

"Hmm. Looks like she just started it today. The box is next to it. When you get that fancy shit, you don't keep the box after you've opened the jar, do you?"

"No."

"And this isn't moisturiser. It's skin-lightening cream."

"What? Why would she need that? She has beautiful skin."

"Peer pressure. From social media, the music industry, fashion magazines, society as a whole. Half of these creams are illegal, and most of them are nasty."

"How do you know?"

"Dev picked up a case last year where a girl had been using one of them. First her face got scarred, then her kidneys failed. She bought the stuff over the internet."

"Vina's skin *was* darker last year," Travis said. "I just figured she'd been somewhere sunny on vacation."

"So you think this cream's from...what? A bad batch? A dodgy supplier?"

"Take your pick. But at the very least, we need to get the police and Trading Standards involved."

"Do you know who to call?"

"I'll deal with it. But they'll want to talk to you as a witness too. Who was the girl?" Zander turned to Travis. "Was she with your lot?"

"She's a singer. She's supposed to be on stage with us tonight."

"That's not gonna happen, mate. What time's the show?"

"The support acts start at seven. Fuck, someone needs to go to the hospital with Vina."

"What about her family?"

"I think it's just her mom. She came to some of the TV shows last year."

"What TV shows?"

"*Sing! Live.*"

"Zander doesn't watch much TV," I explained. "It was a reality show where the contestants performed songs in front of a live audience with only fifteen minutes' notice of what they had to sing."

"It was fuckin' karaoke," Travis muttered.

"Do you know how to contact her mother?" Zander asked.

Travis shook his head. "Is the number in her phone? Can you get it from there?"

"Depends if it's locked."

"Otherwise I'll have to ask Gary."

"Who's Gary?"

"The asshole in charge."

"You don't get along?"

"He's the kind of person who makes coffee by yelling at the machine until it complies."

"Want to borrow some body armour?"

Travis tried to smile, but it was the same forced expression he used when signing endless autographs. I was starting to learn his moods better now. The grit of his teeth that meant he was holding his temper in check. How his eyes softened when he was truly happy. And like now, the way he chewed his lip when he got upset.

"Wouldn't make any difference. Gary attacks with words, not weapons. Just look after Alana, okay?"

Zander nodded. "Always."

CHAPTER 23 - ALANA

ZANDER INSISTED ON picking Travis and me up in the evening. The show had gone on, as it always did. Meredith offered to sing Vina's part, but in the end, the guys switched back to the original set list and sang alone.

"Replacing Vina after a tragedy's disloyal," Travis had said, and the others agreed with him.

Gary dispatched Jeanne to the hospital to sit with Vina while I stepped in to help Courtney with her list of tasks—yes, fetching Gary's coffee was one of them—although with Vina under sedation, there was little Jeanne could do.

"They washed everything off, and now Vina's got a dressing over her whole face," she reported.

"Did they say how bad it was?"

"No one would tell me much because I'm not family, but the doctors all looked kinda shifty."

Which meant the news wasn't good. And worse, nobody knew where her mother was. Gary's HR person had her contact details, but she didn't answer when Travis called, and nobody wanted to leave a voicemail in that situation. Zander said he'd track her down, and not for the first time, I felt an overwhelming gratitude towards my brother.

Zander had borrowed one of Blackwood's SUVs,

and I curled up against Travis in the back seat. Until then, I'd held it together, but as his arms tightened around my torso, all the pent-up fear and stress washed out of me.

"Shh, don't cry."

"I can't help it. Vina's been nothing but nice to everyone, and she didn't deserve this."

"Why the hell does this shit keep happening? Marli, Jae-Lin, Reagan, Vina. This fuckin' tour's jinxed."

"I don't know. It's either really bad luck or...or..."

Or it wasn't. And I couldn't decide which prospect was scarier.

"Or what?"

"What if all these accidents aren't accidents?"

Travis stared at me, his eyes showing a hint of horror as my words sank in.

"Who are Marli and Jae-Lin?" Zander asked.

"Friends of Travis. Marli died of an overdose a few weeks ago, and Jae-Lin went into anaphylactic shock at a party right after I started with the band."

"I read about the overdose. Why didn't you tell me about the other girl?"

"I didn't think it was important." And I also hadn't wanted to freak Zander out. "She had an allergy to shellfish, and she carried an EpiPen."

"She ate shellfish even though she knew she could die from it?"

"She didn't eat anything at all," Travis said. "I spoke to her afterwards, and she stuck with rum and Coke that night. Coke the drink," he added hastily. "She thought it must have been cross-contamination on her glass. The hotel kitchen's doing an investigation, but so far, they've basically denied it was their fault."

"Four girls, four weeks, four incidents. Do they have anything in common apart from Travis?"

"It wasn't Travis! He wasn't even in the country when Marli died."

"Lanie, I'm not saying it was Travis. Just that he seems to be the link here."

"If there *is* a link."

Zander sighed. "Yeah, if there is a link."

The prospect of Travis somehow being involved in the four incidents in more than a superficial way sent chills through me. No, he hadn't been there for Marli, but he'd had the opportunity to push Reagan down the stairs, and he could've spiked Jae-Lin's drink before he retreated to the stairwell with me. And Vina? He'd gone upstairs for ten minutes when we got back to the hotel yesterday. Long enough to tamper with her face cream?

No! How could I even be thinking like that? Travis had never shown the slightest inclination to harm anyone, and he had no motive for hurting Jae-Lin or Vina. Reagan, yes, but nobody liked her. If I were Travis, I'd have pushed the bitch under the damn tour bus after her sneaky nighttime tryst.

A change of subject was in order.

"I want to visit Vina in hospital tomorrow. Will you have time to come?"

Travis nodded. "I'll make the time. We've got an interview with a radio station at eleven, but nothing after that until five."

"The talk-show appearance?"

"Yeah, and it's pre-recorded. Doesn't air until eight thirty. Gives them plenty of time to bleep my fucks out." He glanced sideways at Zander. "Shit."

"Don't worry; he swears too."

Travis lowered his voice. "I should be better around you."

"I like you just the way you are."

Dove was home when we got in, and she gave me the mother of all hugs because we hadn't seen each other for weeks. She was closer to my age than Zander's, and she acted more like the sister I'd never had than my brother's wife. Though our living arrangements might appear awkward to some, I'd enjoyed having another girl around for the last few months.

"It's really true?" she asked, keeping her voice low. "You're doing bad things with a rock star?"

I leaned close to whisper in her ear. "The worst."

"Holy hell." She stood on tiptoe to look over my shoulder. "I know I shouldn't say he's hot because I just married your brother, but he should come with a fire extinguisher."

I smiled, remembering last night. I couldn't help it. "He comes with a sprinkler system instead."

Dove's expression didn't change for a moment, then her eyes bulged and she made a funny choking sound. "Don't let Zander hear you say that. Not if you don't want your hottie to get castrated."

"My lips are sealed."

"Liar." Her expression grew serious. "Zander said one of Travis's colleagues got hurt today?"

"Chemical burns on her whole face." I shuddered. "From her face cream. It was horrible."

"Will she be okay?"

"I don't know. The doctors are being cagey at the moment."

Zander heard us talking—one of his more annoying

traits was that he was as nosy as me—and waved his phone.

"I forgot to say—someone from Blackwood visited Vina's house today, and one of the neighbours said her mum went on an overseas volunteering trip. She's building a school in Kenya, so she might not have phone reception."

"So we can't contact her at all?"

"Blackwood's got an office in Nairobi, but unless Vina can give us an idea of where her mum's staying, it'll be like hunting for a needle in a haystack."

"I'll ask her tomorrow if I can."

"Do you guys want anything to eat tonight?" Dove asked. "Or a drink?"

I shook my head. I'd nibbled on food from the catering area this evening, but mostly I'd felt too sick to eat. At least now that my secret was out, I hadn't had to dodge Max and Bryson, and their calm presence had made me feel marginally better.

"Travis?"

"I ate earlier."

Dammit, I hadn't even introduced them properly. "This is Dove."

He leaned down to kiss her on the cheek, and she turned red.

"Good to meet you. Thanks for letting me stay in your home."

Dove gave me a wow-the-rock-star-has-manners look, then fanned herself when he turned away. Yes, I knew exactly how she felt. I may have spent the last two nights naked with the man, but I still had to pinch myself.

It felt weird leading Travis into my bedroom under

a pair of watchful gazes, but the alternative—being apart—was far worse. And when the door closed behind us, I relaxed for the first time all day. At least, I did until I saw what Dove had left on the bed for us. Travis picked up the first box.

"Furry handcuffs and a blindfold?"

I turned the same colour as my soon-to-be-dead sister-in-law had. "It's Dove's idea of a joke." Payback because I'd done this to her once. "If you'll excuse me, I'll just go and burn it all."

"No, no, I like this. Love eggs? Marshmallow-flavoured condoms?" He came dangerously close to choking. "A butt plug?"

"I'll kill her."

"Well, I'm gonna send her a thank-you note. If marshmallow doesn't do it for you, how do you feel about pineapple?"

"This is so embarrassing."

"Nah, blue. Embarrassing is when you realise the girl you like found some random woman handcuffed to your bed."

Yes, but I could look back and laugh about it now.

"You really didn't know who she was?"

"I just woke up and she was there."

"Speaking of handcuffs..." I twirled Dove's gift on one finger.

"Not tonight, blue. I want your arms around me."

"R is for romance?"

"This isn't romance. Romance is when I take you to California and we drive up into the hills with a picnic and spend the whole day eating and talking and making love. Then I bring you home and cook you dinner and we watch some chick flick because you like it, and I spend the whole night kissing every inch of you on a bed of fuckin' rose petals."

Holy hell. A man who could cook? "Wow. So we're skipping R for now?"

Travis lifted the hem of my shirt, slipped his hands underneath, and peeled it off over my head. Two seconds later, my bra had disappeared and my jeans were on their way too.

"S is for slow, sweet sucking," he said, lifting me onto the bed.

"You spelled that last word wrong."

His throaty laugh sent shivers through me. "Never was that good at school."

"You learned about the important things. T is for teacher, right?"

"Baby-blue, I'm gonna teach you everything."

Chapter 24 - Alana

"OMG! OHMIGOSH, OHMIGOSH, ohmigosh!"

I turned away from the sink in time to see Tessa drop the bakery bag she was carrying. A donut fell out and rolled across the kitchen floor. Dammit, that looked like a chocolate creme.

Her mouth opened and closed like a demented goldfish's as she stared at Travis, and when he put down his coffee and smiled at her, she began fanning herself.

"I'm dreaming. Tell me I'm dreaming. Actually, don't. I'd rather stay asleep."

"Tessa, this is Travis."

"I know that! You think I don't freaking know that? Why the heck is he in your freaking kitchen?" Travis looked at me, and Tessa looked at Travis looking at me then began hyperventilating. "Holy crap. You did it? Like, *it*?"

"Travis, this is my friend Tessa. Sometimes she doesn't think before she speaks."

Travis's grin got wider, and I knew he was trying not to laugh. "Hi, Tessa."

"He said my name." Tessa backed towards the door. "Excuse me. I'm just gonna go and die a happy death on the sofa."

"Is she always like that?" Travis asked once she'd

disappeared.

"Pretty much. She gets a little star-struck. Be thankful you're not Rush, or we'd be giving her CPR right now."

Dove walked in. "Is Tessa okay? Ooh, are those donuts?"

"I don't think she was expecting to see Travis here."

"I guess I can understand that. Zander's still trying to come to terms with the whole thing himself."

"He wasn't as upset as I thought he'd be."

"Well, he'd have to be the biggest hypocrite in the world if he complained, wouldn't he?"

Dove stooped to pick up the bag and the stray donut as Tessa poked her head around the doorjamb.

"Travis is still here," I told her.

He held up his mug. "Haven't finished my coffee yet."

"Uh, sorry I acted like an idiot. I always do that."

"At least you didn't faint. That's more awkward. And you get extra points for being fully clothed."

"Girls visit you naked?"

"More often than you'd think."

"How about Rush?"

"Does Rush visit me naked?"

She rolled her eyes. "No, duh. Do girls visit *him* naked?"

"Don't even think about it," I warned.

She stuck her tongue out. "Spoilsport."

"Why are you here, anyway? And how did you get in?"

"Zander let me in on his way out jogging. And I came over to talk about the thing we discussed the other night."

"The thing?"

She cut her gaze to Travis. "You know, the *thing*."

Ah, she meant the record label, but I didn't want to tell Travis I'd been poking around in his business. Not now, not right at the beginning of our relationship.

"I see. The thing. Can we talk about the thing later?"

"Absolutely." She picked up the bakery bag off the table. "Donut?"

"Do you two always talk in code?" Travis asked.

"Not always, just sometimes. What donuts did you bring? Tell me there's another chocolate creme."

"There is, but Zander reserved it."

"Zander said he wanted a bacon roll," Dove told us.

"Then I guess he's super hungry."

I bit into an apple pie donut, not so much because I craved sugar but more because I needed to get the taste of synthetic pineapple out of my mouth. A month ago, if anyone had told me I'd become a connoisseur of flavoured condoms, I'd have gotten a stitch from laughing. But as it was, Travis had allowed me a couple of hours' sleep then woken me up early to continue my alternative education.

"Want me to cook the bacon?" Travis offered.

Tessa practically swooned, but thankfully Dove kept her head. Probably because she was still at that loved-up stage with Zander.

"If you don't mind. You can cook?"

He shrugged.

"Do I need to go out and get extra bacon?" I asked.

"Nope. Marlene sent me home with half a pig this weekend."

"Dare I ask?"

"She won it at poker. We'll be eating bacon and sausages and pork chops for weeks."

Travis did indeed know his way around a kitchen, and by the time Zander got back, the apartment smelled like a vegetarian's worst nightmare. Good thing Courtney wasn't there.

Except Zander didn't sit straight down and start scoffing the way I expected. No, he wiped the sweat off his face with his T-shirt then leaned against the counter, looking sombre.

"What's up?"

"The lab just emailed me the results of the tests on Vina's moisturiser."

"The police ran the sample already? I thought that usually took ages."

More than once, Zander had interrupted an episode of *CSI* to tell me just how unrealistic their timescales were.

"Nah, they'll take weeks yet. I sent a sample to our lab too."

"The police let you do that?"

Zander just stared at me.

"Of course the police didn't let you do that. You touched the stuff? Are you crazy? What if you'd gotten burned like Vina?"

"I just smiled nicely at one of the housekeeping ladies, and she found me a tiny jam jar and a teaspoon. Don't worry."

Of course she did. She'd probably have offered Zander her firstborn too if he'd asked.

"Well? What were the results?"

"That shit was full of acid."

"*Acid*?" Whoa. "How? Was it made that way? Or did

someone spike it?"

Zander hesitated. "There *could* have been a manufacturing fault."

"But you don't think so?"

"When Dev did his investigation last year, he tested dozens of these creams, and one of them was the same brand as Vina's. That batch didn't have the same crazy pH level."

"But how would somebody do that? How would they get the stuff into Vina's bathroom?"

"Very fucking carefully." Zander sighed. "Unfortunately, when the police receive their own lab results, they're gonna have questions for you since you were there."

"You mean they'll treat me as a suspect."

"I've got some connections, and I can try to... Yes. That might happen."

"Vina lost her room key the day before the accident," Travis said. "What if someone took it and snuck inside?"

That got Zander's attention. "Are you sure? She didn't just misplace it in her handbag or a pocket?"

"We ran into her in the hotel lobby on Thursday evening, and she mentioned she'd lost her key. If she found it again, she didn't say so."

Zander grabbed a bottle of something green and disgusting from the fridge and took a long swallow. I'd tried that stuff once, and I had to eat a packet of gummy bears and a Twix to take the taste away.

"Let's say someone wanted to harm Vina. That person would have to be close to her because they knew what brand of skin-lightening cream she used. Then they went into her room and swapped the jar." Zander took another mouthful. Thought a bit. "No, that's wrong. Maybe the key's a red herring, because it looked more like our culprit switched the unopened box in Vina's suitcase rather than simply decanting the acid mix into the jar in her bathroom. That could have happened any time since she joined you on tour."

"That's sick," Travis said.

"Welcome to my world."

"But how do we prove any of this?" I asked. "Fingerprints on the jar?"

"I'll get the coppers to take a look, but any bad guy with half a brain wears gloves." Another sigh. "I'll shuffle things around at work and see what I can do. Have either of you seen anyone acting odd around Vina? Or her belongings?"

We both shook our heads, but then Travis opened his mouth. Closed it again. Zander waited him out.

"Something's bugging me."

"Go on."

"Have you ever listened to the lyrics of the song me and Vina sing together?"

I doubted Zander had listened to any of Indigo Rain's songs at all. And me? Probably I should have paid more attention to the words, but whenever Travis sang, I tended to zone out and focus on his ass instead.

"Can't say I have," Zander said.

"It's called 'Burn.'" Travis tapped away at his phone. "A duet. And there's these two verses in the middle."

He turned the screen so Zander and I could both see, and as I read, a horrible sense of foreboding sent snakebite shivers up my legs, through my spine, all the way to the tips of my fingers.

Vina
Why did you punish me so bad?
When you froze me out.
You who drove me mad,
Who sowed all the doubt.

You peeled away my skin and left me sore,
You damaged my heart and made me raw,
Like acid.

Travis
How can you look at me with hate?
When you left me cold.
You who chose our fate,
Who bought what he sold.

Your contempt burned into my skin.
Your lies ate me from the outside in.
Like acid.

"Who wrote this?" Zander asked.

"I did."

"Based on what? Artists take inspiration from real life, right?"

"Sometimes I do, but not this time. I watched a horror movie the night before, and JD was moping around the studio because the girl he'd been fucking for the last three weeks just ditched him. So I kind of merged the two things together."

Zander fell silent. I bit my tongue for as long as I could, but there came a point where I couldn't wait any longer.

"What do you think?" I asked. "Is it just a coincidence?"

Instead of answering, he turned to Tessa.

"Tessa, I need you to promise you won't write about any of this. Not with Alana mixed up in the middle of it."

She looked disappointed, but she nodded. "Okay, I totally promise. Do you reckon Alana's in danger, then?"

"Those lyrics... Normally, I'd say I don't believe in coincidences like that, but if someone burned Vina's face over a song... Man, that's sickness taken to a whole new level."

He wasn't wrong there. Nausea churned in my stomach.

"So what now? What should we do?"

Zander's mouth set in a hard line. "In an ideal world? You'd stay in your bedroom and watch Netflix for the next month or so."

"No way."

"Yeah, I figured you'd say that." Zander stared at his green concoction as though tasting it for the first time. "This tastes like shit."

"I've been telling you that for months, but stop changing the subject."

"Fine. You're gonna keep your head down and stay alert. If your stuff's on a tour bus, the bus stays locked with a guard outside. If you're staying in a hotel, you give them strict instructions that nobody's to go in your room. Not housekeeping, not the manager, not anyone associated with Indigo Rain or their tour. Hell, with the entire music industry. I'll get you plug 'n' play miniature cameras, and we'll monitor them at

Blackwood. And you don't mention a word of this to anyone because ninety-nine percent of the world's population don't know how to keep their mouths shut, and we don't want to tip off our culprit."

"Don't you think you're overreacting a tiny bit? Why would somebody out to get Vina—if that's what happened—suddenly have it in for me?"

"I don't know, but you're my favourite sister, and until we get some concrete answers, I'm taking precautions."

"I'm your *only* sister."

That was a long-running joke between us, since it was entirely possible we *did* have another half-sibling lurking somewhere. Our father had fucked anything with tits, after all.

Zander slung a sweaty arm over my shoulders and gave me a squeeze. "Favourite *and* only sister."

CHAPTER 25 - ALANA

BLACKWOOD HAD ADOPTED a strange concept as an employer, or at least, it seemed that way in my limited experience. They actually cared about their staff and recognised that they had personal lives, and if a problem arose, they helped to solve it. Give and take, Zander called it. Yes, he sometimes had to work ridiculous amounts of overtime or travel the length of the country at the drop of a hat, but in return, when the Vina situation arose, he simply made calls to clear his diary for the next week and arranged for some help from his colleagues too. Devan agreed to go to the hotel to see if anyone witnessed our culprit near Vina's room, while Max and Bryson would stick near me at each concert venue for the next week. Technically, bodyguard duty was beyond their remit for the contract with Indigo Rain, but Travis reckoned Ian was too busy to care and Gary wouldn't question it as long as Blackwood didn't charge extra on the bill.

With the women surrounding the band in general and Travis in particular befalling mysterious accidents, Zander was keen to keep as much distance between Travis and me as possible. As it was too late for Travis to sneak back into the hotel incognito, Zander concocted a cover story instead by posing as an old buddy, driving him to the radio station in his sports car and dropping him off in full view of everyone. Better for the world to think Travis had been staying with a male friend than a girlfriend. Travis confided in Rush, Dex, and JD about our fledgling relationship during a hurried conversation in the men's room, and after offering some words of support which, according to Travis, were unrepeatable, they acted as if they knew Zander when Travis climbed into a Blackwood car after the interview.

Then we went to visit Vina.

Jeanne had reported she'd woken up, although she wasn't supposed to be having visitors outside of family. But when Zander and Travis went in with their oh-so-smooth charm offensive, we got offered comfy seats, cups of tea, and the good biscuits with the chocolate on.

What should I say? Asking Vina how she was seemed disingenuous, and I could hardly use the standard British line of "you look well."

"Hey," I mumbled.

Her eyes wouldn't open fully, and white bandages covered the rest of her face as well as her hands. Zander, ever the detective, picked up her chart and began reading while Travis and I sat down, one of us on each side of the bed.

"Alana?"

"And Travis," he said.

"My brother's here too. Zander."

"Hi, Vina. As well as being Alana's brother, I'm a private investigator, and I'm here to help work out what happened to you. I'm not going to ask you how you feel, because I realise you must be feeling pretty damn awful at the moment, so let's focus on getting you better."

Zander was so much better at this stuff than me. I was grateful, but at the same time, I felt bad that his bedside manner was obviously borne out of practice. I'd never got so involved in the hands-on aspects of his job before, or realised how sad it was that he had to comfort victims for a living.

"Do you feel up to talking?" he asked. "Or is there anything we can do to help you feel more comfortable?"

"I can talk, but I don't understand how this happened."

Her words came out muffled because she couldn't move her lips, the stilted speech of an amateur ventriloquist.

"We think we know the 'how,' but right now, we're stumped on the 'why.'"

"It was my face cream, wasn't it? But I've been using that brand for a year, and it's never burned like that before."

"It's possible somebody spiked it with acid."

Vina didn't speak for a full ten seconds. Then, "What?" she asked hollowly, as if she couldn't quite believe what she'd heard.

"Your skin lightener contained a high level of acid. Did it seem a different texture to normal?"

"It was thinner and it smelled funny, but I thought they'd just changed the recipe a bit."

"Where did you get it?"

"From the internet, the same place as always. A website called 'The Fairest of Them All.'"

"When did you put the new jar in your suitcase?"

"On Wednesday morning before I travelled to London."

I didn't know whether to feel sad or angry on Vina's

behalf. Both, really. Angry that society pushed fake ideals onto people, and sad that Vina had felt compelled to adhere to them.

"Have the doctors said much?" I asked, wishing I could squeeze her hand to show my support. But of course I couldn't. The bandages concealed the damage, but I'd seen the state of her hands before she left the hotel yesterday.

"Most of the time, they use all these medical terms I don't understand. 'Cautiously optimistic,' that's what the skin specialist said yesterday."

"That sounds promising."

"They also said that if I hadn't washed the stuff off so fast, I'd be looking at years of surgery. One of the nurses told me I was lucky. Lucky!"

"Sometimes people don't think before they speak."

"I need to thank you for what you did. I panicked, and it was you who put me in the shower, and if you hadn't..." Vina gulped back tears, and I laid a hand on her shoulder.

"I just did what anyone else would have done."

"Shit, I'm not supposed to cry. It hurts when I cry."

"Have you had enough painkillers? Should I call the nurse?"

"They've given me the good stuff, or so they said."

Zander took over again. "We're trying to get hold of your family, but your mum's abroad. Do you know how we can contact her?"

Vina shook her head, then her eyes crinkled as she winced in pain. "Kenya. She's in Kenya on a volunteering program through her church."

"Which church?"

"First Baptist." Vina rattled off a street address in

Colchester. "A nurse already asked. But the pastor said Mum might not even have electricity for weeks, so her phone probably won't work."

"We'll try to get a message to her."

"She's been saving up for this trip for years."

"That won't matter. Trust me, she'd much rather be back here if she knew you were hurt."

"I know, but... She put her whole life on hold for me for so long, and when I won *Sing! Live* last year, we both thought all the work had paid off, only nothing turned out the way we hoped. And now this."

"Can you think of anyone who might have wanted to hurt you? Anyone with a grudge?"

Vina didn't hesitate. "Rebekah Grace."

"She was a runner-up on *Sing! Live*," Travis filled in.

"At the beginning, she was nice to me, when she was beating me in the polls. But then our positions switched, and she turned into an absolute bitch. I'm ninety-nine percent certain she put laxatives in my Fanta before one show."

"That was why you kept running to the bathroom?" Travis asked. "I thought you were just nervous."

"Yes," she whispered.

"We'll check into it," Zander said. "Anyone else?"

"I split up with my boyfriend recently. Three, no, four months ago. He said he didn't like what I'd become, and...and..." She took a moment to get her breathing back under control. "One of the things he hated was me lightening my skin. He said I'd sold out."

"Why did you do it?"

"My manager said it would give me a better look." Her shoulders shook, and she began sobbing again.

"Now I'll have scars instead."

Oh, hell. "I'll get the nurse," I mouthed.

Vina had suffered quite enough for today.

For years, it had just been Zander and me eating at the big glass table in our Chelsea apartment. Then I'd had only a few short months to get used to Dove being there, and now Travis was sitting opposite her, asking if she'd pass the pepper.

He may have acted wild a lot of the time, but I'd come to realise that was exactly what it was: an act. A persona he'd created to shield him from the glare of the spotlight he'd found himself under. Yes, he'd always have an edge, but underneath, he was quite civilised.

And when we curled up on the sofa after dinner, he cuddled me close, twirling my hair in his fingers while we stared at the TV. And I say "stared at" because neither of us was really watching. My mind churned with hopes and plans and fears for the future, while Travis's relaxed expression didn't change even when the movie ended and the news began.

"We're heading to bed," Zander said. "It's after midnight. Don't you have a show tomorrow?"

Travis nodded. "A small one. Some VIP thing."

They'd be playing at the Roundhouse in Camden. Guests included competition winners, music journalists, and fans able to afford the exorbitant ticket prices for the intimate gig. Like at the party in Paris, the band would be playing a stripped-down version of the show, which meant more focus on their skills and no special effects to hide behind.

"We'll go to bed in a minute," I told Zander. "I'm too comfortable to move."

When Zander's bedroom door clicked shut, Travis kissed me. He'd kept his hands more or less to himself all night, but instead of things turning heated now we had some privacy, he seemed more...tepid.

"Are you okay?"

"No." He closed his eyes and took a long breath. Exhaled slowly. "Do you know how long it's been since anyone but my foster mom asked me that?"

"How long?"

"I can't even remember. Then you came along, and four times you've asked me if I'm okay."

He'd been counting? That such a tiny thing should mean so much made me ache inside. "I'm so sorry. Everyone needs somebody to lean on when things get tough."

"Rush, Dex, and JD are too busy trying to cope with their own demons, and nobody else gives a fuck."

"Want to talk about it?"

"I'm scared, blue."

"Scared? Because of what happened to Vina?"

"A little. But mostly because of what's happening with you. And your family, and your friends. You all treat me like a human being. This is the best night I've had in years, maybe ever, and I never want it to end."

"But all we did was eat dinner."

"Exactly."

He did that thing where he lined our fingers up again, palms flat against each other. His fingers were long, elegant, at odds with his sometimes-rough personality. And I had a chip in my manicure. Dammit.

"Everybody likes having a day off."

"It's more than that. I like being normal. My childhood was something I'd rather forget, and even after I moved in with my last set of foster parents, the house was always busy. Three or four kids at a time, and most of them were assholes like me. Don and Mary had the patience of saints with all of us, and fuck knows, I tested it. This...this is peaceful. And you're here. Do you believe in soulmates?"

"I've never really thought about it. Do you?"

"Maybe. I don't want to."

"Why not?"

"Because I like being here with you too much. Too much because now I'm scared—no, fuckin' terrified—that it'll all get torn away from me."

"I'm not going anywhere."

"Two years. Two more years before I can get my life back. Right now, I feel like I'm two people fighting for space in the same body."

"Rock-star Travis would have cranked up the music, knocked back enough alcohol to bring a horse to its knees, set fire to something, then outraged the neighbours by screwing me on the balcony, right?"

He kissed me softly on the cheek. "Reformed Travis would still screw you on the balcony if he thought your brother wouldn't kill him."

"Uh, perhaps we could do that on a day when he's out?"

After we'd arranged a small forest of potted plants next to the railing to hide us from view.

Travis raised an eyebrow. "E is for exhibitionist?"

"We already did E."

"So? We can make up our own rules. There's nothing to stop us from going through the whole alphabet again."

"In that case, can I have the D?"

L was definitely for laughter. I was still giggling when he picked me up and carried me to the bedroom, punctuating every step with a kiss. Tonight, I got sweet yet solemn Travis, and an orgasm so spine-tinglingly intense I couldn't move for a full five minutes afterwards.

"M is for making love," Travis whispered in my ear as I floated on a cloud of pheromones.

Yes. And I'd just fallen in it.

Chapter 26 - Alana

AFTER THE EVENTS of Friday and Saturday, it was good to get back to doing my job, which had now expanded since I had Travis's, Dex's, and JD's Instagram accounts loaded up on my phone too. Although Travis warned me against reading his direct messages.

"I understand. They're none of my business."

"It's not that. Women send me, uh..."

"Snatch shots," Rush said.

JD snorted. "Yeah, clit pics."

"Don't forget the incredible selection of racks," Dex put in.

"And that weird chick who kept sending him photos of her feet."

"And butt bitch."

Good grief. "Rush, that's not very nice."

"Hey, that's what she called herself. She wanted to sit on Trav's face and have him lick her—"

"Enough! I think Alana gets the picture."

Yes, I did. Avoid Travis's DMs or be scarred for life.

Travis had arranged passes for Zander, Devan and a few other Blackwood employees who were out front watching the show while Max and Bryson kept an eye on events backstage. They'd considered a more overt presence, but as Zander had said before, if whoever tampered with Vina's moisturiser was still around, he didn't want to tip our hand.

I couldn't deny I felt twitchy. After Reagan's death, I'd switched out my heels for flats, and this morning, I'd tested my moisturiser on a tiny area of my hand before putting it near my face. Thankfully, I wasn't allergic to anything but assholes, and I was trying to avoid Gary as much as possible.

Breathe, Alana. Max and Bryson kept people safe for a living. They'd look after me.

Travis ran along the front of the stage, whipping up the crowd for the encore as I shuffled closer at the side. With my camera, I was basically invisible. Nobody paid me the slightest attention. All eyes were focused on the four boys, not another tiny cog in the relentless machine that was Indigo Rain.

And that's when I saw her. Just a glimpse at first, but when I looked again, I was ninety percent sure. She stuck out because while everyone else was dancing in time to the music, she was still. Focused. Watching Travis and nothing else.

I snapped a burst of photos then backed up slowly, watching the girl until I bumped into a wall of solid muscle, otherwise known as Bryson.

"Everything okay?"

"I'm not sure. There's a girl in the audience, and I've seen her before. In Paris."

"And?"

"Dex said she was Travis's stalker. She follows him all over the world and pops up in odd places. I guess I didn't think much of it at the time, but now she's here, and so soon after somebody hurt Vina..."

"You think maybe she got jealous of the

competition?"

"Vina and Travis weren't together."

"They were together on stage. And I watched them perform—they sure knew how to put on a show."

Yes, they did, hands all over each other. I didn't care because Travis was a showman acting a part, but I saw how it could look like something it wasn't to a person on the outside.

"I guess. Maybe."

Bryson wore an earpiece, and he recounted my story to the others. "Zander wants to know where she is and what she looks like."

"Red camisole, honey-blonde hair down to her shoulders, positioned near the front." I peeped out again. "Roughly in line with JD's drum kit. She's just standing there, not moving around like everyone else. About my age, but perhaps an inch shorter. Oh, and she's called Peyton."

Like the freaky nanny in *The Hand that Rocks the Cradle*.

Bryson shifted so he could see too. "Okay, I've got her." He relayed the description to Zander, guiding him towards Peyton. It became an agonisingly slow race— would Zander reach her before the band finished the encore and the crowd began to disperse? I wished I could get a message to Travis, ask him to sing just one more song.

But I couldn't, and he finished with a flourish, tearing off his shirt and throwing it into the crowd. JD lobbed his drumsticks too, and the lights dimmed as the band ran off stage.

Shit.

Bryson stood his ground, talking calmly. "Forward,

forward... She's to your right. Red top with those little straps that break easily."

How did he know what to say? I couldn't even see Zander in the crowd.

Rush lifted me six inches off the floor and gave me a sweaty kiss on the forehead while Travis stared daggers at him from a few feet away. Travis had told his bandmates of the need to keep our relationship secret for now, so either Rush was doing his bit to assist with the deception, or he took joy in deliberately winding his friend up. Knowing Rush, it could be either.

"Get some good pictures, Instababe?"

"Yes, I got one of you scratching your balls during the soundcheck. Will that do?"

"Go for it. I've got nothing to be ashamed of."

Travis flashed me a smile before the guys got hauled off by a PR woman, and meanwhile, the auditorium lights had come on. I caught a flash of red as Peyton neared the exit.

"Where's Zander?" I asked Bryson.

"Stuck behind those girls."

He flicked his gaze towards a group of wannabe rock chicks, all done up in black eyeliner and leather. Dammit. Every time Zander tried to dodge around them, one got in his way. Finally, he elbowed his way straight through the middle, but it was too late.

"She's gone out the exit," Bryson told him.

I waited, hoping, but after ten minutes, Bryson shook his head. "She's gone. But don't worry; Zander'll find her again."

How could I not worry? Vina was lying in a hospital in London, and Reagan was dead in Paris. If Peyton's presence in both cities linked their fates, how long would it be before there was another accident?

Tonight would be the last night with Travis in my apartment, at least for the foreseeable future. Tomorrow, we'd be back on the tour bus, heading for Birmingham and the third biggest show on the tour after Manchester and the O2. When they first started booking for the On the Run tour, only half of the dates had been scheduled, but as venues sold out, Gary had added more and more performances. So many that the boys had started calling it the Running on Empty tour instead. Gary didn't care.

And we couldn't even relax this evening, because Devan, Bryson, Max, and Zander were sprawled all over the lounge, drinking beer and ruminating over the case. Then Nye turned up with a bottle of red wine to add some class, and the discussion turned even more serious when he fetched a whiteboard from the storage closet in the hall.

Drunken detecting. I'd seen it many times before. Sometimes, I'd even helped them to make notes when their writing went wonky.

"So," Zander said. "We've got one incident that's pretty likely to be deliberate..." He printed Vina's name in neat-ish capital letters and circled it. "Another that may or may not have been intentional..." Reagan's name came next. "And two that we and everyone else assumed were accidents until the other two episodes occurred." Marli and Jae-Lin.

"And what have we got to connect the two?" Nye asked.

Zander waved his pint glass towards Travis, then cursed as beer slopped over the rim. "Him."

"Better get a cloth, mate. Dove'll get pissed about the carpet."

Bryson tossed him a crumpled-up handkerchief, which Zander dropped on the floor and smushed around a bit with his foot. On any other day, I'd have pointed out the error of his ways, but I was too curious about what else he had to say.

"And the other band members?" Nye asked.

"Maybe." He ticked off points on his fingers. "But Travis dated Marli and Jae-Lin, yes?" He looked to Travis for confirmation.

"Yes."

"And you were on a date with Reagan the night she died."

"Yes."

"What about Vina?"

"Nothing happened between me and Vina. I've never seen her with a guy other than her boyfriend. Ex-boyfriend."

"But you acted the part on stage. And now we've got stalker-girl, who we know has been in the United States, Paris, and London. We have to at least consider the possibility that these accidents weren't all accidents."

"But we also have three alternative scenarios for Vina," Devan pointed out. "An angry ex, a bitter rival, or tampering at the factory. Which you have to admit are more likely."

"I'm not sure about the factory. Those song lyrics bother me. What about the other three incidents? Is there anything in Indigo Rain's music that could relate to those?"

Travis was always quite pale since he never got time to go outside and England didn't get much sun in any case, but now the little bit of colour he did have drained away.

"I've written hundreds of tracks."

Zander's voice softened, turned gentler. "Let's work backwards and start with Reagan. A fall, a broken neck, something like that?

The clock on the living room wall ticked on, the loudest sound in the room until Max put his beer bottle down on the coffee table. He'd opened another and drunk a quarter by the time Travis answered, and my nerves were fraying rapidly.

"Last year, I wrote a song called 'The Bitch's Touch.'" He sang a verse from the song softly.

Each time I see you, I touch you, I hear you,
The agony grows, a mistress so cruel.
Each time I block it, you throw me to the floor,
And yet I still get up and go back for more.

"It could fit," Zander said. "What was the inspiration behind that one?"

"My personal trainer. Gary sent us all to the gym for a month while we were recording in Los Angeles, and they assigned me this ex-wrestler who was built like a tank. I tried to escape once, and she picked me up and put me back on the fuckin' treadmill."

"Your charms didn't work?" I asked.

"She was a lesbian."

"Ouch."

"Tell me about it."

Zander grabbed a notepad and got Travis to repeat the words so he could write them down. Seeing his suspicions in black and white made the situation seem all the more real.

"Next girl," Zander said. "Jae-Lin. Can you spell that for me?"

Travis took the pen and jotted her name down, then carried on writing.

Pain filled me from the inside out, a bitter pill to swallow.

Of our love I never had a doubt, but your thoughts didn't follow.

You saw things a different way,
Even though I begged, you refused to stay.
I choked, I fell, my body lay cold,
While you walked out with the breath you stole.

"The song was called 'Bitter,'" he explained. "I wrote it *with* Jae-Lin, not about her. She was hurting after her ex-girlfriend cheated on her."

The shocks just kept coming. "Jae-Lin liked girls too?"

"Jae-Lin falls in love with souls, not the bodies that contain them."

"That's kind of beautiful."

"She's a beautiful person. You'll like her when you meet her properly."

"Where is she now?" Zander asked.

"Los Angeles. She's a backup singer for another rock band, and they're rehearsing for their next tour."

"Okay. What about the first victim? Marli?"

"Half of our songs mention drugs. And don't ask me

about the fuckin' inspiration, because it's obvious. I can't pretend to be who I'm not, but I'm not taking them around your sister."

Zander didn't look happy—no surprises there—but at least he understood the priorities. "We'll discuss that later. For now, we have a bigger problem to deal with. Was there any police involvement in Jae-Lin's case?"

"They came out, but they were more interested in the smashed-up hotel suite," I told him. Zander opened his mouth, but I leaned across and put my hand over it because I knew what he was about to say. "That's another thing we'll discuss later, okay?"

"I'm making notes. Don't think I'll forget this stuff because I won't. What about Marli?"

"I don't know," Travis said. "I guess they'll have a file, but I wasn't there for any of it."

"When did you last see her?"

"Three days before she died, at a party. Fuck. Either you're right and there's some sick fucker out there, or I'm a bad luck charm for women." He glanced sideways at me. "I'm getting nervous here."

Zander's voice took on a hard edge. "We'll take care of Alana. But I'll need a list of all the other women you've come into contact with recently."

"Can you define 'recently'?"

"Start with the last six months."

"Uh..."

"It's gonna be a long list, isn't it?"

Travis didn't look at me when he replied. "Yeah."

"And while you're at it, write down all the people you've had a disagreement with in the same time period."

Travis glanced at his phone screen. Half past

midnight. "I need to get some sleep tonight."

"Better write quickly, then. And don't mention this conversation to anyone. If the media or police raise concerns, keep your mouth shut and call me."

"Is that it?"

"Not quite. Until we get to the bottom of this, I don't want Alana going to the US with you. I'm not stupid, Lanie. I know you'll want to do that."

"But—"

"He's right, blue. The most important thing is that you stay safe."

"And in the meantime, if you go anywhere, make sure you stay with people you know. Keep your distance from Travis in public. You're only on the periphery of this mess right now, so it's unlikely you're a target, and we need it to stay that way."

What could I say? Arguing with both of them would be impossible.

"Okay. Just don't let this go on forever. Please."

"None of us intend to, Lanie. None of us intend to."

CHAPTER 27 - ALANA

MONDAY STARTED WITH an early breakfast in the hotel, and after last night's discussion, Travis was determined to maintain a clear distance from me in public, just in case anyone was watching. Even though I understood why he did it, having to sit with Rush while he shared a table with Meredith and Zephyr hurt.

Rush was kind of confused too.

"Did you two have an argument?" he whispered.

I shook my head. "We'll explain everything on the bus, okay? Just go with it for now."

"Sure. You want more coffee?"

"I wouldn't say no."

I'd stayed up into the early hours, feeling hollower inside with every girl's name Travis added to his list. Yes, I'd known Travis had been with a lot of girls before me, but seeing it written out in black and white made me wonder whether I'd be enough for him. Whether his eye would start wandering again. He'd reached triple figures, for crying out loud. Then he wrote down everything he knew about Peyton, and he'd started detailing all the people he'd rubbed the wrong way when Zander sent me to bed. There were a lot of those too.

There'd been no naughtiness when Travis crawled under the duvet beside me an hour later, but I still barely slept, worried not just about the future of our all-too-new relationship, but also about how the hell Zander and co. could possibly solve the case with a list of suspects that looked more like a telephone directory.

Rush waved at a waitress, and she practically skidded to a halt by his side, coffee jug in hand.

"Fill us up, babe."

Did he have to make everything sound like an innuendo?

"Anything else, sir?"

"Can you bring a glass of orange juice?"

"Large or small?"

He winked at her. "Take a guess."

Yes, apparently he did.

"Where are Dex and JD?" I asked.

"Dex decided the walk wasn't worth the effort, and JD's unconscious."

Sounded like Monday was off to a good start for everyone.

Half an hour later, I stowed my suitcase in the luggage compartment under the bus and climbed on board for the final week of the tour. The band had a TV appearance to record that evening, then three more shows on Tuesday, Wednesday, and Thursday. Birmingham, Nottingham, and Cardiff. On Friday, they'd fly back to the US for an appearance at Rock Fest in Wisconsin.

So far, we hadn't talked about whether I'd go to the US at some point in the future, and waves of uncertainty washed around inside me as I slumped onto the sofa beside Travis. He wrapped his arm around my shoulders, which helped a little, but this whole relationship thing left me feeling rather seasick. The other three guys sat opposite, and JD promptly fell asleep.

"So," Rush said. "Why were you two avoiding each other earlier?"

Travis started the story, and I filled in bits where necessary. By the end, Dex had elbowed JD awake, and the three guys stared at us with a mix of horror and fascination.

Rush spoke first. "No fucking way. That shit's all connected?"

"We can't be sure. But my brother does this for a living, and he thinks we should at least consider the possibility."

"Peyton's weird, man," Dex said. "Remember in Chicago when she turned up in the hotel restaurant with that gift for Travis? Done up fancy with a ribbon and a damn bow?"

"What gift?" Travis asked.

"JD was supposed to give it to you."

Travis raised an eyebrow, and JD looked puzzled.

"Uh, I must have left it on the table or something."

Great. "So we don't know what it was?"

"Sorry."

"Has she ever tried to contact any of you apart from that time?"

Travis had never given her his number, thank goodness, so at least she hadn't been able to call him.

Rush shook his head. "But she DMs Travis on Instagram."

What? "Travis, why didn't you mention this last night?"

"Because I never look at my fuckin' messages anymore. Rush does, because he's an asshole."

"Hey, when all these girls have been thoughtful enough to send porn, it's a shame to waste it."

"So that's what Peyton sent?" I asked. "Porn?"

"Nah, she writes poems and long, rambling essays on true love and the meaning of life. Apparently, there's one kindred spirit for everyone, and you're hers, buddy."

Oh, this got creepier and creepier. "We need to send those messages to Zander. Rush, if I give you his number...?"

"Yeah, I'll take care of it."

"Any more Peyton stories? Or did you see anyone else acting strange around Vina? Or Reagan?"

"Or Marli and Jae-Lin?" Travis added. "Could Peyton have gone to those parties?"

I recalled my own experiences trying to get into my first-ever Indigo Rain shitshow. "The guy on the door tried to bar *me* the night of Jae-Lin's incident."

"Derek? He might have stopped you, but he never checks the staff." Rush winked at Travis. "Remember that enterprising blonde who dressed up as a waitress last year?"

Travis didn't look at me. "I remember."

"So if Peyton had worn a wig and a uniform..."

"Yeah, she could've gotten in."

And so could anybody else. I didn't envy Zander his job, but I was pleased he'd proven to be good at it because he'd need every ounce of his skill to solve this case.

On Monday night, I'd hoped to sneak Travis into my

room again, but an error by the hotel staff meant they'd overbooked, and I ended up sleeping on a folding bed in Meredith and Verity's room instead. Better than kipping on the bus, for sure, but I missed my comfortable bed at home as well as the man who'd shared it with me. I couldn't even call him. We'd discussed letting the support acts in on the secret, but Travis pointed out that the more people who knew, the more risk there was of somebody making a drunken slip-up. Or of Gary finding out, and he'd surely have something to say about the matter.

"Thanks for letting me stay here tonight," I said.

Meredith grinned and chucked me a tiny bottle of wine from the minibar.

"Anytime. Us girls have to stick together. Do you want chips? Or candy?"

"Are there any Maltesers?"

A bag came flying in my direction, and I ducked just in time.

"Thanks."

The girl time was kind of nice. A little escape from the waves of testosterone. I missed Tessa like crazy, and while the boys were fun, I couldn't have a sensible discussion about make-up or shoes without Rush taking the piss out of me and the others looking confused.

Verity dropped down onto the bed beside me. "So, what are we doing this evening?"

"Uh, sleeping?"

"No way! We're going out for dinner. I want to see Birmingham."

She pronounced it "Birming-ham," American-style, not "Birmingum" like the British did. Either way, I wasn't sure I wanted to start exploring the city at ten o'clock at night. But Meredith was already hunting for shoes.

"Hurry up and drink your wine, bitches. The clock's ticking, and I'm hungry."

"What about the guys?" Verity asked. "Should I call them?"

My brother said to stick with people I knew if I went out, so this would be okay, right? Just a quiet dinner with friends.

"Zephyr and Skinny are meeting us in the lobby. Travis says Indigo's staying in tonight. They've gotten so boring over the last couple of weeks."

"Probably because Gary's being a dick."

"Gary's always a dick. Alana, do you need to borrow shoes? What are those, ballet pumps? You can't wear those."

Anyhow, that was how I ended up on stage in a dodgy pub in Birmingham, singing karaoke with four members of two rock groups, full of curry with my feet aching from Meredith's ridiculously high shoes. I'd never, never have done anything so crazy sober, but that evening, I got an idea of the buzz Travis must feel on stage, even if my audience was only a bunch of hammered guys in Arsenal shirts who'd hung around after the football finished earlier.

We didn't leave until the landlord kicked us out in the early hours, and I staggered along the pavement between Verity and Zephyr, our arms wrapped around each other's waists, wondering where the hell the hotel was. Meredith got a piggyback from Skinny.

"Does anybody know..." Oh dammit, now I had the hiccups. "Where...where we're going?" And the giggles.

"Left," Verity said. "I think it's left."

It wasn't left. At some point, a pizza delivery guy on a moped took pity and helped us into a taxi, warning us not to puke. Meredith serenaded the driver on the trip back to the hotel, and I crawled out of the elevator on my hands and knees before passing out halfway onto my bed at a time normally reserved for night-shift workers and insomniacs.

Fuck.

"Is there something you want to tell us?" Rush asked, holding up his phone.

"Yes. I'm dying."

I'd made it onto the tour bus—just—and ignored Ian's muttered complaints about me being late. My stomach hurt, my head hurt, my eyes hurt. Did the stupid guidebook have a "no puking" rule? My recollection was hazy, but I was fairly sure the answer was yes.

"I meant about last night. You joined a band?"

"Huh?"

He thrust the phone into my face, and after a few seconds of earnest concentration, I managed to focus on the screen. Oh look, there I was on stage with a microphone in my hand, midriff bared as I waved my arms in the air. Shit, shit, shit. Not only was the picture on some random person's Instagram, but Zander was gonna kill me. He'd told me not to do anything stupid, and I'd certainly say that counted.

"Oh. That. It was Meredith's idea. Or Verity's. I don't remember which. Please don't shout."

"I'm speaking normally, babe." He pushed me gently towards the lounge at the back. "JD, get her a bottle of water, would you?"

"What the fuck happened?" Travis asked when I collapsed next to him on the sofa.

"Meredith and Verity happened," Rush said. "They always pull stunts like that."

"I'll kill them. Alana isn't cut out for this shit, and she's supposed to be keeping a low profile."

"We used to do exactly the same thing," Dex pointed out. "Until we got too big." He shuddered. "That near-riot in Milwaukee…"

Travis took the bottle of water from JD. "Drink this, blue. You need to stay hydrated."

"I think I've got the flu."

"No, you've just got a hangover."

"Try having another drink," Rush suggested. "Hair of the dog. Works for me."

"Shut up, buddy. Another drink is the last thing she needs." Travis smoothed my hair and pressed a soft kiss to my forehead. "Did you have breakfast?"

"Feel too sick."

"You should eat something if you can."

"No way."

"Then close your eyes for a few minutes. And when we get to the venue, stay here for a while and get some sleep."

"You're so sweet." I reached over and stroked his cheek. "I'm sorry I got drunk."

"We've all been there, blue-eyes. We've all been there."

CHAPTER 28 - ALANA

AFTER THE BIRMINGHAM concert, I stumbled back to the bus and crawled into my bunk. I'd totally phoned today in. Slept until noon, done the bare minimum on social media, which included liking comments and replying to one or two on the boys' behalf, then taken photos of the evening show. Meredith and Verity slayed it on stage, leaping around and whipping up the crowd, and I genuinely didn't understand how they did it. We'd all drunk the same vile concoctions last night, and they'd had even less sleep than me, yet they managed to entertain thousands while I could barely function.

"How do you feel?"

Oh, hello. Travis slipped in behind me and wrapped me up in his arms.

"Better now you're here. I missed you last night."

"Really? I don't think you even noticed I wasn't there."

His tone was light, playful as he nuzzled my neck and nibbled my earlobe.

"I missed you before we went out. Things got hazy after that."

"Did you have fun?"

"Honestly? I'm not sure I could live that kind of lifestyle. Going out every night, feeling like I've been hit by a truck every morning..."

"It gets old."

"You don't mind that I'm not cut out to be a party animal?"

"I meant what I said about the time I spent at your home."

"What are we gonna do?" I whispered.

"When? Now?" His hands moved downwards. "I was thinking of playing the alphabet game again."

"I meant in the future. Next week. The week after." Curiosity got the better of me. "Which letter?"

"Z is for zipper." He undid my jeans. "And U is for underwear. There's something so fuckin' hot about pushing a woman's panties to the side and sliding into her." He demonstrated with a finger, and suddenly, I didn't feel so tired anymore. "You're soaked already, blue."

"We're on the bus. Not allowed, remember?"

"Ian's at the front, on the phone to his girlfriend. He won't even know."

"Rush is above us. Dex and JD are opposite."

"Then you'd better not scream my name. Just murmur it quietly."

"You're such an asshole, Travis."

"But I'm your asshole." He did something magical with his finger, and I bit my tongue. "R is for rule-breaking. What do you say?"

"I say I'll never get enough of you."

I heard the rip of foil in the darkness, then Travis scooched my trousers down a bit more and eased into me from behind.

"So fuckin' tight, blue. I love your ass. Did I ever tell you that?"

I had no idea. My brain didn't function properly

when Travis did wicked things to me.

"I don't think so."

"Well, I do. I love every single part of you, Alana Graves."

Aw, that was so... Wait! What? "Uh, you love me?"

"Yeah, baby, I do. I'm fucked. I love you, I've got three days left in England, and I don't know how I can keep you."

He spoke softly into my ear so nobody else could hear, but the gravity of his words wasn't lost. Travis Thorne loved me, but he still had two years left in music-industry jail, not to mention a potentially homicidal stalker. I loved him too. A young love that would blossom and grow if it didn't wither and die first.

He stroked harder, setting a rhythm that sent ripples of heat through my whole body. I squeezed my thighs together, trying to prolong my inevitable release, only for Travis to slip a hand into the front of my knickers. Was he trying to kill me? *Here lies the body of Alana Graves, whose heart gave out while being rocked by a rock star*. Travis groaned, I moaned, and he put his other hand over my mouth.

"Just in case," he whispered.

Shit, shit, shit. A starburst ignited, and I stiffened then turned to jelly. Travis followed, muttering a stream of nonsensical filth into my ear as he came. Once he pulled out, I twisted in his arms.

"I love rule-breaking." I kissed him softly. "And I love you."

"We've got a difficult path ahead, blue."

"And we'll walk it together."

The bus rumbled on towards Nottingham, and I snuggled up against Travis, finally back where I belonged. I thought we'd gotten away with our illicit activities until Rush's voice came from above.

"Promise you're not gonna start shitting on the bus next."

My cheeks burned.

"Shut up, buddy," Travis told him.

But he smiled in the darkness—I felt it—and I smiled too.

Wednesday—Nottingham—and at least I had my own hotel room again. And privacy. And Travis in my bed until he crept back to the room he shared with Rush at six thirty. My phone rang at six forty-five, and I figured it would be Zander with an update, but Tessa's name flashed up on the screen instead.

"You didn't answer my email yesterday."

"What email?"

"Alana Graves, I spent ages writing out a long, heartfelt email, and you totally ignored the whole thing?"

"Sorry, I... What did it say?"

"Okay, so I was kidding about the heartfelt part, but it was long. And it's getting longer. Do you have time to talk? In private?"

"Private? Is this about the *thing*?"

"Is lover boy in the room with you?"

"No, he's gone, and I'm alone. Why? What have you found that he can't hear?"

"Okay, so Red Cat Records has literally the worst website ever. I mean, it's got nothing. No address, no 'about us' section, no blog. No-thing. So I started thinking, what have they got to hide?"

"And?"

"Don't get mad, but I got a couple of people to help me."

"Tessa, you promised you wouldn't tell anyone! What if somebody decides to write a story on the band?"

"It's not people at work, or even on our course. It's Ziggy and Amin."

Having been bullied mercilessly at school, Tessa now went out of her way to befriend people who didn't quite fit with the "in" crowd. I'd followed her lead and met a whole bunch of interesting people because of it, including Ziggy from the Ukraine who solved maths problems for fun and could eat absolutely anything without putting on weight, and Amin, who'd come to England from Sudan six years ago and barely moved away from his computer since. They always saved us seats in the library, and if either of us felt down, Ziggy provided chocolate.

"Dare I ask why?"

"Because numbers hurt my brain, and Amin's better at finding things on the internet than I am."

"And what has he found?"

"Whoa, whoa, whoa. Let me start at the beginning. Red Cat currently has six big acts, plus another dozen smaller bands waiting in the wings. And the six biggies are all touring. Incessantly, just like Indigo Rain. They never stop. Think of it as a giant machine where they take young, hungry bands, drop them in one end, and what comes out at the other is garbage. A waste product. Because nobody ever hears from them again. Five years, gone. Five years, gone. It's like a cycle."

"That's pretty much what Travis told me. Five years, and he doesn't want any part of the business anymore."

"But you'd expect to hear *something*. A solo career. A few gigs or appearances on TV. But there's nothing. Their social media pages die. None of them appear in the news either, or reality shows, or making a tit out of themselves in nightclubs. They just issue one last statement saying they're taking a break, then vanish without a trace. You can still buy their albums, but that's it."

"That's weird. Really weird."

"Tell me about it. Red Cat's great at spotting artists on their way up, at moulding them into exactly what the public wants to hear at that time, but none of them have longevity."

"Maybe they all decided to retire and live off their millions?"

"Who does that? Nobody sits around at home doing nothing forever."

"So where do Ziggy and Amin come in?"

"Ziggy's helping me to compare Red Cat to other record companies. Their statistics—estimated turnover, the number of employees we can identify, the track records of their artists. Amin's looking for contact details for the acts they dropped. So far, we've found nine, and here's where it gets interesting."

"Go on."

"Do you remember Tower Ten?"

"I used to love their songs! But then they..." I trailed off.

"Disappeared without a trace? Right. Another victim of Red Cat. Anyhow, their drummer emailed me back and said he couldn't answer any of my questions because he signed a Non-Disclosure Agreement."

"An NDA? What for? Travis didn't mention that he had one of those."

"Can you double-check? At the moment, I've got no idea what it's for, but I'm gonna keep digging. I just wanted to keep you updated."

"Of course, and thanks, I think. I don't know what to make of all this."

"Me neither, but I've got a horrible feeling it's not good."

And the day only got worse. When I caught up with him in his dressing room, Travis confirmed he'd never signed an NDA, and none of the band members ever spoke to the other acts represented by Red Cat. Everything was kept separate—separate staff, separate tours, separate PR work. Styx and Stones and Vendetta came from different labels, and both were only there for the UK part of the tour.

"Red Cat'll be getting kickbacks, for sure," Travis said. "We had bigger acts wanting to tour with us, but those were the two they picked. Vendetta's new, and Styx hasn't managed to break the UK yet. But why all the questions, blue?"

"Tessa's a better journalist than me, and she thinks the situation's odd. The way the record label operates."

"They do things differently, for sure. That was how they sold the contract to us. They stay small so they're able to move nimbly when they spot new trends in music and marketing. Lean and mean, or so they said."

"Lean and mean? Gary seems to spend a lot of money on expenses."

"Right. Which is another reason we always screwed

around in hotels. He wastes money on expensive suites and room service, so we figured we might as well do that too."

"Is there any chance I could get a copy of the contract?"

"I can ask Frank. But it's pointless; we can't break it. A lawyer already looked into that. Two years, blue. Two years, and we're taking the cash and running."

A knock sounded at the door. "Travis? Your guitar tech wants you."

Courtney still wasn't a brilliant PA, but at least she didn't grate on my last nerve like Reagan had.

"Gimme a minute."

Travis tangled one hand in my hair and kissed me. Hard. I was breathless when he pulled back and grinned.

"I like snatching kisses." He backed away. "And vice versa."

Huh? Oh, that filthy... I blew out a slow breath as the door closed behind him. Filthy or not, I loved every inch of that man.

CHAPTER 29 - ALANA

"YOU'RE NOT COMING to the US with us?" Verity asked.

I shook my head. "No, Rush basically let me tag along on the UK tour for my university work placement. It was either that or write copy for a crappy website. But since I'm technically an American citizen by birth, I hope to visit someday."

"If you do, you're welcome to use my spare room. Or Meredith's. She never minds people crashing, but it's party central at her place."

"I'm not sure my liver could take it. Or my head." I touched my fingertips to my temple. "I've had a horrible headache since I woke up. Painkillers haven't made a dent in it."

"A migraine?"

"Not quite so debilitating, but going to a rock concert sure didn't help."

"What pills did you take?" Verity asked. "Somebody around here probably has something better."

Undoubtedly. "I think I'm just gonna finish this drink and get an early night."

And order room service for two.

Because my head didn't hurt, not at all. I just needed an excuse to go to my bedroom, where Travis would join me for our last night together, at least for the moment. First thing tomorrow, he'd fly back to LA and I'd catch the train to London, a different girl to the one who'd left on the bus to Sheffield five weeks ago. Part of me actually would be going to America: my heart, because Travis held it in his hands.

Half an hour later, he knocked softly on the door.

"Fuck. That was the longest thirty minutes of my life."

"What did you tell them?"

"That I had to make a phone call." He waggled his eyebrows. "P is for phone sex, baby, but tonight you get the real thing."

"You've got such a one-track mind."

"Two-track. What's for dinner? Smells good."

"Steak, with chocolate mousse for dessert."

"My three favourite things to eat."

"Three things?"

His gaze dropped.

Oh, of course. This was Travis.

Except despite his words, he wasn't all about the D. In fact, the first thing he did after he'd stripped me naked was turn up the heat and rummage in his bag.

"What are you doing?"

He didn't answer, just got out a sketch pad and pencil and pulled up a chair.

"You're drawing me?"

"I haven't picked up a pencil in months. I can't when I'm stressed. But you've put me in a better place, and I just want to play for a few minutes." He smiled, which was sneaky because I could never say no to him then. "Please?"

"You won't show it to anyone?"

"For my eyes only, blue."

Being immortalised on paper was a strangely erotic experience. With each stroke of Travis's pen, tingles skittered across my skin, and to draw me, he had to look at me. His gaze heated every inch of my body.

And he really could draw. When I could take it no more, I crawled across the bed to look at the paper he'd been shielding from view. Wow. This was no amateur Picasso with random body parts all over the place. He'd drawn my head and shoulders, delicate lines and soft shading with a mysterious smile I didn't even realise I'd worn.

"Where's the rest of me? Why did you get me to pose naked if you only wanted to draw my face?"

"Why not?"

"Oh, you're such a lech."

"Wanna draw me?"

"No, because I can't draw." Travis would end up as a stickman with three legs. Tripod. "I want to ride you like a wayward cowgirl."

"A wayward cowgirl?" He tilted his head to one side in mock puzzlement. "No, I can't picture it. You'll have to demonstrate."

"Okay."

I reached out to do exactly that, but he held my hands against his belt buckle then leaned down to kiss me instead.

"And we have to finish the alphabet tonight."

"Where did we get up to?"

"V."

"Which is for...?"

Now he grinned. A filthy, promise-laced grin that made my girly bits clench in anticipation.

"Viagra, baby."

No way. "Are you serious?"

"About you? Always." He took a little blue pill out of his pocket and swallowed it before I could stop him. "W is for wicked thoughts, and I've been having those all day."

"And let me guess... X is for X-rated?"

"See? We're perfectly in tune with each other." Travis flopped down onto the bed beside me, arms flung wide. "Saddle up, blue."

Neither of us got any sleep that night, and I discovered I wasn't quite as averse to drugs as I might once have thought. Legal ones, at any rate. One tiny tablet led to hours of sweet sin, and by the time the sun appeared through the gap in the curtains, I could barely stagger to the bathroom. Travis suffered no such problems as he held me up in the shower.

"I love you, Alana." He trailed his tongue along my jaw. "Once, my ambition was to be a rock star, but now I've got a new goal. I want to be able to say those three little words to you in person every morning."

"Two years, Travis, and I love you too."

"Will you wait?"

"For you? I'd wait forever."

"Patience sucks," he said.

"Not as well as you do. I'm gonna miss your dirty mouth."

"Y is for you, blue. I'm gonna miss everything about you."

"What's Z?"

"The Zs I need to get on the plane." He yawned, and I couldn't help following suit. "You wore out my cock."

"I'd say I'm sorry, but I'm not."

"Me neither." Travis pulled me close for one last

soaking-wet kiss before grabbing my towel. "Not one bit."

Two hours later, it was over, at least temporarily. My relationship with rock's hottest star had officially gone long-distance. Following Rock Fest, for the next two weeks at least, Travis would be working in the studio in LA, recording tracks for one of the two albums they owed Red Cat.

The worst part was not being able to say a proper goodbye. I had to give him the same hug I gave to Rush, Dex, JD, and the rest of their entourage in case curious eyes were watching, and then take an Uber from the hotel to the train station while the others went to Manchester Airport. I got a single message from Travis before he boarded the plane, taken in a toilet stall by the looks of it. No, not a dick pic. A short video of him blowing me a kiss, and then, because he was Travis, making a lewd gesture with his tongue. But that only made me laugh, because like he said before, he was *my* asshole.

Everyone on the tour was going home. They all lived in California, except for Jeanne, who came from Nevada and would be camping out on Courtney's sofa-bed until she could find her own place. And now it was time for me to go home too.

I couldn't do much on the train to London, not when the nosy woman next to me kept trying to peer at my phone, but I quickly mouthed, "I love you," and sent the clip back.

Then I fell asleep, and I didn't wake up until the

train pulled into Euston Station.

CHAPTER 30 - ZANDER

"HERE. YOU LOOK like you need this."

Zander Graves dumped a McDonald's bag on the table in front of his sister, and the delicious smell of a bacon-and-egg McMuffin drifted out. For a moment, he was tempted to jog back and buy one for himself too, but that would kind of negate the five miles he'd just run.

"My hero." Lanie shoved her bowl of soggy muesli away. "Are you working this weekend?"

"Yeah, on your case."

Unfortunately. After a fifty-hour week, he dreaded the thought of going to the office again, but he also hated seeing Lanie miserable. And if some asshole of a singer made her smile, Zander had to do what he could to help them out, even if he absolutely hated the prospect of his little sister moving halfway across the world to shack up with the guy. He still didn't trust Travis Thorne. Max had seen him with groupies, snorting coke, drinking until he passed out... The list went on. But when Zander had discussed his concerns with Dove, she'd reminded him of his own past, which could best be described as colourful.

Had he tried drugs? Once or twice. Had he ever fucked a different girl every day of the week? Yes, and he couldn't even remember their names. Had he got

carried away and drunk too much? More times than he
could count.

Would he do any of those things now that he'd
married Dove? No way.

Zander would be a hypocrite if he didn't give
Thorne the benefit of the doubt, but the man got one
chance. *One* chance. And if he blew it...

"Sorry," Lanie said. "I wish you didn't have to work.
Can I do anything to help?"

As it happened... "You can come to the office and
help me to review CCTV tapes."

The world's most boring job. Mathis had sent
footage from the Hotel Nova in Paris, Zander had
obtained the video from the hotel where Vina got
burned, and there had been a camera in the hallway
outside the suite where Jae-Lin went into anaphylactic
shock. The hotel's security office had been about to
erase that footage, but Blackwood had stopped them
just in time. Somebody needed to review all the film for
common faces, and Zander was especially interested in
Peyton Priestly.

She'd flown back to California right after the show
in Camden, and she was one of the few leads they had
right now. Twenty-three years old, the daughter of a
high-flying management consultant and a cosmetic
dentist, she didn't appear to have a job and spent most
of her time flitting between one party or another.
Thankfully, she posted all about it on social media.

Investigating incidents that might not even be
crimes, cases where little to no evidence had been
collected at the time and memories were hazy, was as
difficult as Zander's job got. The police had ruled out
Vina's competitor on the reality TV show—she'd been

on a club tour in Ibiza for the whole of that month with hundreds of witnesses to prove it—and the only other suspect they had was Vina's ex. He worked as a lab technician in a high school, and the cops liked him because he had access to chemicals, but it didn't feel right. He had no motive. When Zander spoke to him, the man had been suitably sympathetic about Vina's plight, but more concerned with getting home to his new, pregnant girlfriend.

And Zander didn't want to push the connection angle too hard with the police. Why? Because if any investigator stepped back and thought about who the logical suspect was, there was only going to be one person at the top of that list.

Lanie.

Somebody had systematically removed the women most closely associated with Travis Thorne from the picture. Lanie had wanted him, and now she had him. She'd had the most to gain from their elimination. Zander knew she hadn't done it, but the last thing he wanted was for the police in two countries to rake through her life. *Their* lives. Their pasts...

So who else shared that motive? Peyton, possibly. The other women on the tour—Courtney, Meredith, and Verity. Or even Vina. It wouldn't be the first time someone had injured themselves in an effort to cover up other crimes.

Then there was option number two: jealousy. Yes, men suffered from it too. Had Travis upset somebody enough that they'd retaliated in the sickest way possible? That opened up the suspect pool a lot wider— the other members of Indigo Rain, the crew, and Gary Dorfman. From what Max and Bry said, Dorfman didn't have much luck with the opposite sex, striking out more often than he hit a home run, and when Zander spoke to Vina, she'd said Gary had asked her out to dinner and she made an excuse. A business dinner, he'd said, but she hadn't been convinced his intentions were quite so innocent.

Clues were few and far between. The skin-lightening cream could be bought under the counter from any number of stores in London, and since they weren't supposed to be selling it, they tended to be cagey about its existence. The acid was readily available —over the internet and from most builders' merchants, since one of its purposes was to clean patios and brickwork. Another use was in drain cleaner, which meant it could even have been stolen from one of the hotels or a show venue. How often did cleaning cupboards get left unlocked?

Yes, Lanie had gifted him one hell of a case. Solving it promised to be trickier than catching smoke in a gale-force wind, but Zander had little choice. He had to give it his best shot.

"Let's start again from the beginning," he said to his sister. "Tell me about the day you met Travis."

Six o'clock in the evening, and Zander was still at his desk. Lanie had gone home to watch a movie with Tessa, but Zander had stuck around to call Jason, a pal in the Metropolitan Police. Turned out they were as stumped as he was about Vina's case. No third-party fingerprints had been found on either the jar or the box, which was suspicious in itself since *somebody*

must have touched it during the purchase process, and nobody had spotted the boyfriend—their prime suspect —anywhere near Vina in the time frame they were dealing with.

Lanie had sifted through hours of CCTV footage, but she hadn't spotted Peyton. Nor had any new likely suspects popped up. The one interesting snippet of information came during their discussion of the party where Lanie injected Jae-Lin with the EpiPen, and Zander wasn't quite sure what to make of it. Apparently, Jae-Lin had taken ill in a locked bathroom, and Verity had been the one who suggested breaking the door down. Why? Pure dumb luck? Or remorse over what she'd done? If she'd just stayed quiet, Jae-Lin would've died, and the fact that Verity had had a hand in saving the girl moved her down the suspect list a notch.

"Are we working you too hard?"

Zander took his head out of his hands as Emmy Black pulled up a chair beside him.

"No, this is personal."

"Something to do with the Indigo Rain thing?"

Of course, one of Blackwood's directors had needed to sign off on his request for extra resources the previous week.

"Maybe."

"Want to talk about it?"

Did he? Emmy's question was genuine, not some bullshit attempt at chit-chat. She may have been a world-class bitch, but she cared in her own strange way. And she had good instincts. Zander laid out the basic facts to see what she'd make of them.

"Well, there's one obvious suspect, isn't there? At

least for the last three 'accidents.'" She used her fingers to make little air quotes.

"Alana."

"Yup."

"Don't even go there."

"I'm not. On paper she looks good, but her motive's flawed. Let's say victim one was a genuine accident. That leaves three girls. Jae-Lin got taken out on Lanie's second day with the band, yes?"

"Yes."

"Hardly time to build up an obsession, is it? She wasn't a fan of the band beforehand?"

"Never mentioned them, never listened to their music."

"And Alana had no reason to compete with Reagan or Vina. Travis was into her, not the other way around, at least to start with."

"How do you know that?"

"I saw them together. She didn't tell you?"

"Where? In London?"

"LA. They flew there for the funeral of the first dead girl." Emmy told Zander a tale that made him want to shake the full story out of his sister. Didn't she understand he needed to know every damn thing that had happened, no matter how unimportant it may have seemed? "My take on it? They were both fighting the attraction at that point. If I was a betting woman, which I am, I'd put money on there being an interesting reason for Travis taking Reagan to that awards show."

"A cover-up? He didn't want to admit to his feelings for Alana?"

"Nah. He'd have gone stag rather than risk hurting her. The dude took a sex doll on a date once, remember? He knows he can get women whenever he wants, and he doesn't feel the need to prove it every time someone rolls out a red carpet." Emmy scrunched her lips to the side, thinking. "Travis Thorne is oddly secure in his own skin, and he doesn't like pretending to be who he's not. But he's also under the thumb of his record label. The whole band is. I don't know a huge amount about the music business, nor do I have any idea whether it's connected to the whole mess that's landed in your lap, but it struck me as abnormal."

"I kind of wish I'd kept my mouth shut now."

Emmy shrugged. "Sorry."

"This is one of the strangest cases I've worked on. At best, it's a crime against Vina plus a whole series of nasty coincidences. At worst? We've got a would-be serial killer on the loose."

"And we might not be able to conclude on which unless another body turns up."

"That's what I'm afraid of."

Emmy's phone buzzed, and she glanced at the screen. "Gotta go. Call me if you need manpower in LA, yeah? I'll sort something out."

"Thanks."

Give and take. There was always give and take in Emmy's world.

"And good luck."

She glided silently out the door, leaving Zander alone with troubled thoughts and a hope that Emmy was wrong for once. He didn't want the body count to rise, not with his sister so closely involved in the case.

CHAPTER 31 - ALANA

"ALANA, WE NEED to talk."

My brother walked through the door two minutes after Tessa left. She'd offered to stay, but tonight was her godmother's birthday dinner and I couldn't ask her to miss that. I'd be fine, I assured her, even though I'd crossed my fingers under the table. How could I possibly be fine after the news she'd just given me? I'd been about to start on the wine, which let's face it, I desperately needed, when Zander came back all serious. And he didn't sound happy.

"Talk? What about?"

He rolled his eyes. "What do you think? You haven't told me everything, have you?"

Perhaps not every single detail. "Uh..."

"Your little jaunt to LA with Travis?" Zander prompted.

"Oh. That." How did he find out? "You talked to Emmy?"

"Yes, I talked to Emmy. Lanie, I'm trying to investigate two possible murders and two attempted murders here. 'Trying' being the operative word. If you hold back on the details, a difficult job becomes impossible."

"We were only there for a few hours. I didn't think it was important."

"Do me a favour and let me be the judge of that. You've been around Travis for the last five weeks, and I haven't. I need a complete picture of what happened during that time. Every interaction, every trip, every conversation you can recall. We've got suspects coming out of our ears, but the only *good* suspect right now is you."

What?

"Me? But—"

"*I* know it wasn't you. But I'm just telling you how a third party's going to look at it. Now, you've got thirty seconds while I get a beer, then you'd better start spilling. Where's Dove?"

"Out for dinner with Olivia."

I guess until that point, I hadn't truly understood what a predicament Travis and I were in. Coupled with Tessa's revelations, Zander's words broke something inside me, and as he headed to the kitchen, silent tears rolled down my cheeks. This should have been the happiest time of my life—finding the man I wanted to be with—but Red Cat Records, some psychopathic asshole, and the whole damn universe were conspiring against Travis and me.

The hiss of a beer can opening was followed by Zander's muttered curse.

"Oh, fuck. Don't cry, Lanie."

It was like being fourteen again when he wrapped me up in his arms. Those first weeks after we moved in together, I'd spent hours sobbing against his shoulder.

"I'm s-s-sorry."

"We'll fix this, Lanie. Don't I always fix everything for you?"

"Y-y-yes."

Listen to me. Twenty-one, and I'd regressed into a snivelling idiot. Love and loss had destroyed all the self-control I'd spent the last seven years building.

"Just talk to me."

So I did. Sitting at the counter in the kitchen, I told Zander everything, starting at the beginning with Tessa's message to Rush on Instagram and ending with her visit tonight. Five minutes in, Zander grabbed a notepad and started scribbling, and when I got to the part about Reagan and what she'd done to Travis, he gripped the pen so hard I thought it would snap.

"So you're saying she sexually assaulted him and he felt he had no choice but to stay quiet?"

"Yes."

"He didn't tell *anyone*?"

"At the time? Just his bandmates."

"That gives any one of them a motive for—"

"For Reagan, I know."

"Four accidents is a lot, too many to be a coincidence, but we have to consider the possibility that there's more than one perpetrator." Zander rubbed his temples, something he only did when he got really stressed. "You don't make my life easy, do you? And then there's this contract shit..."

Indigo Rain's contract with the record label had also been the subject of Tessa's news, which had added a new layer of quicksand to the mire we were currently drowning in. One of the many ex-musicians she'd emailed had finally agreed to give her a few hints, off the record of course. And what he'd said made me hope Gary Dorfman would be our mysterious culprit's next victim. If anyone deserved to fall down a mineshaft, it was him.

"I don't know what to tell Travis."

"For the moment, you don't tell him anything. His contract might not be the same. Is he sending you a copy?"

"He said he would, but I haven't got it yet."

As if Travis could hear the conversation we were having, my phone pinged, and an email notification flashed up.

Here's war and fucking peace.

I tapped at the screen, and a behemoth of a document appeared, reams and reams of tiny text, scanned in so it was a bit blurry. Travis hadn't been kidding about the length. It went on for almost four hundred pages. I tried reading the first few paragraphs, but it might as well have been written in another language. Legalese wasn't something I understood, and even if I did, I'd have fallen asleep before the end of the definitions.

Zander peered over my shoulder. "This is why I never wanted to be a lawyer."

"That and the fact you'd have had to actually go to your lectures at university. And pass exams."

"Yeah, that too."

"So what do we do now? Tessa's source mentioned two problem clauses, but I'm not sure I'd ever find them in that lot."

Two problem clauses. That made them sound like minor inconveniences, yet they had the power to ruin Travis's life. And Rush's, Dex's, and JD's lives too. The first, the one Red Cat would most likely throw in the band's face at the end of their five-year sentence if the experience of their predecessors was anything to go by, concerned costs. Red Cat could offset "reasonable expenses" against the twenty-five-million-dollar lump sum the band was owed, but there was nothing to define reasonable. According to Tessa's whistle-blower, Red Cat recharged everything from executive travel to studio hire to producer fees, all at vastly inflated rates. Twenty-five million would become one million if they were lucky.

Then there was the non-compete clause that had affected Tessa's source. Red Cat held an option over his band, and they couldn't sign with any other label for ten years. Ten freaking years! Who would still remember their names after that length of time? Red Cat had retained the rights to their entire music catalogue too, so they didn't even get ongoing royalties.

In short, the contract was one-sided, grossly unfair, and watertight. A legal minefield laid out for young musicians with stars in their eyes and a desperate need to pay their rent. Oh, and Red Cat recharged their exorbitant legal fees too.

Why did they work like that? Why not nurture and grow a band so they could have a long and successful career? Well, Tessa's contact had a theory on that too. Following the digital revolution, the music industry had changed, and an act that might once have made its money selling CDs or cassette tapes or even vinyl now made pennies for each "sale" from streaming services, or worse, absolutely nothing if some scumbag decided to pirate their work. Artists couldn't live on that money anymore. No, now the money came from touring, from merchandise sales, from endorsements and personal appearances and private performances.

No act could keep that up forever, and fans wanted to see them at the high point of their career, when they were young and hot. Red Cat had a genius marketing department that could take a good band and launch them into the stratosphere. By the time they began falling, the label already had more cannon fodder ready to replace them.

Once a former star hit the ground—without a safety net, of course—the label's execs gave them one final kick in the teeth. When a victim found their expenses had eaten away at their earnings and they were owed basically nothing, Red Cat would offer just enough money to keep them quiet about the whole scandal. Half a million dollars or so to sign an NDA and go away, never to be heard from again.

That was what most likely awaited Travis, and it made me feel sick.

"What do we do?" Zander echoed my earlier words. "Nothing about this is straightforward. If we're going to dig into this contract, we'll have to get a lawyer to look over it, but I don't want to do that unless Travis agrees."

"Travis said a lawyer already looked at it."

"Sometimes people miss things."

"Okay, I'll talk to him tonight."

"Don't tell him the full story about the penalties."

"I can't lie to him."

"I'm not asking you to lie. Just avoid telling the truth."

"Why? Doesn't he deserve to know?"

"Yes, but not right now," Zander said. "First, we need to confirm that Indigo Rain's contract contains those clauses. Second, what if Travis does something stupid out of anger? Like taking drugs or punching Gary?"

"Punching Gary isn't stupid."

"Lanie, it's ten o'clock in the evening. I'm not spending the night bailing your boyfriend out of jail on the other side of the world."

My *boyfriend*. That felt good and scary at the same time. "I suppose you're right."

"We need to be devious, not impulsive, and that means careful research and planning." Zander's knees cracked as he climbed down from his stool. "Go and speak to Travis, then get some sleep."

The first thing Travis asked about was the contract. Typical. Since we were video-calling, I plastered on a smile, even though my fists were clenched into tight little balls off-camera. In LA, Travis was in his bedroom with the faint sound of music and voices in the background.

"Did you get my email with the contract?"

"Wow. It's enormous."

"Yeah, I know, but did you get the email?"

"Do you ever stop thinking about your dick?"

"Not when I'm talking to my girl." His voice softened. "Miss you, blue-eyes."

"I miss you too. So, so much. Have there been any developments with, you know, anything?"

"Nothing. Any news from your brother?"

"Not on the accidents. But I mentioned the contract to him, and he thinks we should get an independent lawyer to take a look at it. Can we do that?"

"I don't trust many people in this world, but I trust you, and I trust Zander, even if he doesn't like me much. Do whatever you think's best."

The ache in my chest grew stronger with his words, and I longed for his touch. But five and a half thousand miles separated us and would continue to do so for far too long.

"Do you have company over there?"

"There's a bunch of people in my living room, but since Rush invited them, he can deal."

"Won't they ask where you are?"

"I told them I needed to call Catie, and if anyone asks, she'll cover for me." His lips curved into a filthy little smile. "Which means we've got all the time we need, baby." The camera wobbled for a second, then refocused on the considerable bulge in his trousers. "You're wearing too many clothes."

Thank goodness I'd locked the door. "I've never done this before."

Travis's voice lowered to that sexy timbre that sent shivers through me, and all our difficulties receded. They still lurked in the background, but for now, they were out of reach.

"I'll teach you everything you need to know..."

CHAPTER 32 - ZANDER

BEFORE HE WENT to sleep, Zander sent a quick email to Emmy Black, asking if she knew a US-based lawyer with an eye for contracts. With her typical efficiency, she replied at three o'clock in the morning.

Call Rhodes, Holden and Maxwell. Oliver Rhodes is my guy.

The name rang a bell. Rhodes had assisted Max with an issue last year after Max's then-girlfriend and now-fiancée got targeted by a serial killer. Zander sent him an email outlining the situation over breakfast, name-dropping Emmy, and the man's assistant replied almost instantly with an offer of help and a quote that made Zander's wallet scream in protest even with Blackwood's discount already applied. But he needed somebody good, and Emmy wouldn't recommend a dud. By lunchtime, he'd signed an engagement letter and sent Indigo Rain's contract for review.

Then it was into a holding pattern. A day passed. Two. Three. Four. Zander caught up on the work he actually got paid for, and Lanie slept in the daytime, spent the evenings with Tessa and her uni friends, and talked to Travis all night. At least Zander had to believe they were talking. He didn't even want to think about what else his little sister might be doing behind her closed bedroom door.

On Thursday evening, Zander settled back in his office chair after a ten-hour day. He wanted to go home, have a beer, and kick back with a movie, but instead, he opened up Providence, Blackwood's primary data-analysis program. Developed by the US-based IS department, Providence combined advanced search facilities as well as an interface that allowed users to query databases using natural language and receive results in real time. Or, in plain English, it sliced and diced through oceans of data a mere human would drown in and gave Blackwood's investigators some of the answers they needed.

Today, Zander asked Providence about Red Cat. Throughout this week, he'd listened as Lanie, Tessa, Ziggy, and Amin discussed the shortcomings of the company over Chinese and sushi and pizza in the kitchen at home, and they'd piqued his curiosity. While the label's signees slaved away in theatres and arenas the world over, Red Cat's CEO, Leonard Martineau, split his time between a luxurious Beverly Hills mansion and a beachfront villa in the Cayman Islands. Ziggy and Amin had come up with a mathematical model that suggested Red Cat's stable of artists brought in gross profits of over two hundred million dollars a year, so where did it all go? Because it wasn't ending up in the talent's pockets.

"Late again?" a voice asked from behind him. Emmy. "Still working on the Indigo Rain thing?"

"It's turned into an even bigger headache than before."

"Something to do with a contract?"

"Yeah. Chances are, their record label's ripping them off."

"Look on the bright side; at least no one's died this week. If I order pizza, do you want one?"

"Wouldn't say no."

If Zander worked late tonight, he'd have a better chance of getting home to see his wife on Friday. She'd been in Northbury since Tuesday, and he'd been pining over her like all those whipped guys he'd laughed at just a year ago.

"Pepperoni?" Emmy asked. "Margarita? Everything? And don't say Hawaiian or I'll be forced to fire you."

"Everything."

"Good choice."

"You're working late too?"

"By choice. My housekeeper's on holiday, and my assistant thought it would be a great time to redecorate." She rolled her eyes. "Again. The whole place stinks of paint, so I'm camping out here."

Seemed even billionaires had their problems. "Want a coffee? I'm just getting up to make one."

"Strong and black, honey."

Emmy sauntered off, but Zander didn't make it halfway to the kitchen before his sister called.

"What's up?"

"It's happened again." Lanie's voice was tight. Edgy.

"What's happened again?"

"Another girl."

Fuck. "What girl? What happened?"

"Travis messaged to say that Caitlin got hit by a car, and he's on his way to the hospital."

"Who's Caitlin?"

"His ex-girlfriend from high school. They're still friends."

Was this ever going to end? "Okay, sit tight. I'll see what I can find out, then get home as soon as I can. Do you know which hospital?"

"I don't know anything!"

Coffee and pizza got forgotten as Zander called Vance in Blackwood's LA office, a guy he'd worked with on occasion and who owed him a favour. Vance contacted the emergency rooms while Zander tried to work out who Caitlin was and why she'd been targeted. Five accidents. He'd been starting to doubt his instincts by connecting the previous four, but no way was this a fluke.

Soft footsteps sounded behind him, and the normally irresistible aroma of cheese, tomato, and pepperoni drifted across his desk.

"Well, I kept up my end of the bargain. Is the coffee machine broken?"

"Sorry. Alana called. Another girl got hurt. Caitlin. A hit-and-run, it looks like."

"Shit. Badly hurt?"

"No idea at the moment, other than she's in the hospital. Vance Webber's trying to find more information for me."

"Witnesses?"

Zander shrugged. "You know as much as me right now."

Emmy dumped the pizza box on the desk and dropped into the seat beside him. Bryson usually sat there, and she swept a pile of candy wrappers into the bin before reaching for the phone.

"I'll make some calls too."

Caitlin Wiles had been out jogging when a car ploughed into her from behind. According to Vance, she'd gone straight into surgery to fix her broken leg, and her wrist would need pinning too. The doctor said she'd been lucky, but what was lucky about having a lunatic try to kill you?

"This is escalating," Zander said to Emmy. She'd eaten an entire Deep Pan Deluxe while Zander could barely stomach a glass of water. "It just keeps getting worse."

"Or better. Depends on how you look at it."

"Better? Are you insane?"

"So everybody says. But think of it this way—our perp's unravelling. They're gonna make mistakes, and at this rate, it won't be long before they fuck something up."

Although Emmy's glass might have been half-full, there was a good chance of it shattering completely.

"But how many more women will get hurt in the meantime?"

"Again, that depends."

"On what?"

"On how you approach the problem."

"And how would you approach the problem?"

"You don't want to know."

Yes, Zander did. Because with the shit hitting the fan on the other side of the Atlantic, he was stumped as to how he could solve the problem himself.

"Tell me."

Emmy shrugged, as if to say, *Well, you asked for it.*

"Simple. I'd turn the tables on our perp. Flush them out with some tempting bait. Pretty blonde bait."

Oh, fuck no. Emmy had been absolutely right; Zander didn't want to know.

"We're not using my sister as bait."

She held her hands up. "Hey, I never seriously suggested it because I knew you'd say that. I'm just telling you what I'd do. Fifty bucks says we'd catch the asshole within a week."

The bitch was off her trolley. "Either that or I'd have a funeral to arrange."

"Are you suggesting my close-protection team doesn't know what it's doing?"

"No, but…"

"Relax, I'm kidding." Emmy flipped open the lid of Zander's pizza box, wrinkled her nose at the sight of cold pizza, but helped herself anyway. "But we can still assist. I can free up some personnel in LA and use our contacts in the police. Unless…"

"Unless what?"

"How well do you know Travis Thorne?"

"Not that well."

"In that case, never mind."

"If you've got another idea, I'd like to hear it. Alana's miserable as hell, and we're up to five victims now."

Even if Reagan deserved her fate.

"What if we use bait, but different bait?"

"How different?"

"Would Travis go for a cougar?"

Zander nearly spat his water across the desk. "*You*?"

"Hey, I'm thirty-five. I'm not *that* old."

Shit. Insulting the boss wasn't a good move, especially when she knew a thousand different ways to kill a man and undoubtedly had experience at hiding bodies.

"That wasn't what I meant. It was more...aren't you busy? I thought you didn't get out of bed for less than twenty grand."

"Twenty-five." One corner of her lips quirked. "Inflation. But I also hate meetings, and I'd like an excuse not to go to some. I'm in LA next week, anyway."

Meetings? She'd put herself in danger to avoid meetings? Zander raised an eyebrow.

"Okay, okay. I think Alana and Travis make a cute couple. Call me a closet romantic. And I know you hate talking about your past, but you and her went through some difficult times, and... Oh, for fuck's sake... Don't look at me like that. And don't you dare tell anyone I've got a soft side. Think of it another way—if anything happens to Travis Thorne, we'll lose the security contract for Indigo Rain, and it'll affect Blackwood's bottom line. Does that work better for you?"

She was serious about this, wasn't she?

"What if you get hurt?"

"Life's no fun without a little risk. Have you got any chocolate?"

Zander leaned over to open Max's desk drawer. He always had chocolate. Not because he ate it, but in case his fiancée visited him in the office and fancied a snack. While he rummaged amongst Max's crap, he thought about Emmy's offer. Drawing out the culprit could work, and it had the potential to save weeks of effort. If it had been anyone else standing in front of him,

Zander's answer would have been a flat no, but with Emmy…

"Here." Zander tossed her a box of fancy truffles from Hotel Chocolat, and she caught it one-handed. "I can't believe I'm even considering this."

"Reckon Travis Thorne'd go along with the plan?"

"If Alana sold it to him, then probably."

"So talk to her." Emmy held out a hand. "Fifty bucks says I catch the fucker."

Even though Zander had once watched Emmy garden with explosives, up until that point, he'd harboured a tiny doubt that she was as crazy as people said. But now he knew the truth. The rumours were all true—Emmy was a madwoman.

He held out his hand. Why did this feel like making a pact with the devil?

"Fifty bucks."

Emmy used a vicious-looking knife to slice open the seal on the box of chocolates, studied the menu card, and popped one into her mouth. Then she pointed the blade in Zander's direction.

"Why are you still sitting there? Don't you have phone calls to make?"

Chapter 33 - Alana

"EMMY WANTS TO *what*?"

My brother perched on the edge of the dining table, tense. "That's exactly how I reacted."

"She's crazy."

"Said that too."

"And you told her no, obviously." His expression didn't change. "Zander?"

"It would give us the best chance of solving this case quickly."

"Are you out of your freaking mind?"

"At the moment, we've got five incidents in four different jurisdictions. Three of them might not even be crimes, there are hardly any clues, and the only thing they've got in common is Travis. If we can't flush out whoever's behind this, somebody else innocent could get hurt. At least Emmy knows what she's letting herself in for."

"What if *Emmy* gets hurt?"

"Emmy's indestructible."

"No. No, no, no, no, no. No way."

"I need you to convince Travis to go along with this."

"Did you not hear a word I said?" I turned to Dove, who'd walked through from the kitchen. "Zander's lost the plot."

"You can't argue with him. He's impossible. Believe me, I've tried. And I do kind of see his point about Emmy being indestructible."

Dove had met Emmy last year when she got into some trouble of her own. A burning building, dead people, and a psycho-maniac had all been involved.

And now my own family was ganging up on me.

But we couldn't possibly let Emmy go through with this ludicrous idea, could we? I'd heard Jae-Lin's gasping breaths, seen Reagan's broken body and the damage to Vina's face. The last thing I wanted was for another poor woman to suffer.

Although the chances were, that would happen anyway. At least with Emmy involved, we'd stand a chance of catching the felonious freak, and her last outlandish plan—with Red Bennett standing in for Travis at Glastonbury—had miraculously worked. Surely she wouldn't have volunteered if there wasn't a reasonable chance of success?

"Is she trained for stuff like this?"

Zander blew out a breath. "I haven't seen her résumé, but I'm gonna go with yes."

"And what about backup? Would she have backup?"

"A whole army, probably, and I'll be there too. Lanie, please just go with us on this one and talk to Travis."

Zander had made up his mind. We were doing this, even though he shared some of my misgivings, and I could either help or hinder him. That only left me one option.

"Fine. I'll explain everything to him when we get to LA."

"Whoa. Wait a minute. You're not going to Los

Angeles."

"I bloody am. If you want me to play along with this hare-brained scheme, and you're so convinced it'll work, then I want to be nearby so I can see Travis when it's over."

Travis was hurting. He'd called me quickly from the hospital to say Caitlin was in surgery, and I heard the pain in his voice. Even if I couldn't give him a hug right away, being in the same time zone would be a vast improvement on our current situation. If Zander was going to the US, then I was going with him.

Dove started laughing. "She's beating you at your own game, Zee. Don't worry; we'll keep out of your way while you do your detecting."

"What do you mean, *we'll* keep out of your way?"

"Well, I'm coming too, obviously. Marlene's great about us having time off whenever we need it. I'll just make up the hours when I get back."

"Dee, you're not coming."

"But I love LA."

"This isn't a holiday."

"And I'm sure Alana needs some moral support, especially if you're out investigating every day."

"No. Just no."

Okay, time to fight dirty. Zander could be so stubborn sometimes.

"I guess if you're away, that gives Dove and me more space to redecorate."

"Redecorate?"

"We discussed it, remember? I want to put a whirlpool tub in the bathroom, and get one of those doggy water fountains for Bear, and brighten up the lounge a bit because cream's such a dull colour."

"I said no to all of those things."

"No, you said 'not right now.' That's completely different."

Dove saw where I was going with this. "We need more plants too. Some pots on the balcony, maybe. It's the wrong time of year for tomatoes, but a few palm trees would work, and we could add shrubs for colour. What do you think about a hammock?"

"I'd love a hammock. And Bear wants a new bed too. One of those mini four-poster ones with a canopy."

Bear wagged his tail when he heard his name again. He was totally on board with our plan.

"We're not tearing the whole place apart," Zander said. "Think of the mess."

"If you're not here, you won't even notice."

He folded his arms, and I knew we had him. My brother was so easy to manipulate.

"Fine. You can come. But until we catch this maniac, you're staying in the hotel. I can't work if I'm trying to keep an eye on you two at the same time."

"Okay, deal."

I'd won this round, but now the jitters set in. Would Emmy's off-the-wall scheme result in success or disaster?

CHAPTER 34 - ALANA

I ALMOST WALKED right past Emmy at the airport. We all did, and she didn't say a word until we were ten yards away and cursing her for being late.

"Did you miss me?"

It was Emmy's voice, but...whoa. She'd flown to the US yesterday, and in that short time, she'd morphed into a leather-clad rock chick with dark brown hair cut into a choppy bob, perfectly winged eyeliner, and a dark red pout. The make-up made her face look thinner, her already high cheekbones more pronounced, and took five years off her age. Only her jaded eyes gave the game away, even though she'd turned them brown with coloured contact lenses.

Now she gave us a twirl. "So? What do you think?"

Dove still looked adorably confused, but Zander slowly smiled. "In present company, I can't say you look hot, so let's settle for 'you look appropriate' instead."

"I think the lipstick's too much, but my assistant insisted."

The insecure girl lurking inside my head had a momentary panic that Travis might ditch me for her, but then I remembered Emmy was married, and the iron band coiled around my chest loosened infinitesimally.

"I think the lipstick's good," I managed.

"Do you have all your luggage?"

"Yes."

"Then we need to get going. The car's already left to pick up Travis."

My heart pitter-pattered faster at the mention of his name. In less than an hour, I'd see him, and he wouldn't leave my side until morning, when he'd drive to the recording studio with his new "girlfriend" for phase one of operations.

Emmy had left her BMW 4x4 parked in a no-parking zone nearby, and she paused to tear the ticket off the windscreen and stuff it into the glovebox before climbing behind the wheel.

"Does a day ever go past without you getting a fine?" Zander asked once we'd pulled out into traffic.

"Sometimes. In places like, say, Egypt and Iraq, they don't really have traffic wardens."

"Have you ever considered parking legally?"

"Considered it. But then I did the math, and with the amount I earn per hour, it's more economical for me to pay the fine than spend five minutes walking to the parking garage."

There was no bragging in her tone. She just stated a simple fact. Wow.

"What about the time it takes you to do the paperwork?"

"I factored the cost of my assistant into my calculations."

"Welcome to a whole other world," Dove muttered. "Population: Emmy."

"Where are we staying?" Zander asked. "You said you'd arrange it."

"Malibu. At my place on the beach." Emmy pointed two fingers behind her at Dove and me. "And you two are *not* allowed out on the beach. Not until this is over." She put both hands back on the wheel. "Anyhow, I've got good news and bad news. Well, they're sort of the same news. How you view it depends on whether you're a negative nelly like Zander here."

Dove giggled, and I had to laugh too at that description of my brother. All through my teens, he'd been my cheering squad, Mr. Positive, even in the worst of times. But Emmy's unfailing belief that she could do anything, no matter how impossible it seemed, made even the most hardened optimist look like a cynic.

"Hit me with it."

Bad choice of words from my brother as Emmy overtook a slow-moving car and missed an oncoming truck by inches.

"We've ruled out your stalker girl from Caitlin Wiles's hit-and-run. Peyton. She was playing hostess for her mom at a business networking event in Ohio with fifty witnesses. Of course, she could still be on the hook for the other stuff, but..."

"But you don't think so."

"Honestly? No. I've looked at your notes, and while Peyton's presence in Camden may have triggered this whole train of thinking, that everything's connected, I think it's someone closer to the band."

"Who?" I asked.

Emmy smiled in the rear-view mirror. "Ask me that question tomorrow."

Skywater House was appropriately named. Beyond Emmy's back garden, the sky blazed orange and pink as the sun dropped below the horizon, leaving the moon to illuminate the dark blue ripples of the Pacific. She gave us a quick tour of the place when we arrived, and it would have given the presenters on *Grand Designs* a wet dream. Four bedrooms, five bathrooms, open-plan living downstairs, a kitchen done out in granite and stainless steel, and a separate guesthouse down by the water. But the place felt sterile. Unloved.

"Do you spend much time here?" I asked.

"Not really. A couple of weeks a year, maybe? But not all in one go. Another of Blackwood's directors deals with most of our business on the West Coast. I get the UK and Europe."

Dove was right. Emmy lived in a whole different world, but one I was grateful to be spending some time in, especially when I heard the crunch of tyres on the gravel drive outside. Travis walked in a minute later, and I flung myself into his arms. We'd been apart for less than two weeks, but it felt like forever.

"I missed you." I wanted to kiss him, but not with everyone watching. Okay, not with my brother watching. "How's Caitlin?"

"Still in hospital. The doctors are worried about her head."

"Is she awake now?"

"She was for a while earlier, but even talking made her tired."

"Has she said anything about the accident?" Emmy asked. "The police had nothing last time I checked."

"She only remembers leaving the house to go jogging, then waking up in the hospital." Travis looked Emmy up and down. "Hey, do I know you? Were you at LAX a few weeks ago?"

Zander did the honours. "She was. Meet your new fake girlfriend. Uh, do you have a fake name?"

"Unfortunately, yes." Emmy pulled a slim wallet out of her handbag and flipped it open to reveal a California driver's licence. "Don't you dare laugh."

I tried not to. Really I did. But it wasn't happening. "Penelope Beaver?"

"I thrashed our forger at pool the other day, and this was the result. With hindsight, I should've let him win."

Zander couldn't keep a straight face either. "How about Penny?"

"It hardly screams rock 'n' roll, does it?" She huffed out a breath. "Penny fucking Beaver."

"Sounds more like a Bond girl."

"I'm gonna kill him when I get back to Virginia."

"But in the meantime?"

"Fine. Penny." Emmy's expression morphed from sulky to sultry, and she turned back to Travis. "And from tomorrow, I'll be your number one overly emotional, entitled, slightly loose groupie. Hashtag powered by trust fund." She batted her eyelashes. "I can't wait to go to the recording studio. Can I sit on your lap while you twiddle your knobs?"

Travis gave me a "what the hell have I gotten into?" look.

"She's married," I assured him.

"What am I supposed to tell the other guys?" he asked. "They know I'm with Alana."

"Zander? Your thoughts?" Emmy raised an eyebrow, and I realised what she was asking. Did Zander believe that Travis's bandmates were suspects?

"They're okay," I told her, and Zander nodded his

agreement.

"Then call them tonight and explain what's happening. Keep it brief. No details, understood?"

Travis swallowed hard. "Got it."

"Penny scares me," Travis said when we got upstairs to our bedroom. "Emmy. Whatever her name is."

A chef had served us dinner, but Emmy only ate two mouthfuls before her phone rang. After listening for a moment, she'd picked up her plate and disappeared into another part of the house. Dove tried to keep the conversation upbeat, but Travis had stayed on edge through the main course and dessert, and I couldn't say I blamed him.

"Emmy. Her name's Emmy."

"Emmy, Penny, whatever. She looks like she'll break my balls if I accidentally breathe funny."

"At least she's on our side." I walked over to the floor-to-ceiling window that looked out across the beach. Bulletproof glass, Emmy had assured us earlier. "And we don't have to think about her tonight."

Travis joined me, wrapping his arms around my waist and holding me close as we both looked at the stars. It was a cloudless night, and I made a wish on the brightest speck in the sky. *Please let this be over soon.* Travis had trimmed his beard earlier in the week, going from artfully unkempt to a neat goatee, and it tickled my skin as his lips brushed my jaw. Apparently, his record contract forbade him from shaving it off completely.

"No, tonight's ours." His arms tightened as he

looked out at the ocean with me. "One day, I want to buy a house like this. Not just for me, but for us. Two years," he whispered, almost to himself.

At that moment, I felt like a traitor. Because although we still hadn't heard back from the lawyers, I knew, I just *knew*, that Red Cat had done something really shitty in that contract. In two years, there probably wouldn't be enough money to buy an apartment, let alone a beachside mansion.

Rather than talking about it, I twisted to face Travis and kissed him instead. Tonight, we could hide out in our bulletproof-glass bubble where nothing and nobody could touch us—not Red Cat, not a homicidal maniac, and not the real world that existed beyond Skywater House's high walls and neatly trimmed oleander hedges.

I took Travis's hand and led him towards the bed. "I don't care about the house. I just want you."

Chapter 35 - Zander

ZANDER LOOKED UP from his mug of coffee when the front door slammed. Though Dove was dead to the world with jet lag, he couldn't sleep, so at five thirty, he'd gone downstairs so she didn't get disturbed by his constant tossing and turning. Only Emmy was awake at that hour, running on a treadmill in the small gym that overlooked the swimming pool, complete with an iPad full of emails propped in front of her. She'd started work already. The gym was perpendicular to the rest of the house, and Zander had been watching her in his peripheral vision from his seat at the dining table.

But now a small man staggered into the room, wearing a pair of denim cut-offs that showed his ass cheeks, a mesh vest, high heels, and cat ears. Bradley, Emmy's assistant. A trail of glitter sparkled behind him.

"Dying... I'm dying," he muttered before swooning dramatically into a chair.

"Do you need help?"

"Yes. I need Advil, a chilled eye mask, and ginseng tea."

Movement caught Zander's eye as Emmy climbed off the treadmill, and a moment later, she appeared next to him.

"Bradley, what the hell happened? You're dropping

glitter everywhere."

"Paulo split with his boyfriend and decided to start his midlife crisis early."

"You've been dancing all night?"

A whistle dropped out of Bradley's pocket as he leaned down to pull his stilettos off. Fuck, the guy had blisters upon blisters. Huge red welts. How had he kept those shoes on for so long? More to the point, why had he worn them in the first place?

"Shitting hell." Emmy rolled her eyes. "If I carry you upstairs, will you puke?"

"I already did that at Paulo's."

"Fuck my life. Why didn't you stay there and sleep?"

"Because I need to do your make-up this morning. I promised."

"I can do my own make-up."

"Oh, please. You don't know the difference between a smoky eye and a black eye."

"Yes, I do. Want me to demonstrate?"

"I speak the truth. Stop being so touchy."

Emmy held out a hand. "Come on. Bed."

As she walked out of the room with Bradley over her shoulder in a fireman's hold, Zander gave his head a little shake. Now he'd seen it all, and Emmy really did have a soft side.

Despite Bradley's hangover, Emmy appeared downstairs at half past eight looking hotter than Zander would ever admit. Sort of a cross between a dominatrix and a socialite. Travis's jaw dropped too, but he soon focused on Lanie again when Zander glared at him.

"Okay, let's go over the plan for today," Emmy said.

"We're going to the recording studio, yes?"

Travis nodded.

"And the evening's clear?"

"There's normally a party of some sort. At someone's house, or a club."

"I've got a call at eight p.m. PDT that I can't miss. We have to work that into the schedule, and everyone needs a debrief at the end of the day. Zander, I suggest you head into Blackwood's LA office so you can watch what's going on."

"Watch?"

Emmy tapped her chunky metal necklace, her skull earring, and the studded handbag on the table next to her.

"Cameras, baby, and I'm wired for sound too."

"Can I come?" Lanie asked.

"You and Dove are staying here with Bradley. We've got a zillion cable channels, and he can get someone in to do spa treatments or whatever."

"No way! You think I want a freaking facial when all this stuff's going on?"

"Guess not. Well, you're welcome to pace the lounge or comfort eat or sit and stare at the wall instead. And don't even contemplate leaving. The security system monitors the perimeter, and if you set so much as one toe over the line, there's a holding cell with your name on it."

"But—"

"Lanie, Emmy's right. Not about the holding cell, for fuck's sake, but you need to stay here."

Lanie's expression turned mutinous, but she didn't argue. Good. Emmy was doing enough for them already without Lanie being difficult. And Zander was happy to be going to the LA office. From a professional point of view, he was curious to see how they worked, and being able to watch events unfold in real time was a bonus.

Travis merely looked uncomfortable with the whole situation. Not surprising, really. He'd become the epicentre of chaos when all he wanted to do was sing.

Two minutes in the surveillance room, and Zander realised why Emmy had insisted on Lanie staying at the house. She stayed businesslike in the car they took to the recording studio, but the instant she climbed out, she transformed into a giggly, vapid tart, all over Travis as they walked inside. Travis, for his part, looked shocked for a moment, but then he visibly pulled himself together, wrapped an arm around Emmy's waist, and guided her through the door.

"Want a coffee?" Vance asked. He'd been assigned to camera duty today, which meant Zander got to meet him in person. They'd only ever spoken on the phone before.

"Thanks. I didn't sleep so well last night."

"I'm not surprised with all this shit going down. Caitlin Wiles was someone's daughter, someone's sister, and someone's girlfriend."

"Is there any more news on that?"

"The oil refinery along the road caught a suspect vehicle on camera around the time of the incident. A dark-coloured SUV with one headlight out."

"Was the licence plate visible?"

"No, it was missing."

"They took it off?" That suggested premeditation,

which pretty much ruled out the possibility of an accident.

"Maybe. Or it could have been a new car. Here in California, new-car buyers have ninety days to put plates on. When they first purchase a vehicle, they get a small registration sticker that goes in their front windshield instead."

"So if they commit a crime in the first three months, nobody can identify their car? That's crazy."

"Tell that to the lawmakers."

"Can you cross-reference anyone on our suspect list to SUV purchases?"

"Someone's already working on that. Once I've got the coffee, I'll play the footage for you." Vance got halfway out of his seat, then sat down again as Emmy locked lips with Travis. Hell, she didn't take this undercover work lightly, did she? "Well, if anyone in that room's our culprit, that oughta shake 'em up a bit. Think they are?"

"Are what?" Zander studied the scene on screen. Travis had better not get any more enthusiastic about the task at hand, not when he claimed to be devoted to Lanie.

"Are in that room. You've been on this case longer than me—who do you think did it?"

Who indeed? With last night's news about Peyton, Zander had narrowed it down to three or four main suspects in his head. And yes, they were all present today.

"So far, each incident's been reasonably clean. The overdose, the allergy thing, and the acid in the moisturiser didn't even require the person to be in the room at the time. And even the two more violent incidents weren't messy. No blood. Based on statistics, I'd say a woman was behind this."

Vance bobbed his head in agreement. "A fight over a man. Jealousy?"

"Or a case of unrequited love."

"Obsession, more like. Any other options?"

"Gary Dorfman. The guy's shifty."

"What's his motive?"

"I'm not sure about that one yet. He seems determined to get the band to knuckle down and work, so maybe he thinks the women are a distraction? I'd also be interested in finding out if Red Cat Records took out an insurance policy on Travis Thorne."

"Life insurance?"

"This is escalating, and it's got to be messing with his head."

"You think he'd do something stupid out of guilt?"

"No, but if someone took him out and made it look like an accident, convincing the world he was suicidal would be easier after all this."

"At least he's got Emmy with him."

"She thinks she'll solve this in a week."

Vance gave a one-shouldered shrug. "She's sure trying hard."

He wasn't wrong there. Throughout the day, Emmy spoke to everyone at the studio. Rush, Dex, and JD. Verity and Meredith. Courtney and Jeanne, but they'd ruled the latter out because she'd only joined the tour after Reagan died. The crew who looked after the instruments and equipment. Frank, the band's manager. And Gary.

Yes, Emmy's conversation with Gary was the highlight of the day. It had started off innocently enough, with a discussion about Indigo Rain's recent tour, then Gary made the mistake of quietly suggesting that Emmy might like to pleasure him for cash.

Vance whooped with laughter. "Bring the popcorn, boys."

Emmy's voice turned coy. "What, here?"

"I'm sure we can find somewhere more private." Gary waved towards the door. "After you."

She sashayed along the hallway in front of him, and tension in the surveillance room grew. How bad would this be? Should they call an ambulance in advance?

On screen, Gary motioned Emmy into a private office and locked them in. Zander almost felt sorry for the guy, and rightly so. Emmy let him get his trousers down before she slammed him back against the wall. He clawed at the arm pressed against his throat, but a swift knee in the balls diverted his attention.

"I'm here with Travis, and if you ever suggest I prostitute myself again, I'll ram my Amex Platinum up your ass. Do you understand?"

Gary might have tried to nod, but he couldn't move his head.

"I said, do you understand?"

"Yes."

Judging by his high-pitched squeak, Emmy was twisting something sensitive with the hand out of camera shot.

"Good. And while we're here, let me suggest you refrain from making the same offer to other women too. It's degrading."

"O-o-okay."

Gary flew across the room and landed in a chair, and Emmy rummaged through a mini-fridge in the corner for ice, then flung that in his direction too.

"Consider this an unofficial restraining order. Put that on your chicken nuggets and keep the fuck out of my way."

Vance smacked the table with a fist and doubled over. "I love that woman."

So did Zander at that moment, but if Gary was their culprit, it was safe to say she'd just ratcheted up his animosity to murderous proportions.

Blackwood's LA office was about the same size as their five-storey building in London and operated in the same way. Staff had rest areas, sleep pods, and well-stocked kitchens in case they got hungry. At seven thirty in the evening, Zander heated a meatball sub in the microwave and sloped off back to the surveillance room. At least Emmy and Travis had left the studio now. In the eight hours they'd spent there, Indigo Rain had recorded one track—*one*—but they must have played it a hundred times and now Zander couldn't get the beat out of his head. If he never heard it again, it would be too soon.

They'd retired to Rush's apartment, which wasn't any bigger than Zander's, together with a bunch of buddies and half of the crew. All three of their female suspects had gone—Meredith, Verity, and Courtney—which was probably why Emmy had just licked Travis's face. Once again, Zander thanked the bitch for insisting Lanie stay out of this.

A quarter to eight, and Emmy checked her watch. Didn't she say she had a conference call? Zander expected her to make an excuse and leave, but instead, she whispered in Travis's ear and he got up too. The bedroom. They headed into the bedroom for what had to be the least sexy liaison ever.

Emmy sat on the floor with her iPad propped on her knees, knocking the headboard into the wall with one foot while Travis sat on the windowsill. Every so often, Emmy giggled, and it seemed she'd briefed Travis too because he groaned loudly each time she held up a hand—presumably when her microphone was muted. In between acting out a porn soundtrack, Emmy put on her serious face and quietly talked shop to the head of Blackwood's Paris office, first about staffing levels, then about the heightened threat of terrorism in Europe. The woman multitasked like a boss.

By ten, she'd flaunted her dishevelled clothing and Travis's mussed-up hair in front of the group gathered in Rush's lounge, dropped Travis off at Skywater House, and arrived back at Blackwood, pleased with her day's work judging by the smile on her face.

"That was fun. I've only ever been to Ethan's studio before, and it's much quieter there. No groupies, no perverts, no murderous bitches hanging out."

"So you think it was one of the three girls too?"

"Yup."

"Which one? What did you find?"

"What did I find? Nothing concrete yet. All I've got to go on is gut instinct."

"And...?"

"At the moment, I have to agree with your assessment. The most likely suspects are Meredith and Courtney."

"Do you have a favourite?"

"Yes, but I'm going purely on gut instinct, and right now, I don't want to influence the investigation and risk writing off the other suspects, not without proof. So I'll keep my suspicions to myself for now."

"Oh, come on..."

"What did the team find today? Anything more on the SUV that hit Caitlin?"

Damn Emmy and her stubbornness. Every so often in Blackwood's London building, her husband would walk out of the office they shared, his expression veering between homicidal and resigned. He'd pause, take a couple of deep breaths, then stride off to the kitchen. Late one evening, on a day when rumour said Emmy had told a high-ranking politician to go fuck himself, Zander had caught Black pouring the contents of a hip flask into his coffee, and now he understood exactly why the man had done it. Emmy could be the most irritating woman on earth at times.

But there was no point in pushing her because she'd never yield. No, Zander's only option was to grin and bear it. And reach for the whisky bottle himself.

Vance took over. "None of the three girls present today have an SUV registered to them or their immediate family."

"Well, the car came from somewhere. Check out their friends, hire companies, roommates. Is there any forensic evidence?"

"The cops found some paint chips and glass from a shattered headlight. They're analysing it to see if they can get a make and model for the vehicle."

"Any new CCTV?"

"Not yet. We're still canvassing. Think this is gonna

be a slow one."

Caitlin lived in El Segundo, a community that managed to retain a small-town feel despite being a suburb of Los Angeles, according to Vance. She'd been jogging towards the oil refinery when she got hit, on a sleepy side street near Candy Cane Park. The driver had mounted the kerb and knocked her into the parking lot of a nearby apartment building. A Good Samaritan had found her, and since she'd listed Travis as an emergency contact in her phone, the doctors had called him when she arrived at the hospital.

Blackwood investigators had already spoken to local businesses to no avail, and now they were trying private homes and dashcams in the hope of finding some elusive footage or even a witness. The cops had all the forensic evidence, and with their current backlog, they'd take months to process it.

Honestly? This was the most frustrating case Zander had ever worked on, made worse by the fact he had no network here in the US. He was little more than a glorified tourist.

"A slow one? Maybe. Maybe not. But let's make it more fun, shall we?" Emmy reached for a pad and tore off a sheet of paper, shielded the pen as she scribbled something, then sealed the note in an envelope. "Side bet, Zander. If I had to pick one person, this is my guess for who's behind all this shit."

He reached for the envelope, but Emmy held it out of reach.

"Fifty bucks if I'm right."

"Fine, fifty bucks."

"And no cheating. In fact, I'll mail this to the UK and you can open it when you get back."

Gah. Foiled again.

"Tell me again why I work for you?"

"Because I order great pizza, honey. Are you done here? It's time to go home."

CHAPTER 36 - ZANDER

THURSDAY EVENING, AND Lanie rushed across to hug Travis as he walked in the front door with Emmy.

"How did it go today?" she asked.

"Better. Kinda weird because right after we arrived this morning, Gary said he needed to go pick up a bagel, then he never came back."

"Perhaps he got hit by a truck?" Lanie sounded a little too hopeful.

"Nah, he texted Courtney to say he didn't feel well, so..." Travis shrugged. "We got more done than usual because he wasn't there to complain about every damn note we played."

Zander knew exactly why Gary had run off with his tail between his legs. The man was a misogynistic coward. A misogynistic coward who may or may not be party to the scam Red Cat had pulled on Indigo Rain with their punitive contract. When Lanie and Travis disappeared into the lounge, Zander beckoned Emmy into the small study at the front of the house.

"Everything okay?" she asked.

"Oliver Rhodes returned his assessment of Indigo Rain's contract today."

"And from the look on your face, I'm assuming it isn't good news?"

"They're screwed. Rhodes says the contract

language is watertight, and although the band could challenge it as unfair in court, Red Cat's attorneys would most likely drain the resources of anyone who tried to start that fight. The band members would end up bankrupt if they tried to walk away, and if they manage to stick it out for another two years, they'll only have Red Cat's scraps to show for it."

Not to mention the non-compete clause hidden away in a section on overseas royalties. They couldn't sign with a rival label without Red Cat's approval for ten years, and in Zander's estimation, the chances of the assholes at the label giving their blessing were zero. While states like California had ruled such clauses illegal, Indigo Rain's contract had been signed through a subsidiary of Red Cat's based in the Cayman Islands, which made jurisdiction hazy.

"Can I see what Oliver sent?"

Zander handed over his phone and waited while Emmy read the executive summary. How was he supposed to tell Lanie and Travis about this? The guy had to be under enough pressure already without piling on more stress.

"Eh, it's not that bad," Emmy said.

"I'm sorry?"

"It's not that bad."

"Yes, I heard what you said, but are you in a parallel dimension? In what way can that news possibly be good?"

"Because they've got an out."

"What out?"

Emmy highlighted a sentence with her finger and spun the phone back to face Zander. "Here. If Red Cat folds, the contract is null and void, all rights to the band's music revert, and they line up with the other creditors. Granted, there probably wouldn't be much left if the label was insolvent, but it's got to be a good thing overall, right? For them and any other bands who are getting screwed over."

"Hold up. I'm still stuck on the folding part. How the hell would Red Cat go bust? They're raking in millions."

According to Tessa and the other two musketeers back in London, the CEO had just bought a new fucking helicopter, probably paid for with Travis's money. And that was only the tip of the iceberg. Amin had scraped data from online retailers on sales rankings for Red Cat's acts, plus compiled a list of all their tours, gigs, and public appearances. Ziggy had estimated the income and costs for each line item, then extrapolated it into estimated revenue, gross profit, expenses, and net profit. It was good, methodical work. If either of them wanted to work in the analytics business after university, he'd put in a recommendation for them with Blackwood's IS team.

"In 1640, in his *Jacula Prudentum,* George Hebert said 'to him that will, ways are not wanting.' An old proverb, but it's still true today. Where there's a will, there's a way, and we'll find a way, but not until we've dealt with our first problem."

"But this—"

Emmy held up a finger. "One thing at a time, Zander. Hey, did I tell you we're going to Vegas on Monday?"

No, she didn't. "Vegas?"

"The band needs to make a personal appearance at one of the casinos on Sunday and play a private event on Monday, so we get to go on vacay. Fun, huh?"

"You belong in an asylum."

"Don't be such a Debbie Downer. I love Vegas. It's the land of showgirls, poker, and all-you-can-eat buffets. Did you know I got married there? Twice?"

"How am I supposed to explain this to Alana?"

"What, Vegas? Just tell her it's work for Travis."

"No, not Vegas. The contract."

"Simple. You don't tell her anything for the moment. If she asks, just tell her you're waiting on Oliver."

"You mean lie to my sister? We swore we'd always be honest with each other."

And they'd stuck to that promise, even if Lanie had been decidedly hazy over her initial week with Indigo Rain.

"Hey, nobody's asking you to lie. Just be economical with the truth." Emmy tapped away at Zander's phone. "There, the email's gone now. We'll pretend neither of us ever saw it."

Zander snatched the phone back and frantically retrieved Oliver's message from the trash folder. Sometimes, Emmy could be so...so...decisive. At that point in time, Zander felt as if he was clinging to the back of a roller coaster by his fingernails, and he had no choice but to hang on and try not to vomit.

"You said there was something new?" Zander asked Vance.

Emmy had thought this job would be done in a week, but it was Sunday evening, five days in, and so far all they'd got was eye strain from staring at screens, both watching Emmy cavorting in the recording studio and trawling through information. Emmy, for her part, had complained last night that she was getting bored, Travis said he didn't want to go to Vegas, and Lanie didn't want him to go either.

"I found a couple of interesting facts," Vance said. "Not sure what to make of them yet."

"Go on."

"Meredith McVey has a juvenile record."

"Aren't those sealed?"

"Technically, yes."

"Technically?"

"She stole a car. Don't ask how I got that information."

Zander's mind connected the dots, as it had been trained to do. "And we've got a mystery SUV, owned by none of our suspects."

"Exactly. What if she boosted it from somewhere?"

"If she did, then where is it?"

"That's the fifty-thousand-dollar question."

"Did you say you found something else too?"

"Verity Arnold's former best friend in high school died under mysterious circumstances."

"What circumstances?"

"The janitor found her at the bottom of the stairs in the science block with a broken neck. According to witnesses, she and Verity had a falling-out the week before over a guy."

"Fuck." Verity rose up the suspect list again. "A practice run for Reagan?"

Vance's side-to-side nod said "possibly." "How about you? Did you find anything?"

"I'm not sure. Courtney Timmons is an odd girl. Twenty-five years old, she graduated summa cum laude from Caltech, and last year, she quit her research position at a pharmaceutical giant to take a minimum-wage job as assistant to the assistant of Indigo Rain. Her former supervisor describes her as brilliant but scatterbrained."

Vance looked as confused as Zander felt. "Scatterbrained? So why the hell did she take a role where her entire job is to organise things?"

"That's the question I've been asking myself."

"And do you have an answer?"

"Not yet."

"An unhealthy interest in Travis Thorne?"

Zander shrugged. He seemed to be doing a lot of that lately. "Right now? I have no idea. But I need to get some sleep or I won't be able to function tomorrow."

"Have you filled in a request form for a deep background check?"

"It's in the queue."

"Maybe Emmy could get it bumped up. Where is our esteemed leader, anyway?"

"Her husband's in town. I don't know where they've gone, but she sent a car for me and said she wouldn't be back until morning."

"I noticed he accessed the tapes of her and Thorne. Bet he enjoyed those. He's probably taken her to a hotel somewhere to show her who's in charge."

Everyone knew Black was the jealous type, but which of the golden couple was in charge was debatable. Vance's guess about the hotel room was a good one, though.

At least they'd have peace at Skywater House tonight.

CHAPTER 37 - ZANDER

ZANDER LEFT LANIE and Travis in the lounge and pulled the door to the hallway closed to give them some space. Goodbyes were never easy, even if Travis was only going to Vegas for a few days.

Meanwhile, Emmy bumped a second suitcase down the stairs and lined it up next to the first beside the front door.

"Do you have everything?" Bradley asked.

"Yes."

"The purple shoes?"

"Yes."

"Your eyelash curlers?"

"Yes."

"That new burgundy lipstick?"

"Yes."

"Your suppressor? Remember when you forgot it last year and I had to fly with it to Minnesota?"

"I've got it."

"Are you sure? Because Minnesota was freezing, and the air made my skin go all dry."

"Bradley, I've got the fucking suppressor."

Zander didn't want to ask the inevitable question, but he couldn't help himself. "Who are you planning to shoot?"

"Don't worry; it's just a precaution. Didn't you ever

have a security blanket as a kid?"

"It's difficult to kill someone with a security blanket."

"Difficult, but not impossible." Emmy patted Zander on the cheek. "Relax. This is going exactly as I hoped."

Relax? How could he possibly relax? They still had three viable suspects, and now they were all flying to another state.

"So what should I do? Just hang around at Blackwood, watching more video?"

"The video feed for this trip won't be going to Blackwood. It's coming here instead."

"Here?"

"Black's gonna be staying for a while, and when he's busy, the control room in Richmond will monitor me."

Emmy's husband? Great. Sharing a house with him would be like tiptoeing around one of the four horsemen of the apocalypse.

But weirdly, Lanie liked him. Half an hour after Travis and Emmy departed, the front door opened and closed with a quiet *click*. Zander didn't hear any footsteps, but Black appeared in the kitchen moments later and nodded in his direction.

"Graves."

Zander resisted the urge to back away. "Morning. Have you met Alana?"

Black's cold expression didn't change, but Lanie still giggled. "Hi, Mr. Black."

"It's just Black."

"Okay, Black. Can I get you a coffee?"

"Thanks. Double espresso, no sugar." His mouth softened just a touch. "You're smiling, but you're worried."

Lanie's fragile mask cracked. "How can I not be?"

"I realise a stranger telling you everything will be fine won't allay those fears, but know that we're doing everything we can to fix this for you. We've dangled a lure for the person causing problems around Travis, and now it's just a case of waiting for the fish to bite."

"What about the band's contract? Did Emmy tell you about that?"

"Emmy's forwarded the research done so far. We can't solve that one overnight, but we're looking into it. In the meantime, you're safe here." Black handed Lanie a handkerchief for her tears, and Zander had a feeling he carried it for that exact purpose. The man was always prepared for anything. "Just sit tight for a few days."

Lanie wiped her eyes and gave a quiet sniffle. "I'll try."

Black was a paradox of a man. He rarely showed emotion, hummed with pent-up energy, and could intimidate a man with a single glance. But he was kind when the situation called for it. He also had a reputation as a workaholic, but at eleven thirty in the morning, he sauntered down to the beach in board shorts and went for a swim. It didn't escape Zander's notice that both Dove's and Lanie's gazes followed him all the way to the water's edge.

Enough! Concentrate on the task at hand.

Black wasn't a threat. Not to Zander, at least.

"Say hi to Zander," Lanie said, walking in with her

phone held out in front of her.

When she handed the phone over, Zander saw Travis sitting on a roof terrace with the lights of Las Vegas twinkling in the distance.

Travis raised a hand. "Hi."

"You got there okay?"

"Yeah. Emmy reserved the last suite, and Gary got put in a standard room." Travis couldn't keep the smile off his face. "He's pissed, but they said they were fully booked."

"Where are you staying?"

"The Black Diamond."

Figured.

"Emmy owns the hotel. That's why Gary got bumped down to a standard room."

And also why Zander and Dove had got a corporate discount and a free upgrade when they stayed there for their wedding. And free champagne, free spa treatments, complimentary fruit, chocolates, a limo service... The list went on. Emmy may have been a bitch, but she was a nice bitch.

Travis's eyes widened as he looked around the terrace. "You're serious? She owns this whole place?"

"The entire chain."

"Fuck."

"So drink the contents of the minibar by all means, but don't smash up the room or we'll be in trouble with the boss."

"Hey, I'm gonna fold the fuckin' toilet paper back into a point when I'm done with it."

"No need to go that far. Where's Emmy now?"

"On a conference call. I said I'd keep out of her way for an hour, then we've gotta go to this club."

"Good luck. Just do what she tells you."

"Is there anything new on the case?"

"Sorry. Emmy's still our best shot at solving this."

Zander passed the phone back to Lanie and settled back in the chair with his laptop as his sister headed upstairs to get some privacy. The police hadn't made any progress and neither had Blackwood, but at least Caitlin's condition was improving. She'd started walking with a crutch, and the doctors were hopeful she'd be home within a week.

An email pinged into Zander's inbox. He'd worked to keep his London cases under control, ticking along, and Nye and Dev were helping out when he needed boots on the ground. But this message related to Courtney, a short and sweet update from Blackwood's research group.

Subject: Courtney Timmons

Detail: Background check in progress. No birth record found in CONUS for this individual.

No birth certificate in the continental United States? Hmm. Were they looking in the wrong place? Lanie said Courtney came from California, and her accent was definitely American. Was there a problem with Blackwood's search program? Unlikely. Was she born elsewhere? Or...or could Courtney be using a false name?

All Zander could do was request that they keep digging and make a note to discuss this new puzzle piece with Black the next day.

CHAPTER 38 - ZANDER

THE NEXT MORNING, Zander considered going for a run on the beach, but when Black jogged out the door ahead of him, he decided not to get into a race he'd undoubtedly lose and used the gym instead. Between that and breakfast with Dove and Lanie, it was ten o'clock before he walked into the study to tell Black about Courtney's sketchy history. The big man was already watching Emmy on-screen, his hair still damp from the shower.

"They're up early today?" Zander asked.

Black popped a carrot stick into his mouth. "Gary lined up a last-minute appearance for the band. Easy money. Guess he needed to buy a new watch or something."

"That guy's a slug."

"It'll be interesting to see how much of a backbone he has. Do you need me? Or are you just here to watch the show?"

"The research team found an anomaly in Courtney's background check."

A knock at the door of Emmy's hotel room caught their attention. Something or nothing? Black's face remained impassive as he clicked through the camera feeds to the one from the hallway outside where a black-clad figure stood waiting. Female. Dark hair tied back in a scruffy ponytail and a bag slung over her shoulder. Zander leaned forward to take a closer look.

"Game on, Diamond," Black said.

Game on? Every muscle in Zander's body tensed like he'd been zapped with a high-voltage stun gun. They thought Meredith was the one?

Black had two giant screens in front of him, and now each one divided into quarters. He dragged the hallway picture into one segment, and the image from Emmy's body cam filled another. *Click, click, click.* How many cameras had they installed in that suite? One pointed at the door, another at the wet bar, and a third at the sofas. Both of the two bedrooms were covered, as was the dining area.

They had sound too, as Zander found out when Black put a finger to his ear then turned on the speakers.

"I'm coming," Emmy called out.

The only movement came from Emmy's walk to the door, and when she opened it, she kept her voice light. Pleasant.

"Hey, Meredith. Everything okay?"

"Everything's great. I just stopped by to say hi. I mean, since you seem to be sticking around with Travis, I thought we should get to know each other."

"Oh, sure. Good idea. I guess the girls have to stick together in this industry, right? Did anyone tell you I used to be in a band?"

"You did?"

"Yeah, we were called Sisters of the Annihilation. I played bass."

"Can Emmy really play the guitar?" Zander whispered.

Black shook his head. "She doesn't even know which way up to hold it."

On screen, Emmy opened the door wide enough for Meredith to step inside the suite, and even though Zander knew she'd never drink on the job, she put a wobble in her gait as she crossed the room towards the seating area. An almost-empty glass of red sat on the coffee table.

Meredith carried on towards the balcony. "You have a great view. Look at the guy with the dog down there. It's almost as big as he is."

"What's the bitch planning to do?" Black muttered. "Throw my wife over the balcony?"

But Emmy didn't bite. "Oh, I don't go out there. I don't like heights."

"Then why are you in the penthouse?"

"I wanted a bathroom with a whirlpool tub, and this was the last one left."

"Money to spare, huh?"

Emmy shrugged. "Why not? Daddy died young and left it to me, so I might as well spend it. He couldn't take it with him, and neither can I."

"I suppose that's one way of looking at it."

"Better a spendthrift than a penny pincher, that's what my mom always used to say."

"Used to?"

"After rehab, she moved to Tennessee and joined an 'ecological movement.'" Emmy used little finger quotes. "She gave up all her earthly possessions to hug a cactus or some shit like that, but luckily, she couldn't get at my trust fund."

Where did Emmy come up with this stuff? Zander didn't know, but she did a pretty convincing job of looking tipsy as she stumbled away from Meredith and fell in a heap on the sofa.

"Dammit. I should have offered you a drink. Do you want a drink?"

Meredith waved a hand. "Don't worry; I'll make them. What do you want?"

"Pepsi. The caffeine-free one. With vodka and a slice of lemon."

"No caffeine? How do you get up in the mornings?"

"No caffeine, no aspartame. They're both bad for you. And who cares about getting up in the mornings?"

Meredith rolled her eyes, which seemed reasonable to Zander considering Emmy had snorted "coke" at Rush's place on Friday night. Apparently it wasn't really coke, it was only lactose powder, but Meredith didn't know that.

"Lactose powder's great," Emmy had said. "Unless you're Slater from our Richmond office. He's lactose intolerant, and it gave him the shits on an undercover job last year."

What a delightful story.

Anyhow, Emmy had survived the party, although if JD ever tried taking drugs around Lanie, Zander would be having words with the man. And now Emmy had to survive Meredith. Black zoomed in as their suspect rattled glasses at the wet bar built into a corner of the lounge. Zander knew from experience it would be well-stocked with everything from designer gin to five kinds of peanuts.

"Diamond, Meredith's just tipped something from a small bottle into one of the glasses. A clear liquid. Tagging it now."

Emmy angled her body cam down at her hand and

gave the "okay" sign—a circled thumb and forefinger—
out of Meredith's sight, and Black tagged the tainted
glass with a red dot on the screen to keep track of it.
What had she poured in there? And more importantly,
how would Emmy handle it?

"Mack, secure the door," Black said.

Mack was Blackwood's head of information
systems, and she must have had a direct link into the
hotel's security system in order to override the
electronic lock. Black gave a small satisfied nod a
moment later.

Meanwhile, Meredith had filled two glasses with ice
and Pepsi, and now she dropped a slice of lemon in
each. Held onto the knife a beat too long, then put it
down on the tiny wooden chopping board embossed
with the hotel's logo.

"Here you go," she said, setting a glass on the table
in front of Emmy. The glass with the red dot. "Enjoy."

"Glass is with you," Black said.

"Could you do me a favour and get me one of those
swizzle sticks?"

"Sure."

Was it Zander's imagination, or did Meredith have
a spring in her step as she walked across the room?

"So, you're performing at the show tonight?"

"Yeah." Meredith dropped the stick into Emmy's
drink and took a seat opposite. "The casino boss saw a
live stream of our show in Camden and wanted both
bands."

"That's awesome. I can't wait to hear you play."
Emmy stirred her Pepsi, seemingly absent-mindedly,
but she didn't take a sip. Why had she wanted a damn
swizzle stick? As a distraction? Meredith took a long

swallow of her own drink, perhaps as a hint. "How does playing for a crowd compare with being in the recording studio?"

"The studio's easier. 'Cause if it goes wrong, you can just do it again, you know? But I love the energy of a crowd. It's like a drug."

"Have you got more shows lined up?"

"Maybe. We might tour in the US with Indigo Rain, but our label wants us to write new material first."

"And how's that going?"

She made a face. "Slower than I'd hoped."

Black talked softly into his headset, instructing an unknown operative. "Knock and say you're from housekeeping. Don't go in. If anyone opens the door, make an excuse and leave."

Sure enough, a quiet tap sounded through the speakers. "Housekeeping."

Meredith's head snapped around, and Emmy took the opportunity to pour a third of her drink into the plant pot next to the couch. The poor potted palm was taking one for the team.

"Can you come back later?" she called, then smiled at Meredith. "Slow because you have so many touring commitments?"

"That and my songwriting partner's been distracted lately."

Who was her songwriting partner? Verity? No, of course not. Realisation dawned on Zander. *Travis* was Meredith's songwriting partner. Was this her motive for removing all the women in his life? Not out of common-or-garden jealousy but because they threatened to derail her career if he didn't knuckle down and write her damn songs? Cold. That was cold.

Black had obviously come to the same hasty conclusion. "Back off that one, Diamond."

"Aw, that's a shame. But I'm sure you'll get your lyrical mojo back soon. What do you plan to sing tonight?"

And so the small talk continued, through Styx and Stones's back catalogue, the hotel's dining choices, and fashion. Bradley had educated Emmy well on the latter. And during the conversation, she used sleight of hand and the distraction of a staged row in the hallway outside to get rid of most of her drink. Finally, Meredith downed the last dregs of hers and stood, no doubt pleased with her work.

"We'll have to do this again sometime, Penny."

Emmy didn't bother to get up. "I don't think so."

"Huh?"

"I switched our glasses when you went to get the swizzle stick. I don't know what you just drank, but unless you pay a visit to the emergency room pretty fucking fast, I don't suppose you'll be around for much longer."

Holy fuck!

Zander resisted the urge to (a) pump a fist in the air and (b) make popcorn as Meredith turned the colour of Vina's oh-so-deadly face cream. After a moment's hesitation, Meredith made a dash for the door, only to find it firmly locked.

"Good luck with that," Emmy said. "I had my buddy in the security office override the locks."

Fear turned to outright panic as Meredith grabbed the stubby knife she'd used to slice the lemon. Emmy slowly got to her feet, relaxed, even smiling.

"What did you put in my drink, Meredith?" One

swift kick and the knife went sailing across the room. Emmy twisted Meredith's arm behind her back and propelled her into an armchair. "Something that takes a while to kick in, obviously. Did you plan to be out of the way when I carked it? Set yourself up with an alibi?"

Meredith's silence gave Emmy her answer.

"Was it hemlock? That would give you half an hour before your muscles weaken and paralysis sets in. How about arsenic? Do you have stomach pain? Strychnine? Is there a little stiffness in your jaw? Come on, tell me."

"Ethylene glycol," Meredith muttered, almost too quietly to hear.

"Ooh, nasty. Vomiting, seizures, and renal failure. You really need to get to the emergency room for a good dose of fomepizole."

"Let me out of here, you bitch."

That was a bit rich, considering Meredith had just tried to kill Emmy.

"Sure. But first I need answers for my client."

"Your client?"

Emmy's grin was best described as malicious. She was enjoying this. "Yeah, my client. I'm a private investigator, and Travis Thorne hired me to find out why his girlfriends keep dying. So talk me through it. Let's start with Marli."

"Fuck you."

"Tick-tock. How do you like being doubled over in pain? I saw a guy in the later stages of ethylene glycol poisoning once. I'm not sure they ever did get the blood he puked up out of the carpet."

Meredith glanced at the door again, both arms wrapped around her stomach. Emmy had her, and everyone knew it.

"Marli?" she prompted again.

"I never touched Marli. She just gave me the idea. That whore was a waste of space, an addict, and Travis still wanted to spend time with her. Why? She couldn't do anything for him."

"Well, maybe he wanted to do something for her?"

"Bullshit. He didn't need to run around after women. They lined up to please him."

Meredith totally missed the point, probably because she was a selfish witch. Not everything in life was done with an expectation of repayment.

"So Marli was the catalyst. Then you moved on to Jae-Lin."

"They'd split up. She couldn't keep coming back for another go. Every time that happened, he shut me out for days."

"Perhaps he was having fun with her?"

"Fun? Music is his life—he's said that since he was a teenager. And now that he's got his dream career, he doesn't need any complications."

"So you did this for him?"

Her head bobbed. "Exactly."

Zander had never heard logic that warped. Meredith's elevator clearly didn't go all the way to the top floor.

"How?"

"I dropped one of my green-lipped mussel capsules in her drink. Everyone knew she was allergic to shellfish. She never stopped bleating about it."

"And Reagan? What did she do?"

"Reagan was nothing to do with me."

"Then how did she fall down the stairs?"

"Who knows? Probably couldn't walk in those stupid shoes she bought. She was sleeping with Gary too, you know."

"Gary? Euuuch."

"How else do you think she got the job?"

"By being a good PA?"

"That's not how Gary works."

"Yuck. Okay, so skip Reagan. Vina?"

Meredith checked her watch. "She should have been a one-hit wonder, but Travis offered to help with her album. Write her songs in secret. Those were supposed to be *my* songs."

"Perhaps he could've helped both of you?"

"Like he has time for that."

"Why didn't you have a go at writing your own tracks?"

"I did, but the label hated them, okay? It's not like I'm totally lazy."

No, she'd clearly put a lot of effort into trying to kill people.

"And so you what? Snuck into her room and swapped out her jar of face cream?"

"It wasn't exactly difficult. She always left her key in her jacket pocket."

"So, now we come to Caitlin. That was you as well, I take it."

"Travis dated her for two years. Two years of his life, wasted. She ditched him, and still every time she snaps her fingers, he goes running. She doesn't deserve him."

"In your opinion."

"Everyone's entitled to an opinion. And you need to let me go now. We had a deal."

"Where's the car you used to run her over?"

"I borrowed my neighbour's truck. And I'm not a thief—he gave me permission."

"Permission to use it in a felony?"

"He never specified, just gave me the keys and said to use it whenever I wanted because I offered to water his plants while he was on vacation. See? I did that because I'm a *nice person*."

Good grief. Meredith was insane.

"Didn't he ask about the damage?"

"I told him I hit a deer." She fidgeted in her seat. "Now let me go. You promised. You *promised*."

"Yeah, I did." Emmy tapped away on her phone, all pretence because it was Black who gave the order to Mack. "The door's unlocked now. So long."

Meredith leapt to her feet, ran across the room, and yanked the door open. Emmy was letting her go? It seemed that way, but Meredith wasn't done yet. She couldn't resist turning back as she stood on the threshold, poised to run.

"You're so stupid. Nobody's gonna believe a word you say, and when I tell everyone you poisoned me, you're going to jail."

"Stupid? Yes, of course I'm stupid. Dumb as a box of rocks." Emmy barked out a laugh. "I didn't switch the glasses, pumpkin, and while I doubt the ethylene glycol will have done the potted plant much good, I'm not sure its death is a criminal offence. But attempted murder is. Quarter of a glassful of the evidence is still sitting on the table."

Meredith's mouth dropped open.

"Smile, sweetheart. You're on candid camera. From several different angles, and I'm wired for sound too.

It's all transmitting remotely. Ain't technology great? Now, because *I'm* a nice person, I'm gonna give you the chance to turn yourself in before I call the cops. The judge might look favourably on that if you show remorse."

"But...but..."

"I'll give you an hour to consider your options before I pick up the phone." Emmy pulled the door open wider. "Bye, Felicia. Enjoy jail."

When Meredith didn't move, Emmy gave her a little nudge.

"Off you fuck. What's wrong? Did I stutter?"

Meredith took a step forward, and Emmy pushed the door closed, forcing her out into the hallway. Shit. Emmy could be a devious bitch when she put her mind to it, and Zander sure was glad to have her on their side.

"What now?" he asked as Black switched CCTV feeds to get a better angle of Meredith. "We take the tape and what's left of that Pepsi to the police? Can we get someone to find that truck before the neighbour gets it repaired?"

"No. Now, we wait."

"Wait?" Why? "How long for? The full hour?"

"I'm betting on less than ten minutes." Black tilted his head slightly. "Five minutes? Okay, Diamond. Fifty bucks."

Meredith still hadn't moved her feet, but she looked both ways down the hallway. Nervous. Twitchy. She was the only one there, and instead of walking towards the elevator, she headed for the roof terrace at the far end. Did she need some thinking time? Zander couldn't blame her for that. Her grand plan had been derailed, and now she'd want to keep her ass out of a prison cell.

But Meredith didn't stop at the glass-topped table or one of the squashy sun loungers. No, she carried right on to the waist-high rail around the edge, leaned forward over it, and swan-dived off the building.

"Holy shit!" Zander leapt out of his chair, eyes fixed on the screen where Meredith had been standing until a second ago. "Did she just jump?"

He'd seen it with his own eyes, but he could still hardly believe it.

Black merely smiled, the sick fuck. "Ten out of ten for effort, but her technique could have been better."

CHAPTER 39 - ZANDER

EMMY KEPT HER camera and microphone on as she lied her way through the police interview, a sincere and heartfelt chat about how Meredith had poured her heart out over a glass of Diet Pepsi. The pressures the young woman had felt on tour, the lack of time to herself, and how she wanted out but didn't know how to escape. Penny's advice to find a therapist had gone unheeded, and poor Meredith had sought the most tragic of endings. Penny even threw in tears.

Of course, there was little the police could do to dispute the story. Emmy had poured the remains of the Pepsi down the sink, and the video footage from inside the hotel suite would remain in Blackwood's vault forever, along with all the other dirt and secret evidence Black undoubtedly collected. That left the tapes from the hallway outside, which showed Meredith acting alone as she crossed the roof terrace and threw herself over the edge. A clear-cut case of suicide.

As for Black himself, he actually ate popcorn while he watched Emmy spin her tale. Low fat with chilli and lime, apparently. The healthy alternative to potato chips. Zander tried a mouthful, and it nearly blew his head off.

"What about the others?" Zander asked. "Shouldn't

we tell someone Meredith was responsible for trying to kill Jae-Lin, Vina, and Caitlin? The police?"

"For what purpose?"

"Justice? So people can get closure?"

"I'd say justice has already been served, wouldn't you? Meredith's dead. Is closure for three people worth dragging countless others through a gauntlet of investigations and media speculation? Meredith's parents, the band, the victims, their families, Alana—a hundred lives would be raked over. What would you prefer? To wake the wolves or let sleeping dogs lie?"

When Black put it like that... "Point taken."

How many other times had the man made decisions like that? More than a handful, Zander was willing to bet. Did playing God take its toll on a man's psyche? Black always seemed so cold, his secrets locked up tighter than Fort Knox. Zander bet that wanting to protect his wife played a part in Black's decision-making process too, but Zander couldn't blame him for that. He'd do anything to protect Dove if the need arose.

"Good," Black said. "Then let's allow this episode to die a quiet death along with its perpetrator, shall we?"

Zander would never tell, of course. A young person's death was always shocking, but if anyone deserved to be shovelled up off the sidewalk by the medical examiner, it was Meredith. At least she hadn't hit anyone else when she landed.

The media, the talking heads, would of course put their own slant on the tale, one of a talented artist taken far too young. Pressures in the music industry would be examined, which might help Indigo Rain's cause. But the upshot was, Lanie and Travis would be free to carry on their relationship without fear of grievous bodily harm, and although Zander was sad that he and his sister would undoubtedly spend a lot of time apart, he was also happy for her. Travis wasn't a bad guy, and he was clearly smitten. Lanie had found her soulmate just as Zander had found Dove.

"Four out of five isn't bad," Black said. "Assuming Marli truly did die of an overdose."

"Reagan still bothers me."

"Yes. Her death seemed a little too convenient when according to your notes, there was animosity between her and Travis."

"That's putting it mildly."

"And yet he took her on a date. Was there more to it?"

"A touch of blackmail. She threatened to tell Gary that Travis made an unsanctioned trip to the US if he didn't take her to the awards dinner. And those recent sex pictures of Travis that appeared online? The girl in them was Reagan. She sold them."

Zander left out the fact that the sex was non-consensual. Really, that was nobody's business but Travis's, and if he wanted to keep it quiet, then that was his decision. Yes, it had crossed Zander's mind that Travis might have given Reagan a helping hand down the stairs, but given the choice? He'd have probably done that too.

"Ah. Do you want Blackwood to look any further into her death?"

"I don't think so. No."

Black nodded once. "Understood. Did you have a question about Courtney earlier?"

"I'm not sure it's relevant now."

"But it bothered you?"

"Yes, but that was before Meredith's confession."

"What did you find?"

"It's what we didn't find. She's supposed to be from California, but she's got no birth certificate in the US."

"Moved here as a baby? Born under a different name?"

"Maybe."

"I'll ask Mack to look into it."

As a lowly investigator, Zander didn't have direct access to Mack, only the research team. But if anyone could ferret out the details, it was her.

"Thanks. I'd appreciate that."

Sorting out the aftermath of Meredith's death took the rest of the day, and callous bastard that he was, Gary still tried to make Indigo Rain perform their evening show. Only when Penny pointed out how insensitive the band would look in the eyes of the media did he relent, although it was unclear whether that was due to fear of Emmy or a genuine understanding of the public's perception.

Either way, Emmy and a shaken-looking Travis arrived back at Skywater House in the early hours of the morning. He always seemed larger than life on TV, but the last few months had taken their toll and now he looked like a broken man. Lanie was waiting for him, and their silent hug spoke volumes. They'd be there for each other, but she had some fixing to do.

Emmy stood on tiptoes to kiss Black on the cheek. "You owe me fifty bucks. And since we got the bitch within a week, so do you, Zander. I'll accept payment in cash or chocolate."

Black took a fifty-dollar bill out of his wallet, and

Emmy snatched it, stuffed it into her pocket, and turned to Zander. He mock-sighed as he handed over the cash, although in reality, he owed her a hell of a lot more than that.

"Now will you tell me what the hell happened today?" Lanie asked.

"And me," Travis said. "One of my good friends died, and telling me to trust you and keep my mouth shut when the cops turned up wasn't good enough. I stayed quiet. Now I need answers."

"And you'll get them," Black said. "After someone's made coffee."

Bradley raised his hand. "Right on it. I picked up an excellent new blend from Whole Foods today."

Dove put a hand on Lanie's back, trying to soothe her. Dove had been through a world of upheaval this year too, and she'd taken it all like the trooper she was. Zander loved her more with every day that passed.

"Come on, let's get settled in the dining room," she said. "We can talk and then get some sleep."

When the others disappeared around the corner, Emmy's sombre expression turned into a bright grin.

"That went well."

Black broke with his usual icy persona to give her an affectionate side-hug. "We'll make a psychologist of you yet."

"Or a detective. I'm thinking I could be a detective instead of shooting people all the time." She glanced across at Zander. "Only kidding. I don't shoot people all the time." A pause. "It's too messy. Sometimes I get creative, like today."

It suddenly clicked what she meant. "You *knew* she'd kill herself?"

"I thought there was a good chance, so I figured I'd give her the option instead of calling the police right away. Nobody likes a long, drawn-out trial. Except for the lawyers, obviously."

"That's...that's..."

"Ingenious?"

"Sick." And it was. It really was. "But also kind of..."

"Innovative? Clever? Cunning?"

Zander hated to admit it, but... "All of the above."

"I'm out fifty dollars from that," Black said. "After seventeen years, I should know better than to wager with my wife."

Emmy just laughed. "Let's go talk to the two lovebirds, shall we?"

CHAPTER 40 - ALANA

"OKAY, LET'S NOT beat about the bush here," Emmy said.

I gripped Travis's hand. Whatever was coming, it was bad. She'd promised to get to the bottom of this, but instead of targeting Penny, the freak who had it in for Travis had gone after Meredith. I'd been watching the news all day, and every channel showed her plummeting from the building, filmed by a passer-by on a cell phone and quickly uploaded to YouTube. Nobody broadcast the landing, thank goodness. Black and Zander had been cagey, refusing to give me straight answers, and Travis was right. We needed to know exactly what happened.

"Meredith was responsible for Jae-Lin's anaphylaxis, Vina's face cream, and Caitlin's hit-and-run. As far as we can tell, Marli's overdose was a genuine accident."

"What?" I gasped.

Zander nodded. "It's true."

"And Reagan?"

"She denied having anything to do with that," Emmy said.

Travis's nails dug into my palm so hard I feared they'd draw blood, and I used my other hand to loosen his grip.

"Sorry," he whispered.

"It's okay."

"How..." His voice came out as a croak, and he tried again. "How do you know all that?"

"She attempted to kill me today, but I stopped her from doing so and put her in a position where she felt she had no choice other than to confess." Emmy told us a crazy story of Pepsi and poison that left me vowing never to touch another soft drink. Apparently, ethylene glycol tasted sweet and you'd never even notice it until you got sick. "And when I said I'd be going to the police with the evidence, she decided to kill herself rather than risk a prison sentence."

"Couldn't you have tried to stop her?" Travis asked.

"Everyone has choices, and Meredith made some spectacularly bad ones. I know it's difficult to lose somebody you considered a friend. A woman who betrayed me died two years ago, and I still look back and wonder why I didn't see the problem earlier. Why I didn't realise how unhappy she was."

"How did you get past it?"

"I focused on the future. And some good came out of that tragedy. A friend of mine met the love of his life, just like you met Alana. You've both got your whole future ahead of you, so don't waste it by dwelling on things you can't change."

A long moment passed, then Travis let go of my hand and wrapped an arm around me instead. We'd be okay. Not today, not tomorrow, but we'd be okay.

"My future starts in two years. Did Alana tell you about the band's record contract?"

"It's been mentioned, yes."

I looked at Zander, Zander looked at Emmy, and

Emmy looked at me. Which of us should tell Travis? Me. It had to be me, didn't it?

"Uh, we did some research on your contract. I didn't want to say anything until after we sorted out the other thing."

"How bad is it?"

Zander took over. "I'll be honest—it's not great news. Red Cat's hidden several punitive clauses in the small print. It seems your manager and lawyer didn't spot them."

"Or they took kickbacks to keep their mouths shut," Emmy said. Zander glared at her for the interruption. "Just saying."

"What kind of punitive clauses?"

My brother gave a brief outline—the expenses clawback and the non-compete clause—and Travis turned deathly pale. Tears prickled at the corners of my eyes as I struggled to stop myself from crying on his behalf.

"You mean we've all gotta work for two more years, and at the end of it, we'll get basically nothing?"

"I'll kick Gary in the bloody balls," I muttered.

Emmy snorted. "Already did that. Well, it was my knee, but it had the same effect."

Travis stared at her. "You did what? When?"

"First day in the recording studio. The little worm propositioned me, but don't worry; he won't make the same mistake again."

I couldn't help it—I wriggled out of Travis's embrace, hurried over to Emmy, and threw my arms around her. "Thank you. Thank you for everything, but especially for that."

"It was a pleasure, honey. Really it was. And don't

worry about the contract. We'll deal with it, and I'll enjoy that too."

"But how? How will you do that?"

She put a finger to her lips. "Go to work, enjoy each other's company, and forget about it. Black and I will be leaving tomorrow, but if you want to stay in the house for a few weeks, that's fine. Just don't chuck the couch in the swimming pool or any other rock-star shit."

"But—"

"I'm going to bed." The chair scraped across the floor as she pushed it back. "Chuck, are you coming?"

"Not yet, but I am breathing hard."

It took me a second to get the joke, but then I giggled. Oh my gosh. Black had a secret sense of humour as well as an ass you could bounce quarters off. Not that I'd been looking or anything. No, definitely not.

They disappeared upstairs, followed by Zander and Dove. Alone with Travis at last, I stood at his side, unsure what to do until he pulled me onto his lap.

"I'm not sure whether this has been one of the best days of my life or one of the worst, blue."

"If it's the worst, then things can only get better from here on out."

"I still have to tell the other guys about the contract."

"How about not telling them? Emmy said not to worry."

"How the hell can I not worry? She isn't even a lawyer."

"Hey, it'll be okay."

"I need to get my own lawyer." Now he closed his

eyes and laid his forehead against mine. "I can't even afford a lawyer."

"If it comes to that, I'll pay for your lawyer. But please, just give Emmy a chance first."

"Do you trust her?"

Good question. Did I? She *had* solved the Meredith problem, albeit in a dramatic fashion. If she could annihilate Red Cat Records too, I'd buy her a bottle of champagne. No, I'd buy her a methuselah of champagne. If anybody could wipe the smug smile off Leonard Martineau's face, it was Emmy.

"Yes, I trust her."

"Then I'll hold off on the lawyer, but I still need to tell Rush, Dex, and JD. They deserve to know. But tonight, I don't want to think about work or Meredith or solving impossible problems—I just want to lose myself in you."

"Then let's forget all that and go upstairs."

Originally, Indigo Rain had planned to stay in Vegas until Wednesday morning, but since they'd fled the city the previous day and returned to LA, there was nothing on the schedule and everyone got a much-needed lie-in. Bradley organised a breakfast buffet, although it was closer to lunchtime by the time we got downstairs.

"Sleep okay?" Emmy asked from her seat at the table. She was reading through her emails while eating a bowl of rabbit food. Sorry, muesli.

"Better than I thought."

"Bradley's in the kitchen making waffles. Actually, he's making a mess, but he assured me there'll be waffles at some point."

I'd taken two steps towards the kitchen when Emmy started choking. Properly choking like she couldn't breathe. I was about to attempt the Heimlich manoeuvre when Travis thumped her on the back and a lump of muesli splatted onto the floor.

Holy shiznitz. "Are you all right?"

"Yu—" She started coughing again, then her gaze strayed to her computer screen, and before I could help myself, I'd accidentally read the email on it. It was only one short paragraph, okay?

From: Mack Cain

Subject: The tangled web

Courtney Timmons was born Courtney Dorabelle Thorne. Adopted at eighteen months old. Sibling, eleven months younger, listed as Travis Daley Thorne. Coincidence?????

It took a few seconds for the words to sink in, by which point Travis had read them too and was undergoing the same horrified-slash-incredulous-slash-will-this-ever-end reaction as me. Emmy sagged back against the table.

"Ah, shit."

"Am I reading this right?" he asked. "Courtney's my *sister*?"

Zander chose that moment to walk in.

"Courtney's your *sister*? What the hell did I miss?"

"Mack emailed," Emmy said. "My cereal went down the wrong way, much choking, etc. Yeah, looks like I wasn't the only one undercover in that studio."

Travis slumped onto a chair. "I can't get my head around this. How can Courtney be my sister? She's never even hinted at anything like that."

"Maybe she didn't know how to tell you?"

"Or maybe it's not true?"

"How much do you know about your early years?" I asked gently. "Your parents?"

"I landed up in foster care at four months old. I don't remember them at all. But I always figured they were assholes because they never took care of me. Or my... Fuck. Do you really think she's my sister?"

"So far, all we've got is a name," Emmy said. "But it *is* a pretty big coincidence."

"So how do we find out for sure?"

"Simple." Emmy tossed him the phone he'd left on the table. "Give her a call and ask her to come over."

CHAPTER 41 - ALANA

TRAVIS CAUGHT THE mobile Emmy had thrown, then stared blankly at it. "Phone her?"

"She works for you, yes? It's the fastest way to clear this up."

"What if she lies?" I asked.

Emmy shrugged as if to say, *No problem*. "Then I'll call her out on it."

Well, at least one of us was confident. I took the phone from Travis because he didn't seem up to any difficult conversations right now. "I'll speak to her."

One ring, two, and Courtney answered.

"Travis?"

"It's Alana."

"Alana? But this is Travis's phone. Aren't you in England?"

"It's a long story, but I'm in LA. Travis isn't feeling so good, and he's asked if you can run a few errands for him this afternoon."

"Oh, sure, sure. What errands?"

"We're both staying with a mutual friend. Could you meet us here and he'll go over the list?"

"Of course. What's the address? Hold on, I need to find a pen..."

The intercom buzzed half an hour later, and Travis had spent the whole time pacing, freaking out, and muttering that this couldn't be happening. But it was. The hits just kept on coming, although granted, the news about Courtney wasn't quite as bad as Meredith doing a Tom Daley off the top floor of Emmy's hotel.

Bradley showed Courtney into the lounge, offering tea, coffee, organic juice, filtered water, or a wheatgrass-and-goji-berry smoothie.

"Thank you, but I don't think I'll be here for long."

"No, you will be."

"Really? Uh, okay, I guess I'll have a coffee."

"Americano, cappuccino, latte, espresso, or macchiato?"

"A cappuccino?"

"Which beans? Typica, bourbon, blue mountain, or caturra?"

Emmy rolled her eyes. "Just bring any kind of coffee, Bradley. Courtney, why don't you take a seat?"

"Do I know you?"

"Emmy. Also known as Penny."

Courtney looked Emmy up and down, and her eyes widened as she realised they were one and the same person.

"You dyed your hair?"

"No, I took my wig off, but that's irrelevant at the moment."

Emmy took the seat opposite Courtney, and I was kind of grateful she was doing the talking because I had no idea what to say and Travis was tongue-tied too. Now I studied him and Courtney side by side, I saw the similarities. She wore glasses, but they had the same colour eyes. Their jaws were the same shape, although Travis's had been obscured by a bushier beard until recently. And they both had the same athletic build.

"Courtney Timmons. Courtney Dorabelle Timmons. Courtney Dorabelle Thorne." Emmy raised an eyebrow. "Is there something you want to tell us?"

All the colour drained out of Courtney's face in much the same way as Travis had paled yesterday at news of the contract. At least she was sitting down.

"I... I..." She glanced sideways at Travis. "I... Yes." All her perkiness evaporated, and she slumped like a leaky balloon. "He... You were never meant to find out like this. I'm sorry. So sorry."

Finally, Travis spoke. "You *are* my sister?"

"I wasn't certain at first, but everything fit—our names, our ages, your history, our biological parents' names. I hired a private investigator, and he thought so too. And then..." Courtney buried her face in her hands. "Then I might have borrowed one of your old beer bottles and done a DNA test on your saliva."

"And it matched?"

She peeped between her fingers. "Yes."

"But... I don't understand. Why didn't you just tell me in the first place?"

"How? I couldn't get anywhere near you, and you never replied to any of the messages I sent you on Instagram. In the end, I went to your record label to drop off a letter, but the receptionist thought I was there for a job instead and gave me an application form. And after I got the job, I figured if I opened up, you'd think I was a psycho for basically stalking you."

"So you're not really a PA? I guess that figures."

"Thanks."

"Sorry."

She sighed. "It's okay. I'm actually a scientist. The interview with Gary was the most degrading experience of my life, and that's all I'll say about it."

Travis's voice dropped to a growl. "What did he do to you?"

But Emmy interrupted. "Let's move on, shall we? Courtney doesn't want to talk about it. But I'm curious as to why now? You're what—twenty-five?"

"I didn't find out I was adopted until I was twenty-three. If I had, believe me, I'd have done this sooner."

"How did you find out?" Travis asked, curious now.

"I research genetics, and I was looking at hereditary traits for a project. I needed a pair of guinea pigs to test one of my theories, so I used me and my mother. I had a few strands of her hair in a locket, you see. Only it turned out she wasn't my mother. Even now, my parents refuse to discuss the details, but my grandma told me what she knew, and I got curious about my birth family."

Wow. What a way to find out. And Courtney sounded so calm speaking about it, but then again, she'd had time to come to terms with everything. Travis was still processing the revelations. Quiet. I reached over to squeeze his hand, and he pulled me closer.

"You're together?" Courtney asked.

"Yes."

"Oh, thank goodness. I thought you hooked up in England, and I was so happy for Travis, but then you didn't come with us to America and I got worried I was wrong, that he'd end up with another Reagan."

"I was never with Reagan."

"She said you were."

"Then she lied. The bitch sold pictures of me naked, for fuck's sake."

"She told me you agreed to it. That it was a publicity

stunt."

"You spoke to her about it?"

"I... Uh..."

"*When* did you speak to her about it?" Emmy asked.

A long, painful silence descended, and I began to get a really bad feeling. The last two days had been a roller coaster of emotions, and now I wanted to puke. Finally, Courtney spoke in a whisper.

"The night she died."

"Tell us what happened, Courtney. Was it an accident, or did you do it on purpose?"

Oh, hell. Emmy thought Courtney killed Reagan? No way. This couldn't be happening.

But it was.

"An accident. A total accident, I swear." A tear rolled down Courtney's cheek. "I was standing in front of the door, and she pushed me, and I pushed her back, and she just kept going until she tripped over her feet and fell down the stairs." Now the tears came thick and fast. "Travis, I'm so sorry. I only wanted to get to know you, and everything went so badly wrong."

Emmy just chuckled. "Wrong? Nah. Reagan merely got a healthy dose of karma. Forget it ever happened."

"You're not gonna call the police?"

"Of course not. Nobody here is, are you?"

Everyone shook their heads.

"There we go. Sorted. At least we know who and why now, and we don't need to worry that there's a second lunatic still on the loose."

"A second lunatic?"

"Meredith was the first." Emmy ticked off on her fingers. "She did Jae-Lin, Vina, and Caitlin. But she's dead too, so we're all good."

Bradley picked that moment to bustle in with a tray of cups and a carafe of coffee. And biscuits. At least six different kinds of biscuits. Or maybe I should have called them cookies since we were in California and American biscuits were a whole different and very strange concept. Biscuits and gravy? Yeuch.

Courtney barely glanced at the coffee. She stared at Emmy instead.

"Meredith?"

"Turned out she was a few fries short of a Happy Meal. Look, forget all that shit. It's done. Over. The truth's out now, so why don't you and Travis just relax and get to know each other?"

What did Travis think of that plan? He'd been quiet so far, no doubt in shock. In a strange way, this mirrored my own story with Zander. We hadn't met until we were in our teens, although obviously Travis and Courtney's story didn't have the same element of paedophilia involved. Did he want to get to know her?

Yes, it seemed, because he nodded in agreement. "Emmy's right. We should forget the past and move on. Will you stick around for the rest of the day?"

Courtney nodded. "I'd like that."

"Where should we start?" Courtney asked.

Emmy, Black, and Bradley had left for Virginia, and Zander announced he was taking Dove out for dinner. Gary had tried to force Travis into the studio earlier, but Emmy adopted her Penny persona one last time and told Gary that Travis was grieving and he could go fuck himself. Yes, those exact words.

I offered to give the two new-found siblings some space as well, but Travis wanted me to stay and Courtney didn't seem bothered. The local Chinese place delivered, so we sat down to talk over boxes of egg fried rice and kung pao chicken and crispy shredded beef.

"How about we start at the beginning?" Travis asked. "My childhood's public record, but what happened to you?"

"It's simple. You didn't get enough love, and I got too much of it. My first eight years were okay. Really good, actually. I was spoiled, probably a bit of a brat if I'm honest, and I had the life most kids dream of. Vacations to Disney World, every toy I wanted, and I loved school. But when I was eight, Mom caught Dad in bed with his secretary and then the battle started. Hell hath no fury like two parents who both want full custody."

"Who won?"

"Nobody. We all lost. The good days were uncomfortable, and on the bad days, I wanted to throw myself under a truck. They spent thousands on lawyers. Played dirty tricks. Hired private investigators to follow each other. Had screaming matches in the school parking lot, then went to ridiculous lengths to apologise to me. On my tenth birthday, my dad bought me a pony, so Mom bought me a zebra. A freaking zebra! It scared the crap out of me, and all I ever asked for was a junior chemistry set."

"How long did it go on for?"

"Until I emancipated myself at sixteen and moved in with my grandma. She's the only sane person left in that family."

Tears streamed down Courtney's face for the

second time that day when Travis walked around the table and hugged her.

"I wish I could have been around to do this then," he told her.

"Me too. This feels kind of weird, you know?"

"Yeah, I do. But forget the past, remember? We've still got two-thirds of our lives left, so let's not fuck it up."

"What will we tell everyone?"

"The truth. The truth about everything. That I've got a girlfriend I'm crazy about and a sister who brings me the wrong coffee every single day and thinks a G-string is a kind of underwear."

"It *is* a kind of underwear."

Huh? "What kind of conversation were the two of you having?"

Courtney turned bright red, and Travis was the one who answered.

"I told her I needed a new G-string, and she suggested that if I wanted to wear women's panties, bikini briefs might be more comfortable."

"It was an honest mistake," I said.

"I'm sorry for being literally the world's worst PA."

"Who cares? Better to bring me a cappuccino instead of an Americano than be a manipulative bitch like Reagan. But what will you do now? You said you were a scientist?"

"Before I got the job working for Red Cat, I researched the genetics of hereditary diseases. Someday, I'd like to go back to university and do a postgraduate degree."

"Which college?"

"Probably Caltech again. I like it there."

"Caltech." Travis gave a low whistle. "My sister's smart."

"And my brother's a freaking rock star." She pinched herself, then laughed. "If I go back to school, I'll hardly see you though."

"We'll manage somehow."

"But Gary said you'd be on a tour of Asia for half of next year."

"He what?"

"You didn't know?"

"Gary never tells us anything. Nobody does. They just arrange stuff, and we've got no choice but to go along with it."

Travis gave Courtney a précis of the problems the band had been having with Red Cat, ending with Emmy's vague promise to sort everything out.

"Do you really think she can do that?" Courtney asked, her face ashen.

He looked to me, and I nodded. Emmy had never let me down, or Zander, even if her methods were a little unorthodox.

"Yes, I do."

CHAPTER 42 - ZANDER

A WEEK AFTER Meredith's demise, Zander walked into Blackwood's London office with mixed feelings. The Chelsea apartment had been eerily quiet when he got home with Dove last night, but as she reminded him, he hadn't so much lost a sister as gained a brother and another sister. Courtney was the biggest surprise in all of this, but her presence gave Lanie another shoulder to lean on during her US adventure.

"Hey, Zander," Nye called. "Once you've sorted out your mail, I've got a new case for you."

"Tell me it's not a lost dog."

"A parental abduction."

Yes, life was getting back to normal. The new normal, the one where he had a wife waiting for him at home and a dog who ate his shoes. The one where he wasn't sharing a house with an assassin and her husband and tempted to wear a tinfoil hat because the bitch could read his damn mind.

And speaking of mind-reading... He picked up the top item from his in-tray, a handwritten envelope with a California postmark. It contained one sheet of paper, folded in half, with a single word written in the middle.

Meredith.

How the hell had Emmy known that?

Zander sighed and fished around in his wallet for a

fifty-dollar bill left over from their trip to LA, then sealed it in an envelope to go in the internal mail. The woman was a bloody clairvoyant.

CHAPTER 43 - ALANA

THREE WEEKS LATER, Courtney slipped into the rear lounge of the tour bus. The new tour bus. This one drove us all around the United States, but it was exactly the same as the UK bus except the driver sat on the left instead of the right and Courtney and Jeanne had taken over the two spare bunks. Currently, we were living the showbiz lifestyle at a truck stop in Idaho.

"Guys," Courtney said. "I'm not sure what's going on, but Gary just took a phone call and he went absolutely white."

She'd decided to stick around, at least for a while. Until we somehow got a resolution to the contract problem. I'd taken over some of the more organisational parts, and Jeanne wasn't so bad at assisting as long as she had proper instructions. Give her a list, and she'd keep going until she ticked everything off. Plus she made excellent coffee.

But in truth? None of us really wanted to be there. Could this phone call be the start of something?

"Did you hear any of the conversation?" I asked.

"No, because he locked himself in the disabled bathroom."

"What about listening through the door?"

"I tried that, but I couldn't make out any of the words, and then some lady carrying a chihuahua gave me a really weird look."

"Okay, so why don't we—"

My vibrating phone interrupted me, and I looked down to see a text from Emmy. No message, just a hyperlink to an article on celebgossip.com and a smiley face. My fingers shook as I clicked on the link. What had she done?

Red Cat Records raided by the IRS.

Criminal investigators from the Internal Revenue Service this morning descended on the headquarters of Red Cat Records, the label behind so many of today's top music acts. CEO Leonard Martineau takes credit for bringing live music back to the masses with a never-ending series of worldwide tours.

But today, there was no sign of Mr. Martineau as agents left his office with boxes and boxes of documents, which they placed on trucks waiting outside.

Officials offered scant details of the reason for the raid.

"We're here on official business," Special Agent John Evans told reporters gathered at the scene. "Primarily, we're investigating violations of Title 26, which is tax evasion and general fraud against the US government."

Martineau could not be reached for comment, and Red Cat's social media account gave no information on the investigation. If the record company is in trouble, could this be the end for some of our favourite artists?

Updates to follow...

Straight away, I dialled Emmy's number, and she picked up immediately.

"Did you do this?"

"Which part? Gathering evidence of Red Cat's tax evasion and sending an idiot-proof summary to the IRS? Giving a nudge to an IRS agent who may have owed someone a favour to bump the investigation to the top of the pile? Or sending an anonymous tip about the raid to a celebrity gossip website?"

"All of it?"

"Technically, I didn't do the first part, but I may have provided some direction. If you'd like to thank the people who did, Mack drinks white wine and Georgia likes those chocolates with the soft caramel centres."

"Do you think Red Cat will go bust?"

"Hard to run a record label from a jail cell, honey. The execs have all been fudging their personal taxes too. For Gary's information, a sailboat doesn't count as a tax-deductible business expense."

"Jail?"

"This is gonna be a mess. A huge mess, but in a couple of months when the dust settles, your boys'll be free and clear. Just sit tight, okay? We've got lawyers on hand to help you out."

"What about the tour?"

"I'm not sure yet. There'll be some negotiation, undoubtedly, but I expect anything not already booked and paid in full will get covered by the company's cancellation insurance. I'm sure the band will want to take their fans into account when they decide whether or not to bail completely as well."

"Of course."

"And it may be too soon, but if they're interested in

recording another album after this has all unravelled and they've taken a break, then Ethan wouldn't mind talking to them."

"Ethan as in Ethan White? The Ghost?"

"Yup."

Wow. "I'll definitely pass that on. Thanks so much. For everything."

"I'm just doing my civic duty in ridding the world of assholes. Now, stop talking to me and go update everyone. I'm sure they'd like to know what's happening, and I need another coffee."

EPILOGUE - ALANA

TWO AND A half months. That was how long it took for Indigo Rain to wrap up their tour and hold a celebratory barbecue which involved cooking hot dogs over their burning contract at Courtney's place. She lived in the guesthouse at the back of her grandma's property, which made her the only one with a garden.

"I can't believe it's over," Travis said. "Freedom tastes like mustard, ketchup, and fried onions."

Rush popped the top on another beer. "I never thought we'd celebrate being unsigned."

"Yeah, well, it's only for twenty-four hours, so we'd better make the most of it."

Yes, they had a new record deal lined up already, this time with Spectre Productions, Ethan White's label. They'd spent a long time talking to him on the phone and even gone to visit him in Richmond. Ethan was a family man with a steady girlfriend and a young son, so he understood the importance of downtime and having a life outside of work. The initial contract, which had been carefully checked over by Oliver Rhodes, called for Spectre to re-release the band's existing back catalogue, and for the boys to record two new albums over the next three years. They'd tour too, but they'd get the final say in the schedule, and there wouldn't be any live performances for at least three months.

Apart from Travis's solo performance at a Richmond dog shelter's fundraising dinner, that was. He'd offered to play a few numbers on the guitar as a thank-you to Emmy, who was somehow involved with the organisation.

Vina had been discharged from the hospital and was recovering at home. To minimise scarring, she had to wear a clear plastic mask for the next eight months, but the doctors were hopeful she'd make a good recovery over time. Travis had offered to pen an album with her. Frank tried to veto the idea at first, but then he quit, so once a week, Travis and Vina arranged a songwriting session over Skype.

Yes, Frank quit. During the IRS's search of Red Cat's offices, some old emails between Leonard Martineau and Frank Fields had surfaced, and Emmy's IRS contact channelled them back to her. Indigo Rain's manager *had* taken kickbacks to get the boys to sign that awful contract, and guess what? He hadn't paid tax on any of that cash. Now he was in trouble with the taxman too, and he'd agreed to resign quietly and forfeit any future royalties to avoid being sued by Indigo Rain as well.

Ethan had already found the band a new manager. His own in fact. A shared arrangement. Javon was in his mid-thirties, but knowledgeable, and he'd work for the band rather than the other way around. Jeanne had agreed to stay on as PA, and Courtney planned to go back to her old job before starting a PhD program at Caltech in the next academic year.

And me? I was going back to my old job too, even if Travis did shoot Rush evil glares every time he called me Instababe. I'd be their official social media coordinator rather than a hanger-on, as well as sharing Travis's bed every night.

But the day after tomorrow, he'd be sharing mine. We'd be spending the first six weeks of his break in England, catching up with Zander, Dove, and Tessa, plus Ziggy and Amin, to whom everyone owed a huge thank-you. Why six weeks? Because Dex was coming with us to have his knees operated on. The best orthopaedic surgeon we could find worked in London, and he had an osteotomy scheduled for three days' time. Tessa had offered up her spare room for recuperation purposes, although she was quite open with her disappointment that it wasn't Rush coming to stay instead.

"Have you got your camera, Insta—"

"Don't say it," Travis warned Rush.

"Of course I do. Everybody smile."

Click. Another picture for the fans. After Red Cat's collapse, the outpouring of support for Indigo Rain and the label's other acts had threatened to become a tsunami, it was so strong. Tessa had told the full story in *NewsFlash* magazine and been offered a job when she graduated as a result. We'd be having another celebration in London, but perhaps not outside because October wasn't the time for barbecues in England, not unless we all wanted to go to the hospital with frostbite.

I took a dozen more shots and quickly edited one to post on Instagram. As long as I could keep the guys in people's minds during their hiatus, they should be able to pick up where they left off. Still with no money to show for the last few years' work, unfortunately, but the forensic accountants were hopeful of recovering something from the ashes of Red Cat. Plus Spectre had offered a small advance, which would pay for JD's rehab at least. He'd check in as soon as we left for London, although since he got the news that he wouldn't have to tour constantly for two more years, he'd been a different person anyway. JD would be okay. I didn't have to worry about him anymore.

Rush, on the other hand, I was both nervous for and proud of. Inspired by stories from Vina's mum when he'd gone to visit, he'd decided to work on a volunteering project in Africa for the next two months, and he probably wouldn't even have cell phone coverage. Yikes. I was a little ashamed to say that I panicked if I ever went out of signal range, and no way would I ever survive on one of those castaway TV shows.

But that didn't matter, because I'd never want to go on one. I'd seen first-hand the impact fame could have on a person, and Travis was much happier out of the limelight. A barbecue with friends trumped a glitzy awards bash or a VIP party every time.

And now he settled onto Courtney's swing seat and beckoned me over to sit beside him. I couldn't resist running a hand over his face. His new, smooth face. Shaving off the beard was the first thing he'd done when we heard the news, and the second was getting a haircut. He conceded he'd probably grow it all back again, but that day, he got rid of it because now he *could*.

"Thanks for being everything, blue. If you hadn't come along, I'd be on stage in Buttfuck, Minnesota, right now."

"And to think I didn't even like you at first."

"I didn't like me much back then either." He picked

up his bottle of beer and clinked it against mine. "To new beginnings."

"New beginnings? Does that mean we can start the alphabet of sex again?"

"Sure we can." He leaned in closer and nibbled my ear. "Speaking of Buttfuck, A is for..."

"Whoa. Let's save that for the third go around." I plucked a chocolate from the box Rush had bought for me earlier. "How about A is for aphrodisiac?"

"How long do we have to stay at this barbecue?"

"I love you, Travis Thorne. I love your filthy mouth and your sweet tongue."

"Love you too, A is for Alana. Always."

Perhaps bad boys weren't such bad news after all.

Wʜᴀᴛ's ɴᴇxᴛ?

The Blackwood UK series continues in Pass the Parcel, release date TBC.

Tessa Smyles is finally living up to her name. She's landed her dream internship with NewsFlash magazine, the red pumps she's been eyeing up for ages are finally on sale, and there's a rock star camping out in her spare room. Okay, so Dexter Reeves isn't the rock star she's been crushing on for the last three years, but he's in the same band, which has to count for something, right?

But life can change in a heartbeat.

When a madman with a grudge explodes onto the scene, Tessa and Dex are left to make sense out of chaos. Which of them was the target? Where will the killer strike next? The clock's ticking, but they soon find they're in danger of losing their hearts as well as their lives.

For more details: www.elise-noble.com/ptp

My next book will be Stolen Hearts, a thriller starring Emmy and Black, releasing in the summer of 2019.

Even assassins need a vacation...

When Diamond and her equally deadly husband head to Dahab, jewel of the Red Sea, all they want is a relaxing fortnight on the beach.

But the bodies soon start stacking up, and for once, it's not their fault. Together with local cop Khaled, they're soon sucked into the case, but there are too many suspects and not enough clues. Then there's teenager Zena, their self-appointed sidekick who just can't keep her nose out of other people's business. Will the team be able to unravel the mystery before the killer gets personal?

For more details: www.elise-noble.com/stolen-hearts

If you enjoyed Indigo Rain, please consider leaving a review.

For an author, every review is incredibly important. Not only do they make us feel warm and fuzzy inside, readers consider them when making their decision whether or not to buy a book. Even a line saying you enjoyed the book or what your favourite part was helps a lot.

Want to stalk me?

For updates on my new releases, giveaways, and
other random stuff, you can sign up for my newsletter
on my website:
www.elise-noble.com

Facebook:
www.facebook.com/EliseNobleAuthor

Twitter: @EliseANoble

Instagram: @elise_noble

If you're on Facebook, you may also like to join
Team Blackwood for exclusive giveaways, sneak
previews, and book-related chat. Be the first to find out
about new stories, and you might even see your name
or one of your ideas make it into print!

And if you'd like to read my books for FREE, you
can also find details of how to join my review team.

Would you like to join Team Blackwood?

www.elise-noble.com/team-blackwood

END OF BOOK STUFF

I finally got my rock star book! I've been wanting to write one for ages. Originally, Ethan in White Hot was gonna be a singer, but I figured he worked better as a producer/DJ. And now I might end up with four rock star books, because I kinda like the other guys in the band too. We'll see what happens there.

If you're eagle eyed, you may have noticed Alana had a change of eye colour between Shallow Graves and Indigo. This is why we have editors, folks. I'm fricking useless at writing character notes, and I totally forgot I'd given her amber eyes until Nikki, my wonderful editor, said "hang on a second..." Because amber-eyes is a dumb nickname and also because I already have a character called Amber, I've changed Alana's eye colour in Shallow Graves, and we'll just have to assume that she was wearing coloured contacts in the original version :)

Did I mention I love coloured contacts? Easiest Halloween costume ever. Blackout contacts, add vampire teeth and a trickle of fake blood, voila. Unless of course the fake blood stains your face and you have to spend the day explaining to the folks at work why it looks like you've been dribbling Ribena.

I'm writing this from Le Mans, currently freezing my ass off at 6 a.m. in a tent, cursing because I don't know how to work the coffee machine and nobody else is awake. Where's Emmy when you need her? And also croissants. I *need* croissants. And a heater. It's so cold I'm strongly considering going running to warm up. Although I'll perhaps change out of pyjamas first.

But it's worth a little discomfort to be here. Not so much because of the cars—which are awesome, by the way—but because of the people. I'm truly lucky to be part of an awesome team on the Mulsanne Straight. We call it the European post, although a few Americans usually turn up too, and it's wonderful to see so many friends new and old from all over the world. In part, this place inspired the Blackwood series—the coming together of a diverse group of people who have each other's backs, who work together to get things done, and even though we don't see each other in person all that often, when we do, it's like we've never been apart.

Anyhow, enough sentimentality... I've got pastries to buy and warm socks to find. Until next time...which will be either Copper or Stolen Hearts—I haven't decided which yet.

Happy reading!
Elise

OTHER BOOKS BY ELISE NOBLE

The Blackwood Security Series
For the Love of Animals (Nate & Carmen - prequel)
Black is my Heart (prequel)
Pitch Black
Into the Black
Forever Black
Gold Rush
Gray is my Heart
Neon (novella)
Out of the Blue
Ultraviolet
Glitter (novella) (TBA)
Red Alert
White Hot
The Scarlet Affair
Quicksilver
The Girl with the Emerald Ring (TBA)

The Blackwood Elements Series
Oxygen
Lithium
Carbon
Rhodium
Platinum
Lead

Copper (2019)
Bronze (2019)
Nickel (TBA)

The Blackwood UK Series
Joker in the Pack
Cherry on Top (novella)
Roses are Dead
Shallow Graves
Indigo Rain
Pass the Parcel (TBA)

Blackwood Casefiles
Stolen Hearts (2019)

Blackstone House
Hard Lines (TBA)
Hard Tide (TBA)

The Electi Series
Cursed
Spooked
Possessed
Demented (TBA)

The Trouble Series
Trouble in Paradise
Nothing but Trouble
24 Hours of Trouble

Standalone
Life
Twisted (short stories)

A Very Happy Christmas (novella)

Printed in Great Britain
by Amazon

58917249R00239